WILLIAM

The Man, The Myth & The Mafia

[signature]

May, 2019

WILLIAM

*The Man, The Myth
& The Mafia*

Gates Whiteley

Copyright © 2019 Gates Whiteley

The moral right of the author has been asserted.

Apart from any fair dealing for the purposes of research or private study, or criticism or review, as permitted under the Copyright, Designs and Patents Act 1988, this publication may only be reproduced, stored or transmitted, in any form or by any means, with the prior permission in writing of the publishers, or in the case of reprographic reproduction in accordance with the terms of licences issued by the Copyright Licensing Agency. Enquiries concerning reproduction outside those terms should be sent to the publishers.

William: The Man, The Myth & The Mafia is a biographical novel.
While the dialogue found herein is entirely imagined, this story of
William Whiteley's life is based almost completely on
real life events, people, and circumstances.

Matador
9 Priory Business Park,
Wistow Road, Kibworth Beauchamp,
Leicestershire. LE8 0RX
Tel: 0116 279 2299
Email: books@troubador.co.uk
Web: www.troubador.co.uk/matador
Twitter: @matadorbooks

ISBN 978 1789018 868

British Library Cataloguing in Publication Data.
A catalogue record for this book is available from the British Library.

Typeset in 11pt Sabon MT by Troubador Publishing Ltd, Leicester, UK

Matador is an imprint of Troubador Publishing Ltd

*There is a general sense of preparedness which only
a man pursuing a calling he loves can know.*
—Joseph Conrad

*He liked flattery, he liked presents,
and he liked the best cigars.*
—Santayana

Foreword

THE HISTORY OF WILLIAM WHITELEY's life contains no teleology of destiny. He could have wound up as he started—a devoted son—staying at home and eventually taking on the family business. It is a testimony to his industry, his ambition, even his courage, that he charted a different course in midlife.

During his forty-third year, William left his mother's home and the family business in Toxteth Park, Lancashire, England, to begin his life anew. During the thirty-eight years remaining in his life, he went from total obscurity to making a fortune during Prohibition. He created two historic whisky blends—House of Lords and King's Ransom—one of which would become the world's best known and most expensive.

But he was not done.

He spent five of the last eight years of his life bringing an obscure farm distillery to the world's attention and left this world at the age of eighty-one years, having earned the sobriquet "Dean of Distillers."

William's wife, Josephine, twenty-six years his junior, was a prominent figure in his life. Nothing in the record suggests that theirs was other than a happy marriage. They traveled extensively, lived well, and had no children. In the end, the best way to describe William's life may be as a love story. He loved what he did, and many of those who drank some of his finest loved him for it.

Family lore and genealogical research place William as a distant uncle. One of his forbearers migrated from Leeds in Yorkshire to the seaside community of Whitehaven, Cumberland County. From there, the first Whiteley in our clan migrated to the States sometime in 1748.

T. Gates Whiteley

ONE

New York

IN THE SHORT SEVEN YEARS since its opening on the Upper East Side, the hotel had acquired the reputation of a quiet place at a discreet location. Surveying the lobby, he thought it perfect for the put-up job he had in mind.

Accompanied by a very curious concierge, William prowled the meeting rooms, and having rejected the first offerings, now stood before two dark, paneled doors. He paused, studying them a moment before entering the room. What he saw inside reminded him of a baronial library he had once seen in a photograph.

A conference table of ornate design reigned amid polished wood paneled walls and coffered ceilings. Parquet flooring in a herringbone pattern contended with deep-pile carpeting, upon which the table rested. Coupled with the rest of the furnishings, William thought it all came close to reeking of old money.

After the concierge finished his orientation, William sat at the head of the table and took his time adjusting the level of light sheening off the walls and ceiling. The effect he sought was one of quiet elegance and refinement—something in stark contrast to the personality of his guest. Satisfied, he rose to leave the room and join Ridley for dinner.

William and his chartered accountant, Vernon Ridley, had left Southampton on April 14, 1934, arriving five days later in New York. There had not been a moment to relax and enjoy the cruise, Ridley thought, his angular face lined with worry. *How could he be so calm*? he wondered.

Ridley was still trying to sort through the different potential outcomes. In his mind, the least likely one was obviously the best, and the rest, well, he hesitated to consider in any detail.

– § –

In a small Italian eatery across town, Frank Costello ate and drank in the company of his bodyguards and Irving Haim. Born Francesco Castiglia in 1891, and Costello being his favorite alias, he had made the name change official in 1916. Of medium height with dark brown hair and swarthy face, he favored expensive, well-tailored suits. Haim by comparison was taller and nine years younger, with an open, friendly face that now gazed into the dark brown eyes of his "associate."

Costello had just finished describing the assignment he had given to Haim, who said, "So, Alliance Distribution wants *exclusive* rights to distribute both King's Ransom and House of Lords."

"Yeah, that's right," Costello said, still chewing.

"But what we really want is the distillery."

"And if William's…not ready to sell?" Haim asked in a mild tone of voice.

"Your job is to get him ready," smirked Costello.

Irving Haim had met Frank Costello in their early days of rum running, working out of Canada. In 1926, Costello, on trial for bootlegging, had escaped conviction. At no time during his bootlegging career had Haim ever attracted the attention of the authorities, and Costello wanted to know why.

Haim took the money he had made bootlegging and used it to begin running a legitimate business as a tobacco merchant. He was also a broker, buying the cured leaf at auction in several of the many warehouses of Durham, North Carolina, and Danville, Kentucky. Known to be one of the "speculators" who tried to outbid the company buyers, he would occasionally buy a grower's entire load at the front door before other buyers had a chance to make a bid.

After Haim had known Costello for a while, he felt he knew why Frank could not escape the attention of law enforcement. Eschewing violence, Costello made certain his gunmen were under orders not to shoot first.

Yet, there was the necessity of dealing with the rapacious, murderous Al Capone.

After Capone assassinated a rival gang, during what became known as the St. Valentine's Day Massacre, Mafioso led by Costello held a meeting in Atlantic City. Capone soon found he had lost all support, and in the end, had to agree to spend time in jail while things cooled down in Chicago.

The meeting at the President Hotel was widely publicized, and pictures of Costello posing with other gangsters appeared in local newspapers. Despite his professed disdain for strong-arm methods, in the minds of most who knew of him, Costello continued to be associated with the darker side of the underworld.

Over the years, Haim had found many reasons to doubt whether Costello really wanted to escape the connection.

– § –

The telephone rang in the room William and Ridley were sharing. The front desk called to say that a Mr. Irving Haim would like to speak with William.

"He wants me to come down and have a drink with him," William explained to a startled Ridley.

"You want me to come with you?" Ridley offered.

Shaking his head, William said it would not be necessary and left the room.

As the hour was late, there were few patrons in the hotel bar. Haim was alone and rose to meet William when he entered the room. *He hadn't changed much*, Haim thought, extending his hand to the short, unassuming Britisher.

"Good to see ya again, William. Have a seat," Haim offered as he waved the waiter over. With drinks ordered, Haim began to make his pitch. "Frank wanted us to talk before the meeting tomorrow. He's gonna ask you about selling the distillery. Wanted me to see what you thought."

The drinks arrived. William thanked the waiter, but before he could sign the check, Haim reached for it.

"This is on me, William."

"I think not, Irving."

William handed the pen and receipt to the waiter. Raising his glass, he offered his "cheers" and sat back in his chair. He looked at Haim for a moment before he began speaking.

"How did you come to know Frank?" William asked pleasantly.

"We met in the '20s, back durin' our bootlegging days."

Haim traced his history with Costello briefly and then brought the conversation back to the matters at hand.

"So, William, you thinkin' about retirement any?"

"I am not."

A silence fell on them for a moment.

"How did you get your start in distillin'?" Haim resumed.

"I was raised in it, you might say," William began. "My family had a wine, spirits, and tobacco shop, with my parents and I living in a flat above. Later, I went to work for a distiller and blender as a sales agent and after that went on my own."

William paused to take a sip before continuing. "The distillery, we purchased last year…to secure a reliable source for the making of our whiskies."

Haim nodded and sat back in his chair, reflecting upon his own life story. Born in Romania at the turn of the century, he and his family had immigrated to the States in 1905. Originally born Irvine Haimorrtz, and no longer observant, he decided to change his name to Irving Haim and became a naturalized citizen in 1912.

"I grew up in a tough part of Philadelphia on Morris Street, in the First Ward," Haim concluded. "My sisters and I went to work young to take care of our parents."

"And when did you go to work for Frank?"

Haim paused for a moment before he replied. "I don't work *for* him exactly. You might say I work with him…when he needs an honest front."

William allowed a small smile. "Like my distillery, perhaps?"

"That's it," Haim countered.

"And Frank wants it in a bad way. He's willin' to pay, of course…"

"Just like that sub of yours." William set his unfinished drink aside. *The submarine,* he mused. *Yes, that* had *been instructive.* There was a slight edge to his voice, and he looked directly into Haim's eyes, replying, "There might certainly come a time when I *may* be ready to sell. But as of the moment, there is no interest in selling…to anyone."

So, the answer is no, mused Haim. *That ain't good…*

TWO

Golders Green

Surveying the room, looking over the multitude gathered to remember the man he had so loyally served, Hinch felt gratified. His eyes came to rest on the display of floral arrangements placed behind the podium. Realizing there was time before Ridley spoke, he moved forward, finding his attention drawn to the largest burst of flowers and noting an attached card with the signatures of Frank Costello and Irving Haim.

He then saw Miss Josephine beckoning him to join her. Reluctantly, Hinch followed Josephine into a small anteroom off the sanctuary.

"A moment with you, Hinch," Josephine said as she closed the door.

Hinch's discomfort increased as Josephine looked at him intently—and, he thought, with half-accusing eyes. *Was it sixteen years?* Hinch asked himself, noting for the first time the faint signs of aging around those eyes that now seemed to bore into him. Those eyes. Had they always been so blue? So clear and penetrating? Though taller, he began to feel diminished in her presence.

"As I'm sure you know," Josephine began, "William said that he wanted you to stay on after…his demise. I want just that, Hinch. I want you…no, more than that, I *need* you to stay, Hinch."

Josephine paused to judge the effect of her words. William's words. What she saw did not comfort her. With a troubled expression, Hinch began to tell her what she did not expect nor want to hear.

"No, Hinch," Josephine interrupted. "There is no one else I would prefer. You knew William's habits and methods as well as anyone. And frankly, I don't want to have to get used to someone new."

Josephine drew up all of her five feet, five inches of height as if to signal the matter closed.

To her dismay, Hinch turned, brushed past her, opened the door to the sanctuary, and walked out, leaving her alone in her disbelief.

It was difficult for Hinch to make his way through all the congregants, many of whom had a kind word of encouragement for him. He stopped when he had to, patiently receiving and responding to the well-wishers.

"Such a good man… A great man you had there, Hinch… What will you do now, Hinch?"

On it went, until he finally made his way outside the crematory. Breathing in the cold, clean, November air, his mind cleared and his resolve firmed.

He waited while Josephine came along slowly and deliberately through the crowd of friends and well-wishers, acknowledging each condolence. Arriving at the car, Josephine ignored Hinch's opening of the rear door, made her way unassisted to the left side, and placed herself upfront in the passenger seat.

Both sat in silence, while Hinch turned the motor over to begin their departure for Middlesex.

At least I can count on Dora and Alice to occupy Josephine, Hinch thought with relief.

Josephine, on the other hand, was perplexed. Stealing herself for another round of rejection, she turned to look at Hinch.

What she saw slightly unnerved her: the profile of a resolute face, jaw firmly set and lips compressed—a taciturn figure whose eyes looked straight ahead without so much as a flicker of self-consciousness or doubt.

"The lad's a stout one," she once heard William say.

"But his is a good heart, and he will not let you down," William also had said; only this time he was wrong. Hinch *was* letting her down, and Josephine could not see anything goodhearted about it.

Neither spoke during the remainder of the short journey to the house at 32a Wildwood Road in Hampstead Heath. Only six years had passed since Charles Holloway James designed the restrained, Neo-Georgian, red-brick house, with its "stripped" front and pantile roof.

Nearing their destination, Hinch recalled with a quickening of remorse the many hours he and Mr. William had spent walking aimlessly across the Heath. Although neither of them played golf, the nearby course had provided a comfortable feeling of cozy isolation so treasured by the two of them, especially in the last few months before William's death.

"Y' 'ome, ma'am."

With a sharp glance, Josephine looked into the defiant face of the man who had served her William for so long and so well.

"Will I see you again, Hinch, or is your mind made up?"

"Aye," Hinch nodded.

"Then come into the house for a moment. I will need the name of a driver you might recommend," said Josephine as she turned and marched to the door.

Dutifully, Hinch followed Josephine into William's study, where Dora quickly joined them. Her youthful face lined with worry and flustered by the strain of having returned from the funeral just ahead of her mistress, her words tumbled out breathlessly.

"Oh, Miss Josephine, are you all right? Perhaps I might get you some tea...?"

"Yes, Dora, that would be nice...and thank you. You will have tea, won't you, Hinch?"

Hinch nodded and gave the departing Dora a smile of thanks.

"All right, Hinch, let's be honest with one another," Josephine began. "Could you please tell me what this is all about, and why you refuse to stay on? Is it money, Hinch? Something else, perhaps? Or do you just despise me that much?"

His reply delayed by Dora's return, while she put out the tea service, Hinch tried to think of what he might say that would not escalate the tension he felt building all around him.

Josephine listened to his reasoning: He was thinking about going to Todmorden to see his sister. After that, he wasn't sure.

"So, you have no concrete plans and nothing better than what I have to offer. Isn't that right, Hinch?"

Josephine let her words hang in the air while she watched Hinch take his tea. *God in heaven! What is it about Yorkshire men?!* she mused with irritation.

She knew him to be about forty-five years of age. His face was unlined, but his brown hair was beginning to show touches of gray. Tall, broad at the shoulders, and still trim at the waist, she had to admit he was attractive in a way. She almost allowed a small smile to escape her lips as she reflected on how often she had asked that question of William.

Her brilliant, stubborn, but loveable William, and how she missed him now.

"Aye, y' reight. A' got no plans. Happen A'd go n' see a bit o' t' world…"

Hinch's laconic voice trailed off as he saw the incredulous look forming on Josephine's face.

"See a bit of the world? My God, Hinch!" Steeling her nerves, she moderated her tone a bit. "You and William have done all that. What more could you possibly want to see?"

The look on Hinch's face told her all she needed to know, and she began to beat a hasty retreat. "I'm sorry, Hinch. I have no right to presume how you should live your life," Josephine said primly.

Seeing no reaction, she continued. "Let's see if we can agree on this, on something at least. Go see your sister, take that time you say you need for yourself. Can we agree to talk again in what, a month's time?"

THREE

Todmorden

As Hinch gazed out over the Clough, a part of the upper Calder Valley, he thought he had been right to come home. The steep-sided Pennine Valley, with its moorlands and gritstone outcroppings, glistened in the light, falling mist while he reveled in the stark beauty around him. There had been thick, massive woodlands before industrialization, yet he knew some of what he saw remaining was ancient. As a boy, walking with his father, he learned some of the woods dated to the 17th century.

The willow warblers had gone silent, and he was too late to enjoy the flowering of the purple moor grasses, but there had always been something about gloomy, gray days he found comforting—and sometimes exciting.

Wild and mystical, the poets had said about the Clough.

His had been a leisurely departure from London. Then, with the train making every stop along the way, disgorging large numbers of soldiers, he had watched their joyful reunions and reflected on his time in the Great War. His mind went back to the moment he met Ridley.

"Rids," he said to call him. First, it was "Ids," until Ridley insisted he learn to roll his Rs. Rids was Vernon Samuel Ridley, who had proved to be a damned fine accountant and an even better friend.

Maybe Rids will have a line on all this, Hinch thought to himself as he took the turn on the trail that would take him back to his sister's home.

"Ey up," his sister greeted him.

Hinch was a nickname he picked up in the Great War. He would allow no one to use his given names—neither of them pleased him. Percy Gladstone Hinchen, his folks had named him. His sister called him "P.G.," and as sisters went, he had found his could sometimes be uncomfortably direct.

"Wat's got y' tongue?" she asked, beginning her interrogation.

"At's Miss Josephine…," Hinch began by way of reply, then explained why she wanted him to stay on, and why he did not.

"Eee, by gum!" his sister began, expressing her astonishment before she went on to question his gumption.

Shaking his head, Hinch tried to explain. When he was through, he looked intently into the face of his sister for acceptance and understanding.

He found neither.

"So! She 'as not allus treated y' so well, y' say? Wat da y' 'spect?"

Gathering his thoughts, Hinch began to describe how, over the years of service to William, he had never felt disrespect or condescension. He spoke of the difference in Josephine's attitude toward William and that which she displayed toward servants.

"So, y' see, reight, sis?"

She did not see.

Instead, his sister pointed out the obvious. There was a war going on, and though jobs were available, none was better than the one he had.

In response to his sister's probing, Hinch retreated, going out the back door of her cottage, where he soon found himself enveloped in the quiet winter calm pervading Todmorden. Surveying the scene around him, he saw the fine misting had ceased. He had the better part of a month to decide and felt no sense of urgency to do so.

"Wat th' 'ell," he muttered, as a fresh solution to his gloom presented itself. "Goin' t' White 'Art, sis," he shouted, not caring whether he was heard.

The White Hart had never failed to satisfy from the time his dad had first introduced him to the pub. It was not a far walk, and as he eased himself onto a seat at the bar, Hinch was struck by how the place had changed. The old-time pub he and his dad had frequented had been demolished. From the wreckage, a hotel in mock-Tudor style had risen to dominate the corner of the street on which it sat.

What had he heard it called? *Tudorbethan?*

It was early, and the crowd had not yet gathered for lunch as Hinch took his first sip while looking around the room. Dark, paneled walls and matching tables and chairs glistened in the subdued light that filtered through the large, leaded glass windows.

"You here for the duration?" he heard the barman ask.

Turning to respond, Hinch shook his head. "Visitin' family. Y'sef?"

"Came just after the reopening in '35," the barman replied. "The hotel had just begun to generate a fine return for the owners when Herr Hitler interfered."

Hinch nodded his understanding, realizing his own troubles were insignificant compared to those of most folks caught up in the war. He then had another realization. The barman looked to be of an age that disqualified him from serving during Hinch's war. Short and portly, with a balding pate, his smile, though broad, seemed insincere. With the questions that followed, Hinch began to sense the barman was probing a little too deeply into what his business was. Growing tired of what had become a kind of interrogation, Hinch was tempted to pay his tab and depart when the barman spoke again.

"Well, I guess you have already had your war."

"Y' bloody well reight A'ave." Hinch spat out the words.

To his satisfaction, he thought the barman might have flinched ever so slightly. To be sure, he had not done anything heroic during his time in service, but he *had* served. Moreover, he resented the implicit attack on his patriotism.

"Meant no harm, my friend," the bartender said soothingly. "Was it the Army in which you served?"

Hinch shook his head. "A' wuh a driva.' Squadun' 26."

"Yes, he was! And a bloody well fine one at that!" a familiar voice chimed.

Hinch and the barman turned to look at the figure approaching the bar.

"Rids? Ey up?" Hinch asked.

"Well, I thought I might have me self a spot of ale—that is, if the proprietor doesn't object," Vernon Samuel Ridley replied as he cast a cool eye toward the barman.

"Ya know, that mouth of yours needn't be open if there's nothin' a' comin' out, don't ya?" Ridley said, smirking at his friend.

'Ow is it y' 'ere?" Hinch was finally able to ask. Then his mind went back to the last conversation with Josephine. "She sent ya!"

"Not at all, my good man. I brought myself. And myself is here to see if there's any sense left in ya." With a slap on the shoulder of his good friend, Ridley quickly got down to business. "Yes, I did talk with Josephine, Hinch. She told me about your…um, reluctance to stay on and asked me if I knew anyone who could take your place. I told her there must be a million as good as you, and it shouldn't be too hard to find one," Ridley said with nary a smile on his angular face.

Hinch could not help himself. His chuckle began at just that moment when he chose to take another sip, and that led to a coughing fit when a little of the brew trickled down his windpipe. Ridley did not help matters any, sitting there with a grin on his face, apparently uninterested in his friend's discomfort.

"If you can stop making a fool of yourself long enough, why don't you try to explain what's wrong with twenty quid a week and steady eats?"

Trying to find his voice, Hinch heard himself wheeze, "At's Miss Josephine! Don't allus treat a fella' reight."

Ridley took a moment to take in the anguished look on Hinch's face and decided to change direction. "So. You think you'll find better treatment elsewhere?"

Hinch nodded his head, not quite ready to trust his voice.

"Doing what?" Ridley asked.

"Dunno' a'yet," Hinch wheezed.

"Well, my friend, don't be surprised if you have trouble finding a man who still has his car in order. And petrol? That's a bit scarce these days, I've heard."

Hinch shook his head and looked gloomily at his empty glass. He knew what Ridley had said was true, but damned if it mattered where putting up with Josephine was involved.

"A' got some brass n' A' can mak out," Hinch thought to say, as another brew seemed to magically appear on the table.

"Yes, I know. William was very generous…very generous to the lot of us, at the end." Ridley paused as he reflected on the unfortunate demise of their mutual employer. But will whatever you have accumulated last you through the war, Hinch?"

The two men looked at each other as a silence set in between them.

A Yorkshire man through and through, Ridley thought to himself. Then he remembered something. Something he should have asked before.

"Hinch, I didn't think to ask your sister, so I'll have to ask you. Is your mum all right? Did she get through that sickness you told me about?" Ridley was relieved when Hinch nodded.

"She be' a' reight. Ain't no secrets 'tween us Rids. 'A don't lak t' woman."

"It's Josephine we're talking about?"

Hinch nodded his head.

"Well, just what has she done that's so bloody awful?" Ridley asked with that cocky grin on his face.

"Will you chaps be havin' somethin' to eat?" asked the barman.

Hinch was on his third pint and beginning to feel famished. He looked at the barman and Ridley, who said, "Bangers and mash for me."

Hinch nodded; he would have the same.

"All right," Ridley said as the barman left the table, "it's time to get serious. "You and I both know that Josephine can…be difficult."

Hinch nodded.

"She can be aloof, and as William used to say, even disagreeably acute. Still, I find her to be quite charming at times." Seeing no response and taking another tack, Ridley continued. "Did you ever stop to consider that Josephine has a lot on her mind? Now, especially now, she has the weight of everything on her shoulders. It shouldn't surprise either of us to find her preoccupied at times."

The food came and was quickly consumed. More pints ordered, Hinch lit a cigarette as Ridley began packing his pipe. The pungent aroma of good tobacco wafted through the barroom, and Hinch felt almost content. Almost, because he knew Rids was waiting for a response.

Hinch thought about what Rids had said. He could see the sense in it. There was the matter of his bank account—at unprecedented levels due to Mr. William's largess, yet it would not see him through indefinitely. His sister could not take him in for the long term, and the twenty quid… well, he knew that was three or four times what most blokes were making. Ridley was the first to break the contented silence.

"So, where are we, Hinch?"

Ridley immediately regretted his gambit. From Hinch's glowering face, he read the negative response before it came.

"All right," Ridley said hastily. "No need to answer that. Give me a moment. I need to go up to my room to fetch something I forgot."

"Rum? Y' stayin' 'ere?" Hinch asked in surprise, thinking the hotel was fully occupied.

"What did you expect me to do? Lay about the bar all night?" Ridley said, rising from his chair. "In case you've forgotten, William's name still carries some weight around here," he added as he turned and left the barroom.

Hinch did remember. After all, whenever Mr. William had recorded his place of birth, it was most often *Todmorden* he wrote. Whiteley was very much a localized name in West Yorkshire.

Upon Ridley's return, Hinch saw the envelope, and it was with some astonishment that he received it from Ridley's outstretched hand.

"Wat's 'is?" he asked.

"Just open it, Hinch. You may be in for a fair bit of surprise."

Reading the note was a little difficult in the low light of the barroom. He did not immediately recognize the handwriting and let his gaze drift down to the signature where, with mixed feelings, he saw Josephine's name. Rereading the note in full, he found his antagonism beginning to fade.

"Twenty-five quid?"

"Yes," said Ridley, "and there's more to come if you can bear to hear it."

A heavy rain made the walk home somewhat difficult. Several times, Hinch wished he had accepted Ridley's invitation to share the room at the White Hart. Slipping and sliding along the muddy path, he made his way to his sister's house; at one point he paused to regain his balance.

Wot's up? he wondered. *Seems tha' keep tunin' t'streets roun.*

Taking off his shoes, he saw the fire was smoldering still. Relishing its warmth, he eased himself into the comfortable chair before his sister's hearth.

"'Ome at last and nowt alone, A'see," his sister's voice sounded.

Startled out of his stupor, he saw his sister come round to look fully into his stubby-cheeked face, now taking on the glow of another warmth.

"Aye, I bin w'drink, t'be sure. Wat wud y' be doin' at this 'our, sis?"

"'Opefully lookin' at tha' wiser face," she said, withdrawing with a smile and leaving him alone with his thoughts.

Rain continued through the night, adding to the gloom that greeted Hinch as he woke with a massive hangover. The house was not yet stirring when he stumbled into the kitchen in search of a morning restorative. Opening the pantry door and casting a doleful eye, it was with great relief he found the remains of a bottle of brandy, from which he sipped while starting the teakettle to boiling. As the pain in his head began to subside, and his mind cleared, fond memories of the good years with William flooded his consciousness. During this reverie, he gradually became aware of the whistle of the kettle that woke the house.

– § –

Sipping from an early morning cup of strong coffee, Vernon Ridley was gratified to find the dining room quiet and nearly deserted. Two hundred miles distant, Todmorden provided a welcome respite from the turmoil of London. He had needed to get away.

Beginning in August, there had been a lull in the bombing, and Vernon found himself with little to do as a firewatcher. There was some business to tend, but with Josephine's request for help and the chance to spend time with Hinch, Vernon had all the reasons he needed to make the trek to Todmorden. Looking at his watch, Vernon began to wonder what was keeping Hinch, who at that moment entered the dining room.

"Parky out tha'," Hinch offered as he helped himself to a seat.

Vernon looked into the face of his friend, seeking any indication of a decision. Seeing none, he began with small talk about the weather (which *was* chilly), listened to Hinch describe his hasty withdrawal from his sister's kitchen, and went on to the prime minister's speech.

Reading aloud from a weeks-old newspaper found at the hotel, Vernon quoted, "'We will never enter into any negotiations with Hitler,' the PM says, and further, 'he sees no reason why Japan would want to enter the war...'"

"Blimey, and neither do I," Ridley exclaimed, putting the paper down as the waiter approached their table.

"Two bubble and squeak," Vernon ordered.

To his surprise and pleasure, Hinch spoke first. "Bin a' thinkin,' Rids…aba' wat y' said. Summat aba' muh t' cum."

Sitting back in his chair and feeling more confident, Vernon began tracing all the events that had transpired since Irving Haim had purchased the distillery. He then began a brief summary of Josephine's business interests and noted Hinch's surprise over certain specifics.

"Y' workin' for 'Aim, now, reight?" Hinch inquired.

"That's right, but it's still William Whiteley and Co., Ltd. It's a lot like working for William, actually."

"'Ow so?" asked Hinch.

Patiently, Vernon sought to explain how the new ownership planned to expand William's brands worldwide. Yes, the war had interrupted a burgeoning enterprise, but the war could not last forever.

And whisky might.

As Hinch began to take in what Ridley was saying, he reflected upon the many years he had worked for Mr. William. He remembered the exact moment Ridley had introduced them and the excitement he had felt about the opportunity to drive the Sunbeam. The memory of his embarrassment over the teasing flashed in his mind as he recalled that first meeting. Then, from his memories came a succession of images: Minervas, each more luxurious than the one preceding it. His reverie interrupted by the arrival of their waiter, and their breakfast now in front of them, he heard Ridley's question.

"So, what should I tell Josephine? Are you in, or…"

"Y' kin tell 'er A'm 'n," Hinch said, taking his first bite.

Vernon clapped his hand on Hinch's shoulder and spoke with a wry smile. "I think if William were here, he would be chuffed t' bits."

FOUR

Tenerife

MARCH 7, 1901—RMS BIAFRA SLIPPED her moorings and began to make her way out of the port of Liverpool while George and his son William settled into their first-class cabin. Unlike his father, William was of medium height, but with sandy hair that already showed signs of balding. Consistent with the history of skipping generations, George had a full head of hair, with gray showing at the temples, matching the color of his goatee, all set off by his ruddy complexion.

"There, that should do it," George said as he put away the last of his undergarments. "What say we head up to the saloon?"

"You go ahead, Father – I'll be along in a few minutes," William replied.

After George had left the cabin, William reached into his luggage to retrieve his diary and began making entries in his fluid script. *Day 1— Leaving Liverpool on schedule in fair weather, no storms yet, on or off ship. Scheduled to arrive March 6 or 7. Believe all may go well.*

As William put his diary and writing instruments away, the words of his mother sounded again in his mind. In spite of all that had transpired between them in recent years, her bitterness still surprised him.

"Go with your father, if you must," she had said. "His methods are not yours, but you may learn something of value from him, I suppose."

His parents' separation in the end had not surprised him, but what did was discovering how much he missed his father's company. His parents had agreed to part ways without divorcing. William had dutifully agreed to stay with his mother to help run the business. His mother had kept wine and spirits, and his father retained the cigar and tobacco portion.

It had been a family business with the shop downstairs and the flat upstairs, where William had his own room to retreat to at the end of the day. He was an avid reader and did not socialize much. The family said he took after his mother, Hannah, who was quite opposite to George, a very outgoing, even gregarious person.

George had traveled, doing business and securing agreements with suppliers of the goods they sold in their shop. Whenever possible, George tried to cut out the middleman to avoid adding to the cost of the items they sold, which, simply put, were wine, spirits, and tobacco.

William preferred the wine and spirits side of the business. There were indications, even in his youth, that he had a sensitive palate. George never encouraged William to smoke after what occurred on a certain day in the summer of 1881.

They had their establishment at 1 Balk Field Road in Todmorden, where a shipment of Listan negro wines arrived one day, and William dropped a bottle while putting the wine away. William salvaged as much as he could from the broken bottle and, after straining it through cheesecloth, began to taste and make notes.

Soft, fruity, but highly aromatic, his tasting notes began.

Later, when George became aware of what had happened, William showed his notes to his father, asking him to critique them. George was amazed at the subtle flavor notes William had recognized in the wine.

When the subject of this trip to the Canary Islands came up, it seemed a perfect fit for the two of them: George would go to evaluate the late tobacco crop and William the most recent Malvasia vintages.

As he rose to leave the cabin, he paused to admire in a mirror the sack suit he had purchased for the voyage. He adjusted the four-in-hand knot of his tie and took notice of the extra inch and a half of height his laced boots gave him.

His most prominent feature was his nose.

It was a poking nose. Fully formed, it was equipped for poking wherever his curiosity led it. The nostrils were large and flared. They were what they seemed to be—capable of smelling uncommonly well.

His eyes, slightly hooded, were the color of the remains of coffee people leave in the bottom of a cup.

His ears were his second most prominent feature. They were built for listening well—large pinnae and ear canals—without whorls.

His hair, what there was left of it, was the color of sandpaper. He began balding at an early age, the effect of which, in the minds of some, confirmed his intelligence.

His forehead, glossy and high in the style favored by intellectuals, was free of wrinkles, save one. That one was vertical, beginning about an inch above his eyebrows and ending on that line. The effect it gave was one of intense concentration.

Full lips on a level line seemed to hint at a smile that, if it came, would show his small, finely made teeth. When the smile did not come, there remained in its place a faint hint of amusement.

A stubborn chin resided squarely below his nose. It did not jut outwardly but remained firmly placed, anchoring his face, which, though full, was not jowly.

After the ship's transfer from its Congo passenger line, the saloon on RMS *Biafra* was enlarged and refurbished. Sailing out of Leopoldville, and with a tonnage of just over thirty-three hundred, *Biafra* could provide cabin space for sixty first-class passengers, about half of whom seemed to be happily engaged in conversation with his father as William made his entrance into the saloon.

"Ah, William. Meet the major and sit with us. What will ye have me boy?"

George, already in rare form, introduced his son to all the men around the table. The major was apparently in the middle of a story that had something to do with Crimea, as best William could tell. He paused to catch William up.

"Was telling your pa a little about my time with the 17th Lancers at Balaklava and how Captain Morris would let us climb the towers of Cembalo. People think I lost my arm during the battle there in '54, but it was my foolishness on those bloody towers that did it."

William nodded, and as he listened, the words of Tennyson's poem echoed in his mind.

"You saw the 'valley of death,' I gather," William said.

The major nodded and remained quiet for a moment.

"It was bollixed from the beginning, as we know," the major intoned.

"It were Captain Morris' words earlier in the day that have always stayed with me. He told Cardigan, 'My God, man, what a chance we are losing.' As everybody knew then and later, *that* was when the Light Brigade should have charged."

With the assurance of one who has captivated his audience, the major continued with his story about the seminal event of the Crimean War. With a floridity of expression, the major told of the campaign in Crimea, which, though indecisive, provided much in the way of pride and emotional support in Britain.

"You say you climbed the Genoese tower?" queried William.

The major nodded.

"Which one?"

At this, the major paused. "Ah…let's see."

"Perhaps it was the Consol's castle or the donjon? Or perhaps it was one of the surviving wall towers we can still see today," offered William.

"Yes, well…one of those, to be sure," the major sputtered.

"Now," William continued, "did the unfortunate injury to your arm occur before or after the battle?"

"Oh, before, to be sure. As I said, it was this foolishness of mine that led to my loss. Certainly, no heroics on my part," the major wheezed.

William paused, and there began at the table a long silence, interrupted at last by George.

"Well, then, another round for all?"

General agreement gave way to soft murmurings among the men before William was underway again.

"So, the 17th Lancers were on the left, with the 13th Light Dragoons on the right?" With a nod from the major, William continued. "It was nasty and brutish, I have read. Russian canon at the end of the valley, backed by cavalry. Infantry on each side equipped with the Minie, racking our flanks with unrelenting fire! It must have been unnerving, sir…for your mates, that is."

Still no response from the major.

"And then wheeling about to make their way back through the same gauntlet again! The poet has spoken of their gallantry, sir, but we have not. Let us do so," William suggested.

Holding their glasses aloft, each man joined the table in drinking to the Light Brigade.

At this, the major found his voice. "No, as I told you, it was not the fire of the enemy that caused my injury…just a foolish prank on my part. Nothing heroic a 'tall."

"Nevertheless, you must have been very grateful at the time to Morris," William concluded.

"Oh, the captain was a gallant man, to be sure! He rode at the front of the column and never wavered," the major exclaimed with renewed confidence.

"I was speaking of the general, sir," William replied.

"The general? What general?" the major sputtered. "It was Captain Morris who led our Lancers, sir," he said with rising indignation.

"Oh, to be sure," offered William. "And it was General Morris and his French Light Cavalry who drove the Russian infantry off the north side of the valley, allowing the rest of the brigade to withdraw and perhaps escape total destruction."

Another great silence ensued at the table.

This time George did not offer to buy another round.

Finally, William broke the silence. "But let us go back to the site of your misfortune. The tower you climbed—whichever one it might have been…you are saying Captain Morris allowed you to climb it?"

The major nodded.

"I do not doubt your word, sir, not at all," William began. "But I have it on good report that Captain Morris was a disciplined soldier, not given easily to tomfoolery. What did he say to you, sir, when you reported to him with your injury?"

The major appeared to lack a response. Some who were there later said that he seemed to begin to shrink before their very eyes. What the major appeared to lose, William appeared to gain as he forged ahead.

"For example, did Captain Morris tell you that he was concerned for your safety? Did he counsel you about the dangers of sharpshooters who might have found your silhouette on the tower an inviting target? The Russians did, after all, control the high ground around Balaklava after October 25th, did they not?"

"Yes, I believe so," the major croaked.

"Now, about your unfortunate injury. With something as dreadful as the loss of your arm, I assume you were invalided out, eventually leaving the theater. Never to return. Eventually discharged." William paused for a two count. "I gather you weren't a major when you served under Captain Morris. So, how is it you received your promotion?"

One at a time, they left the table. George rose and, shaking his head, motioned to William, who chose to remain where he sat. He thought he saw tears in the "major's" eyes as his face rose to meet William's steady gaze.

"How do you know so much, sir?" he asked. "You are far too young to have been there. How can you assume…?" The "major's" voice faltered as William's eyes locked with his.

"You are right. I was not there. In fact, I was not yet born," William replied evenly. "But I did listen in school when the bravery of the six hundred was lifted up for us children to admire, and emulate someday, when our country would need us again. And the motto of the 17th: *death or glory*. I remember that as well."

William looked on with a rising sense of pity at the deflated figure before him.

The "major" recoiled at his touch as William reached out for his good arm.

"I have no doubt that you served, sir, and I thank you for that. Perhaps I can have the barman freshen your drink?"

At this, the "major" seemed taken aback. "You would drink with me? After all this?"

– § –

When George left Hannah and William in Todmorden, William was in his twenty-eighth year. He had come far in his learning of the wine trade and proved to be exceptionally competent in judging the character and value of the wines they stocked.

"He will do you proud, Hannah," George had once said, reassuringly.

At one point during their time together on Tenerife, William realized that his father had not said a word about why he had left the family. Then he reflected upon his mother, Hannah, who never stopped talking about the disgrace of having an unfaithful husband. She had been shamed, she said. She said these things at the slightest provocation, as when William might mention the receipt of a letter from his father.

"Who is he living with now?" Hannah would ask in her most severe and mocking tone.

When he could bear his mother's bitterness no longer, William would ask how she could be sure of his father's unfaithfulness. She could not, or would not, give him any specifics. Instead, she would remind William of the frequency of his father's travels and the obvious temptations he would encounter. His father's guilt had become an unimpeachable fact in the mind of his mother.

– § –

"We have not the louse. And it is our great good fortune to have our protector, El Teide, to replenish our rich and fertile land."

So began William's education on Tenerife.

His "instructor" was Ernesto Perez, foreman for the vineyard whose operations spanned a period of over one hundred years. El Teide was the volcano responsible for the soil on Tenerife, in which hollow pits were dug for planting and then surrounded by stonewalls to protect the vines as they thrived and grew.

William marveled at the ancient vines, braided together and climbing several meters up and back down the terraced plots. *El cordon trenzado* was the term Ernesto used.

"Our vines are *pie franco*," he said, explaining that meant the grapes grew on their own rootstock.

Thick as his wrists, William thought as Ernesto pulled back the verdant, five-lobed grape leaves to show the size of the vines.

"The grapes will ripen in clusters large…peduncle easy to cut…make hand harvest easy," offered Ernesto.

"When will they be picked?" asked William.

"Harvest begins August…near end. And maybe we go late to September near end. You want sweet wine? Late harvest," Ernesto said, smiling, and continued with the history of his island nation.

The phylloxera aphid, first reported in Languedoc in 1863, caused a great blight that proved devastating to the wine industry in France, as well as in other European countries. Ernesto did not know why—perhaps the favorable trade winds—but somehow the louse never made it to the Canaries, and their wine industry had flourished as a result.

Malvasia de Tenerife had long been the dominant grape in the Canaries, Ernesto said, and did William know it was used to produce the favored "cup of canary" in Shakespeare's *Twelfth Night*? The sweet wine had been immensely popular in the sixteenth and seventeenth centuries, and in the right hands, Ernesto claimed, this Malvasia could produce a fortified wine to rival that of the famous Portuguese island, Madeira.

The phylloxera epidemic, William did know, had one other interesting result. Due to the declining availability of their favorite restorative, citizens of Great Britain began to search for a substitute for their brandy and soda. It was in the wake of these events that he and his father had prospered as wine and spirit merchants.

– § –

The day had begun early for George as he headed for La Palma to inspect the late tobacco crop. On this trip, George wanted to acquire the long leaf filler for his cigar operations. With their return as emigres from Cuba, where they had gone to learn the tobacco trade, the "Indians" of the Canaries had begun to engage seriously in the production of tobacco, rivaling their mentors.

Finishing his notations, George closed the cover of his leather binder and looked at the verdant growth stretching out before him. His thoughts returned to the incident in the ship's saloon. He had regretted the "major's" embarrassment, and yet, he had to admit feeling a certain amount of pride in his son. Perhaps, just perhaps, he had not been a total failure as a father.

George's father, Eli, had been a stonemason, and at first, George followed his father's example. In consequence, he had developed a robust physique that age had yet to alter even now, in his sixty-fifth year.

In his thirties, George found encouragement to try the wine and spirits trade. Starting first as an agent, George discovered he had a winsome personality and an amiability that fostered relationships. Along the way, using the language of commerce, George's Yorkshire accent had disappeared.

Slightly taller than average and somewhat stout, George had a ruddy complexion and reddish hair that affirmed his distant Irish connection. His younger brother, Eli, had entered the tobacco trade, and by 1888 the two of them were operating a business in Sowerby, West Yorkshire. It was in the furtherance of those businesses that George had come to Tenerife.

– § –

William surveyed the lobby of the Hotel Quisisana, finding comfort in the fine Victorian-style interior. That the sun never sets on the empire was true after all, he thought with satisfaction. As he waited for his father to join him, he reflected upon the successful week they had spent in the Canaries.

His mother's words sounded again, and he struggled to make them fit the picture freshly forming in his mind. Her allegations of his father's infidelity seemed ludicrous next to the image formed during their days together on Tenerife. Cuckoldry, adultery—any form of disloyalty—was simply beyond his imagining when in his father's presence.

"The Breña leaf makes all the difference," George was saying, "such intense aroma and floral flavors!"

William smiled in amusement as the smoke from his father's cigar wafted in the light breezes. While hearing his father tell of the day's adventures, he watched for the slightest expression of immodesty, listened for even the smallest exaggeration that might suggest the penchant for dishonesty. He had found neither, and so he began to probe deeper.

"Why did you leave stonecutting, Father?"

Hotel Quisisana sat high above the port of Santa Cruz, where Horatio Nelson had famously lost an arm in July 1797. Nestled in the side of the hill, George and William had a clear view of the ship that would take them home.

Home to what, William was not sure.

He had to hand it to his father; George had not said a negative word. He had, in fact, remained complimentary of his wife's abilities. Not knowing the circumstances, William felt certain a perfect stranger would have thought George happily married still, and with a spouse who shared his business acumen.

William's question seemed to give his father pause, and he continued to puff on his cigar for a moment before responding.

"It was a young man's game," George began.

As he smoked, George told of the rigors of the work and the small remuneration that followed. He told of traveling miles from their home in Todmorden, chasing jobs. He spoke of coming home exhausted, his energy spent and little left to offer his wife and son, other than the food on their table.

"At one time, I thought I could build a cathedral," he concluded. "Then I realized how many blows that would take."

George paused to savor the remains of his cigar and seemed lost in thought, gazing at the tendrils of smoke coiling above his face.

"It was never the last blow that cracked the stone, you see. It was all those that went before."

A question began to form in William's mind, and he struggled to grasp the tiny threads of thought that drifted away with the wisps of smoke from his father's dying cigar.

– § –

The royal yacht, *Alberta*, made its way past a host of ships with their flags at half-mast, carrying a flag-draped coffin containing the body of the royal personage who had ruled Britannia for sixty years. Following behind on the royal yacht, Victoria and Albert, the son who had been "in waiting" almost the entire length of his mother's reign, noted the flag of his ship was also at half-mast.

Asking the captain why, the queen's son was told, "Sire, the queen is dead!"

Edward VII replied, "But the king lives!"

The flag instantly shot up the mast.

Thus began the short reign of the man who had already become the style-setter of the twentieth century.

With scant words of approval and fewer words of praise, Edward, Prince of Wales, had spent his lifetime preparing himself to assume the throne of

England. When a boy, he was not allowed to have friends. Moreover, his father Albert dictated the form and the content of his education.

After reaching the age of accountability, and in spite of several triumphant tours on the world stage, Edward was at no time allowed by the queen to engage in the political affairs of the empire. That the leaders of the world's nations found him charming and engaging had been consistently reported to his mother and to his father before his untimely death.

He was even blamed for his father's demise.

In November 1861, although unwell, with an undiagnosed case of typhoid, Prince Albert traveled to Cambridge, where Edward had gone to complete his studies. The rumor of an illicit affair between Edward and an actress prompted this visit. Although father and son were reconciled, after Albert's return to Windsor, Albert died the following month.

In her grief, Victoria was unable to dismiss from her mind Edward's role in Albert's demise. Over the next forty years, their relationship carried the strain of her blame and remorse.

Originally delayed until the end of the Boer War, Edward's own coronation had to be rescheduled due to an attack of acute appendicitis. Finally, on August 9, 1902, a year and a half after the death of Victoria, Edward was crowned king.

For most, it seemed they had known the king well all his life. "Good old Teddy," who had ended the Boer War, began his reign already beloved by his subjects. That love affair would continue into the next decade, and along the way, George and William's relationship would suffer, while William's promising career would come near to a tragic end.

FIVE

James Munro

While placing the "Closed" sign at the front door and turning to survey the interior of the shop, the initial surge of pride she felt was quickly displaced by a sense of foreboding.

But why would things be different? Hannah reassured herself.

After all, had she not made it clear to William where his best interests lay? Surely, after a fortnight with his father (that villainous, deceitful man!), William would need no further convincing.

Yes, thankfully, she thought, *William is strong enough to be his own man.*

Hannah was the daughter of a Yorkshire farmer, the second oldest of six siblings. Born in Erringdon, she had married George at the age of twenty-two. Their marriage had not been a happy one, except for the coming of William.

Short of stature and thin in body, it was her waspish tongue that made her a force to reckon with. Some who knew her said that her face gave her away before she spoke.

The voyage home had been turbulent, and William was weary from his travels. His father, however, remained his ebullient self throughout, and so for William, it was no easy parting. The journey by train between the port and the station in Todmorden provided William time to think about his life and his station. He and his mum were making a fine living, but

William found during his time away from the shop a restlessness growing within him. He was in his forty-first year, and as far as he could see into the future, he saw only more of the same.

Living with his mum was not hard, really, as she made no demands of his time outside work.

My time outside work? What did that entail?

As William mused, he realized there was little for his mother to interrupt.

Walking from the Todmorden station, he began to reflect upon the routine that had occupied each day of his life the last thirteen years since his father left. Every morning, he would prepare for opening, assist, wait upon their clientele, and turn the daily receipts over to his mum, who compiled the daily tallies with Cousin Gertrude. On those days, when this routine seemed to numb every fiber in his body, William would remind himself that the money was good, and his mum could not remain active forever.

Were those not her very words?

"I'll not live forever, you know," she had a habit of saying when William showed the signs of the restlessness and boredom that alarmed her.

And what of marriage and family?

The tedium of business provided a refuge of sorts, but living at home with his mum did not provide the best opportunity for romance. It was rare for a woman to come alone to the shop, but occasionally a wife would accompany her husband and make inquiries about the characteristics of certain wines. William enjoyed helping people pair wines with food, but those opportunities at the shop were few. He was also aware that he knew no women of his age who were "available," nor had he made many female acquaintances.

His journey by foot had brought him to the point where the shop came in view. He paused to take in the scene around him. Across the street, there were the funky, mismatched residences of neighbors, some of whom were customers. He knew the traffic would pick up and soon those faithful few morning patrons would begin to dribble in. There would be Mrs. Carmody with all the local gossip. *What was her tab now*, he wondered. Old Tom would bring his bottle and insist it be filled only to the half. "Me drinkin' problem ain't what it used to be...not by half," he would say. William smiled, as he always did at the crude logic. It wasn't all bad, he thought as the feelings of restlessness began to subside. Squaring his shoulders, he strode to the door, flung it open engaging the bell, before mustering his announcement: "Hello, Mum, I'm back."

"William, it's so good to have you home! You do look tired, dear. Would you like Gertrude to fix us a cup of Assam?"

Cousin Gertrude nodded her spinsterly head and rushed to retrieve the morning tray. William thought her rather good-looking in spite of her angular features. It puzzled him that she had no prospects and even more that she seemed not to care.

Soon, the two women were listening intently as William narrated the tales of his travels. They were entranced as William described his first sighting of the ancient vines. In their minds, they could picture the vines trained to grow up and down the hillsides.

When Hannah learned the details of the favorable contracts he had negotiated, she congratulated William. Not once, William noted, did she inquire of her husband or of anything about the time he and his father had spent together. William had to bring up his father's role in making the trip a success. For the time it took to tell of his travels, William forgot about the tedium that so distressed him.

Soon enough, clientele began to come into the store, and the day's business began apace. It was back to work, and William rose somewhat reluctantly from the warmth of his welcoming.

In the months that followed, William settled back into the familiar routine that he now found so distressing. The feelings of restlessness and resentment returned, and he began to exhibit an irritability that both offended and alarmed Hannah.

From the time William had started school as a youngster, Hannah came to recognize when her son was bored and what boredom did to him. She had hoped his trip to Tenerife would serve several purposes: as a getaway (or working "vacation") and a change in his daily routine. She hoped her son would return re-enthused. She was disappointed to find her hopes dashed and began to think of what she might do next.

The thought of early retirement had occurred to her. Just another few years and all would be well on that score.

Would William wait that long? she wondered.

– § –

The gentleman had been browsing the whisky aisle for some few minutes before William approached him. It had been William's practice to allow his clientele to amuse themselves for a short while before making their acquaintance. He hoped in this way to develop a reputation for hospitality using the "gentle approach," as it was known among the merchant crowd.

"Good afternoon, sir. May I be of assistance?"

Turning to face him, William thought for a fleeting moment he had met the man before.

"Yes, I do believe you may be of assistance, as you say."

Their eyes met, and before William could extend his hand in greeting, the man introduced himself with a strong grip and hearty voice.

"I am James Munro, and I am a friend of your father."

Hannah had finished reviewing the weekly tallies and correcting a few mistakes Gertrude had made. *Such a willing girl, but much too careless at times,* thought Hannah, resolving not to let the matter rest.

Gertrude had not taken the criticism well, and seeking refuge for her bruised ego, she retreated by way of an interior stairwell to the shop below. She soon overheard a conversation between William and a customer, remaining out of sight until the man departed.

"When may we talk again?" the man asked William.

"Soon, I trust," Gertrude heard William say as the man left through the front door.

Was that about employment? Gertrude thought to herself. When William turned back, he caught sight of Gertrude.

"How long have you been standing there?" he asked.

"Sorry, Cousin William, I just came down. Aunt Hannah is on a tear, and I had to get away." For a moment, their eyes met, and it was then Gertrude felt certain something important had transpired between William and the man.

She was right.

In the weeks following their first meeting, William met with James Munro on four occasions. By the end of their discussions, William was certain he had made the right decision. Munro wanted to hire him to help build his new business. He had just incorporated under the name James Munro & Sons Ltd., to enable and facilitate his contractual arrangement with the largest distillery in America. Cook and Bernheimer had appointed Munro to manage the newly acquired Dalwhinnie Distillery. William was to be their sales agent, with exclusive access to the West African market. All arrangements made to their mutual satisfaction, William had only the duty to inform his mother of his decision.

"You cannot be serious, William. Why, I don't believe a word you are telling me."

The shop had closed for the day, and Cousin Gertrude had left the two of them to finish the tallying and posting. William wasted no time in broaching the subject of his leaving.

"Furthermore, William, I do not see how you can leave us in the lurch like this. You know—"

"Let me tell you, Mother, what I do know," William interrupted. "You say you cannot live forever, and while that is true for all of us, it sometimes seems you might."

Allowing himself a small smile, William continued, "I want more than this life I have been living, Mother, if you can even call it *that*."

"Why, William! What do you mean?"

"I want to do more than run a little shop the rest of my life," he began. "There is an entire world out there, and it seems I have just become aware of its existence."

"This is your father's doing. I can plainly see his hand in this. You cannot deny it, William. He has turned you against me, he...*he* of all people! It was not enough for him to desert us! Oh, no! He will not rest until, until…"

"Until what, Mother?"

William's question was answered by Hannah's wailing and sobbing. With a rising sense of sorrow and the stirrings of guilt, William handed his mother his handkerchief and waited for her emotions to subside. When he thought the moment had come, he began by reminding her of the current favorable state of her affairs.

"The contracts currently in force will carry you through to the time you set for retirement. Gertrude can manage the daily traffic through the shop. So, you're all set, Mother."

Hannah looked on her son with apprehension while reflecting upon the truth of what he said. That she would want for nothing, she knew to be true. Stifling her anger and resentment for a moment, she looked upon her son's face. She was startled to find she did not recognize what she found there.

She had seen her son angry before, but the anger would pass. This was different.

This was the look of a determined young man.

Something caught in her throat, and she swallowed hard; her stomach heaved, and she thought she would be sick.

But he wasn't young anymore.

William held his anger in check, waiting for his mother to respond.

Be patient, be patient. Surely, she will see...

Memories of her years of calculated planning to ensure her son's loyalty came back to her, followed closely by an image she sought to resist.

She saw a face, but it was not that of her son.

The face spoke.

"You have finally done it, Hannah. I can endure your anger and suspicions no longer."

"No! Never! You cannot leave me! I will not hear of it!" she had said that day. The day George had left William and her in Todmorden.

In her disbelief and horror, those words sounded again.

"Nooo," she wailed, retching and sobbing.

Tears obscured her sight of the departing figure, though she heard his footsteps and the bell that signaled the soft closing of the door.

– § –

William began to unpack his suitcases as the SS *Karina* made her way slowly out of the port of Liverpool. The letter from Gertrude had come the day of his departure, and he had tossed it into a suitcase with some of his clothing. Putting his things away, he returned to the unopened letter. With apprehension rising, he opened it and began to read.

At just over forty-two hundred tons, *Karina* carried only eighty-eight passengers, most of them bound for the Canary Islands. William, however, was bound for Tunisia and the port of La Skhirra. The old port had become the center of the export trade in esparto grass, and James Munro wanted his new forty-five-year-old sales manager to add his whiskies to the ever-increasing list of imports.

William's training had taken place in the Leith offices, where Munro had personally guided him through an introduction to the products of Munro & Son and those of Dalwhinnie. Tastings had been a delight for William, for coupled with the pleasures of the palate came a respect for the knowledge Munro possessed for blending. While it was true he shared no secrets at that point, it was impossible to overlook the vast knowledge Munro possessed. William began to look upon his new employer as something of a mentor. As the weeks of training wound down, the only misgivings William felt had to do with the director of the company.

With his arrogance and pomposity on full display, every moment around him became a torture for William. Biting his tongue, William was able to endure a constant hectoring from a man who obviously regarded a majority of the rest of the species to be inferior to himself. Throughout his training, William was schooled in a rude and officious manner regarding the writing of contracts, along with their company rules and practices. Making careful inquiries of other employees, he found the director to be widely disliked, even hated by some. No one had an answer to the question as to why Munro kept him on. It was with relief that William left Leith to set out on his first journey for the company.

Munro's newest agent made his way topside on *Karina* to find the weather had changed dramatically, rather like his spirits. Gertrude's letter had not surprised him. Filled as it was with complaints about his mother's bitterness, he felt only pity for Hannah and sympathy for Gertrude.

Retreating to the dry warmth and comfort of the saloon, William was gratified to find a chair and soon began engaging with one of his fellow passengers in conversation.

"Patten's the name," a man to the left of William said as he offered his hand. "Where are you bound for, sir?"

"Tunisia. Yourself?" William replied as he took the measure of the man sitting next to him. A round, earnest face met William's gaze in a sincere and friendly manner that he found very reassuring.

"The Canaries and Tenerife, to be exact," said Patten. "So, you've been there before?"

When Patten told him he was going to inspect the late harvest of Malvesia, William's interest turned keener, and he spent some time discussing his recent visit.

Dinner provided an opportunity for their conversation to continue, and at the end of their meal together, Patten offered something in return for the interest and helpful suggestions William proffered.

"You will, of course, be dealing with either the French or the Italian emigres in Tunisia. They have all intermarried, and in the main, you will find them hospitable and amenable. There are, however, some you may wish to avoid." Taking a slip of paper from his vest pocket, Patten scribbled a few names and handed the note to William.

Karina made her way south, passing Lisbon to enter the Strait of Gibraltar. It was at the port of Algiers where William decided to stretch his legs. Patten offered to accompany him, as they had a few hours to kill, and the two of them made good use of their time touring the Casbah. William found their similar height made for a matching gait as they strolled along. He noticed Patten showed no signs of tiring and his ebullience was like a tonic. William began to think about what a friendship with this man might be like.

They hired a guide to show them through a few of the magnificent Ottoman palaces, most dating from the early eighteenth century. As they made their way back to the ship, William consulted his Baedeker and found, to his amusement, the port described as "once a nest of piratical vessels." Standing on a street corner just above the port itself, they viewed the comforting sight of French warships, row upon row.

"It seems some of the pirates may have stayed behind," Patten noted.

"Eh? What do you mean?" asked William.

"Check that list I gave you, and you will find a name that matches the one on that sign, dead ahead."

As William fished in his trouser pocket to retrieve the list, he looked in the direction Patten was pointing. There, he saw the name of an import business on Patten's "blacklist" emblazoned across the face of the building in front of them. William felt his curiosity rising and gave Patten a questioning look.

"Why don't we check your theory and make inquiries therein?"

With a shrug of his shoulders, Patten followed William inside.

The room they entered was small, well-lighted, and inviting to the eye. At a small desk with a telephone placed on one corner sat a very attractive young woman who greeted them in a strong French accent.

"Welcome, messieurs, and how may I be of service?"

"Oh, we were just strolling by and noticed your sign," William offered.

"Of course. And did you wish to talk to our manager?" the woman asked.

As she rose from her desk, William could not ignore her lithe and buxom form. With dark hair, widely spaced eyes, and full lips, she was a startling contrast to the women of William's acquaintance.

Glancing briefly at Patten, William said, "We need to return to our ship within the hour, but if your manager is available, we could talk briefly."

William looked at the business card he had received in exchange for his. Thereon he saw the manager's name, an international cable address, and that the firm had been established in 1883.

"A long time even for pirates to stay in business," William observed as he took a sip of his whisky. Upon their return to *Karina*, it was in the saloon that the two friends celebrated their departure from Algiers.

"It has been said that was the year the pirates came," replied Patten. "It was after the Treaty of Bardo, if I recall correctly."

William took another sip and looked intently at his new friend. He was puzzled to find he had bonded so quickly with a total stranger. There was no doubting Patten's experience, and William had been favorably impressed with how the man carried himself. He knew he would be foolish to reject out of hand the man's advice, but wished to know more, so he asked Patten to elaborate.

Patten observed the man before him, and began his summary of what he knew about the ethical standards of the firm (which were low) and the reputation for dishonest dealings (which was high). William took no notes and said nothing to interrupt, waiting politely for him to finish.

Why am I so concerned for his welfare? Patten asked himself before continuing.

"The firm has also enjoyed the protection of the authorities over the years. Their founder was one of the most respected of the early French colonials. It is only in recent years that the firm's reputation has declined."

William listened intently. When Patten was finished, William thanked him for his advice and for his sincerity, adding, "Don't you find it amusing to refer to the French as 'pirates,' given the entire history of the Barbary Coast?"

Putting the card in his coat pocket, William then steered the conversation to other topics of mutual interest. In a short while, the matter forgotten, before retiring for the evening, the two friends made promises to keep in touch. Patten left William's company in a hopeful frame of mind, looking forward to his eventual arrival in Tenerife.

– § –

"So, that will be four hundred cases of King of Kings, a butt of our best for blending, and could I interest you in a program whereby a portion of your shipping charges may be waived?"

Placing the contract he had just negotiated into his new leather case, William strode confidently toward his hotel. Some who may have observed him at that moment might have said he swaggered. There is no denying that William was proud of himself, and in a self-congratulatory frame of mind, he settled into his hotel's bar to celebrate. From his pocket, he took a small notebook in which he began to jot—in a code of his own—the results of his efforts.

William's initial foray into the community of importers had provided results that exceeded even his lofty goals. Buoyed by his initial results, William had gone from success to success. Apparently making a favorable impression from the beginning, after exhausting his meager list of prospects, he found he was being referred to other importers by those he had judged to be their competition.

Along the way, he had hit upon the idea of reducing the shipping charges to provide an incentive to buy. He did not know if this was a unique practice at the time, though it certainly seemed to get the results he desired. At no time did he pause to worry about what his employer might think of this gambit.

– § –

Munro & Son had their offices in Leith, which rested on the shores of the Firth of Forth and had served as the port of Edinburgh longer than

William could remember. The director was sitting at his desk—a rather large and imposing one, William thought—as he entered the office.

Waiting for the invitation to sit, William's consternation rose as the director ignored him while busying himself looking at the contracts before him.

The director was a large man, with a bulk about him that made even his oversized desk seem to be on the small side. As William watched with rising indignation, the director pushed his eyeglasses near to the end of his rather large and bulbous nose. He then looked directly into William's face for a long moment before speaking.

"So, Mr. Whiteley, we are a bit proud of ourselves, I gather?"

William, a bit flummoxed at first by the hint of sarcasm he detected in the director's voice, gathered himself and then asked if something was wrong.

"Wrong?" the director asked in a tone that seemed rich with accusation. "Wrong, you ask? Well, not if you are referring to the letter of the law. Nor are we referring to a wrong in the civil sense of things…that is, in the sense of insubordination, for example." The director paused to judge the effect of his words.

"Then what is this all about?" William asked with a touch of irritability.

"Please sit, Mr. Whiteley," the director replied, and William did so.

"Perhaps you will think me unfair," the director began. "But you see, here at Munro, we take seriously the matter of profit. As you undoubtedly understand, having run a business yourself, profitability is the foundation of success…in any commercial endeavor." Seeing William unmoved, the director continued. "Let us put the pencil to these contracts of yours, which, by the way, we are *obligated* to fulfill *to the letter*." The director paused, as if for effect, before continuing. "As we total the amount of sales, subtract the cost of producing what you have sold—along with your commission—and then subtract the amount for shipping charges you have waived, we arrive at a certain figure that, to you and to Munro & Son, is problematic."

William had listened carefully. He knew the profit margin from Munro's operations. Carefully (and rudely, he recalled) schooled about the prices of all the products made and costs of production, he knew the contract terms he had negotiated allowed, even after waiving a *portion* of the cost of shipping and factoring in his commission, a margin of profit for Munro. William noted when the harshness left the director's voice and his manner shifted to an amiability belying the meaning of the words to come.

"We understand this was your *first time out*, William," the director began, with only a slight tone of sarcasm. "Mistakes do happen, of course. Working for Munro, we also understand, is more than a bit different from your years of self-employment. In those circumstances, you might have been able to be a little more generous to your clientele in regards to the terms of sale."

William then heard a bit of the hard edge return to the director's voice. "At Munro, however, we cannot be so generous. Your commission, such as it is, will be reduced shilling for shilling by the total amount of the shipping charges you have waived."

Outwardly, William seemed unperturbed. His quick mental calculations told the stark truth—there would be essentially a wash. The net result in terms of "commission" paid to him would amount to less than what he had earned at his mum's shop. If not for the company picking up his travel expenses, he would be facing a disastrous deficit.

"What you say sir, is…simply unacceptable. The terms of my employment clearly allow the use of my judgement and discretion and even encourage such in contractual dealings."

At his reply, William observed the already ruddy complexion of the director turning a deeper shade of scarlet. *Not used to any sort of blowback,* William realized. Suddenly, there was a knock on the office door. The director seemed to freeze in his chair for a moment before shouting, "Come in!"

James Munro made his way into the room in a deliberate, unhurried manner. He went behind the director's desk and stood next to him for a moment before picking up the offending contracts from where they rested in a tidy pile upon the desk. After briefly thumbing through the pages, he paused with them still in his hand and looked full into William's face.

"Well done, Mr. Whiteley," he said, as the body of his director visibly recoiled in shock.

His eyes filled with distress and confusion, the director looked at Munro with a silent plea for clarification.

This cannot be happening! the director screamed silently to himself.

"Now, about the matter of shipping charges, William. How did you come upon that idea? Were you reacting to a move by one of our competitors, or did this come out of the blue?"

William looked at Munro, and with a deep sense of relief and satisfaction, he explained how the decision came to be. While on the ship with Patten, William and he had secured an invitation to tour the hold full of crates and other containers. During the tour, they noticed bills of lading attached with the shipping charges clearly stated thereon. They realized a few seemed to vary without regard to the origin, size, or weight of the shipment. It then occurred to him that the shipping charges were, perhaps, negotiable. At the moment of his discovery, he felt he should have known all along that this was so, but in his training, it was emphasized that the list of shipping charges, then in effect, should be rigidly adhered to.

At William's use of the term *negotiable*, he saw the color in the director's face change again, this time going from a shade of red to gray.

"And so, William," Munro continued, "you negotiated a significantly larger order, in your view, by reducing shipping charges. Charges that we might have to pay, given they were not passed along to the client as we normally have done."

"Yes, sir" was William's reply.

"And so, did you end your negotiations there, leaving Munro & Son holding the bag, so to speak?" Munro asked.

"No, sir," William replied as he reached into his case to retrieve documents, which he handed to Munro.

After a brief glance, Munro handed the documents to the director saying, "You appear to have also negotiated lower charges with the shipper, to um…offset what would otherwise be something of a loss of profit.

"Why, this was *very* well done, William!"

Glaring at William, the director sat back in his chair with a resolve forming in his mind.

SIX

Josephine

K*ILDONAN CASTLE* LEFT SOUTHAMPTON EXACTLY fifty-six minutes late on the last day of March 1906. In a first-class cabin registered under the names of Mr. and Mrs. Whiteley, the couple leisurely removed their clothing. William looked upon the girl twenty-six years his junior and marveled how quickly his life had changed.

Josephine was an inch or two shorter than the forty-five-year-old lover she had taken, but she felt in no way diminished. Auburn hair, blue eyes, and a trim, buxom figure, William discovered, made a bundle to handle. As the lovers slipped under the covers, they remained completely unaware of the ship's movements.

Their days seemed to blend into one long, flowing rhythm. "I had no idea you were such a fine dancer," Josephine murmured as they moved to the music. The small dance floor in the lounge was not crowded as William and his partner glided around the perimeter. He held her at a short distance, to give room for their legs as they negotiated the twirling steps that enhanced the pleasure of the waltz. Despite William's suggestion, Josephine hesitated at trying the hover corte, preferring the closeness of the traditional steps.

"In time, my darling, in time," William whispered.

– § –

James Munro was worried.

The reports that lay on his desk had brought alarming news.

Government reports had confirmed what he knew already to be true—sales were declining almost everywhere, it seemed, save Africa. The reports went on to suggest why. There had been a decline in domestic consumption of alcohol, precipitated by a corresponding decline in household incomes. The reports also tracked a growing societal repugnance for the "excesses caused by alcohol consumption."

Munro picked up the sales reports for each of his agents. *At least he could count on William.*

Continuing his review, he now turned to his director's confidential summary of the activities of each agent. Dismayed by the director's focus upon the *attitude* of his "star salesman" rather than his results, he rose from his desk with a question forming in his mind.

– § –

"You have the artist's palate, William," Munro said after the tasting.

"Pun accepted, James," said William, with some feeling of pride.

They were happily ensconced in Munro's office overlooking the Dalwhinnie distillery. William, looking out over the whitewashed buildings and thinking to himself, *patience, lad…in time, in time,* was startled by what came next. It was as if the older man had been reading his mind.

"Have you thought about coming inside to work?"

William, caught a bit off guard by the question, took a moment to smell and again taste the idea he had presented Munro. Noting William's hesitation, Munro suggested they talk further.

Given free run of the place, William had received permission to experiment with blending different whiskies in small amounts. Most of the concoctions he had tossed. When his senses suggested he might be on to something, he took a small amount to Munro for his evaluation. To William's delight, Munroe rarely rejected, but instead would offer suggestions for improvement to his creations. This collaboration had resulted in one experimental blend scheduled for limited production.

When the name was chosen, William was certain it would demonstrate Munro's continuing fascination with royalty and the monarchy.

– § –

With William's newfound affluence, he had moved from his mum's home, renting a roomy flat in Queen's Club Gardens near St. Dunstan's in London. He had not lived there long before he first met Josephine.

Originally from Surrey, Josephine Sharp and her family had lived in Lambeth for more than seven years when she met William. Her father was in the business of selling and repairing sewing machines, and with his wife, Mary Jane, had three children: Josephine; a sister, Constance, known as Connie; and a brother, Frederick.

After dating him for several months, Josephine felt it was time to tell her parents about William. Returning home from work one day, she found her mother in their kitchen. She sat down on a stool next to their dinner table and began her introduction. Things seemed to go along pretty well until the subject of William's age was broached.

Shaking her head and with an all too familiar feeling of despair settling in, Mary Jane paused to look at her daughter. "And so, how did you meet this William?" she asked.

The look on her mother's face did not seem to invite a response, Josephine thought. She saw her mother's head was cocked at an angle that meant she had to be careful what she said. Josephine told of the frequency with which she had waited on William at his favorite haberdashery and how their relationship had developed. She neglected, however, to mention the cruise they had just taken together.

"He thinks I'm bright, Mum, and that I work below my capabilities."

"He does, does he? Is he prepared to offer you something better?" her mother responded—with just a bit of sarcasm, Josephine thought.

"I think he's going to ask me to marry him, Mum."

Mary Jane had been slowly stirring a pot on the stove when Josephine's words fully registered. "Marry you!" she exclaimed as she stopped stirring and turned to look her daughter fully in the face.

"Heavens, girl, he's old enough to be your father! Speaking of which, yours is just home, if my ears don't deceive me. Let's see what he thinks of all this."

"Oh, no, Mum. Please don't! Give me a chance to tell him myself," Josephine pleaded, but too late, as Frederick Sharp entered the kitchen.

"Tell me what, Josie? Is it about another boy in your life?"

Frederick Sharp was not a large man, but he could be intimidating as his daughter was beginning to remember. She did not know if she could take on both her parents at the same time. She saw nothing but incredulity in their faces while they waited for the next installment from the pages of her lovesick adventures.

Josephine was crestfallen as the faces of boys she had been infatuated with flashed through her memory. Often teased by her pa about her lovesick ways, she did not relish more of the same. Feeling her blood rushing to her head, she fled the kitchen in embarrassment.

"We were not speaking of *boys*, Fred," Mary Jane explained to her husband. "Her 'latest' is only three years younger than you!"

Looking steadily into his wife's eyes, Frederick asked, "Who is this man, and what does he do?"

"He's a customer, and apparently a good one. Josie says he sells whiskey."

"A drummer? A forty-six-year-old whisky seller?! Why, I don't believe it!"

Josephine had fled to her sister Constance's room seeking sympathy. She and Constance huddled together, just as the voice of their father reached their ears, summoning Josephine in very certain terms.

"Now, explain to me, Josie, what is going on with you and this... what's his name?"

"William," Josephine replied.

"William who?"

"Whiteley. William Whiteley," responded Josephine.

Looking at her parents and seeing disbelief and disapproval in their faces, she felt anger beginning to rise within her. She also felt a sharp pang of regret, wishing she had never said anything to her mum. The fat now in the fire, there was no turning back. To her amazement, she heard Constance come to her defense.

"Why are you being so mean to Josie? Why do you think only the worst of this fellow of hers? You don't know him, and Josie does—"

"You can stop right there, Connie," Mary Jane interjected. "Your father and I do not need your interference. You may leave the room."

Flashing a look of gratitude, Josephine watched her sister depart and began to realize what she must do. With a tightness in her chest and uncertain she could speak, Josephine reached for her purse, pausing for a moment at the door of the kitchen.

"What do you think you are doing?" Mary Jane asked harshly.

"I'm not sure, Mum. But when I decide, you'll know."

"No. Let her go," Frederick said as he held his wife by the arm. "If Connie's right, we have done enough harm already."

– § –

Kildonan Castle was the last mail steamer laid down for the Castle Line. Requisitioned by the government for troop transport during the Boer War, at nearly ten thousand tons, it had recently been restored to passenger service.

William and Josephine were among two hundred first-class passengers aboard and under sail for the Cape, or as some preferred to call it "the Colony." Even though the ship would sail as far east as the Mascarene Islands, William's business would necessitate they go no farther than the *Kapp de Goede Hoop*, as the Dutch had named it.

Finishing her unpacking, she turned to find William looking out to sea through the porthole in their stateroom.

"Am I allowed to interrupt your thoughts?" Josephine said as she drew close and nibbled at one of William's ears.

William felt desire rising and pressed against her willing, eager form.

It was after their lovemaking, during their moments on the dance floor, when Josephine came to understand an important part of William's method. Thinking the waltz was the only dance he cared for, she asked why. She then learned of his interest in other forms of dancing and his plans to take lessons someday, perhaps to learn certain Latin dances.

"But that will be after I have mastered the waltz," she heard him say.

– § –

George was greatly looking forward to the wedding. Having just returned from the Canary Islands, he credited the fatigue he felt to a hangover from his travels. In his seventieth year, he had begun to feel the effects of aging, at least in his body. His mind was as sharp as ever, he reflected proudly, as he relaxed in his flat above the shop. Jane would be closing soon, and he looked forward to their end-of-the-day cocktail before the evening meal. As he checked the fire in their wood stove, he felt a tightness in his chest.

Damn old age!

"Good girl, Louisa," he said to their servant girl as she brought out the bottle.

"Are you all right, sir?" Louisa replied, as she looked into his ashen face.

"Feeling a little peaked, that's all… Nothing a little hair of the dog can't help."

Jane Crowsdale closed and locked the shop door with a final goodbye to one of their favored customers and turned to tidy up a bit before climbing the stairs to the flat she shared with George.

Must not keep him long.

Returning the box of cigars to the humidor, she reflected on George's carpentry skills as she admired the dark mahogany case glistening in the low light.

Built it himself, and not many of these around.

She turned out all the lights below and slowly began to make her way up, pausing to admire the artwork hanging on the staircase walls.

Entry to the flat above was through a bedroom converted into a study, with a small library she and George enjoyed together. She glanced at the books she had contributed to their cache and thought briefly of her home in Whitehaven. It was likely she and George were cousins, she remembered him saying. Whiteleys were all over Whitehaven, having come principally from Leeds almost two hundred years before. Yorkshire was full of them, as the census would show decade after decade.

George had come to Southport around 1890 from Sowerby, where he and his brother, Eli, had been in business together. Eli had, like his brother, been a tobacconist—until the day he told George he was making a change.

"Pickles, he said," she remarked, remembering what George had told her. "Pickles and spices are his game now."

Jane entered the sitting room to see Louisa bending over George and thinking she heard him speak; she walked around just in time to see him fall forward, out of his chair.

"My God! What has happened?! What have you done to him?" she screamed as Louisa looked on helplessly.

Louisa looked at her mistress in alarm and groaned. "I think he is sick, Miss Jane…"

"Get the doctor, Louisa, and be quick about it," Jane said forcefully.

"Dr. McHugh might still be in his office! Hurry!" Louisa heard Jane shout as she flew down the stairs.

Looking around, Jane spotted the bottle of brandy and managed to get a little down George's throat.

"It's not good…not good at all, I'm afraid." Dr. McHugh had finished his examination of the patient, giving George a few drops of some liquid from a small bottle in his case. The three of them had managed to move George to his bed.

"He will have to rest, and I mean *rest*!" Dr. McHugh began. "He cannot be allowed out of bed, so you will have to secure a bedpan." Louisa nodded, and Jane asked about eating.

"Should he want food, only liquids—until the worst of this passes."

"Is it his heart?" Jane asked anxiously.

"Yes, it would seem so. His pulse is very irregular, and he may not make it through the night. But I will remain in my office throughout the day, so come get me at any hour if you see a turn for the worse."

George seemed to rally shortly after midnight, but Jane did not allow herself to sleep. She remained at his bed, watching his breathing as he went in and out of consciousness. Once, he raised himself from his bed to ask where Hannah was, and Jane was shocked into silence. In all the years Jane had been with George, he had never mentioned his wife until now.

Soon, to Jane's relief, George drifted off to sleep.

Hannah must be told.

She was still his wife, despite their years apart.

Jane had met Hannah only once during a kind of reunion of the clan. She had not liked Hannah then and found her to be rather severe, even bitter. That was several years ago, while George was still in Sowerby.

Why they remained married, Jane could not explain to herself. George had never offered any information, and Jane felt she could not ask about that part of his life.

They had talked about William. To her surprise, George asked that William "not be bothered."

George's breathing became more labored about four in the morning.

She shook him gently, to no avail. With panic rising in her breast, Jane quickly went to Dr. McHugh's office. To her great relief, he responded immediately to her knocking, and the two of them raced up the stairs to the bedroom, where they found George gasping for air. Dr. McHugh went about his ministrations, and soon their patient seemed to relax and breathe more normally.

"That was close," Dr. McHugh observed as he closed his case.

"I have been giving him tincture of Ouabain, but should he have another seizure, I must be here to respond. Why don't you get some sleep, Jane? I'll take this watch."

– § –

"A spot of tea *would* be nice, Louisa," Jane said next morning as their housemaid set the tray on the bedside table and asked how the master was. "Better, the doctor thinks. He has to get through the day without another seizure and then we'll see. And I *am* sorry. I spoke rather roughly yesterday, I'm afraid."

Nodding, Louisa withdrew with relief on her face, and Jane returned to her watch. The tea was bracing, and as she recovered from her sleeplessness, Jane began to form in her mind how she was going to inform Hannah.

A telegram. It's the best way—short and to the point.

She set about composing a brief note for Louisa to take to the operator. Louisa made her way quickly to the post office, and the telegram went out shortly after the operator came on duty.

George suffered heart seizure. Stop. Dr. in attendance. Stop. Will keep you informed. Stop.

Rereading the telegram, Hannah felt herself growing dizzy for a moment. Shaking her head, she read the message a third time. Seated, with the paper in her hand, she saw Gertrude enter the room with their morning tea. Looking at her aunt, Gertrude knew immediately something was wrong. Setting the tray down, she took the yellow paper from Hannah's limp hand and read with concern growing in her face.

"Oh my. Auntie, this is awful. Are *you* all right?"

Hannah nodded.

Silence went on for another moment, before Gertrude rose to leave the room.

"Where are you going, dear?" she heard Hannah ask.

"To put out the 'Closed' sign… I think it best, don't you?"

Again, Hannah nodded.

– § –

Arriving home at 43 Oxford Street, William received a telegram from his mother informing him of his father's death. There would be no service, as George had requested. At the appropriate time, the two of them would spread his ashes over his parents' grave.

Waves of emotion swept through William, and he cried out in anguish, though no one heard him, as he had dropped off Josephine at the store an hour before. Pouring himself an ample portion of the unnamed blend, he went to his study.

He had seen his father only once since their return from Tenerife, and he was grateful now for the frequent letters that had passed between them. The effects of the whiskey were calming, and though it was difficult, he worked his way through the rest of his mail.

If only…if only we had had just one more visit together.

– § –

The vicar looked upon the couple whose marriage he was about to bless. He had seen it before and always hoped for the best.

Why do these young girls marry their "fathers"? I pray she will not be disappointed, he thought, and he pronounced them man and wife.

Josephine's parents came, and she was very happy her father had agreed to give her away. Even her mother seemed impressed with William's obvious affection for their daughter. William had asked an old school friend to stand with him, and the five of them had gathered in the Vicar's study to sign the document solemnizing the marital union.

He had hesitated for a moment when recording his father as deceased, and William was gratified at that moment to receive a reassuring squeeze on his arm from Josephine.

St. Catherine of Hatcham stood at the top of Pepy's Road, New Cross, occupying a commanding position upon the hill. As the newlyweds emerged from the church, a glorious spring day seemed to offer the promise of only good things to come.

Frederick and Mary Jane watched as their new son-in-law opened the door of the Sunbeam for his bride to enter.

"Fancy car, that," Frederick allowed while they waved to their daughter as the automobile moved slowly away.

"Yes. I can't help wishing the best for them both," Mary Jane murmured.

"I just pray she will not be disappointed."

Their flat was centrally located in London, near the British Museum and adjacent to Soho Square, with its amusing Tudor-style hut. Josephine fancied herself to be a quite capable cook, and William seemed to agree. The months passed happily, and William continued to progress well with Munro & Son. He was able to avoid being gone from home until October. Two trips to Africa proceeded to consume that entire month, and for the first time in their marriage, Josephine was alone for an extended period. She did not expect to see William for more than a few days in October, as between trips he had to report to the Leith offices.

– § –

He was a day out of Liverpool and enjoying a small libation in the saloon of the SS *Karina*. Nostalgically, he looked about the room, hoping to spot his old acquaintance, Patten.

Had it been a year?

Sipping his drink, his thoughts flowed naturally to fond memories of the Tenerife journey with his father. So much had happened since then, and...God, how he missed him! And his mother had seemed to be so unaffected by his father's death.

Seemed to be...

She *had* been at the wedding to see them off.

And Josie had been so appreciative.

– § –

The director was again perplexed as he reviewed the contracts William had deposited at the office. William had not remained for consultation, but begged off for a few days at home before his next departure. To his consternation, Munro had readily agreed to William's request, and the director was left to marinate in his private frustration. He was unable to find anything amiss and reluctantly submitted the contracts with his approval.

He is too ambitious, and I will be there to catch him when he errs.

SEVEN

Sacked

It was early in the year of 1907 when William's own sales began to decline.

He had reason to suspect that the heavier whiskies were becoming less popular. Mackinlay had begun producing a lighter spirit, its flavor enhanced by aging in sherry casks, and its popularity increased significantly due to its mild and fragrant characteristics.

"Three years is the critical point, I've learned," Munro heard his director say, "and then we find out who has the staying power. This lad may not have it."

Munro knew that sales had been declining industry-wide since the beginning of the century, and that was true for everyone, not just Munro & Son. There were indications that higher taxes were in the works. Suffragettes were actively, and in many instances, violently, going about seeking the "franchise," giving rise to lurid reports in the newspapers. The British Temperance Movement had grown and was getting traction, albeit with less fanfare than their sisters seeking the right to vote. In many instances, both movements attracted the same supporters.

None of this bode well for the industry, and it was there Munro had placed his focus. Now was certainly not the time he wished to think about losing his star salesman. He was glad William had resisted the idea of coming to work inside. He was right where Munro most needed him to be.

– § –

SS *Salaga* left Liverpool with William aboard. Destinations included Tenerife, Grand Canary, Monrovia, and the isolated and nearly defunct port of Egwauga.

Sitting in the saloon, William smiled. *Nearly defunct—now that is close to home.* The last rift with the director had been a sobering one.

No, William decided. *One must first have a friendly relation to have a rift.*

"My good man," the director had begun, "this *client* of yours has come to my attention, and not for the best of reasons." William noticed the avidity with which the director spoke.

"Just a casual reference check, you see, has revealed a number of reasons to question the advisability of our contracting with *your* client." Again, the emphasis upon the word.

"All right," William began, "what seems to be the problem? Does the firm not pay its bills? Is there a question of solvency? Are the principles politically out of favor with the ruling government?"

The director smiled and removed his eyeglasses to clean them with an oversized handkerchief.

William seethed at the man's pomposity.

"We are, of course," the director began, "concerned about the ethical standards of all potential customers. As you know, Munro and Son did not get where we are today by ignoring the character of the individuals with whom we do business."

"Yes, well, just what are we talking about here?" William interjected.

"What we are talking about, my good man, is tax avoidance, for starters," the director replied with relish.

"Taxes?" William asked, his incredulity enhanced by a growing confusion.

"Yes, taxes. You see, William, it is very easy to check with any country's authorities to determine if a prospective customer is in their good graces in regards to the timely payment of the taxes due…whether those taxes are on business activity, income, or whatever."

The director paused to let the matter linger in the air, but before he could continue his civics lesson, William intervened.

"Are you telling me, sir, that we are responsible for determining whether a *client* is current on his tax obligations? You don't see our boys checking with the authorities before delivering the goods to the local pub! Don't be absurd!"

"Well, you may be right there, William," the director replied with a smirk. "But we do observe the padlock."

– § –

Josephine sipped her tea at The Ritz, pretending to review the agent's analysis of the location.

Had she given away too much?

She was certain William would have been coyer with this agent sitting across from her. She decided it did not matter, as she began to imagine how their new flat could be furnished and decorated.

It *was* puzzling…the mysterious manner with which William had departed.

Clearly, he had been subdued, she remembered thinking, when she watched William complete his packing and preparation for his trip to Africa. She had been relieved when he suggested she look at a new flat coming available.

Fifty-Four Piccadilly! Right next to the venerable Burlington House. And just a couple blocks from the fabulous new Ritz Hotel! *We could do well here…*

The Royal Academy had taken over the old estate in 1867. She heard the agent say h*ow fortunate* it was that the government had been dissuaded from their plans to demolish Burlington House as a part of building the University of London.

With promises to make contact soon, Josephine parted company with the agent. Passing Hatchard's on her way to the new tube station, Josephine paused to admire the busy scene. *We could do well here*, she mused again.

– § –

William observed the figure sitting across from him while the man read the contracts, pausing occasionally to make notations in a notebook he had brought along for the purpose.

Must be at least twenty years younger than me, William surmised wistfully.

A dark head of hair. The mustache he wore was carefully trimmed and set off his swarthy, angular face to a handsome effect. The grandson of a French merchant and sometime slave trader, his family connection to French West Africa preceded the Treaty of Paris in 1783. At least six inches taller than William, and considerably younger, Louis Arnoult Martine stretched his slender, lanky frame while reflecting upon what he had just read.

Daring and adventuresome, he thought as he sought to penetrate the somber gaze of the Englishman.

Although they had not previously met, Louis had known of William's activity in the region.

Munro & Son were fortunate to have him, Louis thought. He faced his companion. "And so, *mon ami*, you wish to do business?"

William nodded. "The terms are agreeable with you, then?" he asked Martine.

"*Ah, decidement plus donc, mon ami*. But, your employer, he will be as enthusiastic?"

– § –

The director's spirits rose as he looked through the contracts on his desk. He congratulated himself for having taken steps to rein in his African agent. He even took time to reread the clauses he had personally written and directed be added to all contracts made by William.

Void unless countersigned, the words said.

Void, and *null*, the director thought to himself as he rose to make his way to the office of James Munro with the damning documents in his hands.

– § –

The dining table was set for two, and the welcoming meal was ready as Josephine bent to light the candles. Her man would be home soon, and she eagerly anticipated the look of surprise on his face.

It had been a perfect fortnight, notwithstanding William's absence. The lease on the Piccadilly flat wanted only his signature, and she looked forward to their last days in the Oxford Street apartment.

It had been here that William carried her over the threshold, and though he had given her free rein to redecorate, it was not *theirs*, as Piccadilly would be. She heard the door open, and she turned to welcome her husband as words of greeting slipped silently from her lips.

He stood motionless for what seemed a very long time, before Josephine moved quickly toward him. To her dismay, his arms did not reach out to hold her, and in his face she saw a look that made her almost recoil. Gasping for breath, she looked for answers in William's eyes.

"I'm sorry," she heard him say. "I'm so sorry, Josie…"

"Why? What happened?"

"I've been sacked."

"But…but why?

The candles had burned nearly to their ends and supper lay forgotten by the time William finished his tale. The whisky had made the pain just bearable, and Josephine felt thankful she had remembered that detail. She had purchased it as a welcome-home gift in a shop just off Piccadilly. The clerk had suggested it was something a connoisseur would appreciate, and it was from a small farm distillery no one had ever heard of.

As William sipped, Josephine remembered another detail. Touching him tenderly, she rose to go into the kitchen. She put dinner into the warming oven and opened the bottle of claret she had also purchased for the occasion. Returning to their dining table with two glasses in her hand, she poured some into one and looked at William questioningly.

Seeing the half-filled glass, he looked into her eyes and felt a warmth building within. He knew it wasn't the whisky. He knew it was, instead, what he needed more than anything else. He looked at the glasses, one empty and the other partially filled.

"You're right, Josie," he said, making his choice and raising the glass for inspection. "Life will go on."

– § –

William Whiteley and Co. was formed May 8, 1908. Shortly thereafter, the owner became an agent for Edward James and Co., Ltd. William had found offices at 121 Victoria Street, not far from Westminster. The couple had celebrated their second wedding anniversary in their new Piccadilly flat. Now, as William began his first trip on behalf of Edward James, the *Walmer Castle* steamed out of Southampton for the Cape. A medium-sized ship of twelve and a half tons, it had been in service only six years and still sparkled like new. Nevertheless, William felt quite a comedown, as he surveyed the second-class cabin. Better than steerage, he supposed.

After unpacking, William relaxed in the saloon, while ruminating upon a letter from his mum. *Gertrude has left me, and as I have no one to help run the shop, it has been closed.*

William knew this was his mum's way of conveying her disappointments as well as her expectations. This was not the first time since George's death that Hannah had expressed her disappointment in William. When learning of William's termination, she told her son it was not too late to do what he ought to have done all along.

"Come *home*, William," Hannah had written.

With only a moment's reflection, William dismissed the idea completely. *She is able to live on her own account. Easily able.*

He did not know why Gertrude had left, but he could well imagine when he reflected upon the bitterness that had prevailed in his mother's life the last few years.

Pushing those thoughts from his mind, William made himself focus on the tasks at hand. Edward James & Co. had sought his services upon learning of his departure from Munro, as William had developed a reputation for acquiring results in the whisky trade. The arrangement was very straightforward and much to William's liking. The company would not only tender to him a nice commission for sales made, but pay for his travel expenses as well. It would be a chance to get back on his feet, financially speaking.

Arriving at the Cape, William began frequenting his old haunts. It had been just over two years since he and Josephine had been there, celebrating their coming marriage. Each restaurant he visited brought back memories of their time together, and in the train of those remembrances came a longing for her presence.

His work kept him busy and in large part was successful, securing orders for whisky and blended spirits that made the trip worthwhile. His chief disappointment came when he discovered most all the contacts he had made on his prior trip were no longer present.

He was starting over in the full sense of the expression.

The offices of Edward James and Co. were in Edinburg's port of Leith, along with Munro and hundreds of other firms attracted since the thirteenth century to the deep-water port. As he made his way to the warehouse where Edward James had their offices, it gave William no little satisfaction to realize he was working for a competitor of Munro's.

He passed the warehouse of Lachlan Rose's lime juice factory, which, since 1867, had provided a solution to the British Navy's problem of scurvy. He noted the facilities for brokering, blending, bottling, and bonding, and thought, not for the first time, *if you made and sold whisky, you need to be in Leith*. There was Glasgow, of course, but that was further to the west.

He had found return passage on a freighter from the Cape that had brought him straight to the port. Here, he could deliver the contracts and be paid on the spot, in accordance with the terms of his agreement with Edward James. After settling accounts, he would make his way to London by rail and then home to Josephine. Feeling a surge of pride and relief, which he felt Josephine would share, he began to plan how they might celebrate his success.

When he saw the guard, William felt reassured. There had been occasional incidents of theft, and Edward James was alert to employee pilfering of small amounts of whisky, often spirited out in lunch pails.

The fellow guarding the entrance gate to Edward James' warehouse and offices was not by himself. He was aided by the presence of a large iron chain secured by a padlock, the size of which William had never seen.

"Wat will be yer business here, sir?" the guard asked.

"I work for Edward James," William began.

"Aye, and did ye now?" the guard replied. "Well ye don't anymore. No one does, ya see. They've gone bankrupt."

EIGHT

Reckoning

J OSEPHINE HAD AGREED TO DRIVE, and William was glad of it. The distance from London to Matlock was about 130 miles, and the Sunbeam, with the top down, made for welcome distractions.

Hannah, after closing the shop in Toxteth Park, had gone to Matlock Bath to take the waters. She sent a postcard from there, showing the view of the village from the Heights of Abraham with a short note that her plans had changed.

She would stay a while.

Sometime later, the manager of Tor House cabled with the news of her death, and William had been summoned by the coroner to identify the body.

As the couple motored on, Josephine marveled at how the 16/20 lived up to its billing of *the silent Sunbeam*. She glanced over at William's reclining figure, hoping he was indeed asleep. She was still cross with him for declining her cousin's offer of lodging. She hoped he knew what he was doing.

The year had been a difficult one, and there was no end yet in sight to their troubles. Hannah's passing had come with William out of a job and them facing financial catastrophe. Doing a quick mental calculation, Josephine thought they might have £450 between them.

Thank God the car was paid for, Josephine sighed.

But would they be able to keep it?

Originally formed as a hydropathic company, the Royal Hotel had gone through a few different owners since its opening. On arrival, the manager greeted them personally, introducing himself.

"Herr Buttgen at your service. Let me know, please, how I may make your stay more comfortable," he said as he turned the register toward William for his signature.

Josephine nearly gasped when she saw the daily charge for the room: £10 2s, including all meals and a fire at night in their room.

Upon arrival, the porter threw open the drapes in the room to show a panoramic view of the Derwent River gorge. She saw William tip the porter generously, and the moment he was gone, she turned questioningly toward her husband.

"How about a fango, or perhaps a sitz and needle?" he asked.

In her confusion, it took a moment for Josephine to realize that in his outstretched hand, her husband was holding a brochure presenting hotel spa services. With lips trembling and anger rising, she sat down on the nearest chair in a state of full incredulity. She struggled to restrain herself and failed to do so.

"How do you expect to pay for this?"

She listened as William began to explain. He thought his mother's estate would provide some answers to her question, pointed out that they had a bit more in savings than she had realized, and finished with a summary of what Munro and Edward James still owed him.

As he talked, she thought him sane and certainly composed, but when he finished, she felt she knew what she had to do.

"William," she began, "I have never done what I am about to do, nor said anything like this before." Pausing to gather herself and her thoughts, she continued, "Let us begin by accepting that all may turn out to be just as you said. If it does, so much the better, as you seem to hope." Breathing deeply, she forged on, her voice rising despite her efforts to calm herself.

"But William! If things do not turn out the way you hope...*if* you are wrong about *any one* of them..." She hesitated for a moment while there swirled in her mind all the catastrophic scenarios related to their near insolvency. Unable to meet his gaze, her eyes quickly surveyed the luxurious appointments of their room.

My God! What can he be thinking? A voice screamed in her head.

Then, seeing the look on her husband's face, she steeled herself against all the emotions churning within, and with a controlled voice, continued, "It does not *seem* possible that things will turn out as well as you seem to think. Of course, I do not know anything about your mother's circumstances, other than what you have told me. And while I am grateful that we have a little more money than I thought, I cannot believe for a moment you will *ever* collect even a farthing from Munro or James."

While she paused to let this sink in, there was a knock on their room door. She nodded to William as he moved past her. As William opened the door, she heard a man's voice.

"Hello, Son."

William blinked and looked with disbelief at the figure before him.

An apparition! Surely, his mind told him.

Stunned, his head starting to spin; he could only stare at the figure in the doorway.

His father, or a man who could easily pass for his double—his father *dead* these last two years—was standing directly in front of him!

And the apparition began to speak!

"I know it's been a while, Son, and maybe you aren't too glad to see me right now, but—"

"How?" William gurgled. "How is it possible…?"

Rising from her chair, Josephine went to see the apparition for herself.

"So, this is Josephine!" George exclaimed as he brushed past William. Giving a startled Josephine a hearty hug, George rubbed his hands together and spoke to them both.

"What a fine couple you make! Why, I…" George paused as the shock and dismay he saw in their faces began to register. "You both look as if you had just seen a ghost!" he observed quizzically.

– § –

It could have been worse, William thought to himself as he put down his copy of *The Scotsman*, dated 22 December 1909. It had been just over a year and a half since Munro had sacked him.

His counsel had been quietly exuberant, telling William, "Well, old boy, you must look upon the matter in this way: You have retained your good name, and you are free to do as you please."

Yes, thought William, *free but broke.* He mulled over the balance in his bankbook and still seethed, remembering the malicious enjoyment the director had exhibited in the confrontation with Munro. William had responded in kind, William had to admit reluctantly, as memories of the language he used came back to him. That, he thought, as much as the offending contracts, was what finally turned his mentor against him.

He had been gratified at the time with the support Munro initially gave him. He could see a gradual change occur on Munro's face as the director went on with his scathing summary. It was not until certain questionable terms in the contracts negotiated with Martine came to be seen in a negative light that the director succeeded in turning Munro.

"You appear to have placed us at something of a disadvantage, William. The appointing of purchasing agents and the creation of a business structure foreign to our interests were outside your purview," Munro said sadly. "And the trademarks, William...that smacks of disloyalty and betrayal, which I cannot and will not abide."

The words still stung.

William knew what he would regret most would be the memory of the disappointment he saw in Munro's face as he left their Leith offices for the last time. He had vigorously defended his actions in an effort to refute the allegations made by the director. He knew he had tried only to represent the best interests of Munro.

Left at the end with only anger and frustration, he had been unable to defend what he had created. Josephine had been like a rock upon which he had clung for support.

Now, taking the newspaper from him, she began to read aloud from the transcript of the trial. "'His Lordship held that the alleged illegal and fraudulent actings on the part of Mr. Whiteley had not been proved... There remained, however, a serious question, viz, whether Mr. Whiteley, while in South Africa, did not commit a breach of contract...by making contracts with third parties of an onerous and speculative character without consulting the governing director.'"

Josephine paused to wipe her eyes as tears streamed down her face. Then, she continued to read: "'The accusations levelled against Mr. Whiteley were bewildering in their number and their variety. The company's counsel very properly admitted that he had failed to prove the alleged fraudulent scheme. His Lordship went further and said that that charge was without foundation and ought not to have been made.'"

"There, William," Josephine cried out, "you are exonerated. You must see that!"

Looking at her husband, Josephine was disturbed by what she saw, and then perplexed by what he said.

"Yes, I see that. But I also still see that look on old Munro's face. He was like a father to me, you know. He trusted me and took me into his confidence…and…and the court held that, in the end, I had breached the contract."

"But, William, look again at Lord Skerrington's conclusion," Josephine cried and began to read: "'In his Lordship's opinion, Mr. Whiteley made all these contracts in the honest belief that he was entitled to make them as manager and director, and with the honest intent of benefitting the company.'"

The court held that William had exceeded his written authority. Munro was entitled to damages in the amount of one farthing for breach of employment contract. William was also required to forfeit any interest in certain trademarks. In the final accounting, Munro was required to pay the sum of £50 for retention of certain items of furniture William had shipped to the company's Leith address. In a counterclaim against Munro, William had claimed the furniture, bought and paid for on his own account, had been unlawfully detained by Munro. It was in one of the chairs from the lot that he now sat in, pondering his future.

For a moment, his mind went backward to that day in the hotel at Matlock.

His father had never known that his estranged wife had lied. After a long and tedious recovery, George, for his part, assumed it was over between William and him. He had been unable to appear at the wedding and thought William's silence was due to that. At the time, George could not blame him. He had not been a good correspondent, much less a father. If William was disappointed in him, George felt he had a right to be. Then, when notified of Hannah's passing, George felt there might be hope for a reunion.

At first, William would not believe his mum had lied to him. He had misplaced the note, or cable—he could no longer be sure which—that had brought the story of George's passing. Gradually, an entirely different feeling came over him, as he reflected upon what was initially sadness over the loss of his mother.

A deep resentment began to form in his mind and heart as William traced what occurred between their return from Tenerife some seven years before and that moment in Matlock. He recalled exchanging a letter or two over that time, but William could not check the rising sense of guilt over how he had treated his father, even when he thought he was alive. The two of them then resolved to do more than just keep in touch.

– § –

As William entered, what came first to his attention was the long humidor glistening in the low light of the shop, with the hint of a promise to delight the palate of a smoker. He breathed in the robust, aromatic qualities of the combined scents of the many different tobaccos. He caught the dominant, smoky scent of the latakia, then notes of anise, leather, and licorice to round out the incense-like experience. To preserve his palate for tasting whiskies, William long ago had given up smoking.

He now found his resolve weakening.

Over dinner that night, William was tempted to take George into his confidence regarding financial matters. Instead, he remained silent while they enjoyed each other's company. Jane had prepared a succulent osso bucco, stewing the lamb shank in one of George's best clarets. In his travels to Italy many years before, George had learned how to prepare the dish. As William finished his last bite, it occurred to him what to say.

"Father, if we must ever have another falling out, I will take this over a cold shoulder."

Their cigars glowed amidst the voluminous, curling smoke that floated like clouds in the failing light of day. "Satisfaction is the key, my boy," George proffered. "A lot may be endured if you love what you do."

William nodded, satiated.

At that moment, it all made sense to him. He might be low on funds, but he had the rest of his life to catch up. He was free of all encumbrances, with no obligation to anyone but Josephine.

Ah, he thought, *if only she were here to savor the moment.*

Continuing in his reverie, he did not recognize at first the names George was reciting. Coming alert to the conversation, he asked his father to write down what he had said. It turned out to be a list of contacts that George thought might still be valuable. William had told him enough so that George realized he might be of help. Looking at the list George handed him, William's interest piqued when he recognized one of the names: Martine.

"You knew Louis?" he asked George, who looked puzzled for a moment.

"Don't recall that name…it was Arnoud that I knew. Arnoud Martine; don't remember if he had another name. Just called him Arnie."

NINE

Pre-Prohibition America

WILLIAM REMEMBERED FILLING OUT THE required customs form and smiling at the questions: "Whether a Polygamist?" and "Whether an Anarchist?" He checked the "No" box for each, then went on to note his purpose for this visit: "business at 93 Nassau St. NY.," and "yes," he had more than $50 in his possession.

Now as he relaxed in the saloon, the *Oceanic*, a White Star liner, made its way out of the harbor of New York, bound for Southampton. His tallies told him this trip would keep him solvent and allow him to get out from under the most pressing of their financial obligations. It was the year of 1910 and he had been in the States for twenty-six days, making the most of each. Thumbing through the contracts, double-checking the signatures and the volume of the orders, he began to imagine the reception he would receive in the offices of certain distillers in Leith.

One thing for certain, none of them would be named Munro.

In 1892, the Prohibition Party in America received only two percent of the popular vote. The Anti-Saloon League formed one year later, and in two short years, it acquired a strong influence across the United States. Incensed by the number of saloons and the behavior of their customers, the ranks of Prohibition Party supporters continued to grow. Beginning primarily in the rural South, one by one, states began to pass laws limiting the use and access to alcohol.

It would be in 1916, after WWI began, that the movement would capture the support that would allow a two-thirds majority in both houses of Congress. Ultimately, this would lead to the beginning of Prohibition on a grand scale. The passage of the Volstead Act would occur less than one year after ratification of the Eighteenth Amendment in January 1919, and its enforcement would create the market William would exploit in the making of his first fortune.

All that was still in the future, however. Before the distillers were put out of business, and the saloons closed down, there was alcohol to be delivered and money to be made. This had been William's first trip to America, a newly discovered market with a potential that seemed astonishing, while that of his homeland seemed moribund by comparison.

To his great pleasure and surprise, William spied Josephine waiting for him in the arrival lounge of the White Star offices.

"You drove all the way!" William exclaimed as Josephine took him by the arm and led the way to where she had parked the Sunbeam.

"It's only seventy miles, silly!" Josephine replied with a coquettish smile.

Tipping the porter, William opened the door to the passenger side for Josephine to slip into. For a moment, William had a curious sensation that something was not quite right. By the time he made his way around to the driver's side, he thought he had the answer. Easing his way into the driver's seat, he looked with fevered interest at his wife's décolletage.

"You have nothing on under your coat...," he began.

Josephine grinned, and leaning toward him, replied in a somewhat husky voice, "Oh, but there's lots for *you* to see."

– § –

Mackenzie looked at the spreadsheets placed neatly on his desk, thumbing through them for a third time. Making notes on a tablet close to hand, he soon leaned back in his chair with a long sigh of disappointment. His gray bearded face, normally so jovial, was now creased with despair as he pondered his clients' position.

No chance…no chance a 'toll…there is no other way out.

With a similar sense of foreboding, William sat in a chair across from his attorney. Their eyes locked for a moment before either spoke. Sitting next to William, Josephine sobbed quietly while her mind raced with anxiety.

"So? We have come to what, exactly?" William asked.

Mackenzie looked at the notes he had made.

"What you fear the most, I suspect, William. Bankruptcy, it seems to me, is the only way out."

The numbness caused by the word crept over him like a blanket, suffocating a response.

How did it come to this?! he wanted to scream the words.

"These things usually occur over a period of time," his attorney continued. "At the end, inflows simply fail to keep pace with outflows. You have been spending more than you make, and for a few years on, William."

Josephine's tears had prevented a response up until now. She looked at their attorney for a long moment, and then in a tremulous voice said simply, "It is my fault, I fear."

"Now, Josie," William cried, "that's no way to think. If anything is true it is that we have *both* been at fault."

Fearing a marital argument leading to recrimination, Mackenzie hastily interjected, "Oh, yes. Yes, indeed. That *is* the proper way to look at things. In truth, you both bear a responsibility, but you are not alone in that. We certainly have Munro & Son, who, though able, have refused to tender the compensation William fairly earned. And then, there is James, who…well, perhaps therein lies a different tale. They did indeed declare insolvency."

That word.

Again, Josie felt herself cringe in spite of her effort to remain in control.

They would have to give up the flat on Piccadilly, and there would be no funds to pay for the voyages that had kept the money flowing. Everywhere they looked, in their despair, William and Josephine failed to see an escape. In the cold, bleak, wintry, early days of January 1912, a Precognition was filed by William showing over £2,300 in debts and only £268 in assets.

A ruling followed the formal declaration to allow the Official Receiver of the Court twenty-four months to file a certificate that his investigation was complete. During that two-year period, William would be unable to act as a director for a company and would be required to inform any prospective lender of his bankruptcy. The court had the power to undo a wide range of transactions entered into prior to bankruptcy. This action was limited in William's case, since all but one of the contracts had been performed.

The joy seemed to have slipped out of their lives.

Josephine saw William in his melancholy exhibit for the first time, a lassitude that both surprised and alarmed her. For days on end, William retreated into the small room converted into an office, where he spent most of his time shuffling papers on his desk. The rent on their flat, paid through the spring, gave them some breathing room. February came, and still nothing changed. All of a sudden, William announced he was going to visit his father.

A letter had come from George, intercepted by Cousin Jane, who, before mailing, scrawled a note on the back of one of the pages.

"Come as soon as you can—George not well."

Rereading the letter, Josephine noted to William, "Just like your father not to mention he is ill."

On a late February day, leaving Josephine alone in her quiet despair, William caught a train that would take him to Southport and his dying father.

William had not driven the Sunbeam after considering the cost of petrol. There was also the weather to consider and whether Josephine might have some need of the car. As he arrived by train in Southport, he was surprised to see Jane there to meet him.

"Since we are literally just across the street, William, I hoped I might speak briefly with you before seeing your father."

As they walked slowly along, she began to add to William's scant knowledge of his father's condition. "He will tell you that he is fine and that you shouldn't have bothered to come," Jane began.

"Did you tell him I was coming?"

"Yes, and perhaps I shouldn't have," she admitted. "There was a concern that a total surprise might prove too much for his heart. You do know about the problem?" she asked anxiously.

William nodded, asking Jane to continue.

"He had a spell about two weeks ago, and that's when I decided to intercept his letter, and—"

"Yes! And I'm glad you did," William interrupted. "You did very well to alert me. I had been thinking about getting in a visit after…," William paused to change course, "…after things slowed down a bit, for me."

It went just as Jane had predicted. After exchanging hugs and thumps on their shoulders, George invited William to sit. The bottle brought out, father and son began to play catch-up. William listened intently at first, paying attention to what George did not say. After some long moments spent listening to his father talk about what was *not* wrong with him, William seized the moment when George paused to sip his restorative.

"Tell me about your heart, Father."

From the look on George's face, William could tell his question had hit home.

"Well," George began, "the old ticker ain't what she used to be. But what is? Take, for example, Jane's old Vulcan out front. She's about six years old and beginning to show her age, too. But she can be fixed, I reckon, and…well, I guess that's the difference."

"I'm glad you saved me the effort of trying to drag that out of you, Dad."

George did not seem to notice the word at the end of that sentence, but William did. As far back as he could remember, this was the first time he had not used the word "Father." There was something going on, and William wanted it to continue.

"So, what do you say about trying one of Whiteley's finest?" George grinned with the offer.

It took a moment for William to realize they were not drinking it.

Downstairs, in a private room George had built long ago for his clients, the two smoked and reminisced well into the night. Jane popped in with a bit of food but did not overstay her welcome. It was very late when father and son agreed it was time to turn in. Helping his dad up the stairs, William was gratified nothing had happened to spoil the evening. As he prepared for bed, he began to wonder just how sick his dad was.

Amazing performance, he thought to himself as he nodded off.

Rising early next morning, William went outside to breathe in the frosty air. Looking at his watch, he knew sunrise was more than an hour away, but there was plenty of light to see. Staring at nothing in particular and savoring the long moment, his thoughts drifted where his mind wished. The moment lingered, and his thoughts seemed to take on multiple meanings. *Plenty of light to see.... Yes. Yes! It could happen that way.*

Soon, he became aware of a presence near him. Unperturbed, he turned and took notice of Jane standing just behind him.

"I'm sorry," she said, almost whispering. "It's beautiful, isn't it?"

William nodded and motioned for Jane to join him as they began walking aimlessly together. They went as far as the Promenade, and then doubled back to Lord Street.

"What a great location he has," William said as he observed the many shops and places of business.

"Your father has done very well, William. I guess you know he owns the property where the shop is located?"

William shook his head. "On my previous visits, I was so intent on getting reacquainted with Dad that I'm afraid I failed to notice a lot."

"Where's me breakfast, woman?" George asked in mock anger.

They had returned to the flat and had the coffee going when George appeared, still in his nightshirt.

"You don't appear ready for it, if you ask me," William shot back.

"Oh, I'm ready, all right," George riposted, and looking directly at Jane, continued, "Hell of a thing, don't ya think? A boy taking advantage of an old da' like me. Keeping indecent hours and drinking up my best whiskies! Ought to be ashamed, that's what I say…"

"Oh, I am," William said. "In fact, I'm so ashamed of me self that I'm going to eat me da's breakfast too."

After finishing a biscuit, George offered this first bit of cheer.

"You know Eli—your uncle, Eli—died last October?"

"No, I'm afraid not," William replied with his mouth still half-full.

"Well, he did. And it was a blow, to be sure. Only sixty-six, he was. Reckon us Whiteleys ain't built for the long haul," George mused over the remains of his coffee.

The day passed slowly and uneventfully, with George puttering about the shop while Jane and William waited on customers. George noted how easily William slipped back into the role he had occupied all those years with Hannah.

God rest her soul, George thought in passing. *It's good to have William close by, but how can he afford to spend all this time here? Doesn't he have his own affairs to consider?*

End of the day brought with it a pleasant state of fatigue, and William looked forward to dinner and the repartee of the previous evening. Things started well with another excellent meal, for which George broke out one of his most interesting wines. It was a *Chateauneuf-du-Pape* that, during a phylloxera epidemic, had somehow escaped being sold to Burgundy as *vin de medecine.*

The whisky was mellow and the fireside warm as William sat alone, pondering his future. *Not really alone,* he thought, looking at his dad, sleeping in the wingback chair next to his.

To tell his dad, or not to tell him—the question kept creeping through William's mind. Was he was only hesitating out of pride? No, there was more to it than that. He definitely did not want his dad to feel obligated to help. It was his problem, and he would keep it that way.

George yawned and tried to sit up in his comfortable chair. He glanced to his left to see William still there and yawned again.

"Guess I drifted off there for a spell. Need anything?"

"Not a thing, Dad. Everything is just right," William said softly.

"Glad to hear that, Son. Now tell me how you're getting along."

Resolutions are strange things, it occurred to William, as he pondered the request.

"Just fine, Dad. No problems I can't handle," he replied, trying hard to maintain his resolve.

Bullshit, George thought, *and I can still spot it a league away.*

"Well, that's good to hear. But if your old dad can ever help in any way, just let him know."

And that is where they left it.

Next morning, Dr. McHugh came by the shop to check on his patient and stayed a while to chat with William. He administered another dose of

Ouabain and made certain there was an ample supply on hand. Taking William aside from the others, McHugh told William briefly what had transpired since the original seizures.

"He doesn't appear to have had any heart damage, but it's only a matter of time, I fear, before he will."

"A matter of time?" William repeated. "How long has he, do you think?"

"One cannot be certain about these things," McHugh said, "but his age and the state of his health overall would suggest months, at best. More likely, less than that."

Later that evening, William took pen in hand to write Josephine a letter. Using some of his father's stationery, he began by bringing her up to date on his father's condition, including McHugh's most recent prognosis:

> *Dearest one, please know how much I miss you. The days here have flown by since I arrived. Each evening I grudgingly turn the page of the calendar, holding in my mind the day's most cherished moment as if it were the last. I am conflicted. While the last days of my father's life seem to flash by, I am longing for that time I can hold you against me and once again know we are one. Each time I think about leaving to satisfy my longing to be with you, I find myself holding back. How can I leave knowing Dad has only days or weeks to live?*

Using the edge of a tablecloth where she sat, Josephine blotted her tears. *Days or weeks...not long,* she thought. After rereading the letter, she rose to go into William's office, where she rummaged through his drawer until she found what she needed. Throwing a few things in an overnight bag, she retrieved the keys to the Sunbeam and made her way quickly down the stairs to the garage. She paused only for a brief moment to be sure she had forgotten nothing, then backed out of the drive and turned toward her destination.

Trying to read the map while driving did not work well, and she was relieved to find a cutout where she could pull over to the side of the road. *Just as well,* she thought in frustration, as she looked at the fuel gauge. Finding a petrol station nearby, she consulted her roadmap while the attendant filled the tank. It was then she realized she had no money.

"Will a cheque do? It's all I have. Really!" she pleaded.

The attendant nodded and looked at the signature.

"Do you have some identification, madam?"

Fishing in her purse, Josephine breathed a sigh of relief as she retrieved her driving license for inspection.

So many delays!

– § –

"He's resting easier now," Dr. McHugh informed Jane and William as they hovered just outside George's bedroom door. "He is not responding to the Ouabain, which suggests strongly he has suffered heart damage. There is really nothing more we can do."

Jane saw the doctor out the door while William went to his father's bedside. As he looked down on the man he felt he had just begun to know, his throat ached, though tears did not yet come. Just then, George opened his eyes. Blinking once or twice, he turned his head to see his son standing over him.

"You can sit, ya know. Might make it a little easier for me to see ya too," George said with a weak grin.

"Sure, Dad," William said, as he pulled up a chair near the bedside.

"Well, I heard the doc say I'm a goner for sure," George began as William struggled to find words for a denial.

"Had to come sometime, but dammit, we were just startin' to have some fun, weren't we?" George asked, as he looked hopefully into his son's eyes.

"Oh, yes. Yes, we were." William choked out the words. The tears made it difficult for William to see what George was holding in his hand.

"I want you to have something to remember me by," George murmured as he placed the envelope in William's hand.

"Are you sure, Dad? Because this is not necessary…and, anyway, I can't…I won't forget."

"Yes, I'm sure. But there is something else I need to ask you, Son. And maybe you can't give me an answer right away."

"What is it?" William responded as he put the envelope in his back pocket.

"I promised Jane she'd be taken care of after I'm gone. And…well, I need you to look in on her from time to time and make sure…" George began coughing and clearing his throat. His face became very red and his breathing labored.

"Brandy!" he gasped as William reached quickly for the bottle nearby.

"Easy, Dad," William said as George tried to drink from the bottle. As he was able to get more of the restorative down, his coughing subsided, but his breathing seemed more difficult.

"Let me prop up your head," William said as he helped his father raise his body to rest against the piled-up pillows.

"Yes, that's better," George allowed. Then, after a long pause, in a weak voice he opined, "And to think, they call it the old man's friend."

Oh, please, let it be in time! Josephine exclaimed to herself. Just a few miles southeast of her destination, she felt impatience like a fire building inside her. The drover did not even bother to nod in her direction as he coaxed the remaining livestock off the road. With her anxiety at its peak, she sped on.

Just let it be in time...

"You have no worries on that score," William replied to his father as soothingly as he could. "Does Jane know what you have in mind to do for her?"

George hesitated for a moment and then directed William to fetch a small wooden box from his desk. Opening it, he drew out some papers and, setting the rest aside, began unfolding one.

"It's my will," he said as he handed it over to William. "As you can see, I've left everything I own at my death to your aunt, Sara Jane."

William nodded, having read what George just told him.

Another fit of coughing was helped by more brandy. While George was catching his breath, William pondered.

"So, how is Jane to be cared for if Aunt Sara is your beneficiary?"

George nodded to clear his throat, and in another moment was able to speak. "Might want to take a look at what I gave you."

William did as requested, retrieving the envelope from his pocket. Opening it, he saw several pages inside. His attention went to the newer sheets first, and slipping from his grasp, the rest fell to the floor. Picking them up, he saw one set of them written on pages yellowed with age, marked "DEED." The newer pages, signed and dated with yesterday's date, effectively transferred ownership of the shop to William.

There was more to read:

Son, it did the old heart good to see how easily you settled in after you arrived. You have the knack for running a shop like mine. Of course, if you decide this is not what you want to do, I won't be around to see it. Remember: Always do what satisfies.

Now, if you decide to stay and make a go of it, I promised Jane you would keep her on. I don't know how long she wants to work, but I promised she would be looked after. I'm trusting in you to make good on my promise.

"And you have it, Dad," William said when he finished reading. George nodded and reached out to cuff him on the shoulder as a knock occurred on the door.

"It's your wife," Jane said as she came in without hesitation.

"Funny," William replied, "I didn't hear the telephone ring."

He rose from his chair as Josephine entered the room.

"I didn't ring. I just came."

– § –

"It's beautiful, William."

Josephine looked dreamily out from their vantage point on The Promenade across the sands to the Irish Sea. They had walked hand-in-hand after leaving Jane with George, still propped up in his bed.

"I'm so glad, so *very* glad you got to see Dad," William said quietly as they stood with their arms about each other.

"I had to come. Your letter told me that I must. And I think he likes me," Josephine said as she looked to William for confirmation.

"He does. I can promise you that. Did you see how his color improved when he realized who you were?" William asked with a squeeze as he began to relate what had transpired before her arrival.

Josephine listened with gathering apprehension. Still hand-in-hand, they turned on London and crossed Lord Street to reach The Promenade, a street that ran parallel to the sea for several blocks. They stood at about the middle distance from where the pier extended so far out it seemed to touch the horizon.

So different from London she thought, with the fresh, salt-filled breeze billowing, the handsome shop windows with their clever displays inviting one's inspection, the obvious success George had enjoyed there, and the elegance that was pervasive about the shop.

"But is it *real*, William?" she heard herself asking. "And is it right for us?"

"What do you mean by *real*?" William replied tersely.

Josephine knew she had to tread carefully. These were difficult times, and her emotions were raw. A part of her rejoiced when learning the news about George's generosity. *Yes*, it would be a reprieve financially, and that was perhaps the most wonderful part. Remembering the hope she saw in William's eyes when he told her, she cringed a bit, realizing he had come a long way toward acceptance of the idea, even before she arrived.

"I mean that I can easily see how your father has prospered, and the charm of Southport seems undeniable. But would we be happy here after the first glow wears off? Then, too, London is so different. I know I would miss it."

Josephine faltered, as she feared she had gone too far.

William pulled away from their embrace as he sank deeper into his own thoughts. *After the glow is gone,* he thought, *yes, it might happen that way.*

"But, the financial end of things," he blurted. "That's undeniable!"

Josephine nodded in agreement, and a silence fell between them. In a moment, she came alongside him, shivering as she put her arm around him.

"It's cold. Let's go back."

"All right," William replied. "But before we do, I need to say that I could not have gotten through any of this without you."

Josephine could not meet his gaze at first. Blinded by the bright sunlight that had just reappeared, and afraid of giving away her deepest misgivings, she kept her head down until they turned to go back. Soon, the two of them saw Jane outside the shop, looking frantically in their direction.

"I'm sorry! I did not know where to find you! And I couldn't leave him…"

Jane's voice trailed off as William raced up the stairs with Josephine right behind him.

George had slipped under the covers in his sleep, and the gathering congestion had caused another attack of coughing and spitting up mucus—along with little specks of blood. William helped George sit up and held the brandy bottle to his lips as George took a little between spasms. Slowly, as the brandy had its palliative effect, his color returned, and he was able to whisper his thanks.

"I can't leave him," William moaned. "And I know Dr. McHugh said there was nothing we could do, but please, try to fetch him now."

Jane left the room and soon after returned with the doctor in tow.

"He's dying, and there is truly nothing left to do. The brandy will be a restorative for a short time, but he won't last through the night, I fear." With that, the doctor retreated, leaving the three of them to their vigil.

Death did not come in the night. The following morning, George seemed to rally and even requested a "full English breakfast." They were in the kitchen when Jane reminded William what Dr. McHugh had instructed.

"Only liquids, he said."

"Yes, well, put me in my father's camp with this one," William argued. "The condemned man is served whatever he wishes, and surely we can do no less."

As Jane turned to her preparations, William reentered his father's bedroom, where he found Josephine huddled next to George, who was propped up in his bed.

William felt his face flush as he fought against the conflux of emotions raging within him. He stood, struggling against the fear, frustration, and anger rising in his chest.

He felt cheated.

Out of mere pique, it seemed, his mother had betrayed him.

For what reasons, what purpose, had she lied?

She had already succeeded in keeping them apart, with allegations of her husband's infidelity. She had had his undivided attention, his loyalty to their business. The fifty-two years of his life flashed in front of his mind, freighted with remorse and regret while he looked with admiration at Josephine sitting next to George. In time, she rose and came to William.

"He wants you now," she whispered.

Moving into the chair—still warm from her presence—he saw George trying to speak. He moved his head closer and heard a whisper.

"A gem...the best."

With that, he was gone.

Unable to hold back his tears, William softly placed his finger to close his father's unseeing eyes. For a long time, he sat looking upon his father's still form, unwilling to let go.

He felt Josephine's arm on his shoulder and heard her ask softly, "Is he gone?"

Nodding, William began to weep. Achingly, he cried out his sorrow. And Josephine never let go of him.

Oh God, it hurts! The thought came as the bitter waters of his mother's betrayal washed over him.

– § –

"You don't have to eat, William, if you don't want to."

"I know," he said as he picked at the meal Jane had prepared for them. Seeing that William was taking it very hard and being a private person, Jane resolved to grieve later when she was alone.

"I think I'll take you up on your suggestion," William said as he pushed his plate aside.

The obituary George had written was delivered to the newspaper without change. "No one knew him better than himself," Jane allowed. The others agreed and then set about to do what had to be done. Whether they stayed or went, the shop had to be attended and some kind of agreement had to be made with Jane to honor George's request. Before William and Josephine found the time to talk, a few days full of activity passed. It was more than a week later when their next revelation arrived.

The three of them got on quite well, Josephine realized as she finished preparations for dinner, while appraising the circumstances that had bound them together. As they sat down for the evening meal, it was Jane who spoke first.

"I have something to say, and…and I need you to listen." Seeing them both nod, Jane continued. "I remember when George promised to take care of me and that he would make sure I'd be all right after…after he was gone." At this, Jane stopped, wiping her tears away before going on. "But my father would have thought me a fool to believe that."

William opened his mouth to speak, but stopped himself in time.

"You see, my parents never approved of me coming here to be with George. They thought it improper. But they didn't understand how things were between George and me." She smiled again and, shaking her head, went on. "It was never about sex, you see." Jane paused, looking into the faces of Josephine and William. "We simply liked each other."

With tears flowing in rivulets down her cheeks, looking directly at William, she continued. "I admired your father very much. He…he was a good man, honest, gentle, and kind." Pausing to wipe her tears, uncertainty clouded her face, and she hesitated. "For the life of me!" she nearly shouted. "I never understood what got into your mother!" She paused, seeming to remember who her company was. "Oh! I am sorry! I should never have said…"

"No! It's all right, Jane," William said firmly. "I don't understand it myself."

"My Lord, what a day!" William cried when he and Josephine were alone.

"Unbelievable, really, this whole week. And to think what she accomplished in such a short time. It boggles the mind," Josephine murmured, pulling the bedcovers over her.

Nodding, William reached for his wife's body to pull her closer, whispering, "But the mind needs a rest, doesn't it, darling?"

With arched brows, Josephine raised her head and whispered, "Can you be quiet? We mustn't disturb Jane."

Kissing her gently, William whispered, "It's certainly worth a try."

– § –

A truck containing all their worldly possessions left London before they did, as the plan was for William and Josephine to be there a few hours in advance, since the truck was slower. As they motored along, Josephine's thoughts went back to the remarkable story Jane had told them.

In her time with George, she had accumulated a tidy bit of money that she thought would see her though for some time.

"I never went with George on any of his trips, and of course, we never took a vacation together. After all, George paid for everything, and so there was very little need to spend my money."

Jane told them she wanted to get out and see some of the world. Now that George was gone, she set about planning to do so. William and Josephine had agreed to her request to return in two weeks or less.

William was at the wheel of the Sunbeam. As they drove along, he could tell Josephine was deep into her thoughts, and so the silence between them was not oppressive. Putting aside her misgivings, she had agreed to "give Southport a try." There was obviously the opportunity to make something of the chance George had given them.

At the thought of his father's generosity, William felt the tears forming and reached for a handkerchief. In doing so, he momentarily lost control of the Sunbeam and had to wrench the steering wheel to get back on the road.

"Are you all right?" Josephine asked in quiet alarm.

William nodded and smiled as they drove on through the countryside.

– § –

"Now, of course, you will want to look at the latest inventory."

Jane began the orientation, pulling out the journals she had kept for George. William could immediately see that there was an ample supply of most sizes.

"Based on previous sales, I would estimate you have about a three-month supply on hand," Jane continued.

Giving a cursory examination, William found no need to disagree. "But apart from those boxes on display," he said, pointing to hundreds of cigar boxes stored on wall shelving, "are there any in storage elsewhere?"

"Not that I know of," replied Jane, "unless there are some in the cellar. But then, I believe there is only the wine stored there."

"The wine?" William inquired. "What wine?"

During the several meals he had had with George in recent months, William never thought to inquire about any of the wines they had enjoyed. He assumed George kept on the premises only what he would consume, going to the nearby wine and spirits merchant as the need presented. Now, in the low light of the cellar, William saw what he thought must be dozens of cases of wine stored on racks. With a torch kept nearby for such purposes, William began his inventory of this unexpected treasure.

"Did Dad keep an inventory of his wine as well as his cigars?"

"I do not think so," Jane said doubtfully. "If he did, I do not know of it."

As he moved slowly along, William noted the nearly perfect conditions provided in the cellar. Occasionally, picking up a bottle to examine the cork, he was gratified to find none spoilt.

Looking at Jane, William apologized, "It's not right that I should keep you. I can do this later."

As he replaced the bottle on the rack, he noted the vintage. *I believe that burgundy was pre-phylloxera…*

Placing an 1885 Grand Cru gingerly on the rack, William picked up the next bottle. It was the same. Excitement rising in his breast, he quickly went up and down the line of racks, carefully rotating each bottle a quarter-turn.

It was a Sunday afternoon, and Josephine was upstairs preparing their dinner as William sat down on a nearby wine crate to gather his thoughts. *How did he acquire this hoard?* William mused. *He must have had these when he was in Todmorden; but where did he store them?*

"Anything going on down here?" Josephine inquired.

"A small fortune…that's what we have." William looked at his wife, grinning.

"Fortune?" Josephine asked, excitement rising in her voice.

"Yes. And I'm still trying to figure out how he did it. It must have been when Uncle Eli and he owned those buildings in Sowerby. I knew they had cellars, but I never…"

"Went down there?" Josephine finished his sentence.

"Exactly. That was, what, 1889? About right for most of these burgundies. Then he came here a couple years later. No! Not here. That was on Eastbank, where he lived first. The date of the deed to him…let's see… Was that 1901?"

"William, are you sure? I mean, it's been moved thrice, and we know nothing about how it was handled."

William looked at his wife with an even wider grin. "I would bet my life that Dad took every precaution. Besides, this was clearly to be part of his retirement fund."

"So, what are we looking at here? Thousands? Hundreds?" Josephine breathed deeply.

Between running the shop and chatting up his clientele, William had found precious few hours for completing the inventory in the cellar. Usually, after dinner, he would take his notepaper that he kept in a portfolio, and with pen in hand, record the vineyard and the vintage. When he got to the Chateau Margaux, 1900, his heartbeat increased significantly. Bordeaux, post-phylloxera, was grafted to American rootstock but still judged to be outstanding. It was the port, though, that capped off the joy of his discovery.

Dinner was especially good, and knowing Josephine's love for vintage port, he had set a bottle upright earlier to allow the sediment to fall before decanting. Josephine smiled when she saw William had hidden the label.

At heart, still a little boy, she mused.

"Now, try this," he said, handing her a stemmed, tulip-shaped glass.

Josephine nosed and sipped. "Black fruit, stylish, intense…luscious, with some cherry…yet young."

Nodding, William poured himself a small portion. Nosing and then taking in a small amount, he let the rich, red liquid rest on each side of his tongue. Swallowing slowly, he then clicked his tongue against the front of his palate, breathing in slowly to savor the finish. "Yes. Young and very promising."

TEN

Martine

Louis Arnoult Martine sat at his desk with the letter in his hand, unopened. His thoughts drifted back to that moment when he received the notice from Munro & Son, introducing their new agent. He had not bothered to reply, and remembered feeling a vague sense of foreboding at the time regarding the whereabouts and well-being of their previous agent. For reasons then unknown to him, their plan had not been allowed to come to fruition.

La plupart des malheureux, Louis Arnoult Martine thought.

Business had not been good of late, but of course, he could always count on his wealthiest clients, especially if there was something that might interest a collector. As he opened the envelope, a list of some kind fell from the folded letter inside. Picking it up, he noted immediately the predominance of burgundies, though it was the Margaux that his eyes fastened upon.

Est-il possible?

It had been said that all of it was gone. Then, he set his attention to William's letter.

> *Old friend, it has been far too long since we enjoyed each other's company. I trust things continue to go well for you and pray your family is well.*

Martine paused for a moment to reflect upon his own father's recent passing. *Ah,* Louis thought, realizing he could not have known, and read on.

> *You will find enclosed a list of various vintages that have recently come into my possession. Before going to auction, I thought I would contact a few of my old friends from earlier days. Perhaps you or a friend of yours in the business would be interested. Feel free to cable me at the enclosed address within a fortnight of receiving this letter. If you find you are without interest, you need not worry yourself further. For, if I do not hear from you, I will assume there are no prospects for doing business.*
>
> *Most sincerely, W. Whiteley*

Putting down the letter, and after making a few brief inquiries, he cabled William regarding his interest. Martine then began formulating, by letter, his reply.

> *Dear William,*
>
> *Yours of the 18th instant arrived containing within a list of treasures that are impossible to resist. I might almost say, "name your price," as a couple of my special clients seem to be prepared for a bidding war. However, I must ask you to assume full responsibility for shipping and warrant the condition of each vintage purchased. The enclosed agreement spells out those responsibilities in detail. You need only sign where indicated and enclose the document with the shipment.*
>
> *I have taken the liberty of assuming an initial payment of fifty percent will suffice to secure shipment, the balance payable upon receipt and confirmation of the acceptable status of each item. Your proposition comes at a good time, and I very much look forward to our continuing relationship. Please give me all the news of your family and your situation. I am most eager to learn of your ventures.*
>
> *Warmest regards, Louis*

As he gazed about the now-empty cellar, William thought about how to use the proceeds from the sale. Certainly, there were the death duties to satisfy, and as he mentally did his tabulations, he arrived at a tidy remainder that would help see them through. *More than that, really,* William considered, as he turned to go up the stairs, taking one last look around before turning out the light.

Business at the shop had increased once word got around that George's son had come to continue operations. With a mixture of satisfaction and apprehension, he observed cash receipts rise as his inventory dwindled. It was clear that Jane had been wrong. There did not appear to be a three-month supply of tobacco inventory. It would be cutting it close if he did not immediately send cables requesting new supplies.

Thank God for Martine's prompt tender of the balance due, he thought as he put the "Closed" sign out and made his way to the post office.

Josephine reflected a moment on what had so recently transpired as she set aside the letter from her friend in London. Outwardly, everyone seemed to be going about their business normally, her friend had written, but rumors of war were in the air. To be here in Southport, and safe and prospering, seemed nothing less than miraculous.

She took stock of their situation as she began to make postings in the journals she kept. Jane had been so helpful before she left, showing Josephine how each entry led to another until the complete transaction was recorded. As she totaled the receipts for the day, she placed them in the bag the bank had provided, and picking up the passbook, made her way out the door, being careful to reposition the "Closed" sign as William had left it.

The Bank of Southport and West Lancashire was located on Lord Street, just a short walk from the shop. Her new friend, the young assistant manager, was there to greet her. Tallying the day's receipts, Josephine was relieved as always that she had not made a mistake.

"I see you have your passbook, Miss Josephine," the assistant manager observed. "Let's determine your new balance."

She watched as the young man entered the figures and brought forward the total balance on account.

"My, we are building a fine business, aren't we?" the assistant manager exclaimed.

Josephine nodded and agreed things were going well.

"Have you and Mister William considered how you might invest some of your holdings? Gilts are very safe and provide a tidy return."

Seeing that Josephine was interested, he bought out tables showing the different interest rates available on British government bonds. Thanking him, Josephine took some information with her on the investments and made her way back to the shop.

"I think cash will be king in the years ahead," William offered.

Dinner finished, they had swept aside the dishes and spread out the information the assistant bank manager had provided.

"But cash provides such a small return," Josephine countered.

Gradually, as a few hours passed, the couple came to grips with their improving financial situation. They anticipated the court would soon declare the matter of their bankruptcy closed and finalize their status. William was ready to move on.

"It has come to my attention that a certain firm in London may be coming up for sale."

"You are thinking of leaving Southport?" Josephine gasped.

William smiled. He reached out, took her hand in his, kissed it, and looked directly into her eyes. "I have never given up hope, Josie, that one day I would be back in the whisky business."

"But I thought we were happy here," she argued. "Haven't you been happy, and haven't we done well enough?"

Well enough? The question reverberated in his mind.

"It may be that well enough is not *good enough*," William insisted, releasing her hand and sitting back in his chair.

Josephine saw her husband steeple his fingers and gaze directly at her. With growing apprehension, she listened as, for the first time, William began to describe the life he wanted for them.

As he went along, she tried to fight against the entrancement she saw in the picture he painted with his words. Gradually, in spite of her doubts, she began to relax as she became able to visualize the future he presented. How long he talked, she was not sure. When he was done, she felt dazed.

"Is it possible, really possible to do?" she asked with wonder.

"I believe it is," William countered with a serenity she had not seen in him for a very long time.

– § –

"Amazing, William! Nothing short of amazing," Mackenzie remarked as he shuffled through the papers he had been provided. With a slight smile on his face, William gazed at the white, bearded countenance of the man he had come to rely on so heavily during the last six years.

He had taken the train from Southport, coming alone, and now he sat across from his lawyer's desk. The court had ruled that his bankruptcy was final. Discharged from all his previous debts, he sat in London, ready to move on—and in rather dramatic fashion.

"I cannot imagine how you did it, and in such a short time. There seems to be no barrier to pushing ahead. No barrier at all," Mackenzie concluded as he reached for a different file. "This man, Wilson, has only just acquired the business, and here he is, ready to dispose of it," Mackenzie remarked.

"Why do you think that is so?" William inquired of his grizzled counselor.

"We may have to view this in two ways," Mackenzie began. "First, there is the obvious possibility that he wishes to try to make a quick turnaround profit. The second is that he may have been trying to do Turney a favor, and now, perhaps he regrets having done so. Either way, I submit to you that his state of affairs can work to your advantage."

So it proved.

Turney & Son was essentially a defunct business, having been wound up altogether. For whatever reasons John Wilson may have had for acquiring the firm, he now willingly signed over all goodwill, trademarks, brands, office furniture, fittings, typewriters, books of account, correspondence, and stationery used in connection with J. G. Turney & Son, located at 21 Mincing Lane, London. The firm's history began in 1891, and their business description was as "distillers, blenders, and exporters of scotch whisky and other spirits."

William had become an entrepreneur. No longer working for someone else, all of his energy, creativity, imagination, and talent could now be devoted entirely to his own affairs. He moved quickly to secure his position by reincorporating Turney as a limited liability corporation to avoid any personal exposure to the financial turbulence of commercial business affairs. He had learned that lesson well.

– § –

"Why, Jane, do come in," Josephine exclaimed as their friend entered the front door of the shop.

"I just thought I'd drop in and see how you and William are getting along," Jane said as she removed her hat and placed her purse on the counter.

"I'm sorry William is not here to see you. He is off in London on business, and I'm running the shop until he returns. Let's have a cup of tea and catch up." Josephine's mind raced with the possibilities.

It proved to be a slow morning, with only a handful of customers dropping in, so Jane and Josephine had the opportunity to reconnect and learn what had transpired since Jane's retirement. She had traveled on the continent, even going so far as Egypt to see the pyramids and sail the Nile. Listening to Jane, Josephine found her thoughts wandering to why she had chosen to reappear in their lives.

Eventually, she found that Jane had become bored with the inactivity she had experienced after her travels were over. She had seen what she wanted to see of the world and began thinking about what to do thereafter. She had also heard how well the shop had prospered, and was hopeful there might still be a position available. That is, if there might be a need.

Smiling inwardly, Josephine assured Jane that she would broach the subject with William upon his return, and they would get back to her soon.

Completing her postings for the day, and going to lock the front door, she was surprised to meet a delivery boy with a cable from William:

Dearest, we are now owners of Turney & Son, Ltd. Details to follow upon my arrival home. Fondly, Wm.

Over dinner, later that same evening, William proceeded to explain how Turney could be an excellent vehicle for pursuing their dream, Josephine marveled at how their lives were changing so rapidly. She felt like a traveler on a fast train watching her life speed by, leaving everything a blur.

Then, she heard William say, "Of course, if war comes, there's no telling what might happen."

"But, do you really think we will have war?" she questioned. "War between cousins just doesn't make sense!"

ELEVEN

August 1916

A<small>DA TRIED TO STOP THE</small> tears, allowing only small sniffles as she worked to stem the tide of emotion that swelled within her. She knew he had to go, and truly, if she could allow herself to think so, she wanted him to do his part.

It was so hard letting go!

They had been married less than a year, and there had hardly been time to settle into their new flat. She loved her new name. Ridley. It sounded strong. They had talked about not having children just yet, and Ada saw their future empty of everything but loneliness. Yes, the war had been underway almost exactly a year before they married. Yes, most of their friends had already been through their parting sorrows, and some men were already home on leave.

She sat on a corner of their bed and watched her husband complete his packing. His smooth, angular face offset by a shock of dark brown hair never seemed more handsome. He smiled and stopped for a moment. His dark brown eyes, more luminous with tears, looked down into hers. With a gasp, Ada rose and, reaching out, she and Vernon clasped their arms around each other. Sobbing freely and without restraint, Ada relished the comforting warmth of Vernon's body against hers.

The pleasure of their bodies fitting together perfectly; the intoxicating scent of her hair; her taut breasts pressed against his chest; her tears streaming in rivulets and wetting his uniform shirt were what he knew he would remember and cherish about their parting.

They were still holding each other when the taxi honked its arrival.

Slowly, they separated, looking searchingly into each other's eyes. Her blond hair, cut short in the earphones hairstyle and now askew, made her face seem sadder, but more beautiful than ever. Finally, Vernon broke the silence.

"I'll write. Every day."

"You better," Ada nodded as she gradually let go, arms falling helplessly to her sides.

She stood immobile as Vernon picked up his things and made his way out the door of their flat without looking back.

She raced to the window and stared down at the taxi, seeing Vernon enter and then the door closing.

She watched the taxi move away from the curb, then out of her sight.

For how long she stood there she did not know; she simply stared out the window at the nothingness before her.

Dearest,

Arrived Netheravon early this afternoon, having thought I knew my right from my left. Our sergeant has disabused me of that notion, with very specific instructions. With drill and practice, my group and I have received the assurance that we will soon be able to turn left and right with great precision.

There are twenty of us in our training group, and I have not had time to get to know any of them well, but that should not be difficult as we are in such close quarters. More soon, but must retire as morning comes much earlier here than at home.

Fondly, Vernon 15/8/16

Darling Ada,

You wanted to know about the food here. Well, not to put too fine a point on it, it's awful. I think we will lose weight since it tastes so badly.

We are beginning to think we are in the Army, as there has been no mention of any Air Corps squadrons. We drill several times a

day while being referred to as "soldiers," not airmen. There is a huge gap between our sergeants and us enlisted men, even more than between the officers and NCOs. Last night, when we were off duty, we passed a sergeant and greeted him, only to get ourselves chewed out for familiarity. To bed early again. Miss you terribly,
Vernon 16/8/16

Dear Ada,
Total domination. That's what the military is about. Already today, I have been chewed out at least six times and for what purpose, I cannot tell. I am writing you this quick note in the early afternoon before we go back to drill. I may be too tired to write later tonight. Still being made into a soldier and no aircraft in sight.
Your loving husband, or what's left of him,
Vernon 17/8/16

Ada put down the last of the three letters after reading them over and again. In her mind, she tried to picture what Netheravon might be like. Everyone knew it was on Salisbury Plain, not too far from Amesbury. If Vernon had thought about it, she was sure he would have described the camp. It was no secret, after all. Reading the letters again, she began to form her reply.

Darling Vernon,
Your letters have all arrived, just as you promised. I see that it may be too much of a burden for you to write daily, so please write only when you have time to tell me more about the camp and your new friends. I long for news about not only what is happening, but also what plans the military has for you.
It has turned cooler here at home, with rain heavy and thundery for the most part. I so look forward to our time together after your training. Please take care of yourself, as there is one here who loves you and misses you terribly.
All my love, Ada
20/8/16

My love,

Thanks for releasing me from my promise to write daily. It has been a most eventful week, and I am full of news. There is a squadron in my future! After all the drilling and soldiering, most of my group will get unit assignments next week. Most think they are certain to be going to France. There are a few thinking Africa. I don't really care, but with the Germans surrendering in South West Africa, it would seem France is more likely.

Weather-wise, it has been dull and wet here. Of course, that makes our drill sergeants happy. The more miserable they can make us, the broader their smiles. Actually, the NCOs don't smile much, except to each other. We hear their conversations from time to time as when they least expect it.

It is tentative yet, but the word is that we will have a few days at home before we leave for our units. Cannot wait to hold you in my arms again, and please, let it be just the two of us. I love your folks but cannot bear the thought of having to share you with anyone. Can we meet in London and stay at some small hotel? Just think about it, darling. A few days together with only the two of us to think about. Promise you will try to get away.

All my love is yours, Vernon 26/8/16

"Mombasa? I cannot believe it! Let the Belgians and the Boche finish each other off! Why—"

Ada stopped talking when Vernon's lips closed on hers. In seconds, all thoughts of the war fled from her conscious mind as she gave herself up entirely. They made love in silence until the darkness outside their room penetrated, surrounding them, enveloping them in a dark, warm blanket.

The first light lit Vernon's cigarette in a soft glow as he inhaled once and handed it to Ada. Taking it, she turned on her side to look full in the face of the man who had just ravished her. "It's a good thing we're married," she said softly as she stroked Vernon lightly on the chin, "for I don't think I will ever get enough of you."

Vernon lay smoking for a while longer, noticing Ada had let her cigarette go out. "Enough of the cigarette, I see." He smiled at her.

Nodding, Ada rose naked from their bed and turned on a light as she went into the bathroom. When she returned, he noticed she had put on a light negligee that only served to enhance her already appealing figure. She sat down on his side of the bed and looked at him until one of them spoke.

"Hungry?" asked Vernon.

Ada kissed him and leisurely placed her body on his, answering his question.

"But Mombasa?" Ada asked again in time. "Won't it be dangerous there?" she inquired between bites. Room service had arrived, and, famished, both had gone about demolishing the food.

"Yes, but Smuts has them on the run, and the Germans are in retreat everywhere. It's been said that theirs is a diverting action just to keep our forces away from the Western Front. As a wireless operator, I'll likely be with the main forces in…" His voice trailed off while Ada just stared at him.

"You don't want to go out at all?"

Vernon spoke after they uncoupled for the third time. Feeling the effects of the food and their lovemaking, Ada had begun to drift off to sleep and now, with some regret, was coming awake.

"Out? Why?" she murmured just before she drifted off again.

Seeing her asleep, Vernon rose, put on his underclothes, and, quietly retrieving his orders, sat down to go through them again.

The 26th Squadron, assembled at Netheravon the year before with pilots from the South African Aviation Corps, had been shipped out to Mombasa in January, equipped with Farman F.27s and B.E.2cs to fly reconnaissance and observer missions. As Vernon reviewed his documents, he knew the three days they had left for each other would pass all too quickly.

He thought they should wait to have their first child until after he returned, but Ada had other thoughts.

"If I cannot have you with me, then I want something of you to hold onto. Someone who will remind me of you every day we are apart."

Driven by their desire, they had taken no precautions during their lovemaking. He reflected for a moment on the enjoyment they had just shared the last few hours and smiled, realizing it would have been very difficult to be prudent. With his thoughts drifting, he soon joined Ada, falling into a deep sleep.

"What are you doing over here?" she asked from beside him. "And without me," she continued as she placed her shapely figure in his lap.

"Oh, to wake up this way, every day," Vernon exclaimed, embracing his wife. "Tell me more about the wireless," she said as she placed the tip of her tongue in his ear.

– § –

"You can call me Rids." Vernon looked at the driver sitting at the wheel of the Crossley as he slid into the front passenger seat.

The driver nodded. "A' reight. Call me Ainch."

Hinch was the first squadron member Vernon had met. Arriving in Mombasa in early October, they met at the port where the ship had docked, offloading equipment and men to augment the Allied forces. Over the days spent reporting in and acclimating to their new surroundings, the two men became inseparable. As the new wireless operator for Squadron 26, Vernon had to be practically everywhere.

The days fled into months, while they formed a fast friendship they were sure would last. In that, they were not to be disappointed.

TWELVE

Southport 1918

"How much longer, William?" Josephine asked.

Reflecting on her question, William realized he had a number of answers to consider. The war had dragged on into its fourth year, while business at the shop had slowed considerably. Dividing his time between Southport and their offices in Leith, he had gone about preparing for the postwar period that was sure to come.

Turney & Son had been a defunct business when William bought it, but it had a name he could trade with; in fact, it had a number of names—brand names—he thought would still command some interest.

"House of Lords." Now that was a name…

"William!"

Josephine's voice penetrated his reverie.

"Yes, I'm sorry. What were you saying?"

"It's not just the war, William. It's everything."

They were sitting in a small office just off the main room, where the humidor sat surrounded by shelves full of unbought tobacco and cigars. With the ledgers spread out before them, the numbers told a story of declining income and expenses that refused to follow along.

"At this rate, love, we cannot hang on much longer," Josephine lamented. "I haven't said a word to Jane, but she knows…I'm sure."

William nodded and sat back in his chair with a small smile on his face that belied Josephine's concerns.

"Well," he began, "we are ready to move forward when this war *does* end. I have had correspondences with several good men who are interested, once they can come home and get back to their lives and their work. And the bank has been very patient, I must say," William concluded.

The bank could afford to be patient, William thought. Because of his previous troubles and the requirement that he self-report his bankruptcy, the bank had insisted on the appointment of two directors when Turney & Son incorporated and became Turney & Son, Ltd.

Although he had a sizable amount of working capital, a small loan was necessary to get Turney & Son, Ltd. up and running. Alcohol was being made in Leith and set aside in barrels to comply with the Immature Spirits Act of 1915—requiring two years compulsory bonding, and later, a third year. Thus, what some had called whisky upon its creation now took three years of aging to earn the name.

"We must be patient. Like the whisky, dear."

William smiled as he finally got around to answering his aggrieved wife's question.

– § –

Ada woke with a start. She had been dreaming, and in her sleep had seen Vernon coming toward her. She knew it was him as surely as she knew the face of the man whose photograph she kissed every day.

The man with him, she did not recognize. He was a shadowy figure whose features she could not quite make out. Both men were sitting in a vehicle, which was coming down a road toward her. When the two men came close enough for her to recognize Vernon, she woke up.

Still somewhat dazed, she rose in her dream-like state to begin dressing for the day, turning on the kettle while she finished. Sipping her first cup, she walked to the front room of her parents' flat. It was still early, and knowing they were likely asleep, she carefully let herself out the door. Standing shivering on the front stoop, she encountered a chilly drizzle that produced a penetrating cold.

What a horrible day this is likely to be! she thought unhappily.

Her father was in the kitchen when she returned. She smiled as they exchanged their "good mornings."

"Your mother is not feeling well this morning," her father began.

"Are Brenda and I too much for her?"

"Well, your mother tried to make me promise not to say anything, but…"

Brenda Ada had been born in June, the previous year—exactly nine months after her father's departure for Mombasa. Ada knew it was hard for everyone, but her parents wanted their daughter and granddaughter to come, and so they did. For nearly a year and a half, the four of them had lived together in a small flat built for two.

"I'll begin today to look for something, Dad."

Her father nodded as Ada went to comfort her daughter, whose crying announced her wakening in hunger.

Ada made her way swiftly through the streets in the cool drizzle that became colder as she progressed. Her destination was the post office, where job notices were posted. She had heard jobs were plentiful, with all the able-bodied men away. It had been only at her parents' insistence that she had stayed at home.

Now, that had to change; she must find a way.

As she drew nearer to her destination, the sight of a gathering crowd discomforted her. She could hear voices shouting but was still too far away to make out what they were saying. As she came within perhaps fifty yards of the crowd, a few people raced past her, shouting, "It's over! It's over!"

"What's over?" Ada shouted back.

Then, she saw the newspaper that a figure in front of her had dropped as he began dancing about, the headline of which read:

> HOW THE GREAT NEWS
> WAS RECEIVED
> LONDON LETS ITSELF GO
>
> THANKSGIVING AT ST. PAUL'S

Sitting down on a nearby curb, Ada gazed in wonderment at the pandemonium going on around her. Shouting voices were coming from total strangers dancing wildly about.

"It's over! The war is over!"

Repeatedly they shouted as they began throwing their newspapers in the air, creating an enormous amount of ink-covered confetti that soon covered the street. Looking down at one front page that had floated to the ground, Ada picked it up and read some more from *The Guardian*:

THE SUMMONS OF THE BELLS

Then the church bells, which we have never dared to ring but once on any great day of war, burst into a confident ringing, Big Ben overall, letting themselves go, like all London below them. The bells acted like a beaten tin, summoning a swarm of bees.

A swarm of bees, Ada mused, surveying the people around her. *That's what they are like!*

Ada rose amongst the crowd still dancing, to head back to her parents' flat. She was halfway back when she realized she had forgotten her mission to find employment. Somehow, it no longer seemed to matter. Vernon would be coming home! She quickened her pace, and, nearly running, she reached her parents' front door, throwing it open and shouting the news that would awaken her daughter, *their* daughter, with the message that would change their lives forever.

"But why? The war is over! I don't understand," Ada wailed as Vernon held her closely. She shook so violently that Vernon feared her falling from his grasp. He kept holding her until the shaking and sobbing subsided.

"It's not my time yet," Vernon began. "Just a few more months is all. They want me to help do some training."

"And I want you home," Ada replied as she removed herself from Vernon's grasp.

Vernon's squadron had returned via Capetown to Camp Blanford, where he learned the Royal Air Force wanted him to stay on through the demobilization. Finally, after serving five more months, he was transferred to the RAF Reserves and allowed to go home.

THIRTEEN

London 1919-24

"It's beautiful, William. But are you sure we can afford it?" Josephine gazed out the massive picture window that allowed an almost unimpeded view of the River Thames.

The apartment had become available while William was in London, just before the war's end. He had paid a deposit to secure the flat with the understanding that a lease agreement was optional over the next seven days. They had one day left to decide, and William's vote was to stay.

Jane had been reluctant at first to consider how she might run the shop on her own. George had always made the trips to restock inventory, and Jane was uncomfortable with the idea of so much travel. This puzzled William at first, but then he realized how the times had passed Jane by. She was greatly relieved to learn that such travels were no longer necessary.

The cable and telegraph took the place of the sailing ships, as William demonstrated, while showing how simple reordering from their suppliers had become.

"As the new owner, you have the right to change the name of the shop," William told her on their last day together. Looking around the showroom that was now hers, Jane reflected on the years that had passed since she first came to work for George.

"I don't think I will change a thing," she said smilingly.

Bursham House, situated comfortably in the London Borough of Richmond on the Thames, allowed convenient access to William's new offices at 12 Harp Lane. It was quite a step up from the small flat above George's shop in Southport. While Josephine set about making their new lodgings comfortable, William began making the rounds, renewing old relationships and keeping an eye out for prospective agents. His whisky had matured and was selling sufficiently well to allow him to return to those blending experiments, such as he once shared with James Munro. Among his brand names, *House of Lords* kept running through his mind.

It has to be perfect, thought William, to live up to the name.

During the halcyon days of 1919, as the country embraced their victory, William prospered as never before. Unable to meet the rapidly rising demand, he expanded his facilities considerably beyond his modest holdings five years hence. Whisky consumption increased to the highest level in almost forty years, according to the government, whose excise tax revenue increased accordingly.

William had found it difficult to bask in his success during the heady times that seemed filled with promise as far as eyes could see. As William's business grew, he sometimes reflected upon a growing restlessness within him, undiminished with success.

What is this? he often wondered. *Will I never be satisfied?*

Those thoughts were on his mind hauntingly, even as he sipped and nosed what he knew to be the best he had done.

It had to be good… No, better than good!

Agitated, he rose from his desk and walked to a large window from which he could look out upon the group of buildings surrounding his office.

It was not the satisfying view of Dalwhinnie or of Munro's offices, he recalled, but it would do for now. As he gazed out the window, he remembered again his father's words: *Satisfaction is the key*. Turning back to his project and raising the glass again, he nosed, sipped, and sighed.

From somewhere in his mind came a picture of his father exhaling the smoke from a fine cigar. Then, he recalled the look of contentment on his father's face and made up his mind.

– § –

"RUM RUNNER ABSOLVED OF ALL GUILT. So held magistrate S. Masson, who ruled George Woodward to have broken no Canadian laws, saying, "There is no burden cast upon us to enforce the laws of the United States."

William reread the short news item that appeared in his newspaper. He reflected upon his scant knowledge of what was occurring in the States. He knew, of course, about the Volstead Act that took effect two years before, but here was a new development: *no burden cast.*

He laid aside his newspaper and, taking another sip of his morning coffee, looked about the room he called his office at their new residence: 12a Colville Square.

He reflected upon their many collaborations while selecting furniture as they moved from one flat to another. The year 1922 had already been a very good one, with the release of House of Lords.

The telephone rang, rousing William from his reverie. After a brief conversation, he hung up the receiver and began preparation for his departure.

So, McCoy was the name.

He put on his long coat and cap and left for his luncheon appointment.

"He says he wants all we can sell him."

Dennis began the conversation as William and his office manager sat together in the restaurant.

"And where does he propose we ship the whisky?" William countered.

"To Nassau," said Dennis, smiling from ear to ear. His normally placid face was lighted with excitement. His dark eyebrows seemed further apart, though they continued to hover over dancing eyes. His customary serious demeanor had been replaced with a gaiety William had not seen before and now found slightly off-putting.

William's own eyebrows shot up as he paused to consider what he had just seen and learned. "How long has he been engaged in this, um…practice?"

Dennis handed over the letter he had received in their Leith office and waited for William to finish reading.

"He says he made his first shipment a year ago—to Savanna," William murmured.

"Why, that's right under their noses!" Dennis realized.

"Yes, I see that, Dennis. He also was cleared for Halifax, he says."

William handed the letter back and began to think. After what seemed to Dennis to be an interminable silence, William made up his mind.

"Tell him he can have all the whisky he wants with full payment in advance. The usual contract terms will suffice, I think, with that proviso added."

"All right, chief. I'll get on it right away," Dennis replied with gusto.

Leaving the restaurant, William made his way back to Colville Square and went into his office to review his appointment book. Opening his desk drawer, he searched for the schedules and began planning the trip.

– § –

Rouses Point, NY. October 19, 1923

"Your reason for visiting the U.S.?" the inspector asked in a somewhat imperious tone.

"Tourism," replied William.

Making his way through the lobby of the small immigration center, he saw a short, stocky, ill-dressed man with a placard, on which he read the designated signal. Nodding at William, the man turned to exit the door, leading him onto U.S. soil. With a nod of his head, he directed William's attention to a large, black sedan. As they neared the parked automobile, a rear passenger door opened abruptly, while William's guide entered on the driver's side.

"Mr. Whiteley?" a tall gent asked as he emerged from the car.

"Yes, I'm Whiteley," William responded.

The man smiled, extending his hand. "Irving Haim. Been lookin' forward to this. How was your trip?"

William's trip had begun in Liverpool, where he contracted for one of two available cabins on a freighter bound for Halifax. That the voyage was uneventful William found to be a pleasure—spoiled only by food of marginal quality. From Halifax, William chose to travel by train to Montreal, and from there by small craft south, along the Richelieu River.

Although it had been a leisurely trip, with reasonably good weather, William could feel every one of his sixty-three years. Therefore, when Haim suggested they do some sightseeing, William was less than enthusiastic. When Haim explained the purpose was to investigate some of the more than thirty dirt roads in the area that bootleggers used in their trade, William's spirits rose. Yes. That was what he came to see. So, off they went, bouncing over the poorly maintained roads.

Careening, coupled with sliding on and off the surface of the road, did not encourage lengthy conversation. This was William's first ride in a *Whisky Six*—the six-cylinder Hudsons and Packards favored by the bootleggers. As they rumbled along, William took the opportunity to assess the man who was his host. He could not be more than twenty-five, if that, William concluded, just before he was thrown forward, his head colliding with the back of the seat in front of him.

Without a word passing between them, the driver rolled down his window and handed a paper-wrapped bottle to a man in a car parked alongside the road, then spun away, bounding over the trail as before. Soon, they came to another stop. This time, the driver got out of the car and opened the trunk. Extracting a cardboard box, he set it down on the side of the road. As the driver returned to his seat, William saw another car approaching. He leaned forward, seeing in a side-view mirror a figure pick up the box as they sped away, bounding once again down the rutted road.

At no time did Haim look his way until after they reached the main highway, where they turned southwest. It was then that Haim told him their destination was Watertown. They would have dinner there and spend the night. Arriving shortly before six o'clock in the evening, William went up to his room and immediately turned on the hot water in his tub. When it was full of water as hot as he could stand, he gingerly slipped into the tub, sighing in pleasure as the heat began to envelop his tired, aching body.

Dinner was a remarkably fine meal, and afterward, he and Haim sat alone in a small room off the restaurant and bar area. The place had been a tavern since about 1805, shortly after the town came to be.

"Tell you why I like Watertown," Haim began. "Nothing but honest money being made here," he finished with a grin.

"What's the main source of wealth?" William asked.

"The Black River flows through here on the way to Ontario, so it's a mill town, mostly. But you didn't come all this way to gab about rivers, William. Let's talk whisky."

William smiled, deciding he liked Haim's direct approach.

"How did you get involved in the business?"

"You mean rum-running?" Haim grinned.

"Yes, that's what I mean. How did you get where you are so quickly?"

Listening to Haim tell his story, William was struck by the similarities to his own. Haim also dealt in tobacco, which provided some cover for his bootlegging activities. Soon, Haim brought the discussion back to the matters at hand.

"Ever been to Saint Pierre?" William's host inquired.

William shook his head.

"Fellow named McCoy was there last year to get his ship, *Tomoka*, repaired. It was full of liquor, and he couldn't land on the coast, so he went on to Halifax. Wouldn't let him unload, so hearing about St. P., he wound up spending the winter of '22 there. Came back with all kind of stories about how he talked the authorities into letting him ship his whisky and use their port for distribution. He told a story about some Englishman who agreed to send him all the whisky he wanted."

"I know a little about that," William offered.

"I know ya do, William," Haim replied with a grin. "That's why I agreed to meet ya."

– § –

This time, Josephine met him fully clothed. When they embraced, William thought he detected a bit of a chill in her welcoming. As she drove them from the port at Southampton, she asked about the trip and the people he met. Sidestepping any reference to Haim, William spoke in generalities about what had occurred, ending his summary with upbeat estimates of the business prospects.

"And so, in the end, I believe this will turn out to be a most profitable venture," William concluded.

"Yes, I imagine so," Josephine replied, "but is it legal?"

William began his reply in a soft and earnest voice, which he hoped would diffuse any anxiety Josephine might feel. He began by quoting the magistrate who had observed that Canada had no obligation to enforce U.S. laws. If that were true for Canada, it would surely be true for His Majesty's government. He then briefly traced the history of rebellion against governments perceived by their subjects as unfair, to include the revolution in the States over unfair taxation. In the end, he was able to clinch his argument by assuring Josephine that shipping to Saint Pierre was legal, thanks to men like "Big Bill McCoy."

"But then, of course," William concluded, "until fairly recently, just the making of whisky would not have been legal at all."

William soon found that even his expanded facilities in Leith could not keep up with the increased demand. He felt obligated to hold back a significant portion of his production for domestic sales and for those with whom he had contracted to provide set amounts, among whom was his old friend, Martine. He had the foresight to contract for purchase some of the production from his fellow distillers early on, but the contracts were short-term. He was literally scrambling about to find enough product to meet the burgeoning demand.

In Great Britain, even with the Scotland Temperance Act of 1913, the influence of the "drys" was limited. At first, only a few distillers went out of business. There was never any prohibition against manufacture, wholesaling, or consumption in private at home. Alcohol was available in restaurants if served with a meal, and so domestic demand, while in decline during the postwar years, remained significant. Through consolidation and certain other economies, it was during this period that some distilleries made their mark, while others floundered.

During the early period of the Prohibition boom, William founded a new company: Glenforres-Glenlivet. Within less than three years, this company was the majority shareholder of J. G. Turney & Son, Ltd.

The principals of this company now sat around the conference table in their Leith offices. Among those present were the majority shareholder and his wife, the manager, and a member of the office staff to take dictation. The meeting did not last as long as some had, with all proposals accepted unanimously. Chief among them was the hiring of a chartered accountant, who also became the firm's newest shareholder.

– § –

As Vernon examined the books, he felt a rising sense of excitement and appreciation. The initial belief that he was coming in on "the ground floor" of a promising new enterprise gave way to a certainty as he completed his first full audit. There were some minor discrepancies, easily corrected, and those were due primarily to a lack of sophistication, or knowledge of the more complex rules of accounting. As he began to dictate his report, there was a knock on the door of his office just before the owner let himself in. The secretary, seeing William enter, rose quickly to leave, but was waved back to his seat as William took the chair available.

"Don't mind me," William began, "I am just observing."

"If you don't mind, sir, I would prefer to dictate my report in private."

William's eyebrows shot up, as they were prone to do when he was surprised.

"Well then, it shall be as you request," William said, rising from the chair. "Just don't keep it a secret when you are done."

– § –

The Christmas holiday brought an unusually large number of greeting cards, among which was one from Jane. She enclosed a photograph of herself standing in front of the old store, where above the door could be seen the sign that still read "Whiteley & Son." Later that evening, when all their guests had left, the two shared a glass of some of the port they had found with the wine in George's cellar.

"What do you think of it now?" Josephine asked.

Ignoring the formalities, William drained the last of his glass. "Like us, no longer young. Full of vibrancy, with a fine, lasting finish. Like us," he concluded with a winning smile.

Looking at her husband, she realized she had forgotten to show him the note Jane had enclosed with the card. "She says that business has been slow lately, but she is hoping things will pick up now that the economy is improving."

William nodded and thought he was in full agreement with Jane's assessment.

"She also says," Josephine continued reading, "she is grateful for your holding payment of the rent in abeyance. She wants to begin payments this month and hopes to catch up soon thereafter."

Again, William nodded and made a mental note to discuss the matter with Ridley after the holiday break was over.

"A working account—with yours, Josephine's, and Jane's signatures allowed—should do it," Ridley suggested. Ridley went on to explain that deposits could be made directly by Jane at her bank instead of mailing a check for the rent as she had mostly done.

"That will be fine, Vernon. Will you take it from here and give Jane the necessary instructions?" William asked. After receiving Vernon's reassurance, William rose to go to his office and paused at the door, knowing Ridley had said something else, though not having heard him.

"Then, of course, you may withdraw from the account at our bank here whenever you wish," Ridley continued.

Leaving Ridley to his meditations, William left the room thinking, *Should that day ever come...*

FOURTEEN

A Failed Experiment

WHEN F. SCOTT FITZGERALD'S *THE Great Gatsby* was published in 1925, the meaning of the term "drug stores" was obvious to all but the most credulous. The New York Medical Supply Co., one of the businesses that William had called on during his first trip to the States, was a forerunner in the business of selling alcohol strictly for "medicinal purposes." Tens of thousands of prescriptions were provided for patients' purchase during the 1920s, when a "patient" could legally acquire a pint every ten days. Some sources reported the average charge ranged between three to five dollars for each prescription.

Physicians and dentists lined up to receive the federal government's permission to prescribe spirits, finding a new and surprisingly lucrative source of income. There were other exemptions provided by the Volstead Act, such as the use of sacramental wine, farm-made cider, and homemade wine.

Pharmacists prospered as never before. Some dispensed the spirit in its original container—which now had on its label the additional proviso that it had somehow been determined to be good for one's health. Others bought distilled spirits in bulk and dispensed them in small containers as individual "doses." Speakeasies wanted the real thing, and a large number of businesses formed to meet the new, illicit, burgeoning demand.

In the early years of Prohibition, when Canada became the primary source of alcohol for the States, small boats and ships from Newfoundland ran the most whisky. Later, the main route for shipping was from Windsor to Detroit. The fishing industry had declined dramatically due to overfishing, but boat mortgages still had to be paid. Nowhere else were conditions worse than those on the Isle of St. Pierre.

Three years earlier, Frank Costello made his first trip to St. Pierre, where he somehow convinced the mayor that a duty of $2 a case would represent a respectable return on investment. For the sleepy port to become suitable for the whisky fleet, warehouses had to be built, piers lengthened and increased in number, and loading equipment acquired. Soon, dockworkers began to arrive from the States, immediately causing a housing shortage and the nearly spontaneous creation of other businesses to meet heretofore nonexistent demands on the lonely isle.

– § –

The freighter left Liverpool with a ballast more valuable than rock or sand and much more pleasing to the palate. Stored in its cargo hull, and placed strategically throughout the ship, were cases of William's finest. Every available space contained cases of specially made bottles filled with House of Lords' blended Scots whisky. William experimented with different glass containers to determine what size and shape of bottle could best make a long journey by sea. Each bottle had to contain the requisite amount of whisky—while being both light in weight and strong enough to survive the journey.

In his cabin, William leisurely went about the business of unpacking the suitcase and hanging his suits and jackets in the small closet. He had brought along his newest acquisitions of informal dress. He still preferred one of the short suit jackets inspired by the uniforms of the Great War, but had eagerly adopted the new Oxford bag—a wider trouser. In addition, he had a number of sweaters to match the trousers, which he thought were appropriate for dinner in the captain's cabin. Surveying his cabin, he felt well-prepared for the simple plan he had formed to accompany his first shipment to St. Pierre.

The captain was a Swede, and although he spoke serviceable English, William was offered little of it. Dinner was edible and plentiful, while conversation was not. When it became obvious that William had overstayed his welcome, he retired to the deck, where he spent long moments wishing for one of his father's La Palmas. Finally, resigned to his fate, William returned to his cabin to write a short note to Josephine and begin reading his copy of Margaret Kennedy's novel, *The Constant Nymph*—given to him along with the promise that it would dispel the gloom of a long voyage. In that, it did not disappoint.

Drifting off to sleep, his senses roused by the faint smell of smoke, William rose to investigate. Putting his long coat on over his nightclothes, William raised the latch on his cabin door and stepped into the small passageway that led toward the steps to the main deck. When he arrived up top, he saw a large number of the crew passing buckets of sand. He watched in amazement the sand thrown into the ship's galley. At the end of the line was the steward, who chose the target area for each bucket. Spying the captain, William moved quickly in his direction.

"A small fire. Not to be alarmed," the captain said in anticipation.

Indeed, as William looked directly into the galley, he could see no flames and very little smoke.

"It is why galley is on main deck," the captain said, engaging William with his most words yet. Seeing things were under control, William retreated to his cabin, seeing all hope of sleep evaporating in the aftermath of the fire.

Located just off the southern coast of Newfoundland, the three communes of Saint Pierre, Miquelon-Langlade, and Ile-aux-Chiens had been fought over by Britain and France for almost two hundred years. France reclaimed the devastated, uninhabited islands in 1816, gradually resettling them with a hodgepodge of settlers, including Newfoundlanders, Bretons, Normans, and Basques. Due to a severe decline in the fortunes of the native fishing industry and the drawdown of men by the military draft during WWI, smuggling had become a mainstay in the lives of the few remaining inhabitants.

From his vantage point on the main deck, William could view the approach to the harbor of St. Pierre. The tiny harbor, protected by a group of small islands, he could see was in a flurry of activity. A figure on the quai signaled with flags the berth the freighter was to occupy. William watched as the ship responded to the captain's orders, coming to a stop well short of the dock. William saw the ship's crew cast large ropes to a group of men, who began securing the looped ends to large posts. Winches began rolling in the lines until the portside of the freighter was secure against the dock. With the gangway soon in place, William went ashore to reconnoiter. He carried his long coat and a small suitcase containing all his belongings.

"I am sorry, monsieur, but the Hotel du Vieux was unable to accommodate you," the secretary replied.

"Quite all right," William responded. "It would have been nice to get off the ship, but—"

"Bonjour! Bonjour!" the figure emerging from the mayor's office said. "I am Mayor Arnold. And you are Monsieur Whiteley, yes?"

William shook hands with the enthusiastic Frenchman, who guided him into his office. Taking the offered chair, William sat down as the mayor continued his welcoming.

"Je vois que vous avez. Oh! Pardon, monsieur! In my haste, I forgot."

"Quite all right, quite all right," interjected William. "I merely wished to make your acquaintance and take in the sights of St. Pierre. Can you recommend a place for dinner?"

Beaming, the mayor spread his arms wide. "You can do no better than dining with me, monsieur."

"I'm sure, I'm sure, but I wish to be no trouble."

"No. No. It is no trouble. It is decided. You shall be my guest, and we shall become fast friends, no doubt. Shall we say eight o'clock, monsieur?"

Making his way back along the street above the Quai, William looked into the abandoned fishing factories and warehouses, which all had doors and windows that seemed newly repaired. As he made his way, he was amused to hear the voices of women from side streets inviting him inside. Tipping his hat, he moved on, taking note of the building activity and passing the hotel that had been too full to accommodate him. On impulse, he retraced his steps and entered the front door of Hotel du Vieux.

"Welcome to Hotel Robert, sir!" the desk clerk greeted him as he turned the registration book toward William. "Do you have a reservation, sir?"

"No, I don't. I heard that you were full, and thought I would check to be sure."

"Where are you from, sir?"

"London," replied William.

"So am I, sir! Now, what accommodations were you seeking?"

With a rising sense of anticipation, William replied, "Just for myself."

"It will be no problem accommodating you, sir. A room has just come available due to…um…an unexpected occurrence. Please sign in here. Do you have any luggage?"

The room was small and plainly furnished, with a single, narrow bed pushed against one side. There was a bureau with three drawers and a desk with a chair in one corner. A small lamp on a bedside table was the only light in the room. There was a small cast iron stove for heating, and in a box alongside, a supply of wood. At the end of the corridor, there was a common bathroom, complete with tub, and hot water was available on request. It was early, and William had no trouble gaining access to the bathing facilities. Later, he sat down at the small desk with his writing materials and began to compose a letter to Josephine.

Dearest,

Here I sit in my room on the isle of St. Pierre, where all around me is bustling activity, all of which seems designed for our purposes. I see warehouses under construction, old buildings being prepared for new use, people working fiendishly at an exhausting pace to make this old, neglected port rise from its obscurity. You would not believe it, but tonight I am to have dinner with the mayor, and at his insistence. Of course, you may be sure it did not take much, as the fare on the freighter was regrettably poor. To compound matters, there was a fire in the galley, and what the captain and crew will be eating is anybody's guess.

A curious thing, this hotel, where I am now sitting, writing you now. The sign above the entrance says Hotel du Vieux du Porte. No one refers to it that way, except the secretary to the mayor, as far as I can tell. Everyone, including the desk clerk (who is from London, by the way), calls it Hotel Robert. I shall endeavor to decode this mystery and report to you promptly on the matter.

Ah, my love. Things could not seem to be going any better than they are. I know you were concerned about my coming out here, but I had to see for myself the place where so much business is to be done. And, of course, I had to shepherd my little collection of bottles. Offloading is underway, and tomorrow I shall do a complete inventory to determine if our experiment is successful. Again, a full report to you will come, my darling. Take the best of care, and I shall return within a fortnight, as planned.

Ever yours, William

Rereading the letter, Josephine held it to her breast. "Thank you, thank you," she murmured. In their bedroom on the second floor of their flat, she found she could feel closer to William there than anywhere in the house. There was no satisfactory view to console her, but Hyde Park was a nice walk away, and their new focus on economy the last five years was paying off.

If William is right…

Pausing for a moment, Josephine reflected upon all that William had said. If she was going to be honest with herself, she still was not sure he was right. She had friends who had raised an eyebrow when Josephine told them of their new ventures.

And they were not even "drys!"

Her closest friend, Maggie, was of the same mind as William.

"He's right, love; you can lay it to heart. A hundred years ago, whisky was illegal. Now, the ones who are against it would like to see you and me without a glass of Madeira altogether. How does that strike you, love?"

— § —

The mayor's home was modest by any standard. The one redeeming virtue was the dining room, where two rooms had become one, with the sliding doors separating them pushed into the wall. As he engaged the man next to him in small talk, he allowed his eyes to take in the assorted guests around the room.

Dinner, served upon a series of tall buffets, allowed the guests to sit while eating in small groups around the large room. William stood, surveying the room.

There are perhaps thirty-five of us.

"Mr. Whiteley, I believe," a new voice said.

"You have me at a disadvantage, sir," William replied as he extended his hand to the man who had come up behind him. Slightly taller than William, with his black, slicked-back hair and pencil-thin mustache, his limp handshake did not inspire confidence, though that would prove to be his game.

"Name's Harry Line. From the States and pleased to meet ya."

"Mr. Line, is it? Well, it is a pleasure. How is it you know of me?"

"The reputation of your whisky precedes your person," Line continued, "in both quality and merit."

William nodded his thanks. "Good to hear. Now, are you a purchaser, or are we in competition?"

Line laughed heartily. "And to think, I thought we Americans were the direct ones! Actually, I may be a competitor, though perhaps not in the sense you meant."

William listened as Line told of his plans and purposes. He represented interests in the States who were buyers, not producers. In that sense, they were not competitors.

"Was wondering if you have already arranged to dispose of all your cargo?" Line's gambit began.

Showing disappointment at William's response, Line continued. "You know, of course, we play the game fast and loose out here. Look around this room, and you will see every man is here for himself, or, for the interests he represents. Same thing."

William took the opportunity to do just that, and with the freedom to look about the room, he took advantage of the reprieve Line had given him.

Fast and loose? That is certainly putting it bluntly.

He turned back to Line. "You are suggesting…what? That I disavow the terms of a contract already made and in the process of being honored?"

William looked steadily into the eyes of the man still seated next to him. Line returned his gaze and smiled, seeing his gambit had failed.

"Oh no. I would never suggest such a thing," he lied.

"You will recall I merely asked about any surplus cargo you may have."

"I'm afraid there is none," William replied, staring at his interlocutor.

When Line chose to leave, William shook his hand. In the back of his mind came the warning that to alienate the man would likely not prove advantageous. With a sincerity that seemed to have the desired effect, William assured Line that there was every likelihood they could do business in the future. William's assumption proved correct, as in the next few minutes, Line introduced him to most of the other guests, who were, as it turned out, mostly buyers like himself.

"But it is not right, still! I have reservation and then I have not."

William could not help but overhear the complainant. To his left and behind him, he turned to see the captain of his freighter engaging the mayor with indignation.

"Yes, *mon ami*, very regrettable. But what can I do? I do not own the hotel."

"*Mes mains sont liees*!" he concluded brusquely, signaling the matter closed.

As William continued moving about the room, he paused to introduce himself to each of the mayor's guests, in the end arriving at the side of his host. The two of them had a brief moment to speak privately. He had found the presence of the captain at first surprising. The mayor explained that he made it a practice to exclude no one involved in the trade that was jolting the economy of his impoverished principality out of its doldrums.

"He was only complaining about your good fortune, *mon ami*," the mayor said with just a slight smile, "and wondering how his passenger came to be so fortunate." For the first time, William realized how a room came available for him at Hotel Robert.

Harry Line sat at the desk in his room at Hotel Robert composing his report. He made note of the many transactions completed according to the instructions he had received from his employer. Checking off each obligation he had agreed to assume, he paused at one point on his list, reflecting on what he regarded as the most important of them all.

Pouring into his glass a small portion of a dark amber spirit, he then raised it as if offering a toast to an unseen companion. Then he began writing again.

> *Subject person firmly refused offer I made, though with style, I must add. Careful to avoid offense. Believe you may rely on him as a man you can continue to do business with.*

Harry took another sip as if to toast his absent dinner companion.

– § –

As William completed his own personal inventory, he felt a strong sense of satisfaction growing within. There had been little breakage en route. The allowance he had made for loss exceeded the actual loss incurred. He thought briefly about looking up Harry Line to tell him he actually had some extra cargo to sell. When the dock agent for his purchaser grabbed at the opportunity to secure the bonus shipment, the matter was mooted.

During his last night on St. Pierre, William had a quiet dinner alone at the hotel. He reviewed again in his mind the figures that told the tale of his new venture, and he thought again about how one of his father's La Palmas would top things off. George's words came back to him: *Satisfaction, my boy. Satisfaction is the key.* With sudden alacrity, he realized that he might truly understand for the first time what his father had meant. It could not have been to just *any* satisfaction that George had been referring!

Being easily satisfied was anathema to William. There was *always* a better way, if one could just find it. Always. It had become a passion of his to seek and to find any way toward improvement. George was surely right. At some point in time, his *good* would be more than *good enough*. He had to learn to trust in his sense of *knowing* when things led to that conclusion. He smiled, remembering his struggles birthing House of Lords.

– § –

The return voyage home on the freighter was short and uneventful. The captain's silence no longer troubled William. Given the circumstances, he welcomed it. As he disembarked at the terminal in Southport, he felt disappointment clutch at his heart when he failed to spy Josephine.

Looking in vain over the crowd in the arrival lounge, he saw no one there to greet him. Disappointment gave way to a rising sense of frustration as he stood holding his suitcase at the taxi quay. Impatiently waiting for a cab that could take him to the rail station, he did not at first hear the messenger boy call out his name.

"Do we have a Mr. Whiteley? William Whiteley?"

"Yes. I'm Whiteley," William replied, raising his arm to signal his presence to a slender, ferret-faced young man.

"There is a message for you, sir. At the information desk just inside." The boy pointed in the direction of the terminal William had just left. Once inside, William hastened to the desk where the attendant stood. After viewing William's identification, he said, "It's your wife, sir. A fellow motorist who stopped to help said her motorcar had a breakdown."

"A breakdown? Did she say where she was?" William asked.

"Yes, sir. She is about a mile away from the terminal, sir. She is with the car, near this location."

The attendant handed William his written summary of Josephine's message.

Hailing a taxi, William could not help feeling some apprehension about his wife's safety. How long had she been there? What might have transpired since she left her message? As William and the driver approached the location given by Josephine, his heart was pounding with anxiety. The driver slowed to a stop behind the Sunbeam, and William leapt out of the taxi, hurrying to his car.

As he reached for the door handle, he saw Josephine's body lying across the rear seat. To his great frustration and rising sense of alarm, he found the car door locked! As he began banging upon the window, a great sense of relief washed over him when his wife sat up and sleepily gazed at her husband. She fumbled with the door lock for what seemed to be an eternity before William grasped the handle and flung the door open.

"My God, you're beautiful!" William whispered as they fiercely embraced.

"No, not very," Josephine murmured as she held on tightly. "I must be a fright, really."

– § –

Hinch looked at the man as they shook hands.

"Best driver that one could ever want. We were in the RAF together— 26th Squadron. He can drive anything, William," Ridley completed the introduction.

The three of them had met at William's residence in Colville Square, where Hinch was introduced not only to the man he was to serve but also to his unusual sense of humor.

"Very good of you to come around, uh, is it Percy?" William interrupted. "Ainch as' the name, sir."

"All right then, Hinch. Have you a car to recommend?" William asked.

"Beggin' y' pardon, sir. A ca'?" Hinch replied with some confusion in his voice.

"Yes. Did Vernon not tell you that we are without a car at the moment?"

Looking at his friend for help, Hinch saw only in Ridley's face a struggle to control expression.

"Well, now, it does appear I may have bollixed this up a bit," Ridley said, looking at William. "Perhaps we should discuss whether you actually need a driver at present, given the unfortunate demise of the Sunbeam."

Hinch, with open mouth, looked at the faces of his two tormenters, searching for some evidence of complicity, or feigned concern, and found neither.

Ridley broke first. Slapping his friend on a shoulder, he burst out, "Oh, you should have seen your face! Priceless, it was. That look of complete credulity."

Hinch sat down, uninvited, his mind racing with embarrassment and a rising anger that simply would not do, he told himself. William sat down next to him and waited a moment before he began to talk about his need for a car.

Hinch looked at the man as he spoke and took a moment to decide. *He seemed sincere.*

The sense of humor? *That* would take some getting used to.

He decided to give it a go.

FIFTEEN

Minerva

"The Goddess of Automobiles," the banner screamed. Societe Anonyme Minerva Motors in Antwerp had been founded in 1903. In 1907, their eight-litre Kaiserpreis won the Belgian Circuit des Ardennes. This prompted one Charles S. Rolls to become a dealer in London, first selling the 2.9-liter, 14-horsepower model. England became the most active market for the company, due in part to Rolls' success.

"Did you ever drive one in the war?" Ridley asked.

Hinch shook his head as he gazed reverently at the Vanden Plas limousine. William had yet to join them, and the two friends spent their time luxuriating in the presence of the massive six-cylinder machine enthroned in the Rolls showroom.

The Dutch had used them in hit-and-run attacks against the Bosch. At first, they armed men with only rifles, then light machine guns, all handheld. Hinch gave the history he had heard, saying it was the trenches that put them out of business in the end. Hinch looked at his friend for a moment.

"Cum obsolete fuh wa' time use. Lak wat 'appened t' you n' me…"

Ridley smiled at the insult.

"At' 'as a double-sleeved engine," Hinch replied in answer to William's question.

He had arrived late for the appointment, but the Rolls mechanic and sales agent greeted him warmly and led the inspection tour of the vehicle.

Hinch noted with appreciation that William deferred to his knowledge of the automobile each time the Rolls representatives made a claim.

"Shall we go for a spin, sir?" the agent asked William.

William nodded and, turning to Hinch, suggested, "Why don't you drive?"

As the passengers reclined in the voluminous and luxurious leather seats behind him, Hinch eased the automobile out of the drive. Ridley turned to look out the rear window at the anguished faces of the mechanic and sales agent left behind.

Gliding away from the Rolls showroom, Hinch worked the gears expertly, so that there was never even the slightest pause in the smooth acceleration of the machine. Ridley looked at William, who seemed preoccupied as he gazed out the window on his side of the car.

They soon left the environs of London and entered the open road, where there was little traffic. As they went along, the quiet found in the interior was what first registered.

William made a mental note of many features as he relaxed in his seat. Chief among them was the quiet functioning of the car, but there was one other thing that captivated his attention. His acute sense of smell told him there was nothing untoward. The pleasant smell of the wood and the leather aside, he found his gratification enhanced by what he could *not* smell.

The air vents were shut; the weather outside was cool and there was no need for ventilation. As they passed a couple of farms, William knew that had they been in the Sunbeam, the odor would have been pervasive.

"Should we go much further, sir?" Hinch inquired of the master.

"I suppose not," William said with a note of regret, as they turned around to head back to the dealership.

"It is beautiful, William. So beautiful. But can we...," Josephine trailed off.

"Yes. We can, and as a matter of fact, we have," William said emphatically.

"Are you sure? Are you really certain?" Josephine said wistfully as she sat back in the deeply contoured seat.

"Yes. I was never more certain of but one other thing," William smiled.

With curiosity rising in her mind, she looked at her loving husband.

"Happy anniversary, darling," he said.

Hinch smiled as he observed the couple from the driver's rearview mirror. He could hear almost every word, except in instances when the road surface interfered. All of a sudden, the glass behind his seat began to rise out of its cavity, and the sound of the voices diminished. He looked again into the rearview mirror, this time seeing only a triumphant look on Josephine's face.

SIXTEEN

Das Boot

THE WAR WAS ON. THE headquarters of the enemy was located in New London, Connecticut. The days of brazen daylight deliveries were long past. Now, with a line of destroyers all along "Rum Row" (the name applied to the length of the Atlantic coast where smuggling of liquor occurred), there was no chance of going undetected, even on the darkest of nights. Searchlights constantly swept the waters. Cutters patrolled close in, between the destroyers and the shoreline, waiting for any sign of movement. Parked out beyond the three-mile limit, captain and crew on freighters loaded with William's finest waited anxiously for the skiffs to come.

Frank Costello walked the planks of one of his newly built rum runners. With low freeboards to present a corresponding profile, they were almost invisible in the water. And they could move. New engines that could propel the craft at top speeds of eighteen to twenty knots made them at least as fast as what the Coast Guard had.

An adjustment had been made, allowing William's whisky to flow freely again as one side waited for the other to respond. With a capacity of more than fifteen thousand cases, the new sleek and fast rum runners could pull up to a freighter and, in less than twenty minutes, pull away fully loaded. Offloading from the mother ship occurred in record time, due to the simple fact that all cargo could be lashed down on the main deck of the runner. The weight actually lowered the profile of a ship, rendering it almost impossible to see in the dark waters, and it did not slow them down. Radio relay stations were set up to alert the runners to Coast Guard activity, and the booze began flowing again.

The main problem was logistics—always logistics. Even when safe ports could be found, they could not be used frequently. Of course, there were boats that did not get through, and when a capture occurred, news of it made all the papers. The public read about these successes, and they occurred frequently enough so that the unsophisticated and unaware thought most of the booze was not getting through.

A casual visit to a Chicago or New York speakeasy gave away the lie of those assumptions. These meeting places, where a small window in the door opened to determine the identity of the patron, represented democratic institutions—watering holes devoid of class distinction. It had been said that a man could rub shoulders with his mechanic and think nothing of it.

At one point, the *Ladies' Home Journal* sought to cast a different light, observing that on a recent visit, their reporter, who was doing *strictly* undercover work, claimed, "The fashionable rich demand their rum as an inalienable class privilege."

– § –

"Ja, das boot ist gut."

The captain had been all over, checking every corner of the boat, lingering longer than expected in every section. He had loitered a bit longer at the torpedo stations, even going through the process of preparing them for launch—but just up to the point of launching, for there were no torpedoes at hand.

"*Es ist auch sauber,*" he said in parting as he made his way out the conning tower. His height made it necessary to lower his head often as they toured the tight confines of the sub. The agent thought he had done it with a surprising ease that must have come from practice.

Handing him an envelope containing the specified amount, the agent was surprised the captain did not even look inside. He remained motionless, simply gazing in something like admiration at the submarine.

No, it was more than that, thought the agent. Something more like affection, combined with a longing to possess, like admiring a beautiful woman.

As the agent turned to go, he quickly found his arm imprisoned in an iron-like grip. He was not a strong man and quickly realized the danger. His wrist looked thin as a twig while clasped in the captain's massive hand. Frantically, he tried to pull away from the captain who, with a feverish look in his eyes, squeezed even harder.

Recovering from his shock, the agent yelled. As loudly as he could, he screamed for help.

Immediately released and reaching for a railing, he moved too quickly in his effort to escape. He felt himself slipping, and, try as he might, he could not get a handhold or foothold.

The surface of the submarine glistened in the morning mist, providing the perfect conditions for his fall. When his head hit the unforgiving iron side of the boat, he had only a slight sensation of collision and lost consciousness as his inert body slid silently into the water.

– § –

William flexed his back and sought to move about the confining space. Impossible to stretch out completely, his five-foot, seven-inch frame exceeded the capacity of his bunk bed. How many hours had they been out to sea? Was it ten? He found the confines of the sub mildly disorienting.

Coffee could be had at any hour in the small mess room, and that was where he decided to go. There, he found Ridley pouring over the figures in his journals that he so faithfully kept. At William's greeting, Ridley did not look up, merely waving a hand to acknowledge a presence. For a moment, all William did was sip his coffee (it was good and strong). Then, he interrupted Ridley's meditations.

"Vernon, can you spare a moment?"

No response. He repeated his question.

Ridley sighed and closed the journal he had been inspecting. "All right, William, as you are paying the bills…"

William did not so much as give a nod in response. For a moment, there was a silence between them.

Finally, William asked, "What do you think of our captain?"

Ridley paused before answering.

"He came highly recommended. Well…" He paused to reconsider. "…actually, there was no recommendation. Just the absence of any reason not to hire him."

"Did you interview him?" William asked.

Ridley nodded.

"So, then, on what basis did you hire him?"

Ridley set aside his spectacles on the mess table and rubbed his eyes. Blinking for a few moments, his face screwed up in concentration as he tried to remember the progression of events.

He recalled meeting the captain for the first time in their Leith offices. Fortunately, a new employee had proved fluent, so there were no translation problems. Then, he remembered the look on the face of his interpreter when he asked her what she thought about the captain.

"She seemed to hesitate, she did," Ridley offered. Seeing the questioning look on William's face, Ridley grinned. "Sorry. What happened is, after the interview, I asked this young woman who served as translator what she thought of our good captain."

"And?" William proffered.

"That's when she hesitated. She looked away for a moment and then said something like, she was sure he would be fine, or something of that nature."

"Something of that nature?"

"Yes. Why the third degree, William? Is something wrong?" As Ridley continued to reflect on the interview, he remembered that no other candidate had stepped forward for the job. While he would have preferred someone bilingual, he had to accept that finding a captain who was intimately familiar with a reconditioned WWI U-boat was no easy task. The man *was* qualified. Of that, there could be no doubt.

During the interview, the translator was very precise about certification and reported that the captain's papers appeared correct in every respect. She even went so far as to contact one of the references, who confirmed the captain had indeed commanded a U-boat during the Great War.

Captain Schmidt removed the stub of his cigar from his teeth and flung it into the water, watching it disappear in the depths. He then directed his full attention to the stern of the freighter and tracked the tow line all the way to where it connected to the bow of the U-boat. The bow line also received his attention, as did the stern line and its fitting. Nodding his head in satisfaction, he began to work again on his plan. These meditations were interrupted when William joined him in the conning tower.

Nodding, William looked at the space on the water that separated the sub from its host. "We have been fortunate with the weather," William began, noting the seeming lack of comprehension on the captain's face. "Yes, of course," William said to himself as he turned to look down the ladder and beckoned to a crewmember to join them.

In addition to William and Ridley, who were the only passengers, there was the captain and a crew of five. The captain decided on the number of the crew required, though William insisted at least one of the crew serve as interpreter. That crewmember now stepped up at William's command.

"Ask the captain how we are doing and if he has any concerns we should know about." The crewmember did as was requested while William watched the face of the captain carefully when his response came.

"Captain says no problems yet, though he expects the tow lines to foul sometime." The crewmember—whose name was Hans—looked at William for further instruction.

"Ask him if he will have dinner with me," William ordered.

The captain smiled and nodded at William with what appeared to be sincere appreciation. "And you will join us as well," William said to Hans, who was both surprised and gratified, as he had never eaten at the captain's table on any ship.

Returning to his small cabin, William changed shirts and put on one of his sweaters before making his way to the stern storage area. Opening the watertight door, he found the light switch and made his way through the lines of barrels secured by wooden chocks and tie-downs. Finding the case of wine secured between two barrels, he retrieved two bottles and made his way out, pausing only to turn out the light and secure the door.

"The captain wishes to offer his compliments on the wine," Hans conveyed to William.

The dinner went well. There were many toasts during the meal to everyone's health and the success of the voyage. With the dishes removed from the small table, the captain rose and spoke briefly to Hans before leaving the mess. Seeing the expression on William's face, Hans rushed to reassure.

"The captain begs your pardon and promises to return shortly."

When he did return, he had a bottle of cognac in his hand and four glasses.

Ridley had remained quiet for most of the time during dinner, but he was the first to compliment the captain.

"Ist guten Cognac."

The look of alarm William saw in the captain's eyes was quickly suffused with a smile and a nod of appreciation.

So, is he afraid that one of us knows German?

Towing the sub had been an expensive proposition, but—in William's mind—necessary for providing another layer of protection. Josephine had sounded the alarm when William first told her of his plan. She was beside herself with worry as she confronted William with her fears.

"Please explain why this is not to be regarded simply as *madness*! A submarine whose reliability is a matter of hearsay, and a captain and crew you know nothing about. William, this is absurd on its face!"

William smiled his response, and in that gentle, patient voice, he tried to assure his frantic, angry wife that he was, indeed, not crazy.

"Tow? You are going to *tow* it? Across the ocean? To where?" she demanded.

"To St. Pierre. And if our trial runs prove successful, on to Halifax, under its own power."

Reflecting on Josephine's questions, William was doubly glad for the security represented by the freighter. Relaxing in his cramped cabin was difficult, but the effects of the wine and the cognac soothed his nerves, and he soon fell asleep.

The captain's cabin was somewhat larger, with a bunk that could contain his large frame and a small built-in desk with chair. The captain could not relax and found himself restless in spite of the sedative effects of the meal and the alcohol. Looking at the crewmember wedged into the small chair, he spoke emphatically, in a low voice.

"Wir mussen aufpassen, das wis nicht belauscht oder gemeinsan gesehen werden."

The crewmember agreed and added that if either of the two passengers understood just a little of die Deutsche, it might prove most unfortunate.

Despite the absence of heavy weather, the lines connecting the freighter to the U-boat fouled several times, causing long periods of delay while the crews of both ships labored to solve the problem. First, the fouled line would have to be untied from the sub's fittings and retrieved by the crew on the freighter. Then, the same line with a floating device on the distant end would drift down to the sub, to be retrieved and reattached. The freighter would then slowly move away while the tow line played out to the length that would allow both vessels to move in sync. Afterward, there would be long periods of time when the freighter would climb a swell while the sub was descending. It was during those moments when the captain thought they would actually make it through to St. Pierre.

Launched late in the summer of 1916, the U-boat (*Under Sea*) had not had a distinguished career, with only six patrols to its credit and only one ship sunk. In May 1918, after developing mechanical problems, it was interned in a Spanish port. At the end of the war, the ship, scheduled to be broken up, escaped its fate when purchased by a privately owned firm. After repairs and refitting, it sailed from its Spanish harbor and seemed to disappear from the nautical record. Well-maintained in the time before William acquired it, Captain Schmidt thought it a "gut boot." It was certainly acceptable for the purposes he had in mind.

The captain, almost exactly thirty years younger than William, was a tall man for a submariner, athletic, with broad shoulders and a vice-like grip. He had served, though without distinction, as a U-boat commander in the Great War, and after hostilities ceased, he quit the service near the very end of 1919. Since that time, he had bounced around the world, taking command of several types of ships, though never staying on one job very long. He had a reputation for being a competent mariner with no black marks on his record. Among the few who knew him best (and they were not given to speaking out of turn), he was regarded to be distant, aloof, and perhaps…what was the word…disillusioned? Some said he seemed a little bitter.

At the prearranged signal, with all lines removed from the U-boat, the sub began to make way under its own power into the port of St. Pierre. Standing in the conning tower with Ridley and the captain, William looked for old landmarks on the shore and tried get his bearings. He was amazed by the transformation that had occurred during his absence.

The captain expertly maneuvered his craft into one of the available berths, and within an hour, William and Ridley were off the boat and on their way to Hotel Robert. The captain elected to remain on board. During the next several days, his mission was to find the additional number of men to round out the crew for conducting the tests William had specified.

Signing the hotel register, William noted with mild disappointment the absence of the London-born clerk who had welcomed him almost two years before. This new clerk, apparently of Eastern European extraction, was not as friendly, and made no effort to provide help with their luggage. Having agreed to share a room, he and Ridley unpacked for their stay before heading out to see the sights of St. Pierre.

As before, William first headed for the municipal offices in hopes of paying his respects to the genial mayoral host of his previous visit. In this, he was also disappointed. The previous mayor was out of office and had returned home to France. William was told the newly elected official was in conferences and likely unavailable to meet William.

"Perhaps another day, monsieur, if your business in St. Pierre will detain you a sufficient length of time," the secretary consoled. William left his card, noting thereon his hotel address.

William and Ridley walked along the Quai, noting the bustling activity as dockworkers moved cases containing a variety of different whiskies from ship to warehouse.

"This is amazing, William," Ridley began.

"Yes, and there are many more distillers represented here than before."

"The competition, like the plot, thickens," offered Ridley, smiling at William's grimace.

They had walked only a few hundred yards when a still, distant figure attracted William's attention.

There is something about that profile...

William strained his eyes to identify the man. Whoever he was, he had gone aboard a ship close to the pier by the time William and Ridley arrived on the spot. Pausing for a few moments, the two men waited hopefully for another sighting.

"Who do you think he might have been?" Ridley asked.

"I don't see how he could be here, or why." William paused his reply. "Whoever he was, he reminded me greatly of an old friend from Africa."

Captain Schmidt and his accomplice had been busy with their assignment to find additional crew. Working the docks together, they had approached many men, but found only a few that met their requirements. Most of the men they approached were content with their current arrangements. One captain of a freighter that was due to depart on the morrow told them he was leaving behind two men who had not signed on for the return voyage. He could not recommend them to the captain, as they were malingerers, but he was certainly welcome to them.

"Welcome to his castoffs, he means," the captain's accomplice muttered.

The captain grunted in agreement.

Soon the two men stopped to assess a group of dockworkers who had stopped for the midday meal. Circulating among them, the suddenly affable captain began to chat up the prospects. When he learned that three of them spoke his native language, he adopted his most persuasive manner.

"We have possibly five?" his accomplice queried.

The captain agreed, adding that they would know more when they met the men after work.

The weather was mild, and the wind was gusting only five to six knots as William and Ridley made their way to Miquelon and the *Dune de Langlade*, where it was hoped their tests would occur. From his previous visit, William had learned that August and early September were the best months, with less rain and fog to hamper their activities. Under a nearly cloudless sky, the two men enjoyed the short trip to the largest islands of the archipelago.

Located just off the southern coast of Newfoundland, the eight islands, totaling slightly less than one hundred square miles, were part of the northeastern end of the Appalachian Mountains. Known as the "Mouth of Hell" a generation ago, the water between Langlade and St. Pierre was a graveyard for more than six hundred wrecks that had occurred over the past 125 years.

Their boat running at slow speed, William and Ridley inspected the full length of the isthmus that separated the two islands: Miquelon and Langlade. The sandy tombolo proved to be just over six miles long. At William's request, the operator beached the powerboat to allow the two passengers to disembark and inspect the long, sandy beach.

"It would be hard to lose anything here," Ridley noted.

"Yes, it appears we may have found the perfect spot," William agreed. "In its most narrow place, we have, what, a hundred meters of width?"

Ridley nodded his agreement with William's assessment as they turned to return to their boat.

The cruise back to St. Pierre went smoothly, and upon their return to Hotel Robert, they found a feverishly excited desk clerk confronting them as they entered the small lobby.

"Gentlemen! We have been anxiously looking to your return! The mayor's office, it called many times since you left. And now, I am afraid it is late, too late."

"Is there a message for me?" William asked calmly.

With a flourish, the clerk produced a scrap of paper upon which he had scribbled something that William was unable to decipher. Handing it to Ridley, he glanced at its content and shook his head in response.

"Perhaps you could simply tell us what was said," William said in a measured tone.

With an exaggerated patience that both men found trying, the clerk narrated a summary of his conversations with the mayor's secretary, the gist of which was that the mayor would very much like to make William's acquaintance, and that if it were possible, would he please join him for cocktails that very evening. In the end, it was discovered that the clerk had been right about one thing: They were too late for cocktails.

In the small dining area near the bar, Ridley reflected on the day as they finished a late dinner. "Forty gallons is about 314 pounds, and the container makes the total weight about an even four hundred. Do we know how that compares to the weight of the warhead?"

William nodded and considered Ridley's question. "It's very much the same, as I recall. But then, I think we can rely on our good captain to tell us."

Aboard the sub, the size of the crew had doubled overnight. As the captain looked at the ten men gathered around him below deck, he spoke frankly about the mission, using Hans as interpreter for those few who did not speak German. He told them there would be torpedo testing while submerged and various avoidance drills in anticipation of the nature of their endeavor. "Evade, avoid, and escape" were the words William had used when instructing the captain.

"Ja, Amerikanische gewaseer," the captain answered.

With Hans interpreting, he told the men their mission was a practical one—to deliver whisky onto American shores by use of torpedoes. In place of the warhead normally composed of sixty percent TNT and forty percent HND would be forty gallons of House of Lords.

After the laughter subsided, the captain began to question the sailors about their experience. As he listened, he congratulated himself, noting there were no English-speaking members among the crew. When the real purpose of his plan was revealed, he doubted that anyone present would object. Most were German, after all, and loyal to the Fatherland. If it turned out he was wrong, he could deal personally with any objections.

For their part, the crew was very pleased, if not to say excited about the compensation promised and the perceived lack of danger. Winding things up, the captain pointed out that the orders to avoid confrontation along with the element of surprise worked greatly in their favor. With the sub's seven torpedo tubes, they would send to thirsty Americans deprived of their favorite Scots restorative 280 gallons per volley. By using freighters outside the new twelve-mile limit to restock their torpedo "armament," the captain estimated they could fire three volleys per night.

The trials began two days later when the weather improved sufficiently for William and Ridley to observe operations from the safety of the powerboat. They watched for several hours as seven torpedoes were fired onto the sandy isthmus, retrieved by the crew of the powerboat and returned to the sub for reloading and re-firing.

It soon became apparent that the sub would have to get as close as possible to the shore before firing its payload in order to ensure the accuracy desired. Their inventory of thirty-two torpedoes, excluding those used for practice, was held in reserve for when the actual operation got underway. By the time the test firing was over, all but three of the practice torpedoes were salvageable for future use. What was more gratifying to discover was that none of the "warheads" containing plain water showed any signs of leaking. The experiment was regarded to be a success, and the principals withdrew to finalize their plans. The captain and his crew were left to practice their diving and evasion skills while William and Ridley returned to their hotel.

Having conveyed their regrets the previous day, William and Ridley presented themselves to the mayor's secretary a short time before their appointment. Upon being ushered into the mayor's office, William found there a dignified, urbane fellow who remained seated when they entered, waving at them to occupy two chairs in front of his desk. Pleasantries exchanged, they got down to business.

As the mayor and the director of Glenforres-Glenlivit began to get acquainted, William thought about how the new mayor differed from the first.

This man is here to do business, he realized.

Gone was the bonhomie, and in its place a serious and apparently sincere effort to address William's needs or concerns. Was the assigned pier satisfactory for his needs? Were the warehouse facilities to his liking? Had he had any trouble with anyone working in the dock area? Any disappointments? Any requests for the mayor or his staff?

When the mayor saw that there were no concerns or need he could satisfy, he asked William if he could ask one small favor. William responded in the affirmative as he tried to think what the mayor might want of him.

The mayor then asked if he, Mr. William Whiteley of Glenforres-Glenlivit, could explain how it occurred that the Isle of Miquelon was attacked on a previous morning by a submarine that bore a remarkable resemblance to one presently docked at the pier assigned to William.

– § –

The captain looked with admiration and appreciation at his passenger, now conversing freely on the bridge of his ship. *If only there were more like him*, the captain mused; such savoir-faire and intelligence he rarely encountered among the passengers who traveled on his freighter. Usually, the captain had to content himself with deck hands in transit, drummers whose sole focus was on the goods they sold and foreigners with whom he could not converse. He was an educated man and looked the part. Tall, bearded, and well groomed, he carried himself in a manner that allowed some to find him aloof, even arrogant.

"*Decidement, donc mon bon, capitaine.* It is my pleasure, really," said Martine agreeably.

"I shall be sad to see you leave," the captain replied with obvious sincerity, "but you still plan to make the return journey, no?"

Martine nodded. "Yes, as of the moment, I see no reason to stay. The charms of St. Pierre are…um…limited, is it not so?"

With a chuckle, the captain nodded. "Most certainly. One walks the quai a couple of times, and he has seen all of it. Unless, of course, he ventures onto the side streets, where he may find certain pleasures." The captain paused.

Martine shook his head. "Non, mon capitaine. There was a time, perhaps, but no longer. Sadly, no longer."

For a moment, both men were silent. Each was lost in his own thoughts of different times, different places.

"Ah, I see a lorry approaching. Perhaps the owner of this last bit of cargo has finally appeared," the captain noted with a nod toward a vehicle that turned onto the loading dock.

As a mate approached the lorry, a tall, well-proportioned man emerged wearing a sea captain's uniform.

"What is this? A captain coming to pick up his cargo? It must be precious indeed!" smiled the captain of the freighter with whom Martine was conversing.

"Guten abend, kapitan," Captain Schmidt smiled as he extended his hand.

The contents of the crate that Schmidt took possession of was labeled "spare parts." It had been the only remaining piece of cargo, and the captain of the freighter had given it a closer look than he might ordinarily have done. He had noticed that the international warning, "explosives," had been marked through. That fact alone was not controversial, as cargo containers were often in short supply and reused. Customs had cleared the crate, and there was no reason for the captain to act on his suspicions, even if he had any.

"Spare parts, eh?" the captain asked Schmidt.

Failing to understand, Schmidt simply nodded his head, making the final tie-downs to secure the crate on the lorry. As Schmidt swung his frame into the passenger seat next to the driver, Martine watched with mild interest.

"You think something is amiss, *mon ami*?"

As the lorry moved away, the captain shook his head. "No, not necessarily. I could well be wrong, but…I wonder."

With the end of the day fast approaching, Martine decided to have one more good meal ashore before his freighter left the following morning. The captain had begged off, again with seeming sincerity, regretting that his duties kept him from the further enjoyment of Martine's company. Making his way down the Quai, he realized the lorry was still in sight. Walking only a few hundred feet to the pier where the U-boat was docked, he watched as the crew under Schmidt's command gingerly offloaded the crate and lowered it through a hatch.

Continuing his walk, he began to think about which restaurant he would favor that evening. Coming to the entrance of Hotel Robert, he paused for a moment to be sure of his choice.

"Dieu misericordieux! Est-il possible? William!" he shouted.

For his part, Ridley would later say, he had never before or since that encounter on the streets of St. Pierre seen his friend William so visibly moved. Embracing one another and uttering repeated words of welcome and surprise, the two men were for several moments completely enthralled in their chance meeting.

At last, William shook loose from Martine's grasp and introduced Ridley. Without hesitation, Martine bussed each cheek Ridley possessed and shook his hand warmly. Of course, there was room for the three of them, the waiter announced when he saw the size of the bill in Martine's fingers.

Ridley had never known the circumstances surrounding William's dismissal by Munro and listened avidly to the narrative spun first by Martine, who extolled his friend's insight, wisdom, and creativity. For his part, William was suitably modest and, in the process, pleasingly frank.

"Looking back from the vantage point acquired over the years that have passed," William began, "it was simply a regrettable misunderstanding, and I was as much at fault as anyone." Looking at Martine, he continued, "I know at the time we both thought we were doing the right thing. The truth is, I overreacted. I set out to prove something to that 'devil of a director,' and it proved costly," William concluded, as the memory of Munro's disappointment surged with regret.

The conversation then moved on to Martine's circumstances—how he happened to be in St. Pierre. His wine and spirits business remained, and hearing of the development of the Prohibition trade, he came to investigate. Always on the alert for new opportunities to expand, he resolved to see if there was yet room for one more player.

"And what have you determined?" William asked pointedly.

Martine paused before answering, "There is a great deal of activity to be seen; *c'est indeniable*. But for how much longer? It is said the Americans are already more vigilant, that it is exceedingly more difficult to infiltrate their defenses. Is this not so?" He turned to William for answers.

Captain Schmidt was not pleased. He had looked forward to retiring early after securing the contents of the crate earlier in the evening. Listening to the owner of the vessel speak, he took note of the gentleman who had accompanied Ridley and William.

He is one to be wary of, he thought, and observed the trio. *What is this? A tour of the sub! At this late hour!*

As the meaning of Han's interpretation became clear, the captain thought frantically about how he could dissuade.

"The captain says it is rather late," Hans began. "He is concerned that the crew might be disturbed."

"Tell the captain that on the way in we saw most of the crew are awake and apparently happily engaged," William countered. "In any event, if the captain chooses not to accompany us, we will go on our own."

Seeing he was defeated, the captain nodded and put on his jacket to join the tour.

"Oh, there is one other thing," William said. "Ask the captain if he has an empty bottle we might use."

Making his way to the hold where most of the whisky was secured, William bent down to draw off a generous amount from one of the many barrels. As he nosed the open bottle, his senses were alert to a welcome change in the bouquet. In his reverie, he forgot for a moment where he was.

"Well, William?" he heard Ridley ask.

"Oh, yes. Sorry," William responded sheepishly.

Glasses produced, the five began to sample.

In the few moments of silence that remained, William rolled a small amount around in his mouth, savoring his creation thoroughly. Breathing in to evaluate the finish, he was astonished at the differences he could detect. Three voices spoke their praise.

"Magnifique!"

"Schatzbar!"

"Astonishing!"

"It *is* rather wonderful, isn't it?" William replied immodestly to the praise of the three men. At that moment, William would later say, he made one of the most profound discoveries of his lifetime as a distiller and blender of whiskies. The "marrying" of the many characteristics of the whisky caused by the motion of the ship during its voyage produced remarkably desirable enhancements—in every respect. He would also later admit those discoveries nearly cost him his life.

The hold in which they stood was cramped and crowded, with a low ceiling that made standing impossible, and soon, each man found a place to sit while savoring William's "new and improved" blend. Martine was the most restless, and feeling the effects of a mild claustrophobia, he roamed about as much of the space as he could. He noted the careful positioning of the barrels and the care taken to prevent their movement.

As he poked about the hold, he happened to look in the direction of the captain.

A look of alarm? pondered Martine.

Martine thought something had moved behind those eyes.

"Tell me again, William, about your plans," Martine inquired as he continued his roaming.

William began a brief summary of what lay ahead, before their departure. He described the testing that had taken place and the torpedo warheads replaced with containers of similar shape, designed to hold the whisky, and that all there remained to do was to fill them before launching.

"And you say they are like the shape of a warhead?" asked Martine.

"Yes, approximately," William replied. "The engineers tried to make them similar so they could be detached and reused."

"Do they look like these?" Martine asked, leaning over a line of barrels in the darkest corner of the hold.

"What do you mean? There are none in here, as far as I know."

As William rose from where he was sitting and moved toward the spot where Martine's inquisitiveness had taken him, a sharp blow to his head felled him. On his knees, he tried to rise and received a kick in his side as a reward. Dazed and nearly unconscious, he was unaware of what was happening around him. He saw movement and tried to throw his body forward in an effort to avoid further blows. To his relief, they did not come. He could hear the shouting of voices but could not make sense of what was said. Then, he lost consciousness.

His head ached unbelievably, and his stomach was nauseous. He tried to sit up, holding his head in both hands. He ached; it seemed pain shot through every part of his body. He shook his head once, but stopped because it hurt so much.

Slowly, memory returned, and he quickly opened his eyes to see where the dangers were. He thought he could smell the aroma of a fine cigar. Havana? La Palma? He could not be certain.

As his vision began to clear, he thought he saw a dark figure sitting on a barrel nearby. A figure with what did indeed look like a cigar in his mouth. Then he heard a voice calling his name—a voice he thought he had heard before.

"William, *mon ami!*" the voice cried.

Slowly, he began to recover his senses. How long had he been out? It could have been hours, he conceded. His attention was drawn again to that voice.

I should know that voice, he thought irritably.

"William, are you all right?" another voice asked.

Two voices. Two different voices. This was very confusing.

His head jerked back as the smell of a strong substance invaded his nostrils. Suddenly, his head cleared, and he saw in an outstretched hand a bottle—a bottle he recognized and took from Ridley with gratitude forming on his lips.

"Thank you, Vernon," he managed to say.

"Take your time, *mon ami*. All is well, as you can see," the voice he should remember said.

William turned his head slowly to his left, as it still hurt to move. There, just three barrels away, sat the captain. Straight ahead, near the door to the hold, stood Hans. Ridley knelt on the floor beside him, and Martine, the owner of that familiar voice, was sitting just to his right with a pistol in his hand.

"What…happened?" William managed to ask.

Once William was steady enough to walk, the five of them began to make their way out of the hold. When they came to the first ladder, it was Martine, just behind the captain, who said, "Halt, Capitaine."

As the captain waited, Martine motioned to Hans to come forward. "You will go first, it is understood?"

Hans nodded.

"You will go quietly, and if any crew are seen, you will wave them away, understood?"

Hans nodded vigorously.

"Tell the captain, please, that should he at any moment say anything or try to do anything untoward, he shall be shot. Tell him that, please."

Hans nodded and did so.

No crew members sighted, the five of them proceeded up the ladder. All indications were that the crew had retired. It was to be expected, given the hour. Slowly and without incident, the five men departed the sub and came together on the pier. Martine, holding the pistol in one hand, produced a small length of rope in the other, which he handed to Ridley. With instructions from Martine, Ridley formed knotted sections, and used them to secure the captain's hands behind his back.

"You will see, *mon capitaine*, the more you struggle, the tighter the bond. It is useless, you see?" Martine spoke as he helped raise the captain to his feet.

For a moment, the captain's body tensed as if he were contemplating resistance. Shoving the pistol into the captain's back, Martine said something in a low voice, and the captain's body sagged in resignation.

For a moment, Martine and the rest stood immobile on the pier as they considered their next move.

"The harbor police, that is no good," offered Martine. "They are thoroughly corrupt."

Hans and Ridley were silent while William tried to think. His head still hurt abominably, and his stomach churned with the tension of the moment.

"All right. I think I have the answer," William said to Martine's raised eyebrows.

"What made you think of him?" Ridley asked later that morning as they struggled to get food and coffee down.

William's stomach gradually welcomed the food and the coffee as he tried to overcome the headache that would not go away. Shaking his head slowly, he eventually found his voice.

"He was the only one I could remember meeting." William paused, gently rubbing the knot on his head. "The only person who might actually be able to help us, I thought."

Then, Ridley told William what had happened after the lights went out in his head.

"You should have seen Martine—" Ridley began.

"Yes, I should have liked to," William interjected.

Frowning, Ridley continued, "I could not believe how quickly he moved. He was like a panther. After the captain hit you on your head—"

"With what did he hit me?" William again interrupted.

"His fist! He just walloped you and then kicked you in your side as you went down."

William nodded in agreement, rubbed his head again, and asked, "So, what happened next?"

"He was about a barrel away from the captain at that point, and with no hesitation at all, he leapt." Ridley paused in an effort to time his delivery of what transpired. Seeing he had William's complete attention, he continued.

"The captain is a big man, as we know, but he went down at Martine's first blow! That came when, at the end of his leaping, his forearm caught the captain square on his chin." Here, Ridley paused again to demonstrate what had occurred, throwing his right forearm forward, and in doing so, upset the cup of coffee sitting in front of him on the table.

The waiter came forward quickly to clean up Ridley's spill, and William noted Ridley showed no sign of embarrassment.

"When the captain went down, Martine was on top of him in an instant, but there was no struggle, as he was out cold."

"So, what about the pistol? Where did that come from?" William asked.

"He had it hidden in a holster on his leg," Ridley replied with a knowing smile.

"His leg?" William asked in a tone that suggested he might not be familiar with anatomy.

"Yes, his leg. Or his ankle, to be exact. Martine told me while you were out that he always carried his pistol on trips like this one. When you were coming to, he was telling me this was not the first time in his travels that he had had to use it."

William thought later, the mayor could not have been more willing to help. Roused from a deep sleep—aided by the excellent cocktails and champagne he had finished drinking only a couple hours before—he quickly took charge of the prisoner. Seeing there was no possibility of getting back to sleep, and what with all the excitement, he invited the four of them to have breakfast with him on condition that they leave nothing out of their fascinating story.

To everyone's alarm and regret, Martine begged off with the necessity of having to return to his ship, which was soon to depart St. Pierre.

"Surely you are not leaving us," William implored. "We have so much yet to—"

"Ah, *mon ami*, you must forgive me and try to understand."

It was difficult for all of them to see Martine depart so abruptly, and with so much left for them to do. They were without a captain to command their sub; there was the matter of what to do with the illicit cargo of live warheads hidden in the hold of their vessel. Then, there was the matter of the crew, all recruited by a captain now in custody, and whose loyalties were in question. The whole project was near collapse, and the man who had helped them narrowly avoid catastrophe was walking out.

"Let me at least walk you back to your ship," William had insisted.

Every step William took caused his head to throb and his body to ache. As they moved slowly along, Martine continued to explain the necessity of his departure. He spoke of the business affairs he had to attend to and the need of his presence at home. He promised William that they would meet again, and as soon as he could put his affairs in order, he would come to London.

Soon they reached Martine's ship, with William resigned in his disappointment. As they shook hands and exchanged farewells, Martine handed William his pistol.

"Why are you giving me this?" William asked uncomprehendingly.

"*Mon ami*, listen to your friend a moment. You have just seen the danger you face, is that not so? Believe me, there is more to come. You are in a very dangerous business, *mon ami*, and it would be unwise for you to go on unarmed. Do you not see?"

– § –

They spent the days following Martine's departure trying to solve the seemingly intractable problems they faced. The mayor put his chief of police personally in charge of the retrieval of the warheads from the submarine. It soon became apparent who the accomplices were among the crew; so, in the end, there were three crewmembers—along with Hans—who remained on the morning after the munitions were removed. These men, promised full pay and continued employment, secured the sub, while the principals went about trying to salvage the project.

As the days passed, William's awareness of his predicament became more acute. He found he could rely on Hans acting as first mate to maintain security and keep the sub operational. The mayor proved helpful again, personally selecting a security team to prevent any theft of William's cargo. The leader of that team was a nephew of the mayor, who regarded the successful fulfillment of his assignment to be a matter of family honor.

William knew he was running out of time; he did not like having his options reduced by circumstances or events. He preferred to control events rather than react to them. So, he acted.

– § –

The day had gone better for Josephine. Her friend, Maggie, remained close by during William's extended absence. It was not long before the two of them came to be inseparable.

Hinch would later recall this was a period when Josephine seemed to ignore him, even take him for granted. Once Josephine got over the first thrills of driving the massive, elegant Minerva on her own, she began to rely on Hinch to cart Maggie and her around.

The three of them had been out almost the entire day, attending to social obligations and getting in a bit of shopping. Hinch maneuvered the machine to the curbside to allow Maggie to disembark and waited while the two friends made their farewells. As the glass was up, he could not hear their conversation. That suited him well, as he had little interest. Josephine spoke loud enough for him to hear that it was time to move on, and with a small irritation festering, he did so.

Now that she was alone with only her thoughts to distract her, Josephine began to ruminate on the circumstances, as she understood them. William had cabled her, giving only the briefest outline of what had occurred. It was more than enough information to cause Josephine alarm and regret. She found it hard to believe that her husband had put them in such an untenable position.

A foolish venture, very foolish…

Almost immediately, she brought herself up short.

What was I thinking just now?

Even as she began instead to focus on William's well-being rather than his foolhardiness, she found she felt no better.

– § –

The assistant United States attorney general was fielding her last question from the reporters who had gathered for her press conference. It had been her policy to have frequent meetings with the press to enhance public awareness of her department's successes and foster citizen support.

"Madam General," the reporter began, "I have a two-part question. First, how would you describe your efforts to close the speakeasies that plague our society, and second, how is your office responding to the threat presented by the nations of the world who will not support our efforts to combat the evils of alcohol?"

Mabel Willebrandt had often dealt with these very questions in the political, social, and official venues she inhabited over the past six years since her appointment to the position by President Harding. Known to her detractors by such sobriquets as "Prohibition Portia," she had rigorously enforced the Volstead Act and the Prohibition amendment. Recently, she had begun prosecuting known crime figures for income tax evasion in an effort to circumvent the problem of intimidated witnesses in Prohibition prosecutions. Now, as she formed her answer to the reporter's inquiries, she thought how she might add a refreshing note of candor.

"As regards the closing of the speakeasies, it has proved to be rather like trying to dry up the Atlantic with a blotter." She smiled at the ensuing laughter before continuing.

"From the legal standpoint, it must be observed that the difficulty of handling rum-running ships under foreign registry is far greater than those under American registry. We must keep in mind that our allies around the world are not responsible for the enforcement of our laws. That is our job—my job—and I will continue to give that job my full energies."

Beginning late in the year 1924, the Coast Guard began to recognize the existence of a chain of radio stations along Rum Row. The successes of radio code breakers led to the seizure of several freighters and, in time, the discovery of the identity of many corrupt Coast Guard officials. Chief among these was Officer Samuel Briggs of New London, Connecticut, who admitted he had taken bribes to redirect honest captains and their patrol boats away from Frank Costello's rum runners coming ashore.

The ingenuity of rum runners and their bootlegger customers involved nearly every imaginable method to get booze on shore and to the speakeasies themselves. Newspapers filled with stories of the discoveries of illicit booze found on tugboats working the harbors, along with less romantic vessels, such as coal barges, garbage scows, lumber barges, and fishing boats. Anything afloat garnered suspicion from the authorities.

Under surveillance, sometimes for long periods of time, privately owned yachts, sailing ships, speedboats, and even a Royal Mail Steam Packet were stopped, boarded, and searched for contraband liquor. Within the three-mile limit—later extended to twelve (and sometimes outside)—no vessel was safe. That there was no such thing as "honor among thieves" was often demonstrated by the actions of certain gangs trying to muscle in on the rum runners' racket.

Earlier in the year of 1924, the *Mulhouse* (a French liquor ship) was highjacked on Rum Row three miles off the American shores by forty armed pirates from nine different vessels. As the story spread of the looting of more than $800,000 worth of liquor, it soon became obvious to the rum runners that no ship was safe. Whether due to the Coast Guard patrols or the predations of their own kind, the stakes were raised.

– § –

"So, whadda' ya got, Irv?"

"A guy's got his submarine parked at St. Pierre and needs a captain to bring the booze over," Irving Haim said to the man wearing a dark fedora.

"What's he gonna do? Shoot it to us in torpedoes?"

"Yeah, what he says," Haim replied, looking at the man he had only recently begun doing business with. Dark and swarthy looking, with his expensive suit, hat, and $200 Italian-designed shoes, Haim thought he could have passed for an aging Hollywood star.

Frank Costello was anything but.

The "Prime Minister of the Underworld," as he came to be known, was now fully occupied in the crowded world of bootlegging spirits. He could get gin (cheaply), and he could get bourbon and rye. What he wanted most of all was scotch—*good* scotch—and lots of it.

News of the dangers of drinking "bad booze" regularly appeared in most newspapers. Though the victims of drinking denatured alcohol tended to come from the poorer ranks, not a few socially prominent people had died from consuming alcohol laced with noxious chemicals, such as brucine, a plant alkaloid similar to strychnine.

Alcohol would always be available for industrial use during Prohibition, and this alcohol, filled with chemicals to prevent human consumption, was often stolen and "renatured," or restored for human consumption. Already in New York, for more than 750 unfortunate souls, the job had not been done carefully enough.

Costello had enough trouble just finding enough of the "good stuff" to meet his customers' demands. He knew the penalties for selling bad booze sometimes proved more stringent that even the law allowed.

"This House of Lords, you've had it?" Haim inquired.

"I'm not just a scotch man," Costello smiled. "But yeah, I've had it. Pretty good, don't you think?"

Haim nodded. "Rumor has it, it's the best. I couldn't say, since I don't drink much."

Costello looked at his new associate and thought, *Yeah, okay. Don't know if that's true.*

There would be plenty of time to find out. For his sake, Costello hoped the young man wasn't lying. It wouldn't do to deal with a man who couldn't be honest about the little things.

"There just ain't too many of them around," Haim continued. "You got maybe a handful that left the Navy after the war was over, and ain't none of 'em lookin' to drive a German sub."

Costello shrugged, thinking there was always a way. "So what are you sayin', we got no options here?"

Haim shook his head. "No, not sayin' that. Just that you maybe ain't gonna like what I'm about to say." Seeing Costello was waiting for him to get to the point, if he had one, Haim pressed ahead. "You know, they still got this German sub driver over there in jail waitin' for the French to deport him, if anyone will have him."

"Whatsamatter? He don't want to go home?" Costello asked contemptuously.

"Seems he can't go back to Germany. Some problem there with the police, or maybe the military. He didn't exactly light it up durin' the war, they say."

Costello thought, *Don't wanna go home, does he?*

– § –

William watched Schmidt's face as Hans again handled the interpreting. Was there a smugness about Schmidt's manner that conveyed to his interrogators that he knew they needed him more than he needed whatever they were offering? He certainly hadn't been shy about explaining his plans to wreak havoc once he had absconded with William's sub. Captain Schmidt apparently thought he could get back in the good graces of his beloved homeland by avenging his country's losses in the Great War.

With the captain's hands manacled, he now sat with an armed guard in the room where Hans and William quizzed him.

"He says double that amount, and he might consider it," Hans reported.

William looked at the captain for a long moment and, without shifting his gaze, told Hans, "Tell him it's my last offer. Take it or leave it."

Hans did, and Schmidt shook his head.

"Nein," he said with a grim smile.

William rose to leave and, without looking at the captain, said to Hans, "Then I will look at other possibilities. Don't tell him anything. Just leave things as they are."

Hans nodded as William left the room.

The long walk in the municipal building took him to a hallway, where he knew one way led to the exit and the other to the mayor's office. As he hesitated, a door opened, and a French officer in uniform headed in William's direction, accompanied by a man with a face William recognized. As the two men drew near, William saw the face of the young man he had first met at Rouse's Point.

The young bootlegger, Irving…*now, what was his last name?*

Willliam remembered.

The officer passed him without a word or a nod of acknowledgement, but he thought Haim winked at him as they went by.

William remained where he stood as the two men opened the door to the interrogation room where Hans and the captain remained. With curiosity overwhelming him, he moved in the direction of the door and stood there. All he could hear was the low murmuring of the voices within. He tried the door, finding it locked. After a moment, he slowly turned away and grudgingly retraced his steps, this time to the exit and on to Hotel Robert.

Captain Schmidt held his emotions in check as he took the measure of the new interrogators now standing before him. They were standing, not sitting, one obviously a French officer of some service (he could not be sure which) and another man, obviously an American.

What was an American doing here, and why his interest in the affair?

Soon, he heard Hans (the man he had hired!) introducing the two men.

The Frenchman, he was told, was with immigration services, and the American was introduced as a businessman. Schmidt did not acknowledge the presence of either man, but directed all his attention to Hans.

Two can play this game, he thought to himself.

After all, did he not have the Englishman at his mercy? What could they do to him if he refused whatever it was they wanted him to do? Keep him in jail? He had been in jails before.

"The officer wants to discuss the terms of your deportation," Hans began.

Schmidt looked only at Hans and asked what he meant.

"This French officer has been in contact with the German authorities, who say they would very much like to have you in their custody."

"The French are sending you home," Hans interpreted.

Ridley received the second beer with a sense of pleasure quietly growing within. Across the table sat William, concluding a summary of his thoughts about selling the submarine and hoping for a wash as they withdrew from their smuggling business.

All along, Ridley thought of the project as just another business proposition, with a bottom line that needed to be satisfied. He had already made certain to inform William that they were dangerously near the breakeven point, if not past it. It warmed his accountant heart to hear that William seemed ready to withdraw from what looked certain to be unprofitable, not to overlook risky.

Very risky.

Martine's parting comments had registered with William, who was beginning to see he might be out of his league.

"So, you wish for me to begin looking for a buyer, is that correct?" Ridley questioned.

Ridley saw with sudden alarm that William seemed to be hesitating. It was at that moment Irving Haim entered the bar room, alone and unaccompanied by the French officer—or Hans, for that matter. He did not wait to be invited, sitting down on the other side of the table, facing William and Ridley.

"We think we got your problem solved, William," Haim said as he drank from his cup of coffee.

Ridley was eager to hear more, and he was a bit irritated to see the look of doubt on William's face.

"All right," William began, "please tell me more."

Haim took a leisurely sip of his coffee and looked around the room. There was no one else there, and the bartender was preoccupied going back and forth to the kitchen, with provisions and supplies in his hands.

"Well, it's like this, William," Haim began. "We're gonna buy your boat and put the captain to work for us."

A buyer for the boat! Fabulous news! Ridley could not believe his ears. He rejoiced to himself.

William did not.

"Look, William," Haim continued, "you got a situation here that maybe ain't exactly your…uh…what do you Brits call it? Cup of tea?"

No response from William.

"And if you think about it, there really ain't a lot of choices, is there?"

Seeing no response from William, Haim fell silent. He drank his coffee, ordered a refill, and, after waiting for the bartender to go back to his duties, he looked at William.

"Frank wants your boat, and he's willing to pay for it. He don't want you to get hurt…" He paused for a beat. "…and he hopes you'll see this is the best way out. 'Cause you are out, William. Just let me make it clear, before you respond, we want your scotch, and we want your boat. What we don't want is your competition."

– § –

Josephine pulled the covers up, taking care not to wake William. She lay in their bed luxuriating in that stage of pleasurable moments between sleeping and waking, letting her thoughts drift. Their lovemaking was spiced both by her longing that developed in William's absence and her anger over what had taken him away from her. She was relieved to learn that William had managed to dispose of the submarine—that infernal vessel that could well have taken him and all their dreams down with it!

The evening *had* compensated for much of her frustration. Their dinner together at The Criterion had been simply *fabulous*, and such attention they had received, celebrating their anniversary.

Twenty years! She let the number roll around in her imagination.

Turning her head slightly, and gazing at the sleeping body of her husband, she soon felt a warmth building within. He had been funny, she had to admit, when telling her of his conversations with the American mobster.

"I saw I had been thinking too large," William had begun as they sat amidst the Roman arches and golden opulence of The Criterion. Taking another sip of their favorite vintage port, William sketched the process of his thinking.

"It was a matter of realizing I could be the supplier or the chain. I couldn't be both." He paused to look into the eyes of the woman he loved. "Perhaps it was the blow to my head that cleared my thinking. In any event, Haim did make me an offer I found difficult to refuse."

SEVENTEEN

A King's Ransom

JOSEPHINE WAS SUCH GOOD COMPANY that William brought her to their Leith offices on most every trip. As Hinch drove them in the Minerva, William consulted his diaries and talked with Josephine about what he was seeking. Josephine listened without comment, not wishing to interrupt William's creative process.

"I want this new blend to be the best thing I have ever done. If I can find that perfect *balance* that will provide from the first sip…an awareness…the impression that I seek…" He paused for further reflection.

Turning to Josephine, he asked, "Have I told you about the problems with most blends?"

She shook her head.

"You can taste the grain alcohol added." He paused for a moment. "Sometimes, you get fire and spice, and sometimes it just burns the palate." Noting what he thought to be her rapt attention, William continued, "There are then the various malts to be added, little by little, until one thinks the desired effect is achieved. Then, your formula must rest. It must be set aside for the marriage to be consummated." He paused for a moment, smiling at the metaphor before continuing. "Blending is rather like serial marriages. An experimental union is attempted, and, if unsuccessful, it is set aside, and a new relationship gets underway."

With a mild sense of discomfort, Josephine left William to his metaphorical musings and began to take note of the country through which they were passing. Nearly a day's drive from London, they always went straight on through to Leith, never stopping to explore or investigate. The Lake District and the Cumbria valleys seemed to offer such charms as to be irresistible.

But not to William. Sighing, she thought, perhaps, one day…

One day…

Returning to her thoughts about the business, she knew it obvious to anyone who observed the age difference that existed between them. She did not think either of them had aged visibly to any degree, but it was inevitable that someday the unthinkable would happen. She had to prepare for that day, all the while hoping it would remain a long way off. *Before we get there,* she thought, *we must find time for* ourselves.

– § –

Captain Schmidt was having difficulty adjusting to the demands of his new bosses. The pay was good, and the crew the Americans had assembled were adequate. There was still that rush of adrenaline every time out when he maneuvered the sub in position to fire their whisky-laden torpedoes onto the shores of Montauk Beach, Long Island, South Hampton, and even Martha's Vineyard.

Success had followed success as the scouting provided by Costello's men kept them moving from point to point with a frequency that had avoided detection thus far. He had learned which Coast Guard boats were friendly and which to avoid at all costs. There had been frequent contact with four different patrol boats that either confirmed the targeted port or waved them off.

The sub was of the UC class, designed for minelaying and working close to shore. Technically, like all other subs, it was a submergible, with the ability to stay underwater for only short periods of time. The usual approach was to shoot the whisky ashore at night and withdraw from the target area while submerged, surfacing after reaching the twelve-mile limit.

Freighters housed the torpedoes, maintaining and refitting their whisky warheads, as other vessels retrieved and returned the cigar-shaped missiles for reuse. Hard work, good surveillance, and some luck had enabled the rum runners to escape detection.

His bosses drove him hard. *Too hard,* Schmidt thought. Maintenance and repairs necessary to keep the U-boat operational were tedious, time-consuming, and—to his bosses—undesirable interruptions in the flow of profits. He had begun to look for a way to get out of the forced labor that made him feel like an indentured servant.

The 88mm deck gun on the U-boat had been made operational, but there had not yet been a need to use it. As the U-boat continued its surface run toward the twelve-mile line, Schmidt readied himself to take advantage of any opportunity to get out of his predicament. He knew there were Coast Guard patrols all over the area in which they were working. How difficult could it be to encounter one and then surrender his sub? Would not his crew go along once they realized their situation was hopeless? He resolved to go ahead with his plan to surrender and hope that the crew would use their common sense and not resist.

They had reached the point where they would normally submerge to begin their approach to the shore and find their target. Schmidt did not give the command to dive, so the sub continued its surface run. The helmsman began looking nervously at Schmidt, who failed to respond, staring at his charts instead.

When they reached the eight-mile position, the helmsman spoke. "What's up, Captain?"

Again, Schmidt refused to respond.

Just a little farther, he thought to himself.

Soon, he hoped the vaunted surveillance of the Coast Guard would locate their new prize. He then felt the point of an object pressed firmly in his back an instant before a voice behind him shouted, "Dive!"

As the helmsman responded to the order, Schmidt turned to see who had usurped his command.

– § –

Irving Haim stood before the desk behind which Frank Costello sat, forming a steeple with his fingers.

"So, after they bumped him off, how'd the sub get back?" Costello asked.

"Helmsman knew how to drive the boat, and our man knew enough German to read the controls. But it looks like a no-go from here," Haim replied.

Costello nodded.

"Well, we had a good run. Worse comes to worse, we can sell it for scrap." Haim read again the short notice in the morning paper:

MYSTERIOUS DISCOVERY
Off the coast of Long Island, the body of a white male was discovered floating in the water. No identification has been made as yet, and police suspect foul play of the mob variety.

– § –

Ridley was enjoying one of the fringe benefits of working for Glenforres-Glenlivet and Whiteley, Ltd. Sipping and tasting the trial blend, he had an awareness of deeper, fuller, richer flavors, compared to other tastings. Looking at the small amount of whisky remaining in the glass, he took note of its mahogany shade, swirled the remainder, and drank it down.

Looking across the tasting table, he saw William shake his head. "No, Vernon. Sip it—don't drink it." He poured a small amount in Ridley's empty tasting glass. "The point is, we may be here a while. Take your time, because I need a sober response. What do you think so far?"

Ridley was not experienced in drinking blended whiskies, preferring beer and ale—a habit picked up in the war years. He knew William wanted his honest opinion, but he felt that he served another purpose as well.

"You represent the man who does not usually drink whisky," William had once said, adding, "I am keen on having a whisky that will attract a new clientele—one that may not have drunk whisky at all."

– § –

As the end of the year of 1927 came closer, William felt he would have his breakthrough any day. For hours on certain days, he would stay away from his tasting table and avoid all contact with those who smoked. He restricted his diet to bland food in an effort to prepare his palate to be clean and fresh. He drank water as his only beverage while he waited for his next tasting, giving the whisky and alcohol time to get better acquainted.

In the evenings, Ridley retired as early as his duties and William would allow. His hours and days were filled with doing calculations for each of the sample blends William set aside for his trials. Each method (or blend) had its own cost structure. There were the costs of aging to consider—the barrels, the labor, the warehousing—in addition to the cost of production. He tried to stay in step with William so when the grand moment came, he could show his tallies and project price, cost, and profit margins.

When he was done with work, he loved to read before turning out the lights. That evening, as he prepared for bed, he looked at the book cover and felt that faint rush of excitement he often felt before cracking open a new one. It was a biography of Richard I, entitled, *Coeur de Lion*. As was his habit, he first read the summary of the story on the dust jacket:

> *Richard, the Lionheart, while enroute home from a Crusade is shipwrecked. In disguise, he and his band try to make their way to the Hungarian border. They are recognized, captured and thrown into prison by Leopold, Duke of Austria, who feels disgraced by Richard. He demands of England a ransom and if it is not paid, he will turn Richard over to Philip II of France.*

As he began to read the first chapter, a wave of fatigue swept over him. Closing his book, before turning out the light, he realized he had not written Ada. *Tomorrow, for sure,* he decided as he drifted off to sleep.

Josephine woke with a start. It had been very late when she gave up on her husband and went to bed. Now, hearing his arrival, she whispered, "William, why so late?"

As he entered their bed, he snuggled with his wife, putting his arms around her, and then answered with a whisper of his own, "I've got it. I think, finally, I have it!"

Coming near fully awake, Josephine looked in the dark at the face of her husband. "You really mean it?"

"Yes, this time I believe I do."

"Oh, William, this is wonderful. You have been working so hard and so long. We must celebrate."

There was a brief pause while William pulled up the covers. "Well, all right. If you insist."

Josephine sat upright in the darkness. "You mean now?"

They began laughing at almost the same instant.

William arrived at his Leith offices late the next morning and, having breakfasted, allowed time for his palate to clear before plunging back into his work. He liked to have a break between test-tastings, especially in those moments when he felt he was close to achieving something of value. There was a knock on his door just before Ridley entered.

"Vernon, you have come at just the right time," William greeted. "I have found what I want, and now it needs a name. You must sip and think about what we may call it."

Ridley had slept exceptionally well, rising early to complete his letter to Ada. Sitting at the tasting table, looking at the pour William had made, his mind was at peace and ready to focus on the new challenge. No words, other than the customary greetings, had passed between them.

Lifting his glass to nose it, he caught a scent from the whisky that reminded him of the caramel candies his mother had once made. Taking his first sip, he felt a sudden rush of flavors that simultaneously sought out and teased his palate. The whisky could only be described in one word, Ridley thought.

"Delicious, William. Simply delicious."

William nodded his appreciation. "Yes, it may very well be. But I do not believe we can copyright that as its name."

Ridley blushed slightly. "Whatever you may choose to call it, it is worth a king's ransom."

– § –

As the port of Leith had grown, there were times when warehouse space came at a premium. The old wine warehouses had changed contents after phylloxera devastated the European wine industry in the 1860s and now overflowed with spirits, aging.

Companies were holding back their stocks due to the economic uncertainties of the moment, while, perhaps because of lingering aspects of Prohibition, individual consumption declined.

What space William had acquired was no longer adequate for his plans; so, as he began his search, his thoughts turned from the land to the sea. He remembered the discovery that occurred in the hold of the U-boat just before Schmidt's attack.

Preparing to leave his offices, he encountered Dennis, who asked if he could say where William might be found, if wanted.

"The harbor master," William replied, as he set off in the Minerva with Hinch behind the wheel.

The harbor master was dubious. He pointed out to William that with the advent of steam, the problem sailing ships once had acquiring suitable ballast had long been solved by the ballast tank. He could think of no reason why the owner of any steamship would be willing to sacrifice cargo space to carry William's whisky around free of charge. Nevertheless, he gave William the names of several ship owners he might contact and sent him on his way without consideration for the distiller's negotiating skills or ingenuity.

William knew there were still merchant sailing ships working the windy passages of the Cape of Good Hope, massive three- and four-mast ships known as windjammers. With steel or iron hulls and steel rigging, they sailed with half the crew found on the graceful old clipper ships. They carried the lower-value cargos, and William sought out those ship owners to pitch his plan to.

Ridley conscientiously reviewed the numbers, adding the cost of insurance for the whisky serving as ballast. With the cost and shortage of warehousing considered, it quickly seemed a desirable option. William's research had determined there were close to four thousand of these "floating warehouses" still in service. All of a sudden, his storage problems solved, on February 28 of the following year, he registered King's Ransom as a trademark, thereby adding another to the list of his eponymous whiskies.

The year of 1928 was not without its disappointments, as Josephine's mother, Mary Jane, passed in September. Josephine grieved more for her father, left alone and despondent over his loss. With her sister, Connie, in India, there was no one else to look after her dad, and so, Josephine found herself with Hinch at the wheel making trips more frequently to her father's home.

"Would you like me to go with you?" William had asked in the beginning.

She had reassured him it was not necessary, but she knew the truth of the matter. Despite their acquiescence, her parents had never really approved of her marriage. She found her father was uncomfortable in William's company, a reaction she thought due to their being of similar age. In her parents' view, marrying a man only three years younger than her father was still incomprehensible, if not to say bizarre.

– § –

"Stock prices have reached what looks like a permanently high plateau," wrote Irving Fisher, the Yale economist, on October 15, 1929. Fisher was one of Prohibition's leading intellectual defenders. He had also predicted that it might be a generation or more before the Eighteenth Amendment could be repealed and greatly doubted it could ever be done.

His timing is exquisite, thought Ridley.

As he read the London newspaper nine days later on the day that became known as Black Monday, Ridley felt he could afford to smile at his sardonic witticism. Then, he began to think about what he would do if he suddenly found himself out of work or his personal fortune devastated.

A drink would help.

So thought the majority of Americans.

Prohibition had always had its detractors, and their numbers began to climb rapidly after the bottom of the market fell out, and the impact of the Great Depression began to tear at the fabric of all levels of society. An anti-dry social movement began to grow, and so rapidly gained strength that newspapers began to speak of a "social repeal" underway. A prominent Long Island resident, who chaired a Women's Republican Club, shared this observation with President Herbert Hoover:

I have always been in the ranks of the drys, but sentiment is changing.

Prohibition's arch-defender, Assistant Attorney General Mabel Willebrandt, resigned her office in 1929 after President Hoover passed her over, failing to nominate her for the office of Attorney General. Her influence and her support of Prohibition while in office proved to be sorely missed by the "drys," whose influence continued to wane.

With support for Prohibition declining, along with tax revenues due to the economic catastrophe underway, the government began to look more favorably at legalizing beer. The Anti-Saloon League, a major political force in keeping Congress populated with "drys," soon saw its flow of monetary support decline to alarming levels. Its influence soon followed along the same path.

Franklin D. Roosevelt's election late in 1932 had the effect of rapidly coalescing forces of the Repeal Movement. On the fence during his campaign, he openly supported Repeal upon assuming office. Three months later, in February 1933, the Twenty-First Amendment to the Constitution of the United States came up for debate. Shortly before the end of the year, the requisite thirty-sixth state ratified the Repeal amendment. Large celebrations broke out spontaneously across the entire country, heralding the first alternative to a "dry" Christmas in more than a decade. The Great Depression lasted another six long, tortuous years before hostilities in Europe awakened the dormant American economy.

– § –

Just before the middle of the thirteenth century, about 1237 AD, members of a guild, or livery, began "licensing" their members to carry out their craft or trade within the one square mile of London proper. Six hundred years later, the freedom expanded to include those people who lived or worked in the city.

On the third day of April 1930, William applied for admission to the Freedom of the City of London, listing that he was "carrying on the business of distiller" and occupying a residence at 20 Templars Avenue, Golders Green NW 11, London. On the application, he listed for the first time his place of birth as Little Moor, Sowerby, Yorkshire, and included information on his father: George Whiteley, late of Chapel Street, Southport, Lancaster, wine and cigar merchant.

Escorted to the court by the beadle, with the chamberlain presiding in his courtroom at Guildhall, William was handed by the clerk the parchment with his name inscribed by a calligrapher, along with a copy of "Rules for the Conduct of Life."

Invited to read "The Declaration of The Freeman," it began with the words "I do solemnly swear that I will be good and true to our Sovereign King George the Fifth…"

A quiet celebration followed as the new Freeman, Josephine, and a few of their friends gathered at The Criterion. Toasts continued throughout the evening, and one among Josephine's favorites came from the friend who first used a title that was to honor William for the remainder of his days.

"I propose a toast to the 'Dean of Distillers,'" their friend said to a chorus of "huzzahs."

– § –

SS *Lafayette* made her way slowly into her berth in New York Harbor. It was the 29th day of October in the year of 1931, and she had taken seven days to make the voyage from Plymouth, England—days full of anticipation and apprehension for at least two among her passengers.

Before leaving their shared stateroom, Ridley checked for the third time that he had all the documents and papers needed. On a hunch, he checked the bathroom, and found in the tension of the moment he had indeed forgotten his razor. William, waiting patiently at the door, nodded as Ridley quickly put his razor away. The two of them then went topside to disembark.

Clearing customs took longer than expected, as their travel documents showed they were in transit to Canada.

"Will you be staying in the U.S. for any time during your journey?"

"Not long," William replied, noting the officer's friendlier manner when compared to the one he had encountered at Rouses Point so many years before.

The interrogation completed, the two men made their way to the taxi stand.

Nearing their hotel, William asked to see the bill of lading. "When we check in, please call and confirm all has safely arrived."

Ridley nodded and did as requested, confirming the delivery of the contents of the shipment to a Canadian warehouse just across the border.

He hoped it would be enough.

– § –

His customers wanted all the good hooch he could provide. Rumor was too many people still were dying of adulterated alcohol meant for industrial use. The Feds called it *denatured*, which meant anything from strychnine to methyl alcohol was being added to discourage human consumption. It was one thing to bump off a competitor or a disgruntled hoodlum; killing a customer was another thing entirely.

It just wasn't good business, thought the Prime Minister of the Underworld.

He had been briefed about the shortages. It was getting harder to get the booze in; yet, another twenty thousand cases were needed to satisfy the demand. It had to be the good stuff. Like William's.

– § –

In their shared room, William and Ridley went through their plans for the next day's meeting. After reviewing their notes and papers, they both went down to have the concierge show them the meeting room. Doing a walk-through, William pointed out to Ridley where everything was to be placed and reconfirmed all arrangements with the concierge.

"You anticipate ten at a table, but wish to be able to accommodate twelve, is that correct?" the concierge asked.

"Bodyguards?" Ridley asked William after leaving the concierge.

"Yes. If I'm right, that would be the only reason for the number to be twelve."

– § –

William and Ridley went about arranging the conference room table. On two other small tables, the contents of two cases were displayed according to William's precise instructions. In front of each chair at the main table, glasses were placed, along with small carafes of water. Table linen of the hotel's finest quality attractively presented the glassware, which sparkled in the light of the chandeliers. As William surveyed the room, he was careful to ascertain that all arrangements met his expectations. Then, the two men sat down to wait.

Inhaling the smoke from his cigarette, the bellman checked his watch. Five more minutes left on his break, it told him. Taking a comb from the rear pocket of his tight-fitting pants, he slicked back his hair and looked at his reflection in the glass wall behind him. Satisfied with what he saw, he began to think about that hot chick working in the hotel bar. He could show her a thing or two if she ever wised up and went out with him. He was about to stub out the remainder when he saw the limo ease its way to the curb. While he stood behind a column, his interest was drawn to the man who exited the front seat while buttoning his suit coat.

"Holy shit," he exclaimed as he slowly withdrew to avoid attracting attention.

The concierge listened patiently while the bellman excitedly told him of his discovery.

"They're packin,' and there must be six or eight of them," he gasped. "Went right on in and took the elevator up to the eighth floor! You think we should call the cops?"

"You haven't been here long enough to know about these things," said the concierge. "Best not to interfere in what doesn't concern us. A fella could get hurt. You know what I mean?"

The long, black limo slowly pulled away from the hotel after depositing its passengers. The leader of the group of eight then motioned for the rest to follow him as they entered the hotel, thinking they were unobserved. Though at close quarters, they all crowded into an elevator to ascend to the floor where William and Ridley waited. Ridley was at the door to welcome the party of eight and, after exchanging greetings, invited them in, where William rose to greet his guests.

"Nice room," the leader said as his bodyguards cased the space.

"Please sit down. We have a lot to discuss," William invited.

Frank Costello accepted William's invitation, handing his coat and hat to one of his bodyguards. William noted there was no telltale bulge to indicate the mobster was packing. It was apparent to William that only the bodyguards were armed. What he did not know was that Costello had sworn off carrying a gun more than fifteen years ago.

Looking across the table, Costello saw a balding man of average height; of an age he would have guessed to be about seventy years. Except that he did not need to guess. He knew William had had his seventy-first birthday in June, and he knew this unassuming Britisher made the best Scots whisky in the world. But there was a problem. He could not get enough of it.

He knew William's story: the sacking by Munro, the bankruptcy, the death of George (now, there was a man, he had been told), his marital status, and his love for expensive cars. He also believed William was a man he could do business with, in the manner he preferred. William seemed aware of his limitations. After all, what had the episode of the submarine on St. Pierre shown, if not that?

As Costello mused, William gazed directly at him before he spoke. "Mr. Costello," he began.

Raising his hand with a dismissive wave, Costello said, "Call me Frank, and I'll call you William."

Nodding, William continued, "I am pleased you and your fellows could join us today. You've met Vernon, and now the two of us would like to make another introduction."

There were small sounds of moving as all but Costello shifted their chairs. Only his eyes moved as they locked with William's.

Smiling, William nodded to Ridley, who then rose to make his way to the tables, holding the cases of bottles. Moving about the room, and with a sense of pride that his hands were not shaking, Ridley put a small bottle of dark amber liquid in front of each participant. When finished, he returned to his seat next to William.

"Please join me, gentlemen," William invited as he removed the cork stopper from his bottle and waited for the others to do so. "Now, please pour a small amount into your tasting glass—the curved one there next to the water glass."

As he watched each man pour, William saw Costello dispense all his glass could hold. Pressing on, William invited his guests to nose the glass—demonstrating the technique—and then to savor a small amount. To his mild dismay, Costello drank down the contents of his glass, slamming it onto the table.

"You been holdin' out on us, William."

Grinning more than smiling, William replied, "I have, Frank."

Costello looked at William and waited for his explanation.

"Not quite four years ago, I came up with a new eight-year-old whisky. That whisky you have been receiving along with House of Lords."

Costello nodded and, pointing to his empty glass, said, "Okay, I want all of this new stuff you got to sell."

"Unfortunately, Frank, I have none to sell you."

Costello wasn't sure he heard right. "Whadda' ya mean, got none?"

Sitting back in his chair, William looked at Ridley and nodded. Reaching into his valise, he pulled out the bill of lading, which he handed to William. Glancing briefly at the document, William gave it over to Frank. He waved it away, and the man on his right took it from William's hand.

After a few moments of inspection, the man leaned over to whisper something to Costello.

"Only five thousand cases? That's peanuts, William," Costello sneered.

Smiling, William nodded. "Yes, I can understand how you might see it that way."

A long moment of silence occurred, with something of a stare-down underway.

Remember, son, William could hear his father saying. *In negotiations, often he who speaks first loses.*

"Eeet ees a geeft, Frank," the man on Costello's right said in a low voice, breaking the silence.

Fuming inside, Costello frowned at his consigliore and turned on William. "What's the deal here? You got whisky, and I want it. What's wrong with that?" he barked.

"Timing." Before Costello could interrupt, he continued, "You are about a year, perhaps two years too early."

If this guy thinks I'm gonna wait another two years, he's got another thing comin', Costello fumed.

His consigliore was speaking, and Costello half-listened, hearing something about the difference aging made between eight- and twelve-year whiskies. Another part of his mind was occupied with a need.

"What the hell you thinkin'?" Costello interjected. "My people don't care how old it is."

This much was true. If William had known how much his whisky was being diluted in the bars and speakeasies of New York City alone, he might have been even less agreeable.

Unmoved by Costello's interrogation and raising his bottle, William invited his guests to refill their glasses and enjoy a small portion of the limited release of his finest creation.

Costello looked at the remains of the small bottle of whisky that sat on the table in front of him.

This guy's got balls after all, Costello realized. *Ain't nobody ever told me no and got away with it…except maybe Haim. And that turned out all right, most of the time.*

He took a moment to reflect on what he had tasted.

Damn good. Maybe good enough to wait for… But why should I?

At that moment, there was a knock on the door.

All eyes watched as one of the bodyguards edged to the door and opened it a crack. Retrieving an envelope from an unseen hand, the bodyguard took one look and hastily delivered it to his boss. Costello opened the envelope and removed a folded single piece of paper. After he read the contents, he looked at William.

His consigliore was whispering, "A geeft; the man has ge-veen someting of value. *Ora e il momento per respetto, si?*"

Costello sat motionless for a long moment, during which the air seemed to escape from the room.

"All right, William, we'll do it your way…for now."

William smiled, and for some reason, from the memory banks of his mind, he had a flashback to his childhood and to a certain day when he came home from school with scratches on his face and torn clothing.

"You poor dear," his mother had said when she first saw him. "How did this happen?"

Instead of explaining about the tussle he had with classmates, William ran up to his room, where his father later found him brooding.

"You got the worst end of it, I reckon," George had said.

Ashamed and embarrassed, William could only nod his head. George put his arm around him and spoke in a gentle voice, "Was there more than one of 'em?"

Again, William nodded.

"Well then, we'll have to consider certain methods of self-defense."

With his hand, he lifted William's downcast face up to look him in the eyes. "Are ye' game?"

Having his young son's full attention, George talked about how to deal with bullies. He demonstrated how and where men were most vulnerable and counseled going for the biggest one first.

"You bring him down, and the rest will likely run," George predicted.

Costello had not run, but he had backed off.

For William, that was more than good enough.

EIGHTEEN

Edradour

To the east, above the village of Pitlochry and near the ruins of Lindores Abbey, where *Aquavit*, "the water of life" was first created by the Grey Monks of the Tironensian Order, sat the Edradour (EDD-ra-DOW-er) Distillery. It was originally a farm distillery. The earliest records of whisky-making date to 1823, though this distillery did not register until 1825.

Alfred Barnard wrote in 1886:

The Distillery, which was built in 1837, is situated at the root of a steep hill, on the road side, and consists of a few ancient buildings, not unlike a farmstead, past which flows one of the most rampant and brawling streams in the district.

"That stream stems from Moulin Moor and is known as the Edradour Burn," Ridley remarked as they made their way from the Atholl Palace Hotel to the Edradour.

They had parked the Minerva at the hotel, leaving Hinch to his tinkering, and set out to find the footpath that would take them through Black Spout Wood. As they entered the wood, William anticipated the sight and sound of game or small animals scurrying along and across the well-trodden path.

Birds would surely fly, he thought, and looked up.

The sun filtered through the trees, providing ample light to guide their way. They stopped at one point to listen for the sounds of the forest. There were none. Only the swishing of their clothing against the forest fern and other plant life gave them any sensation of sound or movement.

"There must be thousands of eyes watching us," William said quietly.

Walking normally, they felt certain they would come upon some startled forest animal at any moment. Crossing the burns on footbridges, they made their way through the woodland. Pausing for a short detour, they admired the Black Spout, an impressive waterfall cascading down some sixty feet to Edradour Burn.

It was not until the moment they cleared the wood and began their climb to the high road that would take them to the distillery that they saw their first other resident of the woods. A hawk dove sharply to the ground and rose triumphantly with its prey in its claws, sailing away from them in the direction they were going.

Peter McIntosh was there to greet them and serve as their tour guide. He had owned the distillery since 1907, having taken over following the demise of his uncle, John. As he began to speak, the weariness caused by so many years of frustration and failure weighed heavily upon him.

"What you see is pretty much how Barnard described it nearly fifty years ago," McIntosh began. "You've got enough water power to drive several water wheels. There is your barley barn, malting house, and mill."

They observed the Mash Tun, Still House, Wash Still, and Low Wines Still.

A spirits store, cask shed, some outhouses, and a stable rounded out their tour before they came to the first of three warehouses.

"You'll want a wee dram or two, I'm thinkin'," McIntosh said as he led them inside.

Soon after, they settled into a small office, where Ridley began his "meditations," as William had come to call them. Handing several large account books to Ridley, McIntosh said, "You will see that cask sales declined precipitously in the years before we closed. Nevertheless, we have on hand approximately 5,400 gallons of malt."

The confidence and pride that belong to hope.

Where had he heard those words or first read them? William wondered as he reflected upon what McIntosh had said.

And when hope is gone, William then pondered, *what remains?*

The pub in the old hotel was small and cozy, and the peat fire provided a welcome warmth for Ridley and William. The Moulin Hotel had provided rest to travelers since 1695. It was a short walk from the distillery, and they had had time to pause and reflect upon a twelfth-century crusader's grave in the church graveyard across the road.

"The inventory alone is worth the price they are asking," Ridley began. Seeing no response from William, he continued, "There is nothing amiss in the books, either, that I can see. And then, there is the freehold that the duke seems anxious to sell."

William sipped his ale and thought for a moment before responding. "There *is* the smell of anxiety, I think."

Ridley paused to take this comment in.

"An air of desperation, I should say," William finished, as he took a longer draw from his glass.

"Well, he did mention the drop in cask sales, which was readily apparent before they closed in '29. And that decline has been underway for a long while, as we know."

Nodding, William continued to sip his ale without comment. He could see the Edradour had been a victim of the worldwide turbulence in the markets and financial industry that, coupled with the Prohibition movement, had caused the closure of countless distilleries. Finally, as Ridley was about to break the silence, William spoke. "Offer him a thousand, and we'll go from there."

Immediately upon completing the purchase of the Edradour, William removed the entirety of the malt stock to his facilities in Leith, where he put the whisky to use making his House of Lords for the export market and King's Ransom for the domestic and international markets. A certain wing of the British government objected to William's use of the name, House of Lords, and went on to forbid its sale in the home market.

The dearth of malt and grain whiskies caused by the closing of so many distilleries had been a setback to his plans for the twelve-year King's Ransom. Now, with the Edradour in his possession, he felt he could at last produce enough to meet the burgeoning demand, both domestic and international. He smiled, remembering the confrontation with Costello that later gave rise to Ridley's question.

After Costello and his gang had left and Ridley was sure they would not be overheard, he had asked his question.

"Why did you not just tell him about the shortages we faced? He would have understood, I think, that one cannot produce what one does not have."

William looked at his erstwhile accountant and friend. "I felt at the time that would have been a sign of weakness," he explained. Pausing for a moment, he went on. "Imagine trying to explain our shortages and production problems at that time. Can you think of any way to do that and come out ahead?"

Ridley could not.

– § –

"Mr. James can see you now. Do come along," the secretary directed. William and Josephine followed the attractive young woman as she continued to speak.

"You know, Mr. James has been quite busy with the new Hertford County Hall. I am so glad he could find a little time for you today."

Leaving the minimalist reception area, they entered a long hallway, making their way nearly to the end.

"Now, here we are."

She stopped before a large black door and knocked.

A quiet voice inside bade them enter.

As William and Josephine entered the studio, Charles Holloway James rose from his worktable and came to greet them.

"So good of you to come. Call me Charles, and sit, please." He waved them toward a couple chairs nearby. Josephine looked around the large office, noting how sparsely furnished it was. There were two drafting tables positioned to take advantage of the natural light that flooded the space. Both a wall of glass running the entire length of the room and a skylight positioned carefully in the ceiling provided enough light to nearly eliminate the need for the lamp positioned next to the desk where James now sat.

James himself was a very tall man with boyish features that belied his age of forty-two years. He moved so naturally and gracefully that it was hard to believe he had suffered the loss of a leg in the Great War.

"So, you want to build a house. Tell me all about it, and where you want to live," James began.

Josephine could not help liking the man. He was so youthful and quietly exuberant. "That's something we need to discuss with you," she began. "William and I just love Hampstead Heath, and—"

"Yes," James interrupted, "you live not far from there now, on Templars Avenue, I believe."

Josephine noticed William's eyebrows shoot upward, a sure sign of surprise—or favorable impression.

"Well, yes, we do," Josephine replied, not minding his interruption.

James continued, "Do either of you play golf? No? Well, no matter. There is a lovely site available on Wildwood Road with a marvelous view of the Heath. What say we find a day to go and take a look?"

– § –

Ridley finished preparing the summary of events for his meeting with William, using a pencil to mark the calculations he wished to focus upon. Checking his watch, he placed his papers in a folder and made his way to William's office. He found William there, absorbed in his own musings, and made his way to the conference table they would share. As he mentally rehearsed the most salient points in his memoranda, there kept running through his mind the apprehension he felt following his last meeting with Haim.

He had been to the States four times since the first meeting with Costello three years before, and on the last trip, he had returned just before Christmas with deep forebodings. He felt pressured by Haim regarding Costello's desire to purchase the Edradour. Apparently, Costello had not forgotten the outcome of their previous meeting.

The pressure came from poorly disguised references to the issue of William's retirement plans. As Ridley reflected on Haim's words, he realized that, standing alone, they might be seen as containing no threat. But, when Haim would ask about William's health, Ridley could sense the question hidden there.

When is William going to get out of the way?

After summarizing his most recent conversations with Haim, he saw with interest a smile of recognition forming on William's face. William began his response, mentioning how much, at the moment, he was reminded of his father.

"Your father?" Ridley inquired.

William sat back in his chair and tried to recall the exact words his father had used. Realizing he could not, he began paraphrasing what George had said about the middleman.

"Many hands may take possession of what has been sent to you upon your own request. So, by the time the item arrives at your door, the mere laying of hands upon it will have raised the cost but never the value."

"Transportation costs," William continued, "shipping, for example, are unavoidable if there is a distance you cannot negotiate yourself. But what if the item is available right next door? Better yet, what if you can make the item yourself?"

– § –

SS *Bremen* departed Southampton on a cold, blustery April day in 1934 with William and Ridley aboard. Although William did not know it at the time, this was to be his last voyage to the States. Taking only five days to make the crossing, the two men arrived at New York Harbor on April 19 and, soon after disembarking and clearing customs, made their way to their hotel.

They had hardly finished their dinner when, on their return to their room, Haim's call came through. Ridley had offered to accompany William to the meeting in the bar and had to admit feeling some small amount of relief when William said "No." Now, as he finished his letter to Ada, his mind ruminated again on the options he tried to picture in his mind.

William paused to think about Haim's question. The hour had grown later, and there were no other patrons in the bar. The bartender had already been by their table to ask if they wanted anything else and, after a quick look at Haim, withdrew without a murmur.

When William accepted Haim's invitation to have a drink in the hotel bar, he felt certain what to expect. He and Ridley were of the same notion—that Costello wanted the Edradour and wanted it badly. He knew he had Haim's full attention, and he now sought to make him a most persuasive messenger.

As William outlined his concept of continuing to do business with Costello—and Haim for that matter—he emphasized the straight-up manner in which they would begin to engage *legally* in the sale of alcohol. There was surely a pent-up demand to serve, he thought, with the end of Prohibition. His purchase of the Edradour had provided the source he needed to meet the demand for King's Ransom twelve- and eight-year editions, and there was always plenty of House of Lords to ship. Then, there was Costello's business-like model, which he liked to adhere to. Here was the golden opportunity for that honest, legitimate business venture he claimed to want. No front—the real thing. Other than paying taxes and import fees, there was nothing to cause the Feds concern.

Haim listened thoughtfully as William summarized his main points about the advantages of essentially keeping things as they were and had been for the last ten-plus years. For reasons Haim kept to himself, he knew the "legit" business argument would resonate with Costello, but he was still trying to wrap his head around how to get Costello past the word "No."

Another mobster had once jokingly suggested he might someday write a book about his dealings with the Mafia boss and how not many knew what a nice guy he could be. Haim smiled at the recollection of what he said at the time.

"Yeah, after he's dead, you might get away with it. If you're gonna write what a nice guy Frank Costello was, you'll have to leave out that chapter on the 1920s."

He had to admit he admired the Englishman, who he now saw in a different light. In St. Pierre, he thought he had seen a defeated man with few options. Now, he saw across from him an older but more confident fellow to reckon with. *This man might not be buffaloed,* he thought. And that *was* the kind of man Frank Costello could respect. Respect was one thing, Haim thought; agreement, another.

– § –

Frank listened as his "associate" reported the results of the meeting. He respected Haim's opinion and felt he could trust him to be on the level, whether he took Haim's advice or not.

"He likes things the way they are now, and there's somethin' to be said for that, ain't there?" Haim asked.

Seeing no response and fearing the worst, he plowed ahead with his reactionary message. "Somethin' also to be said for the last ten years or so. He ain't never welshed, and he says all he wants is more of the same."

That much was true, Costello thought, reflecting on the last meeting with William. It was Haim's note that had come at the end of the last meeting. Five words that Haim had hastily written:

He ain't got the makins'.

Later, Haim explained it was kind of like his tobacco business. Sometimes he had the wrapper but didn't have the filler. How Haim got his information about William's production problems, he never revealed.

Frank Costello sat back in the seat of the limo parked at the curb of William's hotel. He had listened to the words and the sounds that came with them. What he heard Haim saying was he could not get what he wanted right now, but maybe later. In the meantime, there was dangled that legit tag he so craved.

He was having trouble with the newly elected Mayor La Guardia, who had declared war on the "crooks," pledging even to put Lucky Luciano in jail. He was also on the verge of shutting down Frank's lucrative slot machine business.

Under the guise of selling mints, dispersed when the winning combinations came up, slugs were awarded—that were redeemable for cash. With more than five thousand machines in play in and around the city, hundreds of thousands of dollars were at stake. As Costello left the limo to go inside the hotel for the second meeting with William, something like a reprieve resonated in his mind.

William was waiting.

Ridley was ready for the worst.

The doors opened, and both were immediately surprised by Costello's affability. Gone was the bullying bluster of the previous meeting.

Ridley held his breath.

As William outlined his concepts, he saw Costello nodding his agreement. In the end, they struck a bargain that was to take effect the following year. Costello's Alliance Distributors would be the sole distributor of William's whiskies for the American market. At no time did the subject of the Edradour and its ownership enter the conversation.

To commemorate the occasion, William opened a special bottle of whisky, pouring out a small amount in a tasting glass for those in attendance.

"What you have before you, gentlemen, is regarded to be still a work in progress, although it must be admitted, that work is nearly done. Cheers!"

He raised his glass, nosed, and sipped while Costello threw his down.

"A damn fine whisky," Costello praised.

William smiled at the repetition of the praise that almost made up for the faux pas.

NINETEEN

An Unhappy Mistake

> LONDON TIMES, 6 SEPTEMBER 1935
> *The League of Nations exonerates both Abyssinia and Italy in Wal affair. Fear arises that Mussolini will see no obstacle in his path.*

> LONDON TIMES, 4 OCTOBER 1935
> *Yesterday, without declaration of war, Italy attacked Abyssinia from Italian Somaliland and Eritrea. League of Nations to declare Italy aggressor.*

> THE SCOTSMAN, SUNDAY, 7 DECEMBER 1935
> *An action by the Royal Warrant Holders' Association against William Whiteley & Co., distillers, of London and Leith, and the Edradour Distillery, Blair Atholl, was mentioned upon motion to Mr. Justice Farwell in the Chancery Division, London, yesterday.*

WILLIAM WAS AGHAST. SHORTLY AFTER his return from New York, he learned of the denial of his application for registration of a trademark. The Royal Warrant Holders' Association opposed his trademark on the grounds that it included the Royal Arms of the King as King of Scotland.

The Arms, used since the twelfth century, had once received the poetic description, "the ruddy lion ramping in his field of tressured gold."

Because of the ruling, William and his companies had entered into an agreement to discontinue use of the mark. In October, somehow, the device appeared in adverts in two papers.

> *Mr. F. E. Bray (for the plaintiffs) moved for an interim injunction to restrain alleged breach of an agreement.*
>
> *Mr. Lloyd Jacob, for the defendant company, said his clients had from the first taken up the attitude that they would withdraw all advertisements containing the device objected to. By accident, current advertisements in two publications were overlooked when others were withdrawn...*
>
> *His Lordship, giving judgement, said, "This is not a case in which I think any interlocutory relief should be granted. I am satisfied the defendants are doing all they can to abide by their agreement. There has been an unhappy mistake."*

William felt gratified by the court's ruling. Once again, he had received a favorable decision in the courts of law. On this occasion, he felt more embarrassment than justification. As he sat in his Leith offices, he was confounded over how the mistake had occurred. It was Dennis, his office manager, who spoke first.

"Very regrettable, to be sure, and the agency's fault as well. Why the scheduled adverts were not cancelled, they cannot explain."

"Have they offered recompense?" William queried.

"In a manner of speaking. They have agreed to waive a portion of their fee for future services. One of their account executives had the cheek to suggest their mistake would do us more good than harm. He spoke of the attention that our brand would receive."

Yes, William thought, *I can see how that might be.*

It was certainly the best way to look at the matter. He briefly thought of prospective buyers who might pick up a bottle to examine the label for any discrepancy. Then, his thoughts drifted again to another childhood memory.

He thought he might have been thirteen, twelve years at the most, when he noticed the gag. He felt fortunate to have been there that day, standing by the cash register at his father's side.

"But this *is* tomorrow!" the client had complained.

Laughing heartily, George handed the man his cigar after providing a courtesy clip to the drawing end. The sign posted next to the cash register in the Cheapside, Todmorden shop had read:

"Free Cigar Tomorrow"

If the customer came back, he found that the sign, of course, read the same. At first, George would emphasize the key word—"tomorrow"—meaning the gift of a cigar to be perpetually postponed. Then, sometimes with a chuckle and a wry face, he would hand the man a cigar.

Often, it turned out, the fellow would laugh and accept the joke on himself. Later, George would explain that if he judged the customer to have a sense of humor, he sometimes would push through and let the joke "stick."

"If it's attention you want, it's sometimes hard to tell which is better—the good or the bad," George had said.

Then, he told the story of the day when he decided to take down the sign.

He had taken the sign to Southport when he left Todmorden, and only brought it out occasionally, he later told William during one of their conversations.

"Usually," George began, "the customer got the joke the day he saw the sign and would get a good laugh out of it. Then, one day, this gent walks in, looks around a bit, and finds a box of what he wants. We have a nice conversation—he was from London, on holiday—and then he spies the sign. 'What time should I return for my free cigar?' he asks. I gives him my card, showing the hours the shop was open, and he takes his leave. It was a pretty busy day, and, naturally, I forgot all about him."

"Well, *he* don't forget. Bright and early, he shows, and I find him waiting on the stoop when I opens the door next morning. Comes right in, as pretty as you please, and starts lookin' over what's in the humidor. Then he says, 'That one looks fine,' pointing to one of my La Palmas."

When George paused, William interjected. "So, what did you do then?"

"Well, it was the look on his face that got my attention, first. Naturally, I had picked up the sign to show it to him again, thinkin' that would do the trick. Now, I don't know if I told you about that sign and how it was set up. It was in a nice frame with a stand on the back, so's I could prop it up anywhere and move it about when I pleased."

Here, George paused to light one of his finest, and William took advantage.

"So, what did he say when you showed him the sign?"

"Nothing. He just ignored it and pointed at the La Palma." With a searching look on his face, George paused, seemingly to recollect something. "Did I tell you he was a lawyer? Well, he was. And after a while, when we got tired of looking at each other, he said, 'You probably have had a good bit of fun with that sign, haven't you?'"

"I agreed that I had. Then, he said something that learned me a lesson. He wanted to know if I remembered the day before, when he asked me when he should return for his free cigar, and, of course, I said I did."

"Then, he went on in some really plain language to show how that became a kind of contract."

William nodded in understanding. He could see clearly where this was heading and was careful not to smile too broadly while his father finished his story.

"So, he says at the end, while he's walking out with one of me finest La Palmas, something about knowing I had no intent to deceive. He emphasized that word—*intent*." Pausing to relight his cigar, George continued.

"When we got to the door of the shop, he stopped, stuck out his hand, and said he was sure I would look back on all this as just a happy mistake."

TWENTY

Martine In London

"You remember, mon ami, my promise on St. Pierre? But perhaps you did not believe me then, *c'est vrai?*"

William did remember, very well, that painful incident. What he found hard to believe after the story he had just heard was that Louis Arnoult Martine was sitting in his library at 32a Wildwood Road. Josephine, with her friend Maggie, was returning from a day in the city and did not know of their guest (indeed, they had yet to meet). Having just left the station, his train—which had been gliding sedately along the rails to retirement—was in danger of derailment.

"Tell me more about your business interests in East Africa. I had no idea you had expanded so far," William queried.

He listened as Martine explained his family's import-export business had always had an office in Djibouti since 1883 and the founding of the *Cote Francaise des Somalis*. His father's death, during William's first year in Southport, meant Louis had to take the reins. Their principal import into French Somaliland was coffee—the best coffee in the world could not get to Djibouti, the main port for Abyssinia. Mussolini had fouled up the supply chain. The Italians had even begun to build small forts across the border and were demanding France relinquish her territory.

"You British, right next door, will never stand for that, and they may well be forced to close the port," Martine continued. "So, I must, how do you say…improvise?"

William reached for his globe of the world, showing British Somaliland cradled between the northern borders of Abyssinia and Italian Somaliland, and realized his government would have no choice but to do as Martine had predicted if Italy invaded. He had read the Fascist leader's claim that, with the population increases among yellow and black races, "the civilization of the white man is destined to perish." His purpose in invading Abyssinia was to correct this situation by establishing permanent Italian settlements.

"Yes, I can see the danger you speak of," William mused, "but surely you can relocate your operations to the Colony."

"*Mon ami*, for us, it has been peanuts from Senegal, coffee from Abyssinia, and the spirits imported into the Cape. The Muhammadans forbid the spirits, and so we had the need to diversify."

At that moment, Josephine entered the library, and William rose to greet her and do the introductions. With a welcoming grin on her face, she shook hands with Martine, who, bussing both her cheeks, insisted she call him Louis, and the stories began in earnest.

"Louis phoned after you left, and, naturally, I invited him out," William began, only to be interrupted by Josephine, who insisted Martine stay for dinner.

"We have been having the most interesting conversation about Monsieur Mussolini," William continued, only to be interrupted again.

"The man is a beast, really," she started, looking at Louis to gauge his reaction.

He nodded his agreement, saying, "In the beginning, we all thought he could make change for the better. What was said about him then? The trains, they now run on time?"

"You men must excuse me—it needs be determined if there is a thing to eat in this house," Josephine waved a kiss at William and gave him a thumbs-up, which Louis could not see.

"*Un femme etonnante*! You surprise me, William. She is beautiful. And a lucky man, you are! I have not the good fortune you have, *mon ami*." Louis finished his drink with a note of sadness.

"I never had the pleasure of meeting your wife, Louis," William said cautiously, "but you have often talked of your children."

Louis nodded. "Yes, they are all grown and gone now. How do you say? The coop is flown?"

William smiled and rose to freshen his friend's drink. Just then, Josephine made her reentry and brought with her a martini shaker and some ice.

"Is a change of pace in order, gentlemen? No? Well, then, stick to the flags of your whisky while I run up another pennant. It does, after all, pay the bills."

"I will help the missus," Dora said. "You set the table and mind the method." Alice did as instructed, going into the dining room and finding the table already covered in Josephine's best linen. She smoothed the few wrinkles left as she began to place the plate ware, glassware, and silver according to the prescribed "method" in her instructions.

Shorter and shyer, Alice was almost a year younger than Dora. Born in London, she had never finished school, entering service at the tender age of thirteen. She occasionally resented it when Dora acted so much her senior, telling her what to do and ordering her about. Dora was Jewish, of course, and that was fine, but she could be *so* German, thought Alice. They had both been in the Whiteleys' employ for almost two years, hired just after the house was finished. It was the perfect house, Alice thought. Big enough for the four of them, even though she and Dora shared a small room and took up very little of the space.

She loved going through the house while cleaning and pretending that she lived there. She did, of course, live there, but not in the sense that her master and mistress did. She could sometimes pretend she lived there, as an owner would, like when the Whiteleys were away. It was in this state of preoccupation with her dreams that she entered the kitchen.

"Oh, am I glad to see you, Alice," Miss Josephine said hastily. "Go and tell the gentlemen in the library that dinner will be served in ten minutes."

"Yes, ma'am," Alice replied dutifully, and as she turned to go, she received further instruction. "And tell Mr. William that he is in charge of the wine."

Louis admired the table while William carved. He could see the wine bottles at the other end, with the labels turned away from his sight.

Nevertheless, he was certain of one thing. The wine was not of a recent vintage and the shape of the bottle suggested a Bordeaux. He felt some excitement rising as he busied himself making small talk with Josephine, who was finishing her martini and taking a few moments to relax from her labors in the kitchen.

Dora helped with serving, and when she placed his plate in front of him, Martine thought the guinea hen appeared to be superbly prepared. By his plate, there were small serving dishes with potatoes and carrots, not overly done. A simple meal, perfect for the wine, and charming of his hosts to remember the native African fowl that roamed the continent he called home.

"May I pour, sir?" Dora asked.

Louis nodded and lifted the glass. He nosed it, twirled it, and set it down. Looking at William he said, "You scoundrel. You held some back."

Josephine may have laughed first, but when William and Louis joined in, Dora was very relieved. She was not privy to the joke and the story that went with it, so she had taken Mr. Martine's words literally. Careful not to spill any of the claret, she finished pouring the first bottle and placed it with the second one. She turned to leave the diners to their meal, as the guest of honor rose and asked her to wait.

Louis raised his glass and began his toast. "It is necessary at times of such occasions as this to acknowledge one's gratitude. *Non, ce n'est plus que cela.* Only friendship can account for this. And you are so very dear and good friends. *Merci!*"

Martine was gone only a short time when William found Josephine full of questions about Martine's business dealings and concerns about losing their newfound freedom. Dinner had gone well, and Josephine was instantly attracted to their guest's charm and manner. Yet, overhearing a small portion of their conversation, and alarmed by what she thought to be a threat, she confronted William, who had just days before promised he would be slowing down.

"It's not what it may seem, dear," William replied. "It's only a few hours a week. He only wants me to consult a little, and the money is not that much."

"The money?" Josephine asked.

"Yes. I am willing to make a small investment to help him establish his London offices. A few thousands is all; nothing earth-shattering."

MUENCHENER ZEITUNG, 16 MAY 1936
The English like a comfortable life compared with our German standards.

The article went on to explain how weak and dissolute the English people had become in the time since the Great War. Then, there was this:

A policy which seeks to achieve success by postponing decisions can today hardly hope to resist the whirlwind which is shaking Europe and indeed the whole world.

The article then concluded with this piece of triumphalism:

Today, all Abyssinia is irrevocably, fully, and finally Italian alone. This being so, neither Geneva nor London can have any doubt that only the use of extraordinary force can drive the Italians out of Abyssinia. But neither the power nor the courage to use force is at hand.

Martine had read the article several times before putting it away. That had been over a year ago, and in the time that had passed, little had occurred to challenge that assessment. Hitler had occupied the Rhineland, and neither Britain nor France had gone beyond words of condemnation during the entire time. Germany was rapidly rearming and rebuilding its war machine with compulsory military service and a burgeoning air force. What was the next shoe, and when would it drop?

A scion of an American family by name of Kennedy had formed its own conclusions during a trip to Europe in the summer of 1937, which included four days in Germany. Some days before, while still in Italy, Kennedy and a friend had met a former German socialist who said the hatred of the Russians was behind all the rearmament. On the way to Pisa, this same German happened to mention that ration cards would soon be issued. In his travel diary, the young American mentioned as an aside that the next war could well come from that direction and that the British and all of Europe were backing away from any support of Russia.

Reports in all newspapers covering the Spanish Civil War told of the Nationalists' victory to come under the leadership of Francisco Franco, with help from both Italy and Germany. The apparently irresistible tide of the twin forces of Nationalism and Fascism seemed on the verge of joining the National Socialism of Adolf Hitler, threatening the domination of all of Europe.

– § –

Cordially received when he arrived at the German Embassy, the MP was very quickly thereafter ushered into the presence of the German ambassador to Britain. Their talk lasted more than two hours, and, near the end, the two men stood before a large map on the wall. The visitor, after hearing of the ambassador's plans and proposals, said at once that he was sure the British government would not give Germany a free hand in Eastern Europe. Further, the visitor said that Great Britain would always remain interested in the fortunes of the continent.

The ambassador turned abruptly away from the map and spoke of the inevitability of war. Then, he added that his fuhrer was resolved. Nothing and no one could stop him.

Winston Churchill was, in his words, "only a private member of parliament" at the time. He paused to consider his response to Herr von Ribbentrop. Then, he said that any such talk of war would mean general war and that England should not be underestimated. After cautioning the ambassador about the longevity of the present government, he concluded by saying that if Germany were to bring England into another Great War, she would again bring the whole world against her, as before.

The ambassador responded heatedly that though England might be very clever, this time would be different. Awed by the might of Germany, the world could not and would not rise against her.

– § –

When Dora applied for a position as housekeeper, it had been necessary to be honest and frank while interviewing for the position. She explained that she had been able to get out of Germany, along with her brother, Peter, but her parents had elected to stay behind. This was about all Josephine had known, but she was soon to learn more, and it would bring great sorrow to the house.

She has received very little mail, Josephine noted about the new housekeeper.

Josephine was sorting through the letters that had arrived. Louis was coming to dinner that evening, and Josephine had finished all the preparation. It was a Friday, and as was the custom, their servant girls Alice and Dora had the rest of the day off. Josephine placed the letter on Dora's bed as she made her way to the library and William. When she arrived, she was surprised to see William had dozed off in his favorite chair. Tiptoeing from whence she came, in order not to wake him, she went instead to her office. It was there that she found Dora.

"Why, Dora!" Josephine exclaimed. "Here on your day off?"

Immediately Josephine regretted her flippancy as she saw the tortured look on Dora's face. She rose and went to Dora, taking her arm and guiding her to the nearest chair.

"Tell me what is wrong, Dora. Tell me everything," Josephine demanded.

Shaking her head, Dora handed the letter to Josephine and, placing her head in both hands, began to weep. Josephine hesitated for a moment, not wanting to read what had caused such sorrow, but seeing she must, she looked at the letter and found her German failed her.

"I'm sorry, Dora. I can't read…"

Then, with alacrity, she knew Martine could help, and he would be there at any moment.

"It won't be long, Dora, before Mr. Martine will be here. He speaks your language very well."

To her dismay, Dora shook her head and, taking the letter, fled the room.

A few moments later, Josephine came to the room Dora shared with Alice. The door was open, and Josephine quietly walked to the bed where

Dora was sitting. She sat down next to her and put her arm around her shoulders.

"Won't you tell me what has happened?"

Dora nodded and began to speak in a voice choked with emotion. "My parents, I have lost them."

"It is a sad business. A very sad thing to lose your parents. Especially in this way. The horror they must have gone through," Martine said with anguish as he put the letter down.

"But the letter says only that they were taken in for questioning by the Gestapo. And the neighbor who wrote was hopeful...," Josephine asserted.

"I'm sorry, but with them, there is little room for hope," Martine said.

For a moment, there was silence in the room where Dora, Louis, Josephine, and William had gathered. William felt that Louis was right. In the letter, a neighbor reported that she had been able to salvage a few photographs and personal belongings before the authorities returned to ransack her parents' home. After they had left, the neighbor went through the debris, picking up small items that might be important. She had found on the floor an empty envelope with Dora's London return address, and this was how she had been able to write.

Dora took William's offer of a restorative, and, sipping the brandy, she found she was able to regain her composure enough to thank everyone for their concern and their support. Looking at Martine, she smiled weakly. "Thank you...for your honesty," she said. "I know there is little hope that I will ever see my parents again." She paused briefly to wipe the tears from her face. "They told me Peter and I must leave, that it was too dangerous for us to stay. But they would not leave their friends who relied on them! My father...oh!" She fell silent, weeping. They all waited, and in a moment, Dora continued. "My father," she struggled to begin. "My *father* did not even have a job anymore. The newspaper where he worked had been shut down by the Gestapo for criticizing the government."

She stopped for a moment and seemed to lose touch with her surroundings. Shaking her head, she continued, "My father was a very loyal man. He would not leave, and now he is never coming back!"

Shortly, after the brandy had done its work, Dora began to tell the rest of her story.

"I remember, when I was younger, my father would be very critical of Jews who left Germany for America. He would say it was because they had done something wrong or could not make a living at home. He was very critical of those who left."

William interrupted, "And this was well before Hitler came to power?"

"Yes," Dora replied. "And after Hitler came to power, my father would not leave the newspaper where he worked. Within less than a year, the newspaper was closed, and then my father did illustrations in a fortnightly for an anti-Nazi group that went underground."

"Your father was a very brave man, Dora," Louis said with a tone of admiration.

Dora was very still for a moment while the tears flowed slowly down her cheeks. After a few moments, she regained her voice. "I suppose I should be proud of him—and Momma, too." Then, with her voice cracking, she said, "Momma told him to go when we all could have gone, but he wouldn't listen."

The days that came and went following Dora's sorrow were a time when she bonded with the Whiteleys. Josephine and William were very solicitous of her need for time to grieve, and they saw that Dora threw herself into her work.

Irving Haim made two trips from the States that year to assure the shipments of whisky went as scheduled. He also took the pulse of William's plans for retirement, assuring him that a buyer waited in the wings. A reporter somehow cornered him, asking why he was in England. "I have secured the year's supply of whisky for the States." Later, when the reporter filed his report, his editor wanted to know why had asked no follow-up question.

– § –

Hinch sat in the Minerva outside the Leith offices of J. G. Turney & Son, Ltd., reflecting on the words Rids had said as he and Mr. William left the car.

"Won't be long. You can leave it parked at the curb."

That had been just over an hour ago, and still no sign of their return.

Inside, the director's meeting was winding down. William had been all business, seemingly oblivious to the regret that some of his directors were expressing.

"We'll miss you, old man."

"Never seen a one like you."

"Can't believe it's over."

"The Dean of Distillers, stepping down."

With uncharacteristic modesty, William waved it all away. "We are not done being friends," he said at the end. "Josephine and I will have a little gathering soon to celebrate this occasion. A right proper send-off, you'll see." *Funny*, he thought, as he realized it was what his father might have said.

After all had left but Ridley, William rose from the conference table and walked to a window through which he could see the buildings that housed his operations. As he took what he knew might be his last look at what he had created, his thoughts went back to that happiest of days in Munro's offices.

He remembered sitting comfortably with the old man, looking out the window at the buildings of Dalwhinnie and thinking to himself, *Patience, lad. In time. In time.*

That time had come. And gone. How could it all have passed so quickly? All of a sudden, he felt old. Smiling to himself, he thought, *I've earned it. The right to feel old—or anything else, for that matter.*

TWENTY-ONE

1938

J. G. Turney & Son, Ltd., had incorporated after receiving permission to use an existing name. Shareholders, listed in the order of their ownership, showed: Irving Haim, Vernon S. Ridley, and Arthur Gavin Dixon. William was not listed among the directors or shareholders. Nor was Frank Costello.

"Darling, at last we are free!" Josephine exclaimed when William walked through the door. They embraced for a moment before Josephine broke away excitedly. "I have the most wonderful news to tell you!"

"Well, let's hear it" was William's reply.

"There is a cabin still available on the *Queen Mary* in September. Look at this brochure, and you can see that we could go as far as Cherbourg, and from there to Paris! What do you say?"

"I say let's have a drink and talk about why we are waiting until then." William smiled impishly.

– § –

The chancellor of Austria obeyed the summons to Berchtesgaden, where he heard the ultimatum. In his response, he pointed out that the shedding of blood would be unavoidable and that a world war would likely ensue.

Adolf Hitler responded in dismissive fashion and asserted that no one in the world could hinder him.

"What about Italy?" the chancellor asked, knowing of Mussolini's support of Austria's independence.

With a smug smile that never left his face, the fuhrer informed the chancellor that he and Mussolini were on the best possible terms, that England would not lift a finger for Austria, and that France had lost her opportunity when, only two years before, Germany marched into the Rhineland with only a handful of battalions.

After the chancellor was dismissed, an aide arrived with news from the front. Digesting the report, the fuhrer was furious. "Operation Otto" had not gone swimmingly. Heavy tanks had broken down, conveys were delayed, and for miles the German army stood immobilized along the road from Linz to Vienna. He ranted, and his generals replied in their most respectful "We told you so" manner. They reminded him that he had refused to listen to them when they warned that the army was not ready for the invasion.

General von Reichenau managed to have the heavy artillery and tanks loaded onto railway cars and taken into Vienna in time to join the light tanks and infantry in a victory parade. This was how the German Army Group IV "conquered" Austria, which had planned a plebiscite on Sunday, March 13. It never had a chance of coming off, and a week later, Hitler made official the annexation of his Austrian homeland.

A different kind of challenge was resolved when Mussolini signaled that Austria meant nothing to him. In response, Hitler promised his undying gratitude and irrevocable pledge to come to the aid of the Fascist leader, should he ever need it.

– § –

William was holding forth on the subject of a certain German officer over cigars and King's Ransom. "At first, he made the effort to be most amiable," William continued. "Nevertheless, one could see something sinister behind his smile."

"I can picture it myself," Martine replied. "An ambassador for evil would look exactly as you describe."

The two men were relaxing together after enjoying one of Josephine's culinary creations. She had yet to join them, and William had taken the opportunity to discuss his thoughts, knowing of her animosity for the German they had met in Monte Carlo.

When Josephine joined them, their conversation soon returned to travel. Sitting next to William, she grasped his hand, kissed it, and said, "You should have seen him in Monte Carlo, Louis."

She looked at her husband, smiled, and said teasingly, "You should have seen him, playing detective. We met this *awful* German officer who nearly ruined our weekend…"

William smiled and, waving away the comment, turned to their friend, saying, "It was unimportant, but now let us talk of Paris. Won't you reconsider?"

Martine, with a conspiratorial smile, and eager to hear of his friend's escapades, nodded for Josephine to continue. This business of William playing detective? The obvious enjoyment Josephine exhibited? *Yes,* he must know more.

Inspector Jules Etienne Joubert would no doubt have approved of the Hotel de Paris as a *suitable* destination, despite his affinity for the Hotel Imperial. If she had read this particular Charlie Chan novel, Josephine would certainly have agreed with the assessment. *Beautiful,* she thought as she looked about their spacious room. And how immense the lobby! With its sculpted, curving arches providing support for the large skylight, natural light flooded the spacious interior, accentuating the elegance of the furnishings and the marble flooring, which seemed to flow forever.

Sighing in contentment as she finished dressing for dinner, she realized she had never thought of William as a gambler.

A risk-taker, yes, but always the calculated risk.

Therefore, she found amusing his interest in the game of baccarat. They had spent a couple hours in the casino where William spent most of his time betting on the bank. He had won a small amount of chips, which he was eager to cash in on their way to dinner. *Still the calculated risk-taker,* she smiled to herself.

The decision to come to Monte Carlo *had* been spur of the moment, though. *So unlike William,* Josephine thought, as she happily noted the differences her husband was exhibiting in retirement. He had *always* been fun in his droll, understated way, conservative in dress and manner, and one least likely to act spontaneously.

Dinner was at the Café de Paris, where the elegant art deco interior greatly intrigued Josephine. After dining, the couple returned to the bar at their hotel. Once seated, the barman came promptly to take their drink orders—martini for Josephine and King's Ransom for William. After William signed the room charge, the barman took special care to note the name of his guests.

The name seemed familiar.

Why? the barman asked himself. Putting the bottle back on the shelf, he saw the signature and made the connection.

"Monsieur Whiteley," he asked William, "are you perchance the maker of this whisky?"

A small crowd of waiters and staff gathered around William and Josephine, respectfully listening to his conversation with the barman.

"It is our best whisky, sir, and our most expensive, certainly," the barman smiled.

William responded modestly that he was no longer in the business and was on holiday, having retired. These comments only served to make him seem more interesting, and as business was slow, the wait staff continued to hang about in the growing circle of admirers.

"*Was ist das?*" the voice boomed. "*Haben sie Keinen Dienst?*"

A German officer in uniform stood behind the small group that had gathered around William and Josephine. One of the waiters who spoke German apologized and seated him at a table away from the bar. The man's voice carried well in the large barroom as he asked, in a demanding voice, for food and drink.

Josephine nudged William, saying, "I have heard since we arrived that the Germans love Monaco, but I don't think the affection is reciprocal."

They were finishing their drinks, when a waiter came over with a message that a gentleman had asked if they would care to join him for a drink. The barroom had begun to fill up and Josephine, looking about the room, asked, "Which gentleman?"

When the waiter pointed at the German officer who was sitting alone, she looked at William and said to the waiter, "Thank him for us but tell him no, we are turning in."

As they left the bar, the German tipped his cap and smiled smugly.

The community of Eze was said to be over three thousand years old.

A part of France since 1860, it was described by some as "an eagle's nest." Perched high on rugged, rocky cliffs across from Monte Carlo, occupants from the past included Greeks, Romans, Turks, and Moors.

Josephine and William slowly made their way up the steep, rock-covered streets, pausing to rest at Notre' Dame de l'Assomption. Inside the church, built in 1764, there was an Egyptian cross, which suggested, according to the guidebook, that the Phoenicians had been there and at some point built a temple to Isis.

William did well, Josephine thought as they paused to rest again.

"Feeling fine," William exaggerated when she asked.

In truth, he was beginning to wonder how he would make it back.

After a brief rest, he felt some of his energy return. He was determined not to spoil the fun and pushed on.

At the top of their climb, they were able to take advantage of the panoramic views of the Mediterranean Sea, revealing nearly all the colors of Royston turquoise. From deepest blue in the center to emerald green near the shore, the water formed a shimmering tapestry over which they looked to the place their hotel occupied along the French Riviera.

"Thank you, William," Josephine said as she took his arm. "I would not have missed this for anything."

The news of Austria's capitulation came while William and Josephine were in Monte Carlo. When the news came through, the Whiteleys had retired for the evening. Thus, it was they awoke to the disaster while breakfasting the following morning.

"Hitler's intentions are fully apparent now," William said after reading the news summary prepared for hotel guests. "This is only the beginning and only God knows where it will all end."

On a stroll along the Boulevard de la Condamine, William and Josephine took the pulse of the city. The gaiety, that just days before had impressed and stimulated them, seemed to have disappeared overnight. The people they encountered no longer waved and exchanged greetings. Couples they passed seemed to want to talk among themselves privately, discouraging interaction. When they arrived back at the hotel, they went directly to the bar in hopes of finding an oasis of comfort and repose.

"*Oberst* Richard Baumann, at your service," the German officer introduced himself.

With an exaggerated bow to Josephine and a curt nod to William, he continued in perfect English, "I have noticed you since I arrived, and longed to make your acquaintance. Will you join me for a cocktail?" he asked, looking at Josephine. "Of course, if the lady prefers champagne…"

"No thank you," Josephine replied.

Just then, she felt a slight squeeze as William let go of her arm and responded.

"We would be delighted to have a drink with you. This table should do nicely," and he went about seating his unbelieving wife.

The waiter came over, Josephine thought, with a curious look on his face, and after taking their drink orders, he departed.

The conversation that followed was of the pleasant kind that new acquaintances engage in. Where they are from, what they used to do before the unfortunate tensions that so recently occurred; whether family, wife, or children.

"Yes, I have pictures," Colonel Baumann said as he produced his wallet to verify his claim.

"Lovely daughters," Josephine said politely.

"Oh yes! They have a father who dotes on them every moment. And how I miss them," the colonel sighed. "But, enough of my family and me. Tell me how you happen to be in wonderful Monte Carlo."

William took the initiative and explained briefly that they were on holiday. He simply said that he and Josephine were retired and enjoying travel.

Herr Baumann was not satisfied and probed for more information.

"Retired? From what, if I may ask."

Understanding that an interrogation was underway, William kept his responses short and to the point.

"I used to make whiskies and now I spend as much time as possible enjoying them."

This riposte brought a spasm of hearty laughter from Herr Baumann, which got the attention of a few patrons who had come early to the bar.

"How droll, William. May I call you William? And you are Mrs. Whiteley, I gather?" Herr Baumann inquired.

Stifling the desire to ask, *who else would I be?* Josephine nodded but did not offer her name. *The less he knew, the better,* she thought.

"Well, this has been lovely. I have so enjoyed making your acquaintance," the colonel said, rising. Extending his hand to William, and noticing Josephine did not extend hers, he bowed, "Delighted to meet you, *Mrs.* Whiteley. And now, I must take your leave. *Keine ruhe fur die muden,* as they say."

When he was gone, Josephine looked at William questioningly. "Why did you allow him to…"

"Because I was curious," William interrupted, "and I still am. You noticed, I'm sure, that he wants to know all about us. Well, I would like to know more about him. And what he's up to."

"May I get you anything?" the waiter inquired.

As William ordered another King's Ransom Josephine asked, "Are we dining in, love?"

Receiving confirmation, she ordered another martini.

"Oh, sir, I nearly forgot," the waiter said. "The officer who just left said to put everything on his tab."

When the waiter returned, William asked, "What can you tell me about Colonel Baumann?"

Hesitating for a moment, the waiter replied somewhat nervously, "I can say very little about him, sir. Except that he has been here a couple times before and has always been quite correct in his manner."

After the waiter left, William turned to Josephine, saying, "That sounds just about right. He would naturally want to make a favorable impression—to start."

"Why do you care, William? He seems such a bore to me," Josephine lamented.

"Monsieur Whiteley?"

William looked up to see the manager of the bar standing before him and responded, "Yes, please join us."

"No thank you, sir. I just wanted to let you know that our man Jacque told me you asked after one of our guests."

William nodded.

"Well, sir, he has stayed with us several times and is regarded to be an excellent gentleman in every respect. Was there something you wanted to tell me? A problem of any kind?"

"No, no problem," replied William. "He was very kind to buy us a drink and I wanted to properly thank him. That's all."

"Very good, sir," the manager concluded. "I am glad all is well."

Looking directly at Josephine, William spoke quietly. "Can you believe that?"

"Believe what?" Josephine said irritably.

Sitting back in his chair, William thought how good one of George's La Palmas would taste right then. He deliberated whether he should continue his line of discussion. Making his decision, he pressed on.

"Let's review the very little we know," he began.

"We have our Colonel Baumann, who is a frequent guest here and who just happens to want to make our acquaintance. He does, and when I ask if anyone knows him, the manager here comes to find out if there is a problem. Doesn't that seem at least a bit odd?"

"No," Josephine replied, "but what does seem odd is I am starving and all you can think about is playing detective."

All during dinner, Josephine tried to get Herr Baumann out of her mind. She did not like to think of him as a soldier. Just plain Herr would do. And why was William so suddenly obsessed with knowing more about him? They were, after all, leaving in a couple days; in the end, what difference did it make?

William would not have said he was obsessed, but he would have admitted to being *curious* and wanting to know more.

For example, did the colonel come on holiday or official business? When he left them at the table, he used the old cliché, *no rest for the weary*, or something close to that. Did that not suggest he was here on business of some sort? Following so closely on the invasion of the Rhineland and now Austria, what did that imply? As his thoughts drifted to cigars and cognac, he let the narrative forming in his mind drift away.

Smiling, he spoke to his wife, "What say we go out on the terrace and I'll have a cigar while you enjoy an aperitif?"

The next two days passed all too quickly for William, as their contact with the colonel was limited to brief "hellos" when they encountered each other at the hotel.

"He actually seems to be avoiding us, don't you think?" William asked Josephine.

"Yes, thankfully," Josephine responded.

It was on their last day in Monte Carlo that William found the opportunity for closure. Coming down earlier than had been their custom, he found Colonel Baumann finishing his breakfast.

"Guten Morgan, may I join you?" William asked, and without waiting for an invitation, sat himself down.

With only a flicker of irritation on his face, the colonel looked at William.

"Yes, of course. But please understand that I am leaving shortly and don't have much time," he said.

"Understandable, Colonel. No rest for the weary, eh?" William rejoined.

"Exactly. Now, how may I be of service?" the colonel asked in perfunctory tone of voice.

William paused a moment before answering.

"You were quite curious about why my wife and I are in Monte Carlo. I simply wish to know more about why you are here, Colonel Baumann," William said. Before the colonel could respond, William went on.

"Once you found my wife and I were simply here on holiday, your interest seemed to subside.

You spoke of having work to do here. What kind of work, Colonel? The kind you and your countrymen engaged in so recently in Austria?"

"Now see here!" the colonel objected, "the meaning of this intrusion has become quite clear. You apparently are misinformed about the Fuhrer's intentions. His connection with the people of Austria is undeniable! Why, they welcomed him with open arms."

"I'm surprised you would say that," William quickly interjected, handing the German officer the news summary provided by the hotel. He paused before continuing.

"Given the explanation provided therein and given the somber response we have seen from the residents of Monte Carlo, I cannot be the only one who is concerned about the...*intentions*, as you call them, of your Fuhrer."

Colonel Baumann rose from his chair and stood, towering over William before he spoke. William observed the menacing stare on his face—a face now contorted with anger.

"You English!" the colonel began maliciously. "You English dare to criticize our Fuhrer? After all your history of conquering and subjecting the peoples of your *empire*, you question *our* rights? *Our* motives?"

Drawing himself up to his full height, his scar of a mouth compressed into a tight, thin smile, the colonel turned to leave, pausing to look down at William, still seated. With his right arm he pointed directly at William and wagging his finger said, "Tell England to stay in her place. The Fuhrer has no designs on your empire, nor does he wish your people ill. But, do not provoke him. Do nothing to hinder or obstruct his plans for the Fatherland."

The colonel paused briefly and then, looking contemptuously at William, gave his parting shot.

"Nothing," he began in a hoarse whisper of a voice, "and no one, can thwart the destiny of our Fuhrer, or resist the might of our Fatherland."

A cold chill passed through William's body as he watched the German officer depart. Soon, Josephine joined him and he began briefly to describe to her what had occurred.

For Josephine, it was a relief finally to begin making their way home.

How puzzling, she thought as she considered William's interest in Herr Baumann.

And why did it have to spoil their holiday?

The three friends sat silently together, contemplating Josephine's story. Martine broke the silence with good news that cheered everyone.

"I have decided to join you in Paris after all," Martine offered.

"Wonderful!" exclaimed Josephine. "At least there we won't have to worry about Nazis spoiling our fun."

Treviso, Italy, Wednesday, September 21

The cries went up from the crowd, reverberating as the chant rose to its highest pitch.

"*El Duce! El Duce! El Duce!*"

Raising his right arm in the Fascist salute, quieting the crowd, Mussolini continued with his speech:

"If Czechoslovakia now finds herself in what might be called a "delicate position," it is because she is not just Czechoslovakia, but 'Czecho-Germano-Polono-Magyaro-Rutheno-Rumano-Slovakia.' I now insist that since this problem is being faced, it is essential it should be solved in an integral manner."

Berlin, Germany, Saturday, September 24

"*Heil Hitler! Heil Hitler! Heil Hitler!*"

The fuhrer raised his right arm in salute to the crowd, bringing them slowly to a restless quiet. In the crowd were those who spoke excitedly of the fuhrer's leadership and his obvious commitment to securing peace. They heard him talk of the need to assure the protection of their fellow Germans in the Sudetenland.

How strong he was to stand against those who would seek to surround and to repress the Fatherland! They then heard him say the Czechs must clear out of the Sudetenland, and they must do so by September 26. He concluded his speech with a solemn promise:

"This is the last territorial claim I will make in Europe!"

– § –

RMS *Queen Mary* moored with patient elegance at her dock in Southampton while her passengers waited to board. With Martine, the

Whiteleys made their way rather quickly at times, pausing only when another first-class passenger had special needs to discuss.

The boarding process was rather efficient, Josephine thought, as her eyes caught a Cunard poster titled *"It's Men That Count."* Reading the copy, she found this wording:

> *Stewards and Stewardesses share the same heritage...many of them have had fathers and even grandfathers in the Line. "Service" and "seamanship," after all, are but different phases of the same ideal...racial to begin with, and crystallized into one high, clear code through Cunard's White Star's near-hundred years.*

What a wonderful sentiment, Josephine thought. *If only the success of this ethnic mixing could be carried to the nations of the world.* Then, the question formed in her mind: *Why does the title refer only to men?*

William arranged the spending of their entire time on the ship in the Verandah Grill. The exclusive à la carte restaurant and bar provided beautiful views as they spent the better part of the day making their way to Cherbourg. Martine soon joined them, and the three friends sat down to have lunch and talk about their journey. Their plan was to go by fast train from the port of Cherbourg to Paris, arriving after dark the same day.

Going in the opposite direction, in the year 1933, four Bugatti engines had whisked the railcars from Paris to Cherbourg in three and one-quarter hours—a 220-mile journey. It was said each of the engines was practically the same as the straight eight-cylinder, twenty-four-valve type used in the Bugatti luxury class automobiles. Martine and the Whiteleys could expect to leave London in the morning and arrive in Paris just after nightfall.

London, Wednesday, September 28

> *Orders have been given to the British Fleet to mobilise in response to the rising threat of invasion by German forces massed at Czechoslovak border.*

"The threat of war feels very real," William said as he handed the news summary to Josephine.

The Cherbourg-to-Paris train arrived on time at Gare St. Lazare in the heart of the city. As the three friends made their way to their hotel, they were relieved to learn that Prime Minister Chamberlain had agreed to make another trip to Munich on a peace mission. They retired with hopeful hearts and fatigue from their travels.

Paris, Friday, September 30

It Is Peace! the headline read.

Some distance down, the article reported that the Czechoslovak government had capitulated and that German occupation of the Sudetenland was to be finalized by October 10.

Constructed in 1758 during the reign of Louis XV, the Crillon Hotel was well-located for their visit to Paris. Looking out a window onto the Champs-Elysees, Josephine began to consider what she wished to see and do on her first full day in Paris. Neither she nor William had ever spent time in the "City of Lights," and they had been reassured by Martine that he could fill their days with sightseeing. But first, he said, they must surrender to Paris and her charms. He recommended that they stroll the avenues, take side streets to investigate what they might find, and eat when and where the mood struck. He would begin the formal tour on their second full day in the city.

"Rather mysterious, don't you think?" she asked William.

"How do you mean?" William asked. "Just because he wants us to get our feet wet and savor the charms of the city before we begin touring in earnest?"

"Well, yes. I do think it odd," Josephine replied. "Why not begin today rather than tomorrow?"

William smiled. "I think we can be sure that Louis has other friends here."

"Yes, of course you're right. I should have thought of that myself," Josephine said as she took her umbrella to follow William out the door.

Walking down the Rue de Rivoli, they soon had the Tuileries Gardens on their right.

"Oh, let's peek in," Josephine exclaimed.

They walked the length of the gardens, exiting near the Louvre. Going north on the Rue de Louvre, they came to Las Halles, the huge marketplace filled with sounds and smells that prepared them for a walking lunch. Watching men trim from large wheels of cheese, they felt obliged to buy some. Then, searching for meats and bread, through their collective efforts they made sandwiches. An inexpensive bottle of vin de rouge made their picnic complete.

Down side streets they went, following Martine's suggestion, where they found music-makers in the streets, fortunetellers, and organ grinders with mischievous monkeys on their shoulders. Stopping at one point to consider having her fortune told, and standing with William before a booth, she was startled to see a Romani woman emerge and come swiftly toward her.

"*N'ai pas peur, mon cher.* You weesh to know ze future, *oui?*"

She looked at William, who shrugged his shoulders. "Why not?" she replied.

Taking her hand, the gypsy woman turned it a little left and then a little to the right. She traced Josephine's "life line" with one finger, which she then put to the side of her nose. Shaking her head and muttering something to herself, which Josephine could not understand, she again took a careful look at the palm of Josephine's hand.

"Regrettable," the woman said with a reluctant tone.

Josephine smiled and waited for the examination to end.

"You weel not leeve long, my dear," the gypsy said. "But before you go, you weel come into a great deal of money."

Looking into the gypsy's face, Josephine felt the first flickering of uneasiness.

"And how long do you think I shall live?" Josephine asked suspiciously.

Looking at William, the gypsy asked, "Your husband, *oui?*"

Josephine nodded the truth of that.

"He ees seventy-eight, no?"

Josephine nodded, struggling to conceal her amazement.

"You weel not leeve as long as he," the gypsy said.

"What a strange woman, don't you think?" Josephine said as she and William walked away.

Soon, they came upon a small café, where they stopped to have a coffee. The streets were busy, like the café, and sitting outside they enjoyed "people watching" while they drank and talked about their plans for touring. Looking at his watch, William saw it was near time to go.

"We should head back soon, since we have an early dinner with Louis before the ballet."

"I can now see why Louis wanted us to have this day on our own," Josephine observed as they neared the Crillon.

William agreed, and upon entering the lobby, he went to the front desk to check his messages and mail. There was a note from Louis confirming their six o'clock dinner plans, along with an envelope addressed to him. His eyebrows shot up as he noted the return address in the upper left corner.

When they got off the elevator at their floor, they saw Martine in the doorway of his room near theirs. He was not alone. A strikingly beautiful woman was kissing him full on his mouth, and neither showed any discomfort while being observed.

Louis eventually removed his lips from the woman and addressed the couple in front of them. "Ah, William, meet my friend Isabelle. And let me introduce Josephine," Louis said, completing the introductions.

Shaking hands, they found Isabelle's to be firm, yet friendly. Nearly as tall as Martine, with a slender frame, her dark hair was pulled up into a messy topknot, evoking a casual elegance. They engaged in small talk for a moment and then Josephine begged off to dress for dinner.

"Will you be joining us for dinner this evening?" William asked.

"*Non*, but later," Isabelle said as she kissed Louis on a cheek, nodding at William as she left.

"Lovely, Louis," William praised. "Just lovely. I hope we get to know her better while we are here."

"Oh, I believe you will, William," replied Louis, "and of course, as she said, you will see her later this evening."

Over dinner, Louis listened attentively as Josephine recounted the day, amused by the anecdote regarding the gypsy fortuneteller.

"They are thieves, you know, and *worse*. It is best to pay no attention to what she said."

Josephine thought she agreed, after thinking about the encounter.

"Hocus-pocus, probably," Josephine concluded. She noticed William offered no assessment of his own.

"After the ballet, William, I would be willing to join you for a cigar, if ladies are welcome," said Martine as they rose to leave the restaurant.

"But of course," replied William with his curiosity building.

William thought the opening act featured a familiar waltz, and he turned to Josephine for confirmation.

"I've not seen *Giselle* before," she whispered.

The performance continued with the conclusion of Act I, as the betrayed peasant girl died in the arms of her duplicitous lover, Albrecht. At intermission, Martine provided aperitifs, and they discussed the relative merits of the dancing and singing they had seen.

"The best is yet to come," Martine promised as they returned to their seats.

Act II was dominated by the Wilis and the murderous Queen Myrtha, all of whom were ghosts of betrayed maidens. Together, they roused Giselle's spirit from her grave. Realizing the evil spirits were intent on cornering her beloved, she resolved to intervene. Nearing daybreak, her love, which had survived her physical death, proved strong enough to break the evil force of the Wilis, who were intent on dancing her beloved to death. Albrecht survived, and Giselle returned to her grave in peace.

"Would you like to go backstage?" Louis offered.

"Can we?" Josephine asked excitedly.

Making their way through the throng of admirers, critics, and sycophants, Louis led them to a door—already open—revealing a small dressing room filled with people surrounding the wicked Queen Myrtha who, William thought, bore a strong resemblance to Isabelle.

The hour was late, and the level low in the bottle of cognac that sat on the table where three cigars were nearing a similar fate. The four had retreated to Martine's room at the Crillon, where they relaxed while getting acquainted. Isabelle had changed out of her costume into loose-fitting slacks and a sweater. The two men had removed their jackets and Josephine began to feel slightly overdressed as she surveyed the scene. She thought about excusing herself to change into something more casual, but decided against leaving, as she did not want to miss any of the conversation.

She did not smoke, and spent her time at first listening as Martine told of how he and Isabelle had met on one of his business trips years before. She thought Isabelle strangely silent and chalked it up to winding down after her performance. In an effort to involve her in their conversation, she asked Isabelle, "How long was it you waited for this night to come?"

The ballerina paused to exhale. "I had been dancing for over four years before I was auditioned for the role of the queen."

"Is that a long time in the world of ballet?" William asked.

"Not especially," Isabelle said thoughtfully. "Many have waited longer, and many more for the call that never came."

"And so, do you know what you will do next?" asked Josephine.

Taking a final puff and delicately placing the remains of her cigar in the ashtray, Isabelle smiled wistfully, saying, "If it were only that easy. No, I do not know. All I do know is that I never want to leave Paris."

– § –

The news digest prepared by the Hotel Crillon offered this sobering news the following morning:

PRESIDENT BENES RESIGNS, SEEKS ASYLUM IN ENGLAND—
POLISH GOVERNMENT SENDS ULTIMATUM—
HUNGARY INSISTS UPON THEIR CLAIMS—
CHURCHILL SPEAKS TO THE HOUSE.

Below the headlines was an excerpt from Churchill's speech:

This is only the beginning of the reckoning. This is only the first sip, the first foretaste of a bitter cup which will be proffered to us year by year unless, by a supreme recovery of moral health and martial vigor, we rise again and take our stand for freedom as in the olden time.

"That is our next PM speaking," William said as he handed the news summary to Josephine. At that moment, they were surprised to see Martine join them.

"*Eh bien bonjour*, my friends. And how is our day?" Louis said as he pulled up a chair.

"It is not good news coming out of Czechoslovakia, I'm afraid," William replied.

"Yes, I have already heard," Louis responded. "News like this is the first to be printed. But, here in Paris, where we sit at the moment, the sun is shining and the air is clear. Our troubles we must not let spoil the fun, eh? Is that not so?"

"Tell us more about Isabelle," Josephine interjected. "How long have you known her?"

Smiling at her curiosity, Louis thought for a moment. "I suppose it must be going on five years now. We met here in Paris—one of my trips on family business. Isabelle is her real name. As you may have noticed, she uses a different name in her profession."

"Yes, I was going to ask you about that," Josephine started.

"The name in the program… You are right, it is different," interjected Martine.

"And so, is she just a friend, or…" Josephine hesitated.

"My dear, we must not pry," William interrupted.

"It's all right," Louis said, looking at William with a look of appreciation. "I would like there to be more, but…" He shrugged. "…she says she is not ready."

Looking at Josephine, he asked, "Perhaps, as a woman, you would have some insight to offer? Isabelle knows I was married and have children. I thought I should tell her of my wife's passing, and…now, I don't know… Perhaps that was a mistake."

"How so?" William asked, realizing he had learned something new about his friend.

"I think I know what he means," said Josephine. "You fear she may be thinking it would be difficult to live up to the image of your wife, the mother of your children."

Martine nodded.

"And then, perhaps, there are the children to consider. Their 'approval,' so to speak."

"*Exactement*—you have found the mark," Martine replied.

– § –

Their tour was to begin with the Louvre, and the three companions set out, retracing the path taken by William and Josephine the day before. Going through the Tuileries, Martine referred with obvious reverence to the memory of the Swiss Guards, slaughtered as they attempted to defend the palace during the Revolution.

"The name, it comes from the site of old tile works. In former times, there were many more fruit trees than we see today."

As they went along, they caught occasional glimpses of the Eiffel Tower while making their way to the museum.

"*Mon dieu*, they are leaving," Martine exclaimed, once inside.

The three companions watched with heightened interest as they came upon workers taking down works of art. Pulling aside a museum guard, Louis found that certain precautions were underway.

After a moment of animated conversation, the guard asserted, "*C'est les allemands. S'ils, ils viennent, ils seront decus.*"

"He says they are beginning to move some things in case war comes," Martine said, translating the full meaning of his conversation.

"Is it already upon us?!" Josephine exclaimed.

The world seemed to be still righted on its axis when they found the *Mona Lisa* in her traditional location. The enigmatic smile of the artist's creation seemed to convey a multitude of possible meanings as they gazed upon Da Vinci's triumph.

What does she know? William mused before they moved along.

Outside the museum, it seemed most of the rest of Paris knew little of the somber proceedings underway inside.

Lunch was at a restaurant favored by Martine from his previous visits. As he looked at the menu, he thought how comforting it was that some things had not changed. From the people around them, Martine heard bits of conversation that proved discomforting. He leaned forward to share some of the gossip he had overheard with his two companions.

"It is being said that Mondrian is also leaving."

Seeing the quizzical look on their faces, he went on to explain.

"The Dutch painter is a pioneer in the abstract, cubist movement. He came here in 1911, and the art world has never been the same."

William nodded his head in understanding. "I do not know anything about him, but I think I understand the threat he saw. The Fascists are a throwback to elemental brutishness. They are the most unlikely proponents of modernism, I should think."

"Yes, I agree entirely," Martine affirmed, "and yet, one hears Mussolini enjoining the Italians to enter the 'modern age.'"

"If all this is as you say," Josephine queried, "how can the world be so blind to these dangers?"

– § –

William made his way alone to the location specified in the letter left at his hotel. It appeared to be just another storefront—until he got close enough to make out the wording. Above the door he entered, there was a sign that read *L'ecole du Cordon Blue*. Behind a small desk, he observed an older woman, who looked up as he approached and smiled.

"Monsieur Whiteley?" she asked.

Josephine was curious. The invitation, which he had showed her earlier, did not include anyone else. So, off he went without her, and, as she sat in the busy café, she felt quite alone. *Of course, in the end, he will tell me all about it,* she reassured herself.

"I am very sorry," the woman began, "but Madame Distel has become quite ill. She begs your forgiveness and asked me to speak to you on her behalf."

"Of course," said William as he sat in the offered chair, "and please convey my best wishes for a quick recovery."

"*Merci*. What Madame wished to ask was if you may have an interest in helping develop a new approach to cooking, using whisky."

To this, William's eyebrows shot up in pleasant surprise.

"Not just any whisky, monsieur, but only yours. You see, Madame only recently became familiar with the Scots whisky, and after many false starts, one might say, she had the pleasant discovery of your Royal blend."

"Cooking? With King's Ransom?" Martine exclaimed.

William had returned to the Crillon from his meeting to find Josephine and Martine in the grill, waiting in suspense. He had hardly sat down before they both began peppering him with questions.

William nodded. "The lady seems to think it would revolutionize the culinary world. She says that they cook with cognac, brandy, and wine, and now she wishes to explore the use of another spirit."

Martine nodded, thinking what a waste it would be of the best scotch in the world, as he envisioned the mistakes from experiments thrown out.

"I hesitated to tell her of the old Welsh recipe, a pot roast, I believe," William offered. "But, of course, she was speaking of the French approach."

"I should feel ashamed," Josephine interjected. "The layers of depth in your blends are remarkable. They are an open invitation to someone who wishes to explore those depths in a kitchen." Then, with a conspiratorial smile on her face, she said, "And I believe I shall do it myself."

Before leaving Paris, William saw a small notice in a newspaper of the unexpected death of Madame Distel. The article reported that she left the management of her school to an orphanage.

Pity, thought William, as he reflected upon what might have been.

The pleasant feeling of nostalgia they might have felt on their departure for Cherbourg was spoiled by the absence of their companion, Martine. Electing to stay behind, he had bid them farewell at Hotel Crillon.

"*Pardonne-moi, mes amis*, I must stay behind. There is much I can do here, and there is, of course, the ballerina herself…"

With a hug from Josephine and a firm handshake from William, the three companions separated, not knowing if or when they would meet again.

"I will miss him so," Josephine lamented sadly, as they found their way to their rail car.

"And I as well," William said with an unfamiliar ache in his heart.

– § –

Ridley sat while William read the summary he had provided. It was a short—and to the point—synopsis of William's financial status. As he made his way rapidly though the figures, William was slightly surprised to learn of the increased size of his estate.

"All right," he began after completing his review. "What do you propose?"

What Ridley proposed was something of a shock to his client and friend.

"All of it? Why on earth? And why now?" William ejaculated.

After going over the "death tax" regulations, William began to see what Ridley was driving at. It was impossible to avoid the tax altogether, but it could be reduced. Though he had no concern about Josephine, or what she might do with their money, the idea of being dependent on anyone else drove him to reject all but a part of Ridley's plan. In the end, he agreed to keep a fraction of his wealth in his own name—more than he thought he would ever need while he was alive.

And this is how it happened in October 1938 that Josephine became a millionaire. Around that time, she believed no one would have reason to regard her as changed in any way by the largess.

She forgot about Hinch.

TWENTY-TWO

1939

Rome, Italy, January 12, 1939

These men are not made of the same stuff as the Francis Drakes and the other magnificent adventurers who created the Empire. These, after all, are the tired sons of a long line of rich men, and they will lose their empire.

So said Mussolini to his foreign minister and son-in-law, Gian Ciano.

"Yes," Ciano agreed. "The British do not want to fight. They try to draw back as slowly as possible…"

"Report to Ribbentrop this was a fiasco," ordered El Duce.

"Yes," replied Ciano. "I will telephone Ribbentrop that the visit was a 'big lemonade.' Absolutely harmless."

He was speaking the day after a meeting in Rome with PM Chamberlain and Lord Halifax.

The prime minister of England, a fortnight later, presented the draft of a speech, approved by Mussolini, in which he outlined the results of their meeting on January 11. The PM continued to believe he was making progress through his personal connection to the leaders of Germany and Italy.

Tuesday, March 14, 1939

PRAGUE TAKEN WITHOUT RESISTANCE—
SLOVAKIA ASSERTS INDEPENDENCE—
HUNGARIAN TROOPS ENTER CARPATHO-UKRAINE.

Below the headlines, William read a brief synopsis detailing Hitler's arrival in Prague, where he declared the remains of Czechoslovakia a German protectorate.

As he put the disappointing news aside, he puzzled over why he should feel so tired. The trip to Paris had been three months ago, and he recalled nothing taxing about it, apart from parting with their friend, Martine.

Oh, well. Old age, I guess.

Hinch appeared in the library, asking William if there was anything he wanted him to do. It had become his habit to check in from time to time, partly because he hoped William would want to go somewhere and partly so he could avoid driving Josephine and her friends. He missed the daily driving of William during the days before his retirement.

"No, but thank you, Hinch. I need driving nowhere," William replied. Then looking outside through the window of the library and seeing the Heath extending out of his sight, he noticed it was a particularly fine January day.

"Is it very cold out?" he asked Hinch.

Hinch assured that it wasn't.

"No? Well, then, we shall go for a walk."

The members of Hampstead Golf Club did not much care for the presence of walkers on their course. Of course, that did not prevent them from walking, and from time to time there had been minor altercations between shot-makers and pedestrians. This was why William stood with Hinch on the edge of the course, watching a few members at play.

"Aver tak up th' game y'sef, Mr. William?"

"I did not," William replied. "Though it occurs at times like this that I sometimes wish I had."

Ethelred the Unready had, in the year 986, granted the land to a servant. For some time after, Westminster Abbey held the title. Manorial rights were maintained through a succession of private owners, and from time to time it happened that parts of the manor were sold off for building. However, the Heath remained, in the main, common land.

Over time, additional grounds had been added, and it was upon these the two men began their long, leisurely walk while they talked of many things. Memories of his early days in Todmorden flooded William's mind, and his thoughts turned again to those days when his parents were together.

"What do you mean by spirits?!" Hannah had demanded.

"I been thinking, cutting stone is a young man's game," George began.

"Ha! And it's your father, Ely, that was doing it for forty years," Hannah rejoined.

"Aye, and it was to the ripe old age of sixty-one he lived," George said sardonically.

"I was about six years old," William said, "when my father changed careers." "From then on, what I remember most are the sights and smells of the tobacco business." He continued to remanence.

With some considerable encouragement, even prodding one might have said, Hinch told William a bit of his life story.

"Dad wuh a fahma,' an' we 'ad nowt a' growin' up." Pausing for a moment to reflect, he continued. "A' learnt t' drive a'fore A' wuh of age. Learnt A' cud drive anythin'."

William smiled and said, "Yes, that is one of your great talents. Another is your ability to drive well in, what may be termed, times of great distraction."

Hinch looked sharply at his master's face, on which he saw only the faintest of smiles.

Their walks became a habit they indulged in, often to the displeasure of Miss Josephine, Hinch quickly learned.

"Hinch, what do you mean by '*can't* drive you today'?" she would ask irritably.

Mr. William would answer for the two of them, and off Josephine would go, reluctantly driving herself.

"Of what value is he, William, if he does not drive?" Josephine queried when they were alone.

"He is of great value to me just now, as a companion," William replied. "I find my energy is being restored by our daily walks, my dear. And I am loath to give them up."

"You cannot walk alone?" Josephine asked, and immediately she regretted her question. "I'm sorry, love. Of course, you enjoy his company. Stupid of me to ask," she said as she remembered all the years Hinch had driven William.

"Now, of course, if the Minerva is getting a little long in the tooth, we could find another motorcar for you. Perhaps something smaller and more maneuverable?" William suggested. The look on her face told William all he needed to know before she spoke.

"Oh no! I, and my friends, *love* that car, darling. But sweet of you to offer."

She put her arms around her husband and kissed him. To her great surprise and pleasure, she felt his excitement growing as they held each other close.

"At our age, William? Do you think…?"

Her question faltered as she began to feel the stirrings within herself.

"You will never cease to amaze me," she murmured as she closed the door.

– § –

The Savoy seemed perfectly situated, he thought, as his cabbie left the hotel. It would take twenty minutes, and after picking up Patty at her school dormitory, they would arrive for dinner right on time.

Not much had changed since his last trip in July. He knew about the threat of war and guessed he would find some evidence of preparation or concern. He saw none.

Right on time, he thought, as the cab pulled to the curb to pick up his waiting daughter.

"Hello, Daddy!" Patty exclaimed as she gave her dad a hug and snuggled next to him in the back seat. Her blond curls danced on her head and her small, oval face radiated with excitement and intelligence.

He gave the cabbie the address of 32a Wildwood Road and sat back, giving his daughter another hug. He listened as she talked excitedly about her first term and a few of the new friends she had met.

"It's only been six months, Daddy," she reminded him, with a flip of her curls, when he told her how much he and her mother had missed her.

Twelve years old and going on twenty, he thought to himself, trying to remember what life was like when he had been that age.

Did I ever feel that young?

They did not have to knock on the door to announce their arrival. A young woman was standing out front to greet them.

"Mr. Haim? And is it Patricia?" Dora asked Patty, who made a face.

"It's Patty, *please*!"

Suitably admonished, Dora led them inside, where William and Josephine were waiting. Exchanging greetings and welcoming the father and daughter, they then went into the front room, where guests were usually placed.

Intrigued by the art deco furnishings and art, visions of the stolid, brownstone building she called home flitted unfavorably through Patty's mind. Josephine excused herself to check on how dinner preparations were progressing.

In the kitchen, she found Alice in a bit of a dither.

"What's the trouble, Alice?" Josephine inquired.

Listening to Alice describe the tragedy of a collapsed meringue, she allowed a smile to play upon her face before going over the recipe again.

"Did you remember the cream of tartar?" Josephine asked.

Alice shook her head in embarrassment.

"Don't worry," Josephine soothed. "We have plenty of time. Just set the eggs out now, and in about thirty minutes, try again."

Josephine checked the salmon marinating in King's Ransom and made certain the sauce she had prepared was warming without burning. Then, with the martini shaker in hand, she left to return to their guests.

"Don't make sense to me," Haim was saying when Josephine returned. "But that certainly does." He grinned when he saw the shaker.

"Martini, may I presume?" Josephine inquired.

"You betcha'," Haim exclaimed, rubbing his hands together as he turned back to the conversation with William.

Looking at Patty, Josephine asked if she would like a soda or tea. Patty chose a soda, and Josephine retrieved one from the ice bucket, asking if a root beer would do.

It would.

Drinks in hand, everyone paused for a toast and best wishes for the New Year.

It was the twenty-first day of January in the year of 1939, and the talk turned to the possibility of war. Haim picked up where he had left off.

"As I was sayin', with all the war talk goin' on back home, I thought I'd see a bunch of soldiers in the street."

William interrupted, "There are several reasons why you may not have." He paused. "There aren't very many to start with."

Haim shook his head and said, "Thought maybe it was that anti-war business like we got back in the States. You know that fella', Limberg, he's in love with Hitler."

"Lindbergh, Daddy, I think you meant to say," Patty said with a slurp.

Irving Haim laughed and winked at William, saying, "What a kid I've got, huh?"

"Ain't this wonderful?" Irving Haim asked as he wiped his plate clean.

"Yes, it is, *isn't* it?" Patty said in a respectful tone of voice. Josephine took a bow and winked at Patty, who winked back.

William was still enthralled with the dance of flavors he was experiencing on his palate. *Scotch never tasted so good,* he thought. His "artist's palate" was working ecstatically, deciphering the code. Irving Haim, slapping him on his shoulder, interrupted his reverie.

"What say we have one of these Havana cigars, William?"

"So when did you start drinking?" he asked Haim.

Irving took a long draw on his cigar and, exhaling, replied, "After I knew things would turn out okay."

He paused for a minute, seeming to consider how much farther to go with his explanation.

"In my business, especially in the early years, it was safer not to. If ya know what I mean."

William assured him that he did.

"She's precious, isn't she?" asked Josephine.

Their guests had been gone only a short time, and the two of them now lay together. Her husband showed no interest in continuing their conversation while Josephine found her mind racing over the events of the evening.

William yawned. Pulling his wife closer to him, he murmured, "Delightful. Precocious, no doubt."

For a moment, Josephine allowed herself to consider what kind of parents she and William would have made. She blamed herself, not knowing really if that was true to say. William would have made a fine father, she thought to herself as he began to snore.

Irving Haim stayed on until March 4, when he left Southampton for New York. He had told William he was going to be in Pitlochry for most of his time and would see him when he returned to London for interviews with prospective employees. He joked with William that he was going to have to increase the number of workers at his distillery by more than thirty percent—from three to four men.

Josephine and William had made certain that Patty should feel welcome anytime.

"You consider our home as *your* home while you're here," Josephine had put it.

They had not heard from Patty often, but William and Josephine made it into London a couple of times to have lunch and take her to places she had not yet been. Haim expressed his appreciation often and promised a visit in the summer when he came to take Patty home.

Saturday, June 10, 1939

PM REITERATES SUPPORT FOR POLAND—
DANZIG IN TURMOIL

The Free City of Danzig, which was created in 1920 as a result of the Treaty of Versailles, finds itself caught in the vise between its Nazi government and the German people who resent deeply the separation from Germany. Pressure is building and the stakes are high for those Polish and Jewish citizens caught in the middle.

On June 19, Irving Haim came to London to take his daughter home. Patty could see no reason to leave, but, resigned to her parents' wishes, she offered little resistance. On their last night in England, they enjoyed a dinner with the Whiteleys.

"When will you be back, Irving?" William asked at their parting.

"Reckon it'll depend," Haim said as he bid William goodbye.

It was the last time either would see the other.

THURSDAY, AUGUST 24, 1939—
NON-AGGRESSION PACT SIGNED BY RUSSIA AND GERMANY!!—
RIBBENTROP IN MOSCOW—BRITISH RESERVES CALLED UP

Excerpts of terms from the Pact: *Both High Contracting Parties obligate themselves to desist from any act of violence, any aggressive action, and any attack on each other, either individually or jointly with other Powers.* The article continued: *This treaty is for ten years. The British Government has put its antiaircraft defenses on full alert, and Dominion Governments have been warned of possible necessity of precautionary stage.*

FRIDAY, SEPTEMBER 1, 1939—POLAND ATTACKED—
BRITISH ULTIMATUM GIVEN TO GERMANY—
CHURCHILL TO ADMIRALTY?

SUNDAY, SEPTEMBER 3, 1939—IT IS WAR!

At 1115 BST, the Prime Minister announced the deadline given Germany to withdraw its troops from Poland had expired. Thus, we are at war with Germany. King George has called upon the "people at home" and the "people across the seas" "to stand calm, firm and united in this time of trial."

In a separate action, France presented their ultimatum in Berlin, saying a declaration of war would occur if the deadline of 1700 was not met.

William stood with Josephine looking up at the mass of aircraft covering the sky. Planes of all sizes—mostly bombers—filled the vast space above them. This went on all day, with the appearance of troop carriers occurring shortly after noon.

Hinch stood nearby, saying to himself, *"Let 'em 'ave 'at boys. Giv 'em 'at gud."*

FRIDAY, SEPTEMBER 15, 1939—
WARSAW SURROUNDED—END IS NEAR

Wehrmacht troops have surrounded Warsaw where the Posen Group and surviving divisions from the Thorn and Lodz Groups have joined to meet the German onslaught. German radio reports their Third Army has invested Prague with attacks from both sides of the Vistula.

"What do you think, William? Is this chic enough?" Josephine asked, modeling her velvet satchel.

"You'll get by in the crowd, I think…" William paused for a two-count. "…if the crowd's big enough."

Sticking out her tongue at his irreverent remark, she produced his container—a well-tailored canvas bag.

"I don't know why I am so good to you, you dreadful man," she said smilingly as they both experimented with putting on their gas masks.

Their levity occurred at a precise moment in time. Though war had been declared, nothing seemed to be happening in Great Britain. It would be nearly eight months before the first bombs fell and the harsh reality of war hit the island nation. Looking back on that period of time that became known as the "Phony War," both William and Josephine had good reasons to regret their naïveté. They were not alone in that. Indeed, the entire War Cabinet, with one notable exception, operated on the apparent assumption that the nation that struck first would lose. Curiously, that is exactly what happened.

SUNDAY, SEPTEMBER 17, 1939—
RUSSIA ATTACKS!—
POLAND'S EASTERN FRONT UNDEFENDED!

Hinch moved the Minerva slowly into place and began filling the fuel tank. When he was done, and before the pump shut off, he filled the spare can he had brought for the purpose. Only two hundred miles per month, the government had said, and Hinch thought there might be enough fuel to make it with the spare.

FRIDAY, OCTOBER 6, 1939—
POLAND SURRENDERS!—DIVIDING OF SPOILS BEGINS

TUESDAY, OCTOBER 10, 1939—
LITHUANIA, LAST OF BALTICS SURRENDERS TO RUSSIA!

Beginning on September 28, with Estonia and followed by Latvia on October 5, and Lithuania today, the Baltic States have all come under the domination of Russia as Germany and they divide up the spoils of war.

William read reports indicating the British Expeditionary Force, having landed in Cherbourg, was now being dispersed north to Flanders and south of Lille, along the Franco-Belgian border. His thoughts soon turned to his friend, Martine, and his ballerina.

"I fear the worst," he said to Josephine, explaining his concerns.

"As do I. What can we do to convince them to leave?" she cried.

At that moment of tension and despair, Lord Haw-Haw came on the air. The German station had become one of their favorites, and, in desperation, they tuned out the BBC and its below-the-head programming.

"Treasonous! Absolutely treasonous!" ejaculated William.

"Well, my dear, you have only yourself to blame," offered Josephine. "If you think it drivel, we don't have to listen," she concluded.

William stared at her with a perplexed, strained look on his face.

"No, *no*! It's the accent," William replied with a note of incredulity. "He sounds like a strangled Noel Coward."

– § –

Isabelle's flat was located in the 9th arrondissement of Paris. It was not large or sumptuous, but Louis and Isabelle found it comfortable and convenient. She had chosen it some few years before because of its close proximity to the Palais Garnier. It was there Isabelle was rehearsing for an upcoming performance when she saw Martine in the theater. She took pains to ignore his presence while rehearsals went on.

At the first break, she saw him coming forward from his seat in a back row. "Why are you here?!" she exclaimed in a low voice as he came close to where she bent down from the stage.

"Ah, *cheri*, it is difficult to be apart," he began.

Cutting him off, she slapped him on the shoulder, grinning as she said, "You big fraud! You do not miss me so. I have been here every day, and this is the first time…" Her voice faltered.

"Yes, it is different now," Martine said in a weighty manner.

– § –

"But I do not want to leave Paris," she began. "You know that, so why—"

"Because it is different now, *cheri*," Martine repeated, interrupting her.

"Different, how? Sergei says we shall stay, and I can do no…"

She paused as Louis held his finger to his lips as to quiet her.

Why do I let this man have the power over me? Isabelle asked herself, and continued to listen as Louis told of friends who had left Paris and those who had told him of their plans to go.

"But the British are here. The Maginot Line, they say it is impregnable. Our army—the best in the world. All this, and you want to leave? No! I will not go." She sat defiantly across the table in the café they had chosen for their evening meal. All around them were signs of the gay nightlife of her beloved city. The aromas of the food and sounds of traffic in the street conveyed a sense of stability that Isabelle had come to cherish since she first came to Paris. No, she would stay. No matter what may happen.

"There is something else," he began. He told her about the history of his family and, in particular, the reasons for their vulnerability.

"I did not know you were Jewish," she said.

"On my mother's side," he replied.

"Why did you not tell me before?" she cried.

"Would it have mattered?" he asked and prayed it did not.

They continued to linger in their favorite café. Their cigarette smoke mingled with that of other patrons as they finished their coffee.

"So, now I see," she began, ignoring his question.

Exhaling, she added, "I see why you have been so insistent about leaving."

"It is not just that," he said. "I have children to think of. They are far more vulnerable than I. My son is orthodox, as is his family. We have talked of nothing but leaving Europe since Czechoslovakia."

"I will think about it," she said, as she stubbed out her Gauloise.

– § –

SATURDAY, OCTOBER 14, 1939—
HMS *ROYAL OAK* SUNK! NAZI U-BOAT IN SCAPA FLOW—
HORRIFIC LOSS OF LIFE

Unlike in the last war, the threat of U-Boat attacks at our Naval Base proved all too real this morning when the 'Mighty Oak,' as she was called, went down under a barrage of torpedoes. Early reports confirm a great loss of life has occurred.

"There has been an air attack upon the Firth of Forth." William read the news report to Josephine, who asked, "Do you think we shall also be hit?"

"Fortunately," William responded, "the Germans seem interested only in military targets at the moment."

There had been no word from Martine since William's letter of a fortnight ago, and both were beginning to worry.

"Oh! I nearly forgot," Josephine cried as she handed William a poppy. "Hinch came in with them a while ago. He said no matter what, *his* war would be remembered."

NOVEMBER 30, 1939—RUSSIA ATTACKS FINLAND— FINNISH FRONTIER TROOPS WITHDRAW!

In a coordinated attack, Russian troops, accompanied by mobile armored units, invaded Finland early this morning. From Petsamo in the north, and all along the eastern border to the south at the Mannerheim Line, the Russian forces have penetrated more than twenty miles at this last report.

– § –

"It is a charming story, that *Madeline*," Isabelle said as she put the book down.

Martine looked with curiosity at the cover, which appeared to show the Eifel Tower in a forest.

"It is a children's book, yes?"

Isabelle nodded. "But also much more than that."

As Martine picked up the book, Isabelle went on. "I find it relaxing to read these stories, so uncomplicated. Not at all like what we have now."

Martine tried to ignore the obvious reference to their ongoing quarrel as he read, "'*In an old house in Paris that was covered in vines, lived twelve little girls in straight lines*'

"If it is all in rhyme save me the trouble and tell me the story," he insisted.

Exhaling the smoke from her cigarette, she spoke out of a fog. "I will tell you the part most amusing."

From somewhere within Martine cringed, not knowing why.

"The little girl, Madeline—a redhead, by the way—has an attack of appendicitis. She has her appendix removed, and later, when her classmates visit her in the hospital, she proudly shows her scar to her eleven friends." Pausing only to exhale, Isabelle continued. "They return to their boarding school, where they wail and cry, making an uproar, demanding their appendix also be removed."

Martine immediately seized upon the parallel. "So, you see why I want to leave Paris, but you do not see the danger to yourself?"

"No, what I see is Sergei promising we will be safe. The show will go on. There may be danger; yes, I see that. But I am not Jewish, and I do not think like one of those little schoolgirls."

"Yes. You are not…and I am. Jewish that is." He stopped, hesitating for a moment as the fear of a certainty began to form in his mind.

She looked at him for what seemed to be a very long time before she spoke. "It does not matter. And yes, I do love you, if you do not already know that. But, I cannot go with you. I cannot leave Paris. Not now…"

"So, the answer is no?" Martine asked with his heart pounding.

Her silence was her only response.

– § –

DECEMBER 30, 1939—
RUSSIAN TROOPS REPELLED!—
VALIANT FINNS PREVAIL FOR NOW

All along the 'waist' of Finland, Russian attacks have been repulsed. After allowing the Russians to penetrate some thirty miles, Finnish counterattacks and ambushes by their troops experienced in forest fighting have driven Russia's crack troops from their objective. No one expected this, and many are celebrating the wisdom now of not having courted Russia as an ally.

The "City of Lights" was never more beautiful than during the Christmas of 1939. All seemed in readiness for the festive celebrations as in years past. Shops sold out, as last-minute shoppers found to their frustration and regret.

Posters in travel agencies assured travelers that "Everyone flies nowadays," and went further with sanguine directives such as, "Don't mind Hitler. Take your holiday." The latest fashions were on display for those discriminating clients who could still afford them.

Many could.

There were, of course, those who were making their final arrangements to leave the city, among them a number of Jewish refugees, artists like

Mondrian who believed their art would attract the negative attention of the Nazis, and actresses such as Marthe de Florian.

Martine was not among them.

As they lay together, drowsy from their lovemaking, Isabelle prayed, "Not now, *mon dieu, pas maintenant*." She knew that if he asked her at that moment, she would fly with him anywhere.

"Not now," she whispered to herself. "Not now…"

TWENTY-THREE

1940

"At last," Josephine announced, "we have heard from Louis!" She brought the unopened letter into the library where William sat.

"What does he say?" William asked with hope in his voice.

Reading the letter aloud for the first time, the sadness it evoked made speaking the words increasingly difficult.

"So, that's it, then. He's not coming, and all because of her," Josephine wailed.

Taking the letter from her, William read it himself. In his mind, he could see Isabelle at their last dinner together, so confident and so assured. He thought about what he might do if he were in Martine's situation. He looked up at his tearful wife for a moment and thought to himself, *Yes, I can see how I might do the same thing.*

He gave her back the letter and said, "His love is very strong. Let us hope it is strong enough for whatever comes."

– § –

Hinch continued to accompany William on their daily walks across the Heath, and each one provided a new revelation. He heard more about William's childhood and how his family moved often.

"When I look back," William said, "I sometimes think we were like a band of gypsies, moving all over Yorkshire. I can only assume my father was looking for the best location for his shop."

Some of his recollections were sad ones, Hinch knew, like the story told about his uncle John Bentley coming to visit in Langfield.

"Looking back, I think at the time, it must have been obvious something was wrong in my parents' marriage. I remember having queer feelings about some things I overheard, but at the time, they did not point to their separation."

Refreshed from his walk, William sat in the library rereading Martine's letter. Like a scent rising from a perfume blotter, he could sense the despair coming from the page, as he again read the closing lines: *And so,* mes amis, *I stay, not knowing from day to day what will be my fate. I feel joy in knowing my children are safe. In my despair, I know they have done what I cannot do.*

William and Josephine had been able to assist Martine's son and daughter, along with their families, guiding them through an orientation to their new homeland. The fact that they were not Jewish refugees from Germany was beneficial. Martine's son was well-educated and sufficiently skilled to secure a job with a firm in London, where he could assist with the war effort, if called upon.

– § –

As William sat in his camp chair with pride blooming in his heart, he watched all the young soldiers and their girlfriends at play. The Easter Fair at Hampstead Heath had come off nearly as usual. Phonographs had replaced organs, but the volume was sufficient for all to hear the music. As the day came near its end, an old veteran from the Great War toddled by. Seeing William sitting alone with Hinch in his old uniform, he ventured over to offer his regards.

After a few moments of conversation, in which William learned the man was only recently retired from the Army, the old soldier looked at the many Tommies still on the Heath.

"Theirs will be a harder war, I fear. Not like this 'phony war' we have been having."

Nodding their agreement, Hinch and William rose and, saying goodbye, began to make their way home.

24 MAY, 1940—
HEADQUARTERS, GENERAL GERD VON RUNDSTEDT, ARMY GROUP A.

Adolf Hitler was in good humor as he addressed his victorious commanders: "You will see for yourself if I am not correct when I predict this war will be over soon, very soon, even perhaps in as little time as six weeks."

A general silence prevailed among those officers who had seen, to their amazement, their fuhrer seeming almost prescient. He had been right about Austria, Czechoslovakia, and Poland. Now, it seemed both the British and French Armies were delivered into their hands. His next order they found to be both confounding and confusing.

"Herr General," the fuhrer addressed von Rundstedt. "You will not advance beyond the Lens-Bethune-St. Omer canal line."

"Mine fuhrer! May I ask why?! We have them in our grasp; surely you do not wish to let them go!" exclaimed the general, who knew his forces were already past the canal line.

Smiling, Hitler began to utter words that amazed the entire officer corps present. He spoke with admiration of the Empire and the Roman Catholic Church as bastions of freedom and order—essential elements in maintaining stability in all the world.

He spoke of giving Britain room to negotiate a peace, a peace contingent only upon letting Germany have her way in Europe. He then concluded his remarks:

"We have France on bended knee. She will be out of the war in days, mere days, mind you. It is enough. Now, we must see if the British Lion will yield to reason."

– § –

The Hawker Hurricane fighter, having survived the onslaught, now flew alone. Looking all about him and seeing no targets to pursue, the pilot turned for home. Checking his fuel gauge reassured him while he saw below him the flaming wreckage of the enemy bombers. As he approached the coast, he could see for miles the mass of weaponry and humanity crowding the beaches.

Suddenly, coming out of the cloud cover, four enemy fighters began their strafing run. He was too far away to intercept them, but as the lead fighter began its climb to circle and return, he saw his chance. Concentrating the fire from his eight Browning machine guns aimed at the full silhouette of the enemy aircraft, he watched with satisfaction as it exploded before his eyes. Pulling up to escape the full force of the blast, he spotted the remaining 109s begin their climb and circled to confront them.

The firing began almost immediately as the three remaining enemy planes fully engaged their lone target. Their shells ripped through the canopy, shattering around him as fragments ripped his flying suit.

But he was alive!

He kept firing as the enemy fighters pulled up to avoid collision with his craft. His senses told him he had hit one, and he turned to see the telltale black streak flowing from the 109.

On the beach below, most of the soldiers stood transfixed as they saw—for the first time—one of their own engage the enemy that had for days pounded, killed, maimed, and destroyed almost unopposed. Many began to shout their support and cheer their pilot on as the Hawker rapidly circled to meet the enemy again.

Others were less sanguine shouting their frustration.

"Where the hell has he been?"

"About bloody time!"

What the pilot saw was that his odds had improved.

This time, he faced only three of the enemy, one of whom was clearly damaged.

Their leader fired first, and his shots went home.

The British pilot reacted as the rounds struck him, and he slumped forward in his seat, struggling to right the craft that wanted to spin out of control. With both hands on the throttle, he forced himself upright and pointed his weapon at the oncoming enemy.

Just…hold…on, his mind told him as he hit the boost.

The damaged aircraft was slow to react, and lost the two seconds of time necessary to avoid the Hawker now aimed directly at him and closing too fast.

3 June, 1940—
Luftwaffe Rains Terror on Paris

More than 200 planes of the German Air Force were directed by Reichsmarschall Goering to continue their attack, targeting many industrial sites, munitions, and buildings in Paris. The Minister of Interior has threatened public officials with dire penalties for anyone leaving their post.

4 JUNE, 1940—
EVACUATION COMPLETE—BEF RETURNS—
OUR FIGHTING FORCE INTACT—
OPERATION DYNAMO COMPLETE SUCCESS

The pages of history will be replete of the Miracle of Dunkirk, in which more than 338,000 men were evacuated from the jaws of certain death. Rarely before in history have we seen certain Defeat, at the last minute, snatched out of the omnivorous jaws of the Enemy.

These words described the results of the evacuation plan of the new prime minister of England. He had been on the job less than a month and only three weeks before addressed the House of Commons, whose members were told they could expect nothing more than "blood, toil, tears, and sweat" in the years ahead. With the miracle of Dunkirk, he paid on that promise early.

12 JUNE 1940—
SURRENDER! AT ST. VALERY-EN-CAUX—
PARIS TO REMAIN OPEN

Today, the remnants of the BEF and the once proud French Army were forced to surrender to Field Marshall Erwin Rommel. General Weygand declares Paris to remain an open city. We are to prepare for occupation with no armed resistance. In short, what we are witnessing is total capitulation.

"It is not too late. If we leave quickly, we can make our way south and to freedom," begged Martine.

The feeling of seclusion and safety her apartment had always provided no longer registered, and the tension in the room was almost more than she could bear.

Isabelle could not look into the face of the man whose life was likely now forfeited. And because of her.

But, no! It was not just her. He had decided to stay, even after she refused to go. She had not led him on with false promises. It seemed nothing had changed, and yet…everything *had*.

"I do not want to go," she began. "My life is here. My people are here—I cannot desert them now, especially now…"

Her voice gained strength as she saw what she must do. She forced herself to look into Martine's eyes. "You do not understand. You are from France, but…you are not *of* France."

What flashed in his eyes chilled her heart. "Then, it is I who must go," he said as he turned for the door.

He took a long last look back, and his piercing eyes engaged hers. Searching there and finding the truth, he disappeared from her view.

In the hallway, he waited for a moment. When she did not follow, he left the building and headed for the rendezvous he had arranged. The driver would ask questions, he knew. A fare for one was not the original agreement. He knew he might have to pay for the one who did not accompany him. He hoped that would be the only price he would have to pay for her absence.

– § –

"He's left Paris!" Josephine cried, rushing into the library with the letter from Martine.

"How and when?" William demanded.

Looking at the postmark, she frowned. "It's dated June 17, and he says he will be getting on a ship the next day."

William read the entirety of Martine's letter. "He says he will call when he arrives in England, but he does not know where or when."

— § —

Montlucon was alive with rumors of Italian aircraft, having just the day before bombed and strafed civilian targets.

"We can go no farther." His driver gestured emphatically with one arm and turned a belligerent face toward Martine. His eyes bulged and his open mouth quivered with tension.

Martine looked on at the angry crowds as they came to a standstill in the center of the town.

"You have a car!"

"Help us!"

"Do you have money?"

"We have no food!"

The clatter of voices reached its shrillest note as Martine ordered his driver to push through. Cursing and waving one arm wildly about, his driver began hesitantly moving forward. Hands pummeled the sides and windows of his car, and he feared at any moment the glass would shatter. Slowly, obstinately, the car made its way, and then, suddenly, the road opened, and the crowd seemed to pass away.

"That was close, monsieur!" the driver shouted before the tension he felt began to subside.

It had taken them a week to get this far, all the while passing thousands of refugees on foot, hundreds of broken-down automobiles, and wrecked military vehicles. For Martine, they were a depressing sight. For his driver, a source of fuel. Weapons and ammunition spread over the road glistened in the sunlight like fragments of broken mirrors. During those anxious moments, while the driver siphoned fuel from stranded vehicles, Martine had shared his food and his money with those he met along the road, until he reached the limit of what he thought he had to keep for himself.

They had driven night and day, stopping only for an hour or two to rest. Often, they dozed off amidst the snarling traffic when it would come to a stop.

"Eveille! Eveille!" Martine would shout, hitting his driver on a shoulder, and they would start again to creep along amidst the surging crowds. On occasion, they would fall in with other vehicles, exchanging rumors and reports of German pursuit.

They had already learned that the port of Bordeaux was closed. It was to be avoided at all cost, and so they maintained a southeasterly trek toward Marseille. It was at Toulouse where they fell in with remnants of the Polish Army.

When the firing began, the driver lurched off the road to the apparent safety of a shallow ditch. Martine, thrown to the floor of the car and dazed, struggled upright to see the cause of their sudden halt. As he looked out a window, he saw soldiers firing their rifles in the air and throwing them to the ground. Soon, three men in unfamiliar uniforms crowded at his passenger door. He rolled down the window.

"What do you want?" Martine cried.

One of the soldiers spoke in a pleading manner. *"Jazda! Jazda!"* he cried and tried to open the back door of the car.

"Do not let them in!" his driver shouted, as he started to move the car forward.

Making him stop, Martine looked back at the faces of the three men and made his decision. Stepping out of the car, he opened the back door and motioned for the men to enter.

Cursing, the driver drove away before the last man to enter could close the door.

They reached Tarbes by nightfall and pulled to a stop where a number of other vehicles had gathered to wait until dawn. Many had lost their headlamps, along with the spares they had brought.

The driver made his inspection of their car and reported they had one working lamp, if Martine wanted to chance it. Using sign language and the few words of French the Polish soldiers understood, he informed them of the decision to wait until first light to continue their journey. He received no argument, and soon saw all three were fast asleep.

During the night, they were awakened by the arrival of other cars whose occupants brought more rumors and stories of Luftwaffe attacks all along the roads they had traveled. Voices shouted the news.

"Yes, Bayonne is still open! Bordeaux, still closed."

They had shared what food they had among the five of them, to include Martine's last tin of foie gras. The wine had run out long ago, and only the water in the soldiers' canteens was available to wash down their meal.

Their car was among the first to break camp, and without awakening the soldiers, the driver moved onto the road behind two other vehicles. Soon, the road opened up, and they were able to reach speeds of up to 60 mph.

Late in the day of June 23, they entered the seething city of Bayonne. Little by little, they inched their way to the port area, where a shout went up from the Polish soldiers as they caught their first glimpse of a ship docked at the port.

Stepping out of the car, Martine spotted a French officer in uniform and standing like a sentinel. Approaching him, Martine asked the way to the French consulate.

"What are you seeking?" the officer demanded.

Martine explained his situation, showed his passport, and saw a look of relief on the officer's face.

"You will be able to make it on board. Now, tell me about your passengers!"

The officer's face hardened when he saw the uniforms of the men who had gotten out to stretch their legs.

"*Polonais*. No! Not here! You will have to go to St-Jean-de-Luz!"

The driver refused to go any further, demanding Martine pay him off and release him.

Martine let the French officer inform the Polish soldiers of their fate. Then, turning to the driver, he handed him a wad of francs.

"This is for the soldiers," Martine explained. "You know the way, and it is only a few hours…"

The driver looked at the money, sighed, and, shaking his head, motioned for the soldiers to get back in.

"Where will you go anyway?" Martine asked, laughing as he punched the driver on his shoulder. "It is very nice there. Enjoy the sights while you are away from home."

He watched the car with the four men drive away as he fingered the remaining five hundred-franc note in his pocket.

Surely, that will be enough, he thought hopefully.

The officer stood for a moment with Martine as together they watched the driver join the line of vehicles stretched all along the road south.

"They are airmen. You knew, of course?" the officer inquired.

Martine shook his head.

"They came to fight the Bosch alongside the British. Their General Sikorski made your prime minister provide ships to take them to England."

"It was the least he could have done," said Martine as he turned in the direction of the consulate. He joined the queue, which he judged stretched at least half a block. There was no panic in the faces of the people around him, and he fell into conversation with a couple in front. They had made their way from Bordeaux when the German attacks began. While they talked, others joined up behind Martine, and gradually the line moved forward.

It was shortly before noon when the door of the consulate came into view. A few more hours, Martine thought, and then he would find his ship. There was a commotion in front of him, and he craned his neck to see what was happening. A scuffle had occurred between two men, but those around them shoved them aside, and soon the line of people returned to their waiting.

"We are getting close," the girl ahead of him said.

The door opened, and several people in front of them moved inside. Then, a hand reached out and placed a sign on the doorknob.

"What does it say?" someone behind them cried.

Martine could easily read the printed announcement from where he stood.

"Closed for two hours."

– § –

Meanwhile, back in Paris…

William read the words and paused, thinking, *What a casual segue for this moment in time!*

Then, he began again to read the letter. It was from a mutual friend of Isabelle and Martine, asking after him, and if it was known whether he had made his way to London.

Meanwhile, the letter read, *please tell Louis we miss him and think of him often with affection.*

As do we, William thought. *As do we all…*

– § –

The captain of the *Konigan Emma* checked his watch. *Boarding should be finished soon*, he determined.

With their departure scheduled for 8 a.m., he sent his first officer to pass the word that no more refugees could join the queue. Three thousand was more than seven times the normal capacity of his vessel.

But these were not normal times, he had to admit as he took a handkerchief from his pocket and wiped the perspiration from his haggard face—a face lined with the worry and strain of not having slept for the last thirty-six hours.

Martine struggled to make his way through the crowd. Told at the consulate there would be any number of people hoping to get on his ship, he knew he would have to navigate that mob of refugees to reach the officers who were screening documents prior to boarding.

He pushed forward, saying *"pardon, pardon"* all along the way. Though cursed and spat upon, no one sought to block his way. In time, he found he was standing in front of an officer demanding to see his papers. Looking them over, the officer said, "Proceed."

Martine moved forward to the end of the queue of people waiting to board. Looking about, he saw many refugees with knapsacks resting on the quay and standing in small groups. Some had only the clothes they wore, while others had the one suitcase allowed everyone.

"Traveling light, I see," a voice said.

He turned to see a clergyman standing behind him.

"I was the vicar at an English church in the South of France," he offered in response to Martine's inquiring look.

"You are alone?" Martine asked.

"Oh, no, my wife is up ahead of me somewhere. I had to go back to get a suitcase we left on the quay. I say, do you mind if I go ahead?"

Martine smiled and nodded. *What can one more delay matter?* he figured, and let the vicar pass.

There was a commotion up ahead as Martine saw a burly seaman wrestling with the vicar and attempting to prevent him from boarding. Without thinking, Martine rushed ahead, arriving in time to see the figure of the vicar slip past the seaman. Returning to his place in line, he resumed with the others his waiting to board.

SATURDAY JUNE 22, 1940—ARMISTICE AGREEMENT SIGNED— ALL EVACUATIONS ENDED—HITLER CHOOSES SITE OF 1918 SURRENDER AS SUPREME REVENGE

The Armistice will take full effect on 25 June, thereby ending all evacuations from the continent. Refugees crowd every port. Allied soldiers, citizens, and those of various nationalities find themselves caught in the Nazi trap.

– § –

"*Mon ami*, I am two days on that boat! Little food and water—there were, after all, more than three thousand of us," Martine said, while devouring one of Josephine's creations.

"How did our men conduct themselves?" William asked.

"Magnificently." Martine nodded as he tried to finish chewing. "They sang songs, which you could tell were different from the barracks versions," he laughed as he tried to stuff more food in his mouth.

"But what of Isabelle?" Josephine asked. "Or have you heard from anyone?"

This time Martine paused longer than it took to clear his mouth. "I know nothing more than what our friend told you in the letter," he explained as he knocked back the contents of his wine glass.

Sitting back from the table, more at ease now that his hunger had been satiated, Martine swirled the new pour in his glass and raised it, offering a toast to his hostess.

"You have saved a starving man. *Merci!*"

"What's next, my friend?" William inquired as he sat with Martine in the library. Josephine joined them shortly after helping Dora clear the table.

"Back to work, I suppose," Martine replied. "Have you heard if ships are still getting through? I mean, to the Cape, of course."

"Since Operation Dynamo, all the ships, including the liners, have been requisitioned by the government. Troop ships, supply ships, they have all been taken over," William answered with a frown.

Martine was quiet for a moment before nodding his head. "*Mes amis*, it is necessary, then, to decide where I shall sit out the war."

– § –

"It is not so bad, *qui?*" her friend from the opera asked.

Isabelle shrugged and looked at the note she had received from the officer.

"He says he wants only to meet and get acquainted. What harm is there in that?" her friend continued.

Again, Isabelle shrugged. Finally, her mind made up, she handed the note to her friend.

"*Non*. Tell him no, for me."

Waving away the protests of her friend, Isabelle finished removing the makeup from her face and, after changing into her own clothes, left her dressing room.

Sergei was in the hallway, and she stopped for a moment as he took her by the arm. Pulling her aside, he spoke in hushed tones.

"You need not feel obligated," he began. "We are here to entertain, of course. But that ends when you leave the stage."

"I know. And thank you for that," Isabelle said as she kissed both of his cheeks.

He held on a moment longer before releasing her. "Should you need protection at any time, just tell me."

She was able to leave the Palais Garnier without difficulty, and, as she made her way to her flat, she began to breathe more regularly. Along her way, she saw German officers and French girls walking arm in arm. Shaking her head vehemently, she pressed on until she arrived at her flat.

At no time did she pause to dwell on why her friend was consorting with the invader. She knew her friend was from Alsace-Lorraine and was fluent in Alsatian, German, and French. Her friend had been quite open about her family connections and that as a child, she had often visited relatives in Germany. Moreover, her friend had dark hair and did not look Nordic in the least. They had discussed politics from time to time, and she was aware that her friend had no admiration for Herr Hitler. In fact, she had said she despised the man and could never forgive him for the persecution some members of her family in Germany had endured.

Arriving her flat, she was surprised when the concierge handed her a note as she entered the building.

"There are roses as well, Madame. I took the liberty of leaving them in your flat," the concierge said with a knowing smile. Isabelle did not return the smile and made a mental note to later confront the concierge about her inquisitiveness.

Glancing quickly and seeing she did not recognize the handwriting, she began reading the note as she made her way up the stairs. "Imbecile!" she fumed along the way. "What kind of woman does he think I am?"

Crumpling the note, she threw it across the room upon entering her flat. Seeing it lying in the middle of the floor, she stepped forward hastily and squashed it with her foot, kicking the mangled paper aside. Grabbing her coat, which she had just removed, and the flowers that had just arrived, she left her flat hurriedly.

She found them where she thought she would.

Sitting at a table near the stage, which was empty while the band took a break from playing, she saw her friend and two German officers.

She calmed herself as she walked slowly toward the table.

Her friend must have seen her, because Isabelle saw her mouthing some words and the officers turning to greet her. Both rose, and one reached for her hand, which she did not extend.

Seeing a puzzled look on his face, Isabelle launched her broadside.

Speaking quietly and loud enough for only him to hear, she forcefully told him with controlled anger never to approach her again.

The officer's face hardened, and with a cruel twist to his lips, he uttered an oath followed by the word all women know to be insulting.

In a flash, she threw the roses in his face, not minding the thorns as they drew blood.

Using one hand to pull the thorny stems away, he was shocked then to receive her slap across his face.

Their eyes met for a moment before Isabelle turned on her heels and left.

"*Schlampe,*" the officer muttered as he sat down to wipe the blood from his face.

– § –

"Tell me, *cheri*, once again," Sergei asked.

Isabelle went over her story, this time with a little less vitriol.

Taking notes, Sergei interrupted her only once. When she finished, he made a few notations before responding. "And you do not know his name, *corriger*?"

"My friend will know, and—"

"Yes, of course. I will ask her tonight, myself," Sergei interrupted.

There was a pause, and then Sergei continued, "I think it best if you do not come to practice for the rest of the week."

"No, no! Hear me out!"

"I only mean for your own safety. Is there a place you can go, say, out of the city and for just a short time?"

Isabelle shook her head. "*Non*. And I do not want to hide. I will go on as before, and I will practice."

After Isabelle left his office, Sergei picked up the receiver of his telephone and waited for his call to be put through to his friend in the headquarters of the police. When his friend came on the line, Sergei explained the nature of his call, and, after a little bit of back and forth, during which the officer got the information he needed, Sergei rang off.

Members of the troupe had begun to file in. Spotting Isabelle's friend, Sergei invited her to speak with him privately. After a few minutes, the girl departed, and he began to consult his copy of the score that required attention in the evening's rehearsal.

Practice had gone well, and Sergei was particularly pleased with Isabelle's work that evening. She seemed to add a little more…*feu*? Yes, a little more *passion* to her performance.

As she made her way out the staff entrance, Isabelle was surprised to find a gendarme, apparently waiting for her. He tipped his hat and fell in alongside her as she began to make her way home.

– § –

The next morning, along the boulevard and down to Rue Royale, the swastikas were on full display. *It should be enough,* Isabelle thought, *to bring hatred into the heart of every Parisian.*

Every German face seemed to sneer as she passed the sidewalk cafés, where they sat, row upon row, in their gray uniforms. But it was at the Palais Bourbon where her "climax" occurred. There, she saw the monstrous banner proclaiming:

DEUTCHLAND SIEGT AN ALLEN FRONTEN!
(Germany is victorious on all fronts!)

For a moment, Isabelle stood rigidly. Her body tensed, and her mind recoiled at the insult, the injustice…the *arrogance* of the conqueror!

The look on the face of the German officer she had slapped passed before her, kindling a sense of satisfaction that mingled in the flow of her blood, as in her mind she began to form a murderous resolve.

"*Non*! Do not do this! For if you do, I can no longer protect you!" Sergei begged. "And what of our opera? How will we get along without you?"

He saw in her face his defeat before she uttered one word.

"I cannot sit by and do nothing…," Isabelle replied calmly.

"*This* is nothing?!" Sergei exclaimed, waving his arm about to signify his meaning. "Every night you see our quiet resistance here. You see our beloved opera go on in spite of all that is occurring around us. We refuse to give in or allow them to dictate to us what we shall perform." He paused to catch his breath. "And you call this nothing? It is not nothing."

"Of course, it is important for you to carry on. But it is not enough, not nearly enough," Isabelle said evenly. Something flashed in her eyes. "They must be made to pay for what they have done. They must be crushed!"

– § –

The deep, deep green of the Heath spread out behind them, narrowing at the spot where the wood began. On their slender limbs, the mountain ash trees held the promise of the Rowan red berries to come. William's mouth watered, thinking of the cranberry-like jam his mother had made when he was a child, as Hinch and he returned from their walk.

They had started at first light and witnessed the coming of a gradual clarity in the air that promised one of the glories of an English summer.

"Not a cloud as yet, Mr. William," Hinch chortled as they neared the house.

"Are you certain?" William asked urgently.

Ridley had called from Haim's offices in London with a report of the bombing attacks. Reports had come in indicating attacks to the west at Falmouth and Swansea on convoys attempting to reach the Channel. As news reports began to come in, William and Hinch sat near the radio.

Junker 88 bombers, without fighter escort, have attacked convoys trying to reach London along the Channel. RAF fighters have engaged the enemy, but it is too early to provide casualty reports. Stay tuned for further news.

"But the city? Has London been hit?" William asked Hinch urgently.

He remembered Josephine and her friend, Maggie, had left hours before for a shopping trip. Hinch shook his head as the radio erupted.

Reports are coming in just now of attacks further east and all along the Channel, where convoys are presently under attack. RAF squadrons have engaged the enemy, and early indications are our lads are getting the better of it.

The Battle of Britain had begun.

– § –

"This is my friend," the contact said.

The three of them sat with their coffees at a small table. It was early evening, and the casualness of the encounter surprised Isabelle. Sitting outside with dozens of German soldiers around them, the trio appeared to be simply enjoying each other's company.

Robert Guedon nodded to Isabelle to complete the introduction.

Her first impression of Robert proved to be a correct one. Guedon looked the part of an intellectual, with thick, dark, wavy hair perched upon a high brow. The eyeglasses he wore seemed to magnify his large, intelligent, round eyes, one of which seemed slightly askew. His lower jaw protruded slightly, adding to what was already a pugnacious appearance. But, those eyes! When he looked directly at her, his right eye tilted slightly inward, boring into her, while the other one seemed to look away. The effect this had on Isabelle was somewhat unsettling. With his right eye showing rapt attention, the other offered a window into a mind busy calculating on another plane. Educated at Saint-Cyr, and a classmate of Henri Frenay, he had fought in the Rif and was currently recovering from wounds he had received in the early stages of the German offensive. Because of his disability, he had discovered that he was not regarded to be a danger to the occupation forces. He and Frenay had just begun to assemble the first, modest pieces of a plan of resistance.

"I have enjoyed your work, *mademoiselle*," Robert said, offering his first smile. "The opera will not be the same with your departure."

Smiling her appreciation, Isabelle gathered herself and began to outline her plan. "The opera? Yes, it is an important part of my life. But there are things more important than indulging one's passion for music and dance. I wish to do more, and I hope you will agree to help me."

After several moments of speaking quietly, being careful not to be overheard, Isabelle revealed her scheme. When she had finished, Robert shook his head slowly and paused for a moment to light her cigarette. "By your story, you have convinced me of your ardor," he began. "Of that, I have no doubt."

Isabelle saw a change come over his face, and her doubts began to build.

"I was prepared to tell you of a few friends of mine who are gathering in the shadows, who are just now coming together to begin *la resistance*." He paused to look directly into her eyes. "You are far ahead of even our most ardent friends at the moment."

"So, what are you saying? You cannot help me?" Isabelle retorted.

Guedon gazed into the face of the woman he had just met. Outwardly she appeared tense, angry, coiled to spring. He wondered if the passionate hatred so obviously burning within her could be used to good effect.

He let the tension build in the silence between them before responding. "You say you want to kill the invader. That you want to crush him. And how do you propose to do that? Are you well armed? Do you perhaps have a cache of weapons to share with us, should we support your plan? Is dynamite, for example, readily available to you? And what if you are caught? Are you prepared to experience confinement? Can you resist interrogation, and worse? And what of torture? Are you prepared to resist every effort that would be made to make you talk and give up the identity of your fellow collaborators?"

Despite her best efforts to control her movements, Isabelle's body began to squirm. She felt blood rushing to her head and heat radiating from her embarrassment.

"What you propose," Robert began, "is not only dangerous, it is premature. We do not wish to lose this fight before it is even begun."

Her mind churning, she barely could make out the words that came next.

"And what you have suggested, if you were successful, would bring destruction and ruin upon us all."

Isabelle was stunned into silence. As the full meaning of Robert's words began to register, she felt her anger rising. *Premature!* She raged inwardly at the suggestion.

In a controlled voice that betrayed to others around and near them neither her feeling nor the meaning of her words, she conveyed her disappointment and her frustration.

When she was done, she felt exhausted and drained.

All the reasons for her living had suddenly been denied their meaning and value.

Robert smiled rather disarmingly (she thought) and began to respond with assurances that he was both sympathetic and supportive of her plan. There would be a time for such actions, he said reassuringly, but for now, he would appreciate her help as a courier.

A courier! she thought incredulously. *What is he saying?*

If she could put aside her murderous ideas and free her hands for the mundane task of communicating with members of *la resistance,* he explained, then perhaps, one day soon, accomplices would be available for aiding her with her plan.

What came to be called by some the *refus absurde* began with the slashing of tires, the defacing of propaganda posters with their bold Cyrillic lettering, and the disrupting of communications by cutting telephone lines.

Isabelle soon became adept in the many different methods of providing messages of instruction and information to the various factions. Sometimes in disguise, she would ride her bicycle to a meeting point and casually murmur the memorized message to her contact as she passed him on the street. On other occasions, she would carry information of a more detailed nature sown into her undergarments and simply exchange them with another woman of similar build. The forgery of documents became a major focus of the resistance in the occupied zone, and it was while delivering those items of contraband that Isabelle first met Henri.

Guedon read the message twice, memorizing the dates and places before burning the piece of notepaper. Averse to the use of written messages, he chose instead to convey to the courier the verbal message he wished given Frenay., "Tell him we will have the ration cards and tobacco vouchers the soonest. The ID cards will take longer. But, without the paper, we can do nothing."

Henri nodded his understanding and rose to leave, just as Isabelle entered the room. By common practice, there were no introductions made. Later, when events transpired bringing his treachery to light, Isabelle found she could not remember anything distinctive about his appearance.

But Henri Devillers never forgot a face.

"You have heard the news about Pierre?" Robert asked after Henri left.
"*Non*. Tell me, who is Pierre?" Isabelle responded.
"Just a kid," Guedon began. "He got caught cutting telephone lines."
She paused for a moment to absorb the disquieting news. "Why do you tell me this? You wish to frighten me, or what?"
"If I wished to frighten you, I would simply have told you he was shot," Robert replied tersely, pausing only briefly before continuing. "To

warn you, yes. I wish to warn you that this work is dangerous. Moreover, at some point, your absence from the opera will be noticed. Then, they will start to ask questions, like, what have you been doing with your spare time, *mademoiselle*?"

Guedon was not prepared for what came next.

Isabelle began to laugh. At first, there was just a chuckling, but as her tensions sought release, her laughter came in gales as Guedon looked on with rising incredulity.

"My spare time, you wish to inquire about, Herr Guedon?" Isabelle continued in a mocking tone. "There has been none, mine Herr, for I have been at the opera every day! If you do not believe me, please just ask Monsieur Lifar, the director himself." Isabelle paused with a triumphant look.

Guedon studied her closely. *She is surely no fool. Perhaps I have underestimated her,* he realized.

"So, you have this alibi worked out with Lifar? Suppose the Bosch demand proof?"

"They will readily find it," Isabelle replied evenly. "For I have signed in every day in my role as assistant choreographer."

Printing presses and mimeograph machines were too noisy to use just anywhere, and *la resistance* had begun the practice of using abandoned buildings for their purposes. The paper required to print official documents was hard to find, and when it came available, *la resistence* would secret their inventory in different places.

Isabelle had removed the nails securing a plank in the flooring under the carpet in her flat to provide one hiding place. There, she stored certain papers, replacing the plank unnailed for easier access.

In her comings and goings from the Palais Garnier, it was not unusual for her to be seen carrying a stack of papers. She was, after all, the new assistant choreographer—2d Choreographer, to use the formal term—and sketches of her work consumed a lot of paper. And the opera had to have paper, even though it might everywhere else be in short supply.

– § –

"She said she saw a dog running down the street with a child's arm in its mouth," read William. "Name is Jean Taylor—a fourteen-year-old girl who was waiting in a shelter during the raid on Coventry."

Hinch tried to remember if he had experienced anything remotely similar in the last war. He decided he had not.

"They have been catching it in the harbor towns, and now there is this focus on the cities. Has the office reported any damage?" William asked Hinch.

"Nowt a'yet. Cross Street, aye, but no closer."

"I cannot believe our good fortune, and I even *hate* thinking like that," said William, bringing himself up short. "I do not blame our people one bit, taking over the Underground. I think it is criminal there are no proper shelters. Let's check the news report, Hinch," William said, as he turned on the radio.

This just in. Home Secretary Sir John Anderson will be stepping down. It is expected his replacement will be announced shortly. The terrible attacks that have occurred over Coventry are reported to be the worst of all that have occurred thus far. Major buildings have been leveled, thousands injured or killed, and it is reported that Communist party agitators have distributed leaflets demanding the government provide centralized shelters. One final piece of information from the home front before turning to international news: It has been estimated that more than twenty-five percent of the population in the city has left, seeking shelter in places distant as the south of Wales and Gloucester.

"Hello, all," Josephine said as she made her way to William and his embrace. "Maggie and I have just finished our inspection of the bomb damage west of here."

The attack had first hit the City of London, then had expanded to include the suburbs, where Josephine; her friend, Maggie; and others became firewatchers for their neighborhood. Josephine was describing the craters caused by high-explosive bombs dropped near Romney Close.

"Sounds very much like the one Hinch and I saw on our walk near Hampstead Way," William mentioned. "Just east of us, near Wildwood Rose, there were two bombs dropped yesterday."

"Let's see." Josephine paused to consider. "That makes six that have bracketed us already. Are you at last willing to consider using the shelter?"

The government had made available "Anderson Shelters" made of thick corrugated iron and measuring about six-by-four feet. Hinch had helped install one shelter, digging down three feet into the ground to provide further protection. William was not attracted to the idea and preferred to sleep in his own bed, which, though less safe, was not damp and moldy.

"I hold with those in London," he replied, "who gather with their loved ones in the same bedroom, so in case there is a direct hit, they will all go out at the same time."

"I think we all know the central reason for your antipathy toward the shelter, my dear," Josephine said with a sweet smile. "It is on the smallish side and could not accommodate the two of us and all the wine and spirits we have in the house."

"Well," William smiled. "I would consider sleeping in the wine cellar."

– § –

There was still light in the day as Isabelle left the palais. The officer standing outside to join her tipped his hat as she came on. Seeing him clearly for the first time, she felt a slight sense of alarm, realizing he was not the same man who had been escorting her.

"*Ou est* Officer Richard?" she asked irritably.

"*Inevitablement detenu...desole*," he replied.

They walked a short distance before Isabelle became aware of someone following them. Looking back, she saw to her further alarm two officers, one French and one German. It was seeing the face of the German that troubled her the most.

Where have I seen...? Before she finished the question in her mind, *she knew.*

Guedon saw the boy running and hoped he did not see him. The café had provided a view with some cover as he watched Isabelle's arrest without detection.

We are betrayed! His mind then raged with the question: *Who?!*

He stared without comprehension at the newspaper before him and made certain he made no sudden movement.

A figure he saw out of the corner of his eye approached the table where he sat alone.

Was this to be the end? he wondered. Teeth clenched, he looked up into questioning, frightened eyes.

Those eyes belonged to one of his men, and Guedon made himself greet him cordially. "*Mon ami*, sit and have a coffee."

His companion did as requested.

Guedon hoped his effort to appear normal had attracted no one's attention. Pointing at an article in the paper, he shook his head, signaling his accomplice to say nothing. The man nodded his understanding.

The coffee came, and they talked of many things that had nothing to do with their predicament, whatever it turned out to be. Soon, the boy Guedon had seen flash by came back, this time slowly looking as he scanned the faces of the crowd.

Holding the newspaper up to avoid meeting the boy's eyes, and with a foot hidden under the table, he nudged his friend and whispered, "Give him the signal, if he sees you, to pass on."

"Too late," his accomplice replied in hushed tones.

The boy saw Guedon and his friend and paused for a moment, deciding what he should do. He could see the two men talking and began to understand they wished him to go away. With the words of the message he carried repeating in his mind, the boy made his decision and entered the café.

Soon after, a waiter emerged from the café and approached Guedon and his companion.

"For you, *monsieur*." The waiter presented a small tray upon which there was a folded matchbook.

"*Merci*," Guedon replied and tipped the waiter. Then, striking a match to light his cigarette, he put the matchbook in the pocket of his coat. After a few moments of casual chatter, he rose, excusing himself, and went to the WC.

Entering a stall, he closed and latched the door, hurriedly taking the book of matches from his pocket. Unfolding it, he saw the hastily written message:

"Nous sommes trahis. C'est fini."

Tearing the note to bits, he flushed it and left the stall.

Rather than approaching the table where his accomplice still sat, he waited until he caught his eye. With a slight shaking of his head, he gave the prearranged signal and left the café.

"How can this be?" Sergei asked. He listened as the voice at the other end rapidly spoke to him of Isabelle's arrest, a voice of someone he did not know or recognize.

"I must speak with Officer Bernard at once!" Sergei demanded.

"*Inevitablement detenu*," the voice replied before the telephone went dead.

Almost immediately, there was a knock on his door, and, before he could reply, it was thrown open by a German officer, who rapidly entered Lifar's office.

"What is the meaning of this intrusion?" Lifar blustered.

"The meaning?" the officer smiled sardonically. "It is with great regret that I must report the arrest of your prima donna, Herr Lifar."

"Of whom do you speak?" Lifar replied indignantly.

– § –

The cell was warm, at least, she thought, *though not really a* cell *in the sense most would think.*

It was a modestly furnished room in a large palais or private home confiscated from its Jewish owners. She took note of the spartan furnishings and tried to imagine how it might have been furnished before she…before her incarceration.

She knew she had done well thus far, refusing to say anything other than admitting she was the assistant choreographer—the 2d Choreographer, to be precise—for the Paris opera.

The questions from her interrogator had a broad focus, and several times Isabelle had to think hard about her answers. While trying to be factual, she avoided revealing anything she thought would hurt *la resistance*.

She had not been allowed to sleep for more than an hour at a time; at the end of which, her interrogation began all over again—the same questions, over and again.

Guedon passed the next few days moving from safe house to safe house, avoiding all contact with members of his network, relying on the hospitality of friends. His cover at work did not appear to be blown, and he spent his days on the job as he did before Isabelle's arrest. Reports filtered in that his flat did not appear to be under surveillance. Gradually, as one uneventful day after another passed, he began to relax in the belief that Isabelle had divulged nothing.

"And so, *mademoiselle*, let us try again."

The interrogator could not have seemed less threatening. Were it not for the circumstances of the moment, Isabelle might have regarded his healthy countenance and excessively polite manner as a precursor to a possible friendship. Obviously German, his French was flawless and he had a way of carefully considering his words before he spoke. His face was not handsome, but his small mustache, carefully trimmed, and his luxuriant, dark hair, well groomed, gave the impression of a kindly professor. His lively, dark eyes seemed to radiate kindness and concern for her well-being. It was his tone of voice, Isabelle thought, that belied her first impression. It was a voice that meant business, she thought. "I am here to help you betray all that you believe in and still feel good about yourself," his voice insinuated.

They had been over repeatedly the details of her life—born in Lyon, educated in public schools, eventually the ballet school here.

"You say you studied under Madame Zambelli, I believe?" he continued.

"Yes, that is so," replied Isabelle.

"And yet, you do not dance now," the interrogator said rather than asked.

"No, as I told you, I am a choreographer, or I was, until…until this."

"And you find your arrangements here… *uncomfortable*?"

Isabelle nodded. "You have had me tucked away here for almost three days. No explanation, no charges…nothing. What do you want of me?"

Just then, there was a knock at the door, and the interrogator voiced a command to enter.

Looking at the figure silhouetted in the doorway, she stifled a gasp, realizing it belonged to the German she had seen following her on the street just before her arrest. Her mind flashed back to the scene in the cabaret and the face of the German officer she had slapped.

That same face belonged to the man just now making his way into the room.

Looking down at her with what she thought to be a most malicious smile, he now spoke.

"*Mademoiselle*, I see that you are well, yes?" Without pausing for a response, he continued, "You have received every courtesy during your stay with us, I believe."

Isabelle nodded. "Yes, all but one."

The officer looked at the interrogator and motioned for him to leave. "And which is that, may I ask?"

"My freedom."

Nodding his head as if in understanding, he turned from where Isabelle was sitting and walked to the window overlooking the street below. Looking down, he saw a few people passing with heads lowered and shoulders bent against the cold winds blowing against them. Turning then to face his prisoner, he looked at her intently for a long moment.

"I fear you may never leave here," he began.

"Why? What have I done?" Isabelle exclaimed.

"You are a member of *la resistance*!"

"That is not so! You have no proof of such a thing."

He moved so rapidly toward her that she was unable to react until he was nearly upon her. Recoiling, the chair in which she sat fell back against the wall behind her, while she struggled to regain her balance. When she did, she ducked as his hand flashed in front of her face.

Thinking she had dodged a blow, she did not recognize what he held in his hand.

It was a photograph.

As the picture came into focus, she saw the place in her floor with the plank removed to reveal her hiding place.

"If this does not prove that you have something to hide, *mademoiselle*, then what explanation can you provide?"

Her mind racing, she tried to remember what she had last hidden there. Was it the paper? The completed ID cards? The forged travel documents?!

Think! she commanded herself.

She looked again at the photograph just as he withdrew it from her face and placed it on the table next to her. She could not help staring at it.

If somehow she could will it to come alive!

Slowly, in her mind, she began to retrace her steps three days before when she left to go to work on the day of her arrest. What had she in her possession that day?

"You see now it is useless to deny," he began. "We have found your hiding place. We know you have met publicly with those thought to be members of *la resistance*."

Thought to be! Thought to be, she heard him say. *He is not sure—he is guessing!*

"It is futile to deny your involvement, as I am certain you now see," he intoned.

"Where are my belongings?" she demanded.

For a fraction of a second, her question seemed to startle him, she thought.

"Your belongings are secure, I assure you," he responded crisply.

"If that is so, may I see them?"

"Of what use are they to you now?"

"I believe they will prove my innocence."

Slowly, a certainty began to form in her mind.

– § –

"Nothing! They knew nothing! *Salauds!*" Isabelle screamed.

Sergei nodded his head, smiling. "It appears to be as you say. But," he cautioned, "what brought you to their attention? For what possible reasons could they have suspected you, *cheri*?"

Isabelle struggled to calm herself. Breathing heavily and clenching her fists, she began to pound the table at which they were sitting in Sergei's office. Shortly, when her hands began to hurt, she stopped. "They said I had been seen…" She paused to breathe deeply. "…that I had been seen with those thought to be…*thought to be*!" she screamed again.

"Thought to be *what*?" Sergei demanded in a tone of voice that brought Isabelle back from the brink.

"*La resistance*," she said quietly.

The silence between them was brief before Sergei rose to signal their interview was over. He spoke reassuringly, suggested she go home, and take the time she needed to recover. They would talk soon and discuss her role at the opera going forward.

– § –

The door to her flat was slightly ajar, and it was with some hesitation, mingled with fear, that Isabelle pushed it open. She saw him standing in the middle of the room as she stood in the doorway, surveying the damage.

Every table had been overturned. Shades were clinging to the remains of their lamps. With the carpet rolled back, the place where the plank had been removed formed a gaping scar amongst the wreckage. He spoke just then in the same harsh, accusatory voice he had used just before her release from confinement.

"You must know that this is only the beginning for you. Not a day will pass without scrutiny of your every movement, your every action. Of this, you may be sure."

Leaving, he brushed past her, turning as he reached the stairwell to give her one last merciless smile.

Her festering anger drove her to begin the arduous task of working through the damaged furniture and personal belongings spread throughout the flat. In every room, she found her drawers had been pulled out and the contents thrown about. Salvaging what she could, she returned to the living room and went to the hole in the floor.

Dieu merci…

She looked at the hiding place, a place she could never use again. She thought how fortunate she had removed the papers a day before her arrest.

Suddenly, she became aware of a presence in the room and, turning quickly, she saw the boy. How long, she wondered, had he been standing in the open doorway of her flat?

She waited for him to speak, while trying to decipher the look in his eyes. He said nothing and, handing her a note, left as silently as he had come. In the boy's scrawl, she read the message from Guedon.

He never wrote anything, she reminded herself. The words would not mean anything to another who might read them. But, to her, they meant the end of something cherished, something she needed now more ever before—a channel for her hate.

Sergei Mihailovich Lifar had been conducting, without a wand, when he addressed his opera troupe. He had spoken not of the opera, but of the political.

Born in Ukraine in 1905, at the age of twenty-nine, he was offered the directorship of the Paris Opera Ballet. It was hoped with his youth and vigor he could restore what had once been the envy of the world.

"Today, I must tell you of the great dangers we face in the coming days."

He looked around the room at the upturned faces. "If war comes to France and the Germans capture Paris, many of you will be in great danger. I do not have to tell you of the atrocities already reported. It is enough to say that many of you may have good reason to want to leave while you can." He paused for a moment, searching and finding certain faces among the troupe. "As for the rest…those of you who elect to stay… you have my pledge that I will do everything in my power to protect you." He paused again to collect himself. "Our opera will continue to perform."

Those were brave words at the time, she remembered thinking.

That same Sergei sat at his desk, but now the words were different. He had asked to speak to her privately, and now she knew why.

"I am sorry, *cheri*," Sergei began. "It is too dangerous—for you, for the opera…"

Leaving his office, in her anguish she was surprised the tears had not come. What came upon her instead was a feeling of emptiness. A void, a chasm that seemed vastly larger than even the hole in her floor. Now, she realized, she was truly alone.

– § –

The sound of the BBC Christmas music program provided a welcome distraction while Dora and Josephine busied themselves in the kitchen. William sat in the library thinking of the king's speech, which had ended just moments before. Martine seemed to doze in the easy chair next to William's.

With a lull in the bombing underway, a few hours of near normalcy had been seized to celebrate the holiday.

Returning earlier from her fire-watching duties, Josephine had triumphantly presented a chicken, given to her by a fellow watcher. Root vegetables, put up months before, would provide the side dishes. There were, of course, wine and spirits in the cellar to enhance the occasion. Hinch had fashioned a grate that would allow cooking over the fireplace, and kerosene lanterns and candles provided light.

All the light to see, William thought nostalgically, as he indulged in memories from his earlier years.

They had been without gas and electricity, except for a day here and there, for several weeks. For safety's sake, William had had Hinch turn off the power and fuel lines. To fight off the cold, they bundled up, wearing several layers of clothing. Still, they knew they were better off than most.

"Ah, *mon ami*, forgive me." Martine yawned and sat up in his chair.

Martine had continued to operate his London offices, partly to provide employment for his staff, partly to try to hold his business affairs together, and mostly because he found by staying busy, he did not have to think often of Isabelle, or those last, happy days in Paris.

"Not at all, my good friend," William replied. "You and Josephine have been keeping ungodly hours these last weeks. With her watching and you working, Hinch and I have been left pretty much to ourselves."

"Still walking the Heath?" Martine asked.

William smiled and nodded. "Yes. Apart from trying to dodge a now and again bomb, we manage to stay active."

Martine looked at his old friend and thought of those far-away days back in Saint Pierre. *He was old then,* Martine thought, *and here we are, what, seventeen years later?* Perhaps it was the low light of the lanterns, but to Martine, his friend did not look so well. *Yes, decidedly so,* he thought, *not robust at all.*

"Are you well, *mon ami*?" Martine inquired.

"What do you mean? *Well,* as in before? Or, *well* as can be expected?"

Just then, Josephine entered the room with her martini shaker. "We have just enough gin left for two. Which of you gents shall it be?"

– § –

As expected, the pause in the bombing proved short-lived, and on December 29, the second Great Fire in London consumed the city. The prime minister ordered St. Paul's Cathedral saved, at all cost. Surviving the bombing thus far, it had become a beacon of hope for all Londoners. All around it, the debris of neighboring buildings burned as the firestorm raged. But St. Paul's stood through it all, reflecting the obstinate will of a people who, like it, refused to succumb.

DECEMBER 18, 1940—
GERMAN HEADQUARTERS—DIRECTIVE NUMBER 21

The German Armed Forces must be prepared to crush Soviet Russia in a quick campaign even before the conclusion of the war against England. For this purpose the Army will have to employ all available units… For the Air Force it will be a matter of releasing such strong forces for the eastern campaign in support of the Army… The offensive operations against England, particularly her supply lines, must not be permitted to break down.

TWENTY-FOUR

1941

"No, Hinch! Let them go! They have a right to be angry, even at us," William ordered as the unhappy trio hastened away.

Three young men with grime-smeared faces, dressed in tattered clothing, were disrupting a peaceful walk on the Heath.

"G'day, me Lords," one had greeted them in mocking tones.

They met at a point where two trails crossed, and Hinch had taken exception to their behavior.

"Be off, you buggers. This be a gentleman ya see before ya," Hinch growled.

"A gentleman, a gentleman," they sang out in unison as they began to dance around the two obviously prosperous and privileged men.

"Aye, it is gentlemen we see a sittin' out the war and far from London, you are! And far from the trouble as well," their leader sang out as they continued to parody and dance. "And mayhap you'll be able to spare a quid or two fer us starvin' souls, me Lords! And if'n ye don't *want*...then mebbe we will take it from you!"

At this, Hinch had heard all he intended to hear.

Seizing William's walking stick from his grasp, he advanced toward the boys, shouting, "Oh! Y'll nowt be a' wantin' wen A' catch one a' ya."

It was then that William brought a halt to Hinch's purpose as the boys turned and ran. Watching them run away, Hinch muttered, "Th' blighters! Th' little blighters!"

William stood motionless for a long time, watching the boys disappear from view. "And I would have emptied my pockets willingly," he said quietly.

Hinch looked at his master and saw a face fully composed, but an old face, it was.

Th' years 'ave been kind, t' 'em, he thought. But there had been so many of them.

Listening to William's telling of the brief and disappointing encounter, Josephine waited for her husband to finish while thinking of what she and her friend, Maggie, had discussed.

"I've been thinking a lot about the way we are living," Josephine began, "and I have the feeling we can do more."

With a bit of eagerness that even surprised himself, William asked, "What do you propose?"

– § –

Bad weather had brought another lull in the bombing, and the city had taken full advantage: Rubble was swept from the streets, AAA defense positions manned with freshly trained crews, and decoy fires for confusing the bombers readied for ignition after the bombing resumed, as everyone believed it would. Life became a little more bearable, and, for those who still had them, homes again became a place of refuge.

It had been weeks since the Minerva had escaped the confines of the garage, and her engine purred her approval as the four of them neared their destination.

Doors opened by a valet, they quickly exited the car and made their way inside. They had shared a few nostalgic moments when they passed by the location where their old Piccadilly flat had once stood. Now, as they began their descent to their destination twenty feet below ground, Josephine smiled at Martine with gratitude. He had been the one to make William see that he could make the trip.

"Welcome to the Café de Paris," the doorman said as they were invited to enter the nightspot.

Though the hour was early, couples were dancing already to the music of Ken Johnson's swing band as the four of them made their way to their reserved table. Hinch was invited to join them and, looking about, was very glad to have been included. The number of beautiful women in the room, dressed in all their finery and many seemingly unattached, captured his attention. Maggie and her husband had arrived just before, and their table for six was located just off the dance floor.

Shortly after the arrival of William's party, the band's leader, "Snakehips" Johnson, announced they would be taking a break. Soon, the room filled with a cacophony of conversations. As Hinch continued to take in the surroundings while looking for a possible dancing partner, he thought about what was playing out before their very eyes.

London was partying right in the middle of the Blitz. Here, in Soho, there was *living* proof that Londoners would not be cowed. Outside, the bombs and the death they brought were another world away, while inside, life was being lived. Hinch took note of the many uniformed partygoers and reflected on how the war made things different. He knew, for example, that he would not have been allowed inside the club in so-called normal times.

The band returned, and dancers surged onto the floor, doing the jitterbug and the many variations of feverish dancing that went with the music.

Their energy is intoxicating, William thought, as he wished for a waltz.

It was not to be, as the first chords struck announced a fox trot. Hinch excused himself as he left the table in search of a dance partner. Maggie announced she was available as a partner, since her husband did not dance. Martine obliged, and William leaned over to speak above the din.

"The next waltz is mine," he announced to Josephine.

"I am so proud of you," she whispered into his ear as they leisurely circled the dance floor. He held her with only a small space separating them as they danced.

Funny how women think, he thought as the music ended and they made their way back to their table.

"Oh, William! That was wonderful. May I have the next waltz?" Maggie gushed as they filled their seats.

"Sorry, dear. My dance card is full," William smiled graciously. *Just one dance and I'm winded,* he thought to himself ruefully.

The way home was difficult to navigate, though thankfully, the temporary lull in the bombing brought by the weather still held. Back the way they came, Hinch drove slowly, thankful for the powerful headlamps that illuminated the way. Even with the required blackout covers, there was light enough to see.

As they crept along, Josephine fell into fond remanences of earlier days. Visions of dancing with William aboard ship flooded her memories, and she squeezed the arm of her dancer. Stirred from his drowsiness, William patted her arm and pulled her hand to his lips.

"You're a fine, old girl," he said fondly.

"Indeed. I must have been to come this far. With you in tow."

– § –

Isabelle sat in her ruined apartment, feeling she was amongst someone else's relics. Nothing seemed the same. The boy had been gone for some time, and had he returned, she thought he would have been surprised to see her sitting still where he left her.

She had been rocking back and forth, groaning inaudibly. Her rage, now impotent, left her shockingly weak. She had no desire to move, to get up, or to face what lay before her. What was it tomorrow held? She did not know and was struggling to find reasons to care.

Her friend from the opera, meanwhile, was elsewhere.

Not in the small café where the trouble began, but in the offices of the one man who held the solution, she thought, as she responded to his reticence.

"You must see that the situation is manageable," her friend began. "Your choreographer has gone south, for reasons of her own. The second choreographer needs only your request to return."

"But it is too dangerous still," Sergei replied.

Her friend shook her head. "Not dangerous. Not even risky. What will the authorities think if she does *not* return? I will tell you what they will think. Better, I will suggest to you what they will do when they discover Isabelle is no longer working here. Their suspicions will multiply as they consider why she is no longer with us."

"What foolishness is this?!" Sergei demanded. "If anything, her absence will help prevent further scrutiny. Their attentions will be drawn elsewhere—"

"Yes, exactly so," the friend interrupted. "They will be drawn to *you*, and to the rest of us, to see what we have been up to. To see what they may have missed thus far. They will hound us until they find what they *want to find*!"

In the silence that followed, neither spoke nor looked at the other. Underneath a cool countenance, her mind raced with the thought, *the one who speaks first, loses.*

And so it came to pass.

— § —

This just in. Patrons of the Café de Paris will be shocked to learn that last night as the bombing recommenced, that paragon of West End nightlife received a direct hit. Lost in the carnage that occurred was the young bandleader, Kenneth Johnson. Known affectionately as "Snakehips," he was loved by many, and his absence from the nightclub scene will be sorely missed. It is believed that all other members of his band were killed in the blast, along with a large number of patrons in attendance. A troupe of dancers, set to come on stage just before the explosion, escaped unharmed, as they were off stage and behind the full force of the blast. More news will follow when all next of kin will have been notified of this horrible loss.

William sat stunned by what he had just heard on the wireless. Thinking nostalgically of their visit to the café just moments before the news came on the wireless, he now struggled to absorb the horror. Josephine had not yet returned from her auxiliary's meeting, and he dreaded the thought of having to tell her of the loss.

He sat in the darkened library, looking out the window at the growing darkness on the Heath. It had been a cold, clear night, perfect for bombing. With intense dismay, he went over the atrocities that already seemed to have gone on forever.

He longed for the company of Hinch, who, at his insistence, had driven Josephine to her meeting. He wondered about the welfare of their old friend, Martine, whom they had not heard from since their night at the café. He then heard the front door open and a muffled greeting that preceded the arrival of his visitor.

"There you are," said Josephine as she came through the door with a lantern. "It is rather dark in here, darling…"

"Yes, even more so than you think, I'm afraid," William responded, as he began to tell his wife of the sadness he knew.

– § –

19 APRIL

Had a few drinks, then went to the Savoy. Pretty bad blitz, but not so bad as Wednesday, a couple of bombs fell very near during dinner. Orchestra went on playing, no one stopped eating or talking. Blitz continued. Carroll Gibbons played the piano, I sang, so did Judy Campbell and a couple of drunken Scots Canadians.

On the whole, a strange and very amusing evening. People's behavior absolutely magnificent. Much better than gallant. Wish the whole of America could really see and understand it. Thankful to God I came back. Would not have missed this experience for anything.

There was a knock on the door to his room, and, hastily putting his diary away, he called out, "Come in, the door's open."

A porter entered carrying a tray with champagne and a few hors d'oeuvres. Signing the tab, he handed the porter a gratuity in cash.

"Why thank you, Mr. Coward!"

"Not at all," said Noel Coward, as he began to enjoy his bedtime snack.

– § –

"Arretez!"

The rehearsal was not going well.

Sergei took his prima ballerina aside, spoke quietly to her, and then motioned for his choreographer to join him center stage.

"Can we make a change here?" he asked, pointing to a movement on the page.

Isabelle nodded. "What do you wish?" After a brief discussion, the rehearsal began again.

Returning to her high desk, Isabelle quickly made the changes she thought would support Sergei's ideas. During a brief break, she showed him her interpretation. The next movement went more to his liking, and he smiled his appreciation. For a brief moment, a feeling of gratitude penetrated her concentration, before she went back to her sketches.

Her flat was now restored to something resembling its original condition, and Isabelle did not miss the clutter she had lived in before. The floorboard had been nailed in place, and the new carpet found to replace the old, when removed, took some of her bitter memories with it.

She tried not think of Martine often. When certain memories teased their way into her conscious mind, she steeled herself from letting them spread.

She did not try to forget him; that would be going too far. Better to know he was there, locked away in her mind, than lost forever.

– § –

The bombing, long a nighttime horror, made it necessary to work only during the day. Martine's staff, such as they were, consisted of one clerk and a secretary who was presently taking dictation. She paused, thinking Martine was restructuring a sentence in the letter she was typing.

"Shall I read it back?" she asked, her eager, lively, young face shadowed with uncertainty.

Nodding, Martine listened as he tried to refocus his thoughts on the work at hand. *The work at hand,* he thought, and smiled ruefully to himself. Real work was unavailable to him. That personal contact, face to face with his client. The give and take of commerce.

All gone, like the day itself.

His staff, in the process of clearing their desks and preparing to leave the office, avoided eye contact with him. Only when they were on the way out did the two of them give him a wave of their hands and a murmured "good night."

Was it sheer madness to continue these pretentions of normalcy?

His mind turned to thoughts of Paris.

One vignette of their time together played in his mind before he forced himself to think of the hours left in the day. There was time enough to get to his favorite watering hole, and then the rest of the day could take care of itself.

– § –

"Heil Hitler," the colonel said as he gave the Nazi salute and clicked his heels. "Yes, of course, heil Hitler, and please sit," the officer replied. He did not rise from where he sat behind his desk. Tall windows let in an enormous amount of natural light, revealing a cool, gray interior furnished in a thoroughly masculine fashion.

"We are of equal rank—there need be no formality between us," he concluded.

"Certainly. I merely meant to give the proper respect to my replacement," Colonel Baumann responded.

"That is all well and good, but let us get down to your summary reports," the officer countered. "We will start with your list of known collaborators. I assume those that did not leave Paris already should now be in our custody."

"Actually not," the colonel began. "There are a few that we still have under surveillance. They are the ones with an asterisk next to their names."

"Yes, I see that," the officer responded with a touch of irritation in his voice. "Perhaps you will be so kind as to explain your reasoning in each case."

The colonel went over the information collected for each person on the list, referencing the file compiled showing occupation, daily movements, known friends and acquaintances, daily habits, and further details that had been noted by the efficient watchers he had recruited.

"You have been able to secure the cooperation of a number of French citizens, I see," the officer noted.

"Yes," the colonel responded with a note of pride in his voice. "It has been surprising to discover how cooperative Parisians are in these matters. They show no reluctance whatsoever, whether it involves the betrayal of their neighbors, their so-called friends, coworkers, even spouses!" The colonel chortled.

"And so, in these few instances, you obviously believe there is more to gain by watching rather than apprehending?" the officer asked.

"For now, yes. But of course, the situation can change at any moment. One merely needs to judge when the time has come to strike the adder, before it strikes us," the colonel finished with a malicious smile.

The two German officers continued their review of the lists and files of suspects and collaborators who spied upon them, finishing near the end of the day.

"That seems to take care of the matters at hand," the officer concluded. "Before you take your leave, I am given to understand that you are headed for the Russian front. You must eagerly look forward to your next assignment."

"Yes, of course," the colonel responded with what seemed to be a touch of reluctance. "I have sampled the pleasures of Monte Carlo, and there is, of course, Berlin. But can anyone really look forward to leaving Paris?"

She left the Palais by the staff exit to begin her walk home.

Out of habit, she walked with her head down to avoid the eyes of passersby. She was still appalled to see the fraternization between her people and the invader. As she went further along, she had the almost electrifying sensation that something was different. Yes, she was sure. She was not being followed.

To be certain, she stopped to look in a store window to see if anyone behind her reacted. Seeing nothing to indicate she was under surveillance, she began walking back in the direction from which she had come. She retraced her steps by perhaps a third of the distance; still there was no indication of a follower.

She stopped in front of a café and quickly turned to surprise anyone who might be coming up behind her. She saw nothing to indicate she was under surveillance, and, all of a sudden, she felt like shouting for joy. Instead, she sat down for a coffee. It was delicious. *Unusually good.*

As she relaxed in her newfound freedom, she began to take notice of the patrons of the café seated near her. To her pleasant surprise, she saw her friend from the opera sitting alone and waved. Responding, her friend rose and came to her table and asked to join her.

"Please do," Isabelle replied enthusiastically. "I have not had the opportunity to thank you properly for…*negotiating*, I suppose is the word…my return to the opera."

Her friend smiled. *"Il n'y a rien."*

"No, you are wrong," Isabelle insisted. "It is everything to me."

She went on to explain that without her position as choreographer, she would have nothing. "It is something to live for, and without it, I don't know…" Isabelle paused, uncertain how to continue.

Her friend stepped in to avoid the awkward moment and blithely went on about opera gossip and the ongoing rehearsals. As she chattered on, Isabelle realized how, in isolating herself, she had ignored this friendship. Chastising herself inwardly, she resolved to do better. During a pause in their conversation, Isabelle asked if her friend had any plans for dinner. No? Well, then, it was settled. She would cook for the two of them. Yes, her friend could bring something to contribute, and the hour was set.

Cooking for herself proved difficult most evenings. A form of rationing had taken place while the invader took what he wanted with impunity. In time, a vibrant black market had developed, where, for the right price, anything could be had.

Almost anything, she thought, as the face of Martine flashed briefly in her mind.

Her good friend due to arrive at any moment, she polished two wine glasses and set them out. Out of the meager ingredients available, she had fashioned antipasti that would tide them over while the entrée finished cooking. She looked at the bottle of wine she had opened and shook her head thinking about the price she had paid.

Dinner, now followed by coffee, had been more than satisfactory, she knew. Her friend had been a very good listener during the meal. Isabelle now found a need to strike a balance in their conversation, which had been somewhat one-sided, she thought.

"And so, what have you been doing with yourself, all this time?" Isabelle inquired.

"Oh, you know how it goes," her friend began, "there is work, and then there is going home to an empty flat," she finished as she looked about the room.

"Do you mind my asking a personal question?" Isabelle inquired. Seeing her friend shake her head, she went on. "No German officer to liven up your evenings?"

Her friend smiled wanly, and said, "That is all over for me. I came to see how wrong I had been. And I remembered all the trouble I had caused you…" She paused and looked away.

Isabelle felt dreadful. She reached across the table to provide a reassuring touch on the arm of her friend. "You must not concern yourself anymore. It is all behind us now." With a gusto that surprised herself, Isabelle added, "And, as you can see, I have survived! Even more, I have overcome…the difficulties. You know, they are not following me anymore."

As the hour of the curfew drew near, the two friends embraced one another and resolved to meet often thereafter. Later, while cleaning up in her kitchen, Isabelle felt that special warmth that comes from the renewal of old friendships.

Not all is lost, she realized gratefully. *No, not all.*

– § –

Martine stood watching with horror as the House of Commons burned.

The Abbey and law courts already badly damaged, the fire from the AAA batteries proved mostly ineffective. He watched the enemy bombers, clearly illuminated by the high-power searchlights, circling above, apparently unscathed.

All of a sudden, he became aware of projectiles plummeting as a rain of steel fell all around him, and he sought shelter in a nearby doorway. In his mind, he tried to form an understanding of what was happening as the projectiles failed to explode. Several fell near him, bouncing at his feet, still smoking.

He could now see them clearly enough to wonder if they were shell fragments from the very guns firing at the invader. During a pause in the bombing, he had left the shelter of the underground before the "all clear" sounded and now realized how foolish he had been. Just as he began to wonder about his survival, another lull commenced.

"It's very bad tonight, isn't it?" William asked. He had come into the kitchen to find Josephine and Dora gathered around the wireless.

"One of the worst, they say, for this month," Josephine confirmed, "and we're not even halfway along."

An explosion close enough to shake the house then occurred, sending a saucer crashing to the floor. Dora, who had asked to stay the night, bent down to pick up the pieces.

If all our losses were only this small..., William thought.

The newspaper lay on the table next to his chair, the lantern being the only light. Headlines screamed of the terror that was, and had been for so long, raining down on the island nation. He read about the recent attacks on Liverpool and the Mersey, which had continued for seven successive nights and taken the lives of an estimated three thousand people, with tens of thousands made homeless.

The prime minister had said in a public address not long after that in addition to the damage done by the enemy attacks, he had seen *side by side with the devastation and amid the ruins, quiet, confident, bright and smiling eyes, beaming with a consciousness of being associated with a cause far higher and wider than any human or personal issue. I see the spirit of an unconquerable people!*

William's thoughts went back to his early days in Todmorden. He must have been about nine years old when his grandfather, Eli, had passed, he recollected. His father had then moved their family to Cheapside from Erringden, and, though a child then, he could remember their poverty.

There had been little to eat in those days as his father went from job to job, cutting stone wherever he could. His parents fought ceaselessly in those fretful days, and he winced at the recollection of having to cover his ears at night to keep out the sounds of their quarrelling.

He remembered, when he was eleven, visiting his Uncle Eli in Sowerby. Was it there his father began to think of leaving his trade? He struggled to visualize the shop, above which Uncle Eli and his grandmother lived. With some effort, it came back to him—the sights and smells of the tobacco products they sold in the space below.

It was not much of a shop. Just a small space, perhaps large enough for two or three persons at one time to come in and select their tobacco from the one display case that served as a humidor of sorts. He could remember very few cigars amongst the inventory, which contained mostly cigarettes and pipe tobacco.

He must have been eighteen, he thought, when his parents moved to Langfield, and his father opened the shop on Balk Field. In his mind's eye, he could see his father, George, carefully measuring a portion of pipe tobacco for a customer and picking up the minute amounts that may have spilled onto the counter, placing them back in the storage jar. But his frugality had paid off.

In the end, his father had made his way—handsomely. Moreover, he introduced his son to a business that would occupy half his lifetime. In a month, he would be eighty-one years of age, and, truth be told, he was beginning to feel every one of them.

"Mind if I invade the gloom?" Josephine asked as she crossed the floor with the gift of a kiss.

She sat in his lap for a moment and looked into the face in the shadows. She forced herself to dismiss the concerns rising within her. He was so much older, she had always known; only now, it was very apparent. Not like before, when there was the business to take care of, the money to be managed, the house to be built.

"Oh, William," she began.

"Present for the moment, dear," he replied—rather jauntily, she thought.

"You know what I was just thinking about?" she asked.

He shook his head. "No idea, I'm afraid."

"That time we went up to identify your mother's remains and discovered your father was alive! I don't think I shall ever forget the look on his face when he realized we thought him dead."

"Yes, I remember well. But, do you remember what we were doing before his knock on the door?" Her face took on a puzzled look, he thought, as he waited for her to remember.

"I'm not sure. Some argument, I suppose. Was it something very important at the time?" Josephine asked curiously.

"It is a time I have looked back on often, when I wanted to measure how far we have come, together," William replied. "We were having one of our infrequent arguments about money. I was just out of a job, and you were asking me how I expected to pay the hotel bill, as I recall."

Suddenly, her eyes came alive with memory. "Sitz and needle! Yes! I do remember. And we never got a chance to finish that conversation!"

Their thirty-five years of marriage flashed before her eyes as they teared up. She looked at her husband and spoke to him in a voice husky with emotion. "You were right, then. And you have been right ever since, my love."

Several quiet moments passed between them before William spoke. "Yes," he began, "I was right to love you."

"You came into my life at just the right moment. You gave me the gift of your young heart…a heart very much younger than my own."

– § –

The news of Girard's trial brought Guedon's operation to a halt.

His agents worked to avoid detection while trying to learn how much the Gestapo knew. By the time Girard's conviction and death sentence had been announced, Combat Zone Nord was again fully operational.

In the time that passed after Isabelle's release, there had been no contact with her. So, it was with some surprise that Guedon received her message suggesting a meeting. In a safe house, near her flat, the two of them met.

"May I ask why you are doing this?" Guedon began their conversation.

"He asked nothing for himself!" Isabelle exclaimed.

"That is true," Guedon nodded, "but he will die nonetheless. It is a fate which likely awaits us all, *cheri*.

I ask you again, *why*? Why are you so willing to give up the peace you have found? Your work, is it not satisfying to you?"

D' Estienne d' Orves, an officer in the Free French Navy, had been commissioned by General Charles de Gaulle to join a network set up in western France using the code name "Nemrod." The Free French Forces, led by de Gaulle in London, had been frustrated by the ineffectiveness of the network, which, under d' Orves, came alive. Code-named Girard, he was betrayed by his radio operator after barely a month of organizational activity.

During his trial, d' Orves demonstrated such integrity and courage to go along with his obvious patriotism that he became an inspiration for many Parisians. Isabelle now spoke of her admiration and determination in response to Guedon's interrogation.

"You ask about my motives?" she began.

Guedon nodded.

"I suppose they are not much different from yours. You obviously love our country and wish to see it free of the invader." She paused to gather her thoughts before continuing. "When I first came to you, I was merely angry about how I had been treated. You may have thought me hysterical at the time."

Seeing no reaction on Guedon's impassive face, she went on. "The arrest, in a strange way, was a good thing. I came alive to the risks you have always spoken of."

"And you say that, recently, you have noticed an absence of the close surveillance you received before?" Guedon asked.

Isabelle nodded.

"If it is as you say, why do you think it is so?" Guedon inquired flatly.

Isabelle paused to consider the question she had asked herself countless times and been unable to answer. "I cannot be certain. I can only assume they lost interest or had other more pressing concerns."

"Assume?" Guedon responded with an edge to his voice. "You *assume* at your peril, *cheri*."

Seeing Isabelle recoil at his criticism, he went on.

"There has been one development that may explain your lack of surveillance..."

"What is that?" Isabelle demanded.

"The German officer who was so...*infatuated*, if that is the word, has been replaced."

"So much the better, then," Isabelle responded. "But what do we know about his replacement?"

"There has not been enough time to assess his methods," Guedon answered. "But your experience may provide some clues. Can you think of anything different that has occurred, other than the apparent lack of interest in your daily movements?"

"Not really," Isabelle replied, thoughtfully. "Of course, there is my old friend…"

"And who is that?" Guedon queried.

Isabelle told him of the reconciliation with her friend—the one who had started all the trouble and now saw how wrong she had been.

"And she seems sincere…? Believable?" Guedon asked.

Nodding, Isabelle confirmed his thoughts as Guedon brought their meeting to a close.

"Better give me her name, in any case," Guedon instructed. "Inquiries will be made about her loyalties, her associations, all of which I'm sure will be reassuring."

– § –

After a massive attack on Birmingham, there seemed to be another lull in the bombing. To confuse matters further, the news of the deputy fuhrer's flight to Scotland had surfaced in the press. Rudolf Hess had parachuted at the end of a solo flight, landing close to Eaglesham, near Glasgow. Details were still murky, but some sort of peace proposal was rumored to have been the reason for his daring flight.

Hess was Hitler's right-hand man; what could all this mean?

"What a birthday present!" Josephine exclaimed as she watched William remove the last of the wrapping paper, watching it pile up on the floor of their library.

"Beautiful," William said agreeably, as he caressed the hand-carved pipe Martine had given him. "How did you do it?" William asked, recognizing its country of origin.

"It was as simple as asking the shopkeeper, *mon ami*," Martine smiled, with only slight exaggeration. It had taken more than a few hours to find what he wanted: a full-line tobacco shop still open for business.

Josephine thought later that she was not surprised. Even with the horror and devastation visited upon the city, shops prided themselves for not only staying open, but also providing merchandise for those who could afford it. She thought about the pluck of those shopkeepers who provided employment and went about their business as long as it existed. Time after time, she had marveled over the resourcefulness of so many merchants whose establishments seemed to rise from the ashes and rubble to go on.

It was true that rationing had severely limited foodstuffs, and both she and William had agreed to hew to the limits set. Carrots and potatoes were plentiful, as was horsemeat. Occasionally, there were surprises to be found at their nearby grocer.

"Is there anything under the counter?" Josephine asked in a whispering voice.

The grocer shook his large head as he stamped and nicked the edges of the ration book. "There'll be corn beef in a tin and a sardine or two, if ya want," he said, returning her ration book to her with something less than a smile.

"I will take them, and thank you," Josephine replied as she made her departure.

Outside, Hinch waited on his bicycle, holding hers as they positioned the groceries in a basket behind his seat. Peddling along, Josephine reminded him that it was his turn for a bath.

"Aye an' we *all* be grateful fer 'at," Hinch remarked.

He made a point of staying downwind from his mistress.

"Escallope of *what*, my dear?" William asked.

"It's new, and our grocer says it's very nutritious," Josephine reassured.

"Yes, well, what is it called?" William pressed.

"Spam," she said.

William sat in silence, looking at his plate on which he spied strange-looking slices of something resembling a flat sausage.

"Would you like to see the container, dear?" Josephine asked.

"Well, it is tinned, at least," William sniffed.

He looked at the markings on the label: *Ingredients: Chopped pork shoulder; meat with ham meat added.* "Hmm. It says they added sugar, salt, and flavoring as well. I wonder…"

"Let me know what you think of it," Josephine requested with a smile. "The grocer says it may be plentiful."

– § –

"Are you going to use makeup?" Maggie asked.

"I don't dare. William would have a fit when it came off on our sheets." Josephine moved about the kitchen, beginning preparation for the evening meal.

"I will probably go stockingless, myself," Maggie countered after a pause. "I've heard some girls are just drawing a line down the middle, and from a distance, no one can tell the difference. When you think about it, five inches of bath water is enough for shaving the legs…if not much else."

Their laughter caught William's attention as he struggled with nodding off. *Thank God, there is still wood for the fire,* he thought, and looked at the unfinished whisky that sat in his glass as the book he had been reading fell to the floor. It seemed a little more difficult to breathe.

What is wrong? he wondered. He struggled to rise from his chair.

"William! William!"

The voice was clear, but sounded far away. *Very far away…*

"Oh, Maggie, quick! Call the doctor! His number is by the telephone table!" "Oh, darling! Not now! You must lie still," Josephine cried.

"You were right to call," the doctor said, checking William's vitals. "His color is much better, and that is a very good sign."

"What do you think?" Josephine asked worriedly. "Has there been any damage?"

"I do not *think* so," the doctor said, pausing to check William's pulse again. His serious demeanor seemed to her both reassuring and frightening at the same time.

"I have been thinking," William began speaking.

"Yes, I'm sure," said the doctor with a look of complete concentration. "Just let me finish my examination before we talk."

"All right now, what has been on your mind?" the doctor asked as he put his instrument away.

"Well, my father had heart disease, and old Dr. McHugh, his name was, gave my father some drops…of something—I can't remember what."

The doctor nodded. "Probably Ouabain. We can certainly try it."

"One more thing, doctor," William began, "you don't think it could have been the Spam?"

Noting the twinkle in his patient's eyes, the doctor shook his gray head, quietly laughing. "I don't believe we've had enough time to be sure of that," he said as he gave Josephine an encouraging pat on her shoulder and withdrew.

They turned on the wireless just in time to hear the announcer introduce the prime minister, who, after telling of the launch of an invasion of Russia by Germany, assured all those who could hear him:

We have but one aim and one single, irrevocable purpose. We are resolved to destroy Hitler and every vestige of the Nazi regime. From this, nothing will turn us—nothing.

We will never parley; we will never negotiate with Hitler or any of his gang. We shall fight him by land. We shall fight him by sea. We shall fight him in the air until, with God's help, we shall rid the earth of all those who have shadowed it and liberated the peoples from his yoke.

– § –

Isabelle soon settled into her new routine, working by day at the opera and by night with *la resistance*. Like Guedon, she eschewed written messages and delivered the instructions verbally. As the days passed, she tried to remain alert to all the dangers she knew. She told Guedon of detecting no surveillance, and he had confirmed this, having assigned watchers of his own.

"She is in the clear," they reported to him.

Isabelle and her friend had taken to having dinner together regularly, usually at one another's flat, but on some occasions, dining out. As she sat at the table with her friend, Isabelle thought about what Guedon had said:

"Try and determine what interest she may have in joining us. You will do this discreetly, I know."

Thus far, there had been no opportunity that Isabelle could see for doing as Guedon had asked. Their conversation had ranged from rehearsals to rationing, with no easy segue to the subject of resistance. It was with a mixture of surprise and appreciation that Isabelle found her friend broaching the subject.

"I have something to ask," her friend began. "I do not believe you are involved, but perhaps you can put me in touch with someone who is active in the struggle."

Isabelle did not feign misunderstanding. "You are right in what you say, so why are you asking me?"

"I'm sorry," her friend rushed to apologize. "I have made a mistake."

Isabelle laughed and then went on in a casual vein, returning to the safe subject of their daily lives. Later, on her way home, she passed the pre-arranged message to a passerby.

Guedon studied the face of the woman now across from him in the cafe. He saw nothing to alarm him. A serious face, no apparent guile; she was calm. His watchers assured him she had had no contact with the invader since shortly after the confrontation involving Isabelle.

"She appears to have broken off contact with the German officers with whom she once socialized. She lives a quiet life, apparently devoted to her work as a dancer," the report had said. In addition, she was from Alsace, with no known relatives living in Paris.

But why now? Guedon mused. *Why did she wait so long to approach us?*

"It was the d' Orves affair," she began. "His magnificent courage and patriotism on full display!" She paused. "I could no longer sit and do nothing."

Nodding, Guedon thought. *Everyone is saying that, even Isabelle.* Perhaps it was true.

"All right," Guedon replied. "We will be in touch."

Isabelle's mind rang with alarm as she kept repeating the message just passed to her.

Debrayer.

What could this mean? she wondered. *Disengage from what? From whom?*

Outwardly calm, she continued on her way to the Palais.

It was hot, she thought, even for an August day. Arriving, she noted rehearsals had not yet begun. The dancers were still stretching and exercising, and Sergei was not visibly present. Told he was still in his office, she went to his door and, knocking, made to enter. He was on the telephone and appeared to be unaware of her presence. She went forward and sat down in front of his desk.

Soon, he finished and hung up. For a moment, he was subdued, obviously distracted. Then he looked up, as if recognizing her presence for the first time. In his first words came the name that would soon be on the lips of everyone in Paris, both citizen and occupier.

"There has been a shooting, and a German officer has been killed."

"Who?" Isabelle asked.

"Moser was his name. It was bound to come to this," Sergei continued. "Now, we will have trouble of a very different kind."

"What do you mean?" Isabelle exclaimed.

Sergei looked at her strangely, she thought, before going on. "Do you think the invader will let this go? Do you think there will not be reprisals?!"

He fell silent, and Isabelle thought she saw some uncertainty on his face, as if he was trying to make up his mind about something.

"You know that we have among our troupe some who…would be very unwelcome, if their country of origin were known."

Isabelle nodded.

Having made up his mind completely, he asked, "You still have friends who…might be able to help with our problem?"

"You mean papers, of course? Documents?" she asked quietly.

Sergei nodded. *"Exactement!"*

It went as she thought.

Guedon had sounded the alarm over Moser's killing and passed the word to stop all activity until circumstances became clearer. As he mulled over Isabelle's request, he asked again, "How many?"

She told him again the number and waited for him to decide.

With relief, she saw him nod, saying, "It will be done. We can only hope it will be in time."

"Yes, it was on the radio," Isabelle's friend was saying as she brought their full plates to the table.

"Radio Paris?" Isabelle asked, with a note of incredulity.

"Hiegel only plays *our* composers and concerts that feature only French music. Have you not listened?"

Isabelle was silent for a moment while she ate and thought about how much to reveal. "I find myself listening to Radio Londres mostly," she said. "I think they tell the truth, not what we hear in Paris."

"Oh, well, yes. There is that," her friend replied jauntily. "But listen now and tell me what you think."

As she turned on her radio, the voice filled the room with a robust, plaintive song of love for sale. *La fille de joie…*the song began before her thoughts were driven to Martine.

The song ended, and another began before Isabelle could continue their conversation. Her friend noticed.

"You see what I mean," she said pointedly.

Sighing, Isabelle resumed eating, nodding without response and thinking, *Yes. But, the girl of joy…she is not me.*

Over coffee, her friend continued chatting about a café she had been to recently and the chanteuse that had enthralled the audience. "She is called "The Little Sparrow," but I think she should be called the soul of France."

"What is this café?" Isabelle asked.

"Chez Marguerite."

"But," Isabelle protested, "only the Nazis go there, and their collaborators…"

"It may be as you say," her friend responded, "but there is room for us, if you want to go."

"Tonight?" Isabelle asked with alarm.

"The band will play a number that was recorded late last year, '*Oiseaux des iles,*'" the leader said.

As Isabelle listened to the gypsy-jazz piece, she closed her eyes and tried to imagine the different ethnicities that could find something there. The intensity of the crowd's enjoyment was infectious, almost intoxicating, and she found herself swaying in her seat in time with the beat. She only stopped when she found she could no longer keep up.

"Django, Django, Django," the cry went up at the abrupt end of the piece.

"And now, joining us on stage, *La Mome Piaf!*" the band leader announced.

The diminutive figure, dressed all in black, swiftly moved to the microphone and, nodding once to the band, began her song. She sang of a boy with "sooty" eyes who drank at a bar without stopping. He drank to forget a bad trick that life played him. They had been foolishly in love. He smiled sadly and spoke of their stupid, bitter parting.

Isabelle listened to the refrain, this time with eyes fully open, open to what she had denied, open to what she had tried to put out of her mind, which was now opened to…*to what?*

Martine was gone. There was no bringing him back.

She laughed inwardly, bitterly.

As another song began, she drank the wine. A third song followed, as did another glass.

She and her friend touched their glasses and drank.

"You did not see her film?" her friend asked with surprise.

Shaking her head, Isabelle said, "*Non*. I see nothing. I do nothing. Until now." She smiled to herself.

"You are smiling," her friend observed. "You are happy we came?"

Nodding and taking her friend by the arm, she began singing the first chorus of "La Marseille." Her friend joined in, and together they continued their walk home. As they walked, they passed several soldiers. Nothing happened for a few blocks, until they turned off the main street, where they encountered a single, lone officer.

He stood in front of them, watching them approach.

They could see his face clearly in the match light as he lit his cigarette. It was a massive face, with full lips curled into a snarl of a mouth from which a large volume of smoke soon came. As they came closer, shadows failed to obscure the cruelty that mockingly danced in his eyes. Eyes that seemed to undress them and claim them both as his personal property. There was no way to avoid him, and he did not move, so they stopped.

"Ladies! Enjoying the evening, I see."

Their singing had stopped also, and the two of them held on to each other, gazing stupidly, they were sure, into the cruel face still illumined by the match light.

He held it closer and looked intently into their faces.

"If you hurry, you will just make the curfew."

He then brushed past them while they stood watching until he moved out of their sight.

"What was that?" her friend asked in a hushed voice.

"I do not think we want to know," Isabelle replied, ashamed for feeling cowed.

– § –

Martine sat silently surveying his empty office. Idleness did not come naturally to him, and he longed to be doing something, anything, to be active. The lull in the bombing of the city had continued in earnest, as August ran to September, and the Russian offensive by the Wehrmacht went from success to success.

The news, such as it was, described the Russians in retreat on every front, with massive casualties as the unrelenting attacks rolled up all resistance before it.

There was no longer any need for fire watching, or observers calling in their reports of enemy activity; even fire brigades, thankfully, he thought, sat at their posts.

His business was at a standstill, rather like the Doldrums—that equatorial region of the Atlantic where ships of old abounded in calms. It was unnecessary to take orders, as there was no method for delivery. Plenty of ships would sail, but none had room for his cargo.

And yes, he had been foolish as well, he thought, keeping up a front.

Taking his pencil in hand, he did a quick summary of his financial position, nodding his head as he finished, reassured somewhat by what he found.

His friends had been attentive. No doubt, they sensed his disenchantment and sought to respond in ways that good friends do. He thought of William and Josephine, and their invitation to spend the weekend. He had declined with effusive thanks and appreciation, begging off with excuses about work to do.

Did they believe him, he wondered. Knowing William, probably not. He felt obligated not to impose, and so, once again, he looked ahead to another weekend without plans or hopes for any.

The trains were running again. He thought briefly about just getting on and riding as far as he could. But aimless wondering was not his style. He needed a plan. Something to look forward to… He needed a woman.

There it was.

"Ah, but whom?" He asked the empty room, and no answer came back.

– § –

"A' y' sartin'?" Hinch asked as William moved toward the door. "Y' cane, sir."

"Yes, and thank you, Hinch," William said as he toddled out the door. Standing at the roadside, he looked longingly across the Heath, looming large and distant.

It had never looked so intimidating before.

"Well, let's go as far as we can."

There was the first bench they came to after going a short way, and Hinch was glad of it. He noted with increasing concern the perspiration on his master's face, and, as they sat together, he began to talk of it.

"A' we sure, sir? At's been a while since—"

"All right. It's all right, Hinch."

They sat in silence as William took in their surroundings.

This might be, he knew, one of the last days he had to take in the beauty all around him. Though there had hardly been any bombing near them, his declining health had ended his activity. This was the first day he had gone out since his…um, what had the doctor called it? He could not remember the terminology.

He smiled at the recognition of his failing memory. The things long ago, they came easily to him now. But, ask him what he had done yesterday? He was sure he could not say.

"But William! You cannot leave me! What will I do without you?" his mother Hannah had cried.

The first time had been just short of his thirtieth birthday, and he had fancied he might strike out on his own. He began to make inquiries, and, of course, this came back to his mother, who in short order enabled him to see his error.

"Now, why would you want to leave a sure thing?" his mother had asked. "You know all this will be yours one day. And I can't live forever, you know."

Coming to, William realized Hinch had suggested they go back. Sitting on the bench, he looked full in the face of his loyal attendant.

Attendant!

My God! Am I that old and feeble?

"No!" he said firmly. Seeing Hinch recoil at his brusqueness, he grinned and said, "I meant to say, Hinch, that I am not quite ready to go in. And I'm sorry. I was a bit short with you just then."

Seeing Hinch relax a little, he went on. "I was just remembering some things from long ago and, well, they were not happy years back then. Have I ever told you about how I cut those apron strings?"

Hinch shook his head, remembering the story well, but not wanting to interrupt his master's thoughts. He listened while William went on telling about how things finally came to a head, and when he first went to work for Munro & Son.

"And did I tell you about when I learned I could actually tell the difference between the Canaries and the French?"

This time Hinch nodded and said, yes, he did remember *that*.

"Well, there you are! What are you boys up to now?" Josephine came toward the bench where the two were sitting in the twilight.

"Not to blame Hinch, my dear. We were just reminiscing a bit. My fault for keeping him this late," William said as he received her kiss.

"O, 'at be a'reight," Hinch said rising.

"But you've got your own life to live, my boy. I simply lost track of the time, I'm afraid. No girl a'waitin? No blokes to pal with tonight?" William smiled.

"Aye, tis a girl a'workin' at th' pub, an'…"

"Be off, young fella," William said with a faux gruffness and waved Hinch on his way. Then, turning to Josephine, he said those words that she would have cause to remember in the weeks ahead.

"The lad's a stout one. But his is a good heart, and he'll not let you down."

In the news that evening, it was reported that for the first time, a German U-boat had attacked a United States warship.

"When will they come in, do you think?"

"They cannot sit on the sidelines for long," William replied to Josephine's question. "They will find Germany knows no limits to her ambitions."

The letter from Haim sat on the table next to his chair, where Josephine had left it. His mind went back to the time when he and Haim had first met and their rum-running adventures. He picked up the letter to read it again and tried to picture in his mind the face of the younger man he had met that day. He could still see in his mind the car they were in, bounding along the backroads and dropping off whisky.

> William,
>
> We've heard about the bombing there in London for some time. Mildred and I hope you and Josephine have come through it okay. I hear from Ridley there has been some damage to our offices, and some of our people have been badly hurt. Wish there was something more I could do from here.
>
> It seems to me that things here are moving toward war. Lindbergh and his crowd are losing the argument, I think. But maybe it will take something big to get us all in. We got a few ships shot up, but that don't seem to matter enough to FDR and his gang.
>
> Hear you may have had a rough spell here and there and hope this finds you on the mend.
>
> Regards, Haim
>
> P.S. Daddy said I could say hello and thank you again for all you did for me while I was over there. Sometimes I wish I could have stayed and seen what has gone on. Nothing much is happening here. Love, Patty

William thought for a moment about what he had read and then picked up the telephone to make a call. He listened while Ridley conveyed the news of the damage from the bombing and the injuries to staff that resulted. Ridley promised to keep him informed about their recovery.

– § –

The visit to Chez Marguerite with her friend had given Isabelle a new confidence about going about publicly. She began to make a habit of going out after work and socializing in the cafés that she had for so long avoided. It began to dawn on her gradually that she saw less of the invader in uniform. Then, it became a game to try to identify him in mufti. As she sipped her coffee, she thought with a grim satisfaction about the effect of the new reprisals.

It was their bearing, and the way they walked, that now gave most of them away, she thought. When she observed the waiter ignoring certain clientele, sitting in twos and threes at a table, the recognition was immediate. With an almost total absence of French men, it had become normal to see mostly women walking the street of the city. Her fears had abated as she learned she could walk about freely. She applied her lipstick, put it in her pocket, and left the café.

Outside, she could see the fire and the smoke billowing into the cold, clear twilight as she stood transfixed.

"It is the synagogue," Sergei said, his voice taut with anger as he took in the horror.

He was just outside the door and on his way in when she emerged. Both had heard about Drancy and the very public arrests that had already sent thousands into confinement there.

"Thank God for your help," he said as he put his arm on her shoulders.

"They arrived in time, then?" Isabelle asked.

Nodding, Sergei released her, and they continued together, walking.

"The two I told you about were able to leave Paris by train. I received notice only this morning that they had crossed over at Bourges."

"What then, do you think?" she asked.

"I know they hoped to make Marseilles. From there, only God knows."

Guedon was waiting where he said he would be. Without any sign of recognition passing between them, Isabelle sat down at a nearby table. It had become their custom to show no sign of recognition when they met in public places. As he finished his coffee, Guedon rose from his table and departed, leaving a newspaper behind.

The waiter came quickly to clear, and Isabelle took the opportunity to take the abandoned paper. She opened the paper to the section where the crossword puzzle was placed and began to read. His words from long ago during one of their first meetings came back to her. "Never think any written message you may receive is from me," he had said. She smiled as she read the coded message and then began to work on the puzzle itself.

"I'm sorry I'm late," her friend apologized as she sat down with Isabelle.

"Not at all," Isabelle replied as they exchanged kisses. "I was just finishing the puzzle." Talk of work began between the two friends as they compared notes regarding the rehearsal.

"I don't know what we are going to do," her friend offered, as they talked about two absent members of the troupe.

"It will not be easy to replace them," Isabelle agreed.

"Do you know what happened to them?" her friend asked.

Shrugging her shoulders, Isabelle shook her head.

"Do you suppose they may have been arrested?" her friend continued.

Something inside her head warned her against going further with the discussion, and she waved off her friend's concerns. "We would know, I think, if that were the case."

Over dinner, their conversation continued about the club they planned to visit. When Isabelle finished discussing her thoughts about the show they were to see, her friend became quite serious for a moment.

"I have a message from Robert," she said quietly.

Isabelle hoped her face remained composed as she steeled herself to remain calm. She nodded, and her friend leaned over to whisper. Isabelle struggled to memorize what she was hearing, while her mind raced with apprehension. She smiled in comprehension and began to steer their conversation back to their plans for the rest of the evening.

All during the show, Isabelle forced herself to concentrate on the music. Outwardly, she hoped the impression she gave was one of careless indifference to anything other than the entertainment. She laughed in the appropriate places and drank until the fear within subsided.

She filled the time during their walk home together with forced gaiety, and hoped the relief she felt did not show on her face when they parted. She was almost glad she had had a little too much to drink. In her flat, she reviewed in her mind the instructions Guedon had given her long ago, about how to contact him in moments of crisis.

It seemed lunchtime would never come. The hours at work dragged on until the moment came when Isabelle could make her excuses to Sergei and hurriedly depart.

The meeting place selected was some distance from their usual haunts to try to avoid suspicion. When she arrived, Guedon was nowhere to be seen, and she took a table away from the other patrons to sit down and wait.

She admired the calm manner in which he approached her and the casual way in which he greeted her, like an old friend. When she thought it safe enough, she asked the questions that had been burning within her mind.

"Yes, of course," Guedon said, in answer.

Then it was true! Her friend *had* become part of their group.

"But why didn't you tell me?"

A look of surprise flashed briefly across his face. "Did your friend not use the code to confirm our association?"

Feelings of mortification and embarrassment mingled with relief as Isabelle tried to remember the exact words her friend had used. Guedon waited patiently while Isabelle worked to recall what her friend had said.

"I cannot be certain," she began. "It does not seem possible, but perhaps I missed it. Oh! I don't know…"

"It is much better to be careful. Do not trouble yourself further," Guedon said with a reassuring touch on her arm. He then repeated most of what her friend had told her, confirming what needed to be passed on to their network.

"I hope I am not too late," Isabelle said shamefully.

Guedon assured her that was not the case and, soon thereafter, rose to leave. Then he sat back down and, leaning over, spoke softly. "It was her first time. Perhaps she left something out. You were wise to be careful, *cheri*."

After he left, Isabelle sat alone, thinking through all that had happened.

Why had she been so suspicious? How had she missed the signal that would have put all her fears to rest? Mentally, she retraced all that had occurred, beginning with the crossword puzzle.

That was it, she thought. That was where things began to get confused. The message in the puzzle had been about other matters. *More important matters,* she thought. Then, her friend *had* surprised her.

Of that, there was no doubt!

The mind does crazy things, she had to admit. And, these *were* crazy times.

– § –

The lull in the bombing had become a cessation.

The news reports asserted that Hitler's invasion of Russia had taken away the aircraft that had brought the horror and ruin of the Blitz. Their life had returned to a kind of normalcy, and Josephine took to sleeping late. Still drowsy, she reached over to William's side of the bed and realized he was not there.

"Asleep in his chair, again," she said to herself.

Rising and putting on her dressing gown, she tiptoed to the library and found him in his favorite chair. The fire had reduced to smoldering embers, but the room seemed warm enough to make him comfortable. Just then, the sound of the rear door opening announced Dora's arrival. Putting her finger to her lips, she joined Dora in the kitchen.

"Mr. William is still asleep," she announced. Then, whispering, she asked that coffee be made. Martine had been generous in sharing his coffee rations, since he took his meals away from his flat, and they had enjoyed regularly a cup in the morning together. While the coffee was perking, Josephine began to think about breakfast.

She went to the pantry and looked at what there was to choose. The tin of Spam she pushed aside and decided upon the corned beef. *That, with two of the neighbor's eggs, would start the day nicely,* she thought.

Dora whispered that the coffee was ready.

"You take it in, Dora, while I work on breakfast," Josephine requested.

Hearing a loud crash, followed by Dora's scream, Josephine ran down the hallway to the library, where she found Dora standing next to William, frozen in place.

"I…I…I think he's dead, ma'am," Dora sputtered.

Josephine stood still, looking at William's body slumped in the chair.

Her mind raced with conflicting thoughts. Had he had been alive when she looked in earlier?!

If not…when had it happened?

She walked slowly to his side and felt his brow. It was cold.

Could she have got to him in time?

She picked up his wrist and found no pulse. Gently placing it back on the arm of the chair, and with feelings of remorse and guilt, she withdrew to go to the telephone.

"You are all right?" Martine asked, hugging her.

"I don't know. I'm just numb. I don't know what I feel right now," she said quietly.

Guiding her to a nearby chair, Martine held her hand and, producing a handkerchief, gave it to her to dry her eyes. They sat in silence only for a few moments before a vehicle arrived.

"That will be the ambulance," Josephine said.

The doctor, who had been the first to arrive, met the attendants in the library and helped them lift and position William's body on the stretcher. To her great relief, he had told her nothing she could have done would have saved William. Soon, he returned to where Martine and Josephine sat together.

"Is there anything I can do for you?" he asked. "A sedative, perhaps?"

Josephine shook her head. "No. Thank you. Nothing now."

"Well, then, I will look in on you tomorrow, if that is agreeable," the doctor suggested. When Josephine agreed, he took his leave.

"A coffee?" Josephine asked, after the doctor had left.

"I don't want to trouble you…," Martine replied hesitantly.

"No trouble. I would like the company," she said as she rose to move toward the kitchen.

"Oh, no, ma'am. I've got it right here," Dora said as she appeared with a tray.

"Does Hinch know?" Martine asked.

Josephine nodded. "Yes, and I asked him to tell Vernon and some of the others." She drank her coffee and went quiet.

Martine tried to think of those he felt should be contacted. He knew a few mutual friends who would want to know of William's passing, and he began to make mental notes of their names.

"You know, he wanted to be cremated," Josephine said, coming back to the conversation. "I believe he had made arrangements at Golders Green."

– § –

Ridley looked out at the men and women who had congregated to pay their last respects. He took a quick glance at his notes before he began speaking.

"If I may, I would like to begin with some of my earliest memories of our good friend. I first met William some years after he got his start.

"He had become successful by 1925, when, as most of you know, House of Lords had taken America by storm. *All* the world, really.

"But it was the American market that accounted for most of the sales, due to the unwise—but providential policy—of outlawing spirits."

A chuckle ensued, and he paused before continuing.

"I first met William in his Leith offices and was soon impressed by his business acumen. It was not possible then to know of his courage, and by that, I mean both mental and physical.

"Do you know the story of the U-boat?" he asked the assembly.

Many did not know firsthand, but the story had gotten about, and Ridley made the most of the occasion as he went on. "Here is a man in his sixty-sixth year, if memory serves, riding in a submarine being towed from England to Saint Pierre!"

Passing briefly over the unfortunate details of William's injury and the betrayal of the captain, Ridley soon arrived in his story at the time of their first meeting with Costello.

"Now, many of you have heard that William was in business with the Mafia. I am here to put an end to those rumors…as rumors."

He paused to gauge the effect of his words. He saw only expectant faces.

"William indeed had a connection with Mr. Frank Costello, who became our sole agent for U.S. sales. William delivered the whisky to Saint

Pierre, where Mr. Costello's agents took possession and, in a variety of ways, supplied the American market.

"It must also be said that William was something of a creative genius. His ability to blend whiskies, and then to market them, was without equal in our profession."

There were a number of soft murmurings in agreement.

"Finally, it may also be said that his generosity occurred typically in a quiet, modest fashion. As many of you know, we lost a couple of very fine people during the Blitz. When William found out, he quickly stepped forward to take care of their burial expenses.

"And so, in the end, what we have now is an opportunity to give our old friend a proper send-off." Nodding to his left, he continued. "You no doubt have already noticed the trays of glasses and bottles on the sideboards here. In a moment, I will ask you to raise your glasses and join me in a toast to William, with some of his finest."

Hinch surveyed the room, thinking it *was* a right proper send-off.

But wait... Was that Ms. Josephine beckoning to him?

"Wat cud *she* want?" he muttered to himself.

TWENTY-FIVE

1942

"*Nehmen Sie Platz, bitte,*" the officer said.

The woman sat down as requested.

The office was large and comfortably furnished in a decidedly masculine way. Tall windows provided enough natural light to allow the two to see each other clearly. As she looked at the man across from the desk between them, her confidence rose. His face had none of the cruelty she found in that of his predecessor.

"You have something to tell me, I believe?" the officer began.

She nodded, and before she could begin, he spoke again.

"You are from Alsace-Lorraine, yes?"

She nodded.

"You have family there, I believe?"

She nodded again, thinking she must look like a bobblehead doll.

"Tell me about your family."

"I will do better," she said, seizing the opportunity to speak. She took from her purse an envelope, from which she produced a folded photograph and handed it to the officer. He took it with interest showing on his face and studied it for a moment.

"King William," he replied.

"Yes, at Versailles," she responded.

"And what of it?" he said brusquely, handing the photograph back to her.

"It will explain my loyalties," she said.

Arching an eyebrow, he asked, "How so?"

Handing the photograph back to him, she said, "Look closely to the right. The man in the foreground is my grandfather."

Looking at the figure in the photograph, he saw a dark-haired, bearded man in uniform with saber raised in salute to the emperor.

"He was attendant to the emperor," she stated.

"Aides-de-camp. Yes, now I see," the officer replied. "One question, before we begin," he continued. "How did you acquire this?"

"Each man in this painting received a print to commemorate the occasion. Before I came to Paris, I took a photograph of my father's, which hangs in our home in Colmar."

– § –

At the same time, another meeting was occurring. Henri Devillers sat with Guedon and Isabelle in one of the safe houses, seldom used.

"This is the most ambitious of all the plans we have considered to date," Guedon began. Without divulging the names of any of the members of Combat Zone Nord, he outlined the plans to disrupt communications, transportation, and the daily lives of the invader.

"Will they be armed?" Devillers asked casually, seeking to conceal his rising level of interest.

"Enough will be. They will be ready for trouble when it comes," Guedon replied.

After Devillers left, Guedon gave Isabelle her instructions to pass on. "Use your friend in this. There is no time to waste. Speed is of the essence."

Isabelle met her friend in a nearby café, where she had been waiting expectantly.

"It is the big one?" her friend began.

Isabelle smiled. "The biggest we have done. Here is what I need for you to do."

After her friend left, Isabelle rode her bicycle along the pre-assigned route, passing her verbal messages to those who would do the work. The excitement she felt grew with each contact she made. Their mutual excitement was contagious, and by the time she finished her rounds, she felt limp with exhaustion. Her legs nearly failed her as she wobbled her way to her flat.

Guedon had demanded she return home and await the outcome. It would be only a few hours, she knew, before Paris would explode in violence—a violence the invader had earned because of his atrocities.

She found she could not stay awake, and it was cold in her flat. Wrapping herself in a blanket, she lay down on her sofa to be near the telephone when the first reports came in. She had memorized the one-word codes, which would signal a successful attack in the arrondissements targeted.

She began to dream; in it, she saw a mass of forms without faces, milling about in some unfamiliar square. They were human, but did not look human.

They had eyes, which she could see, but no other facial features at all.

Then, they became aware of her presence. Soundlessly, they turned toward her, making their advance in measured strides. There was no sense of haste on their part, but they must have been moving rapidly, because she was running—and they were gaining.

She came to a wall…or was it a door? She found it locked.

Isabelle looked frantically from left to right, but could find no means of escape. She began banging on the door and pleading for someone—anyone—to open it.

Isabelle thought the knocking she heard was from her own hands. She did not know how long the sound had gone on before she became aware enough to wake from her dream. It became louder and more insistent, and finally she rose and went to her door.

Slowly, she opened it while fear choked her throat, as she peered through the crack.

It was the boy.

Immediately, he handed her a folded piece of paper.

She could hear him running down the stairs as she unfolded the paper and read, for the first time, a written message from Guedon.

We have been betrayed! Devillers suspect. Come south at once.
You are too important to lose.
   –G

She read the words over and again, rooted in her terror and disbelief.

At once!

Forcing herself to move, she found that her limbs seemed only vaguely connected to the rest of her body. She thought she might fall, and she gripped the back of a nearby chair, then the frame of the door to her bedroom.

Moving with more speed than assurance, she selected a small bag and threw a few clothes in it, along with a few pieces of jewelry. Without taking the time for one last look, she locked her flat and slid the keys under the door.

When she came to the concierge's apartment, she quietly went by and out of her building.

Immediately, she felt seized with the fear of discovery.

There were few people on the street, as curfew was only minutes away.

She moved in the direction of the safe house, where she was to join up with others fleeing the occupied zone. She saw in the distance a taxi—one of the horse-drawn automobiles that had evolved due to the shortage of fuel. As it and she drew closer, she could make out the face of the driver. He paused just long enough for her to board before making his way forward.

They went perhaps two hundred yards, she thought, before the driver took the taxi down a narrow alley. Almost immediately, a sliding door shot up and open, and the horse took the taxi inside a building. Quickly, two men began to disassemble the harness, leading the horse into a stall. Now shorn of its artifice, the engine of the automobile roared to life. The driver threw the gearshift into reverse and, when out of the garage, sped away, leaving Isabelle in the rear seat, desperately grabbing for door handles to hold onto.

There was no conversation between them while the driver hurled the taxi forward at a frantic pace. Somehow, they avoided the checkpoints Isabelle had seen throughout her trips on her bicycle.

The driver seemed to know his way. At no point did he hesitate or appear uncertain.

Soon, she saw they were on the outskirts of the city. After they had gone some distance—she was not sure how far—the driver pulled over to a cutout in the road.

"Your papers!" he demanded.

Isabelle withdrew her papers from her bag and handed them over.

By the light of a small torch, he studied them, then handed them back without a word. They waited perhaps half an hour before she saw the headlamps of a vehicle approaching from behind. Flashing its lamps once, the car slowed down. As it came alongside, she could see figures inside. Then, the car sped away, while the driver of the taxi accelerated to a position well behind it.

Cars lined up at the first checkpoint for a distance of at least a hundred meters; the driver pulled slowly into position to wait their turn.

At the beginning of their race away from the city, Isabelle had not minded the silence of the driver. She was exhausted and slept fitfully once they were on the road south. Now, as she waited to pass through their first point of danger, her fears brought her fully awake.

"You know your story?" the driver suddenly spoke.

"Yes. I am your cousin, and we are going to see our family," she recited.

"Where?"

"Lyon."

"What does our family do?"

"They are farmers. That is why we are joining them. They need our labor."

Their taxi was only a short distance from the checkpoint when Isabelle saw two officers working the line. Vehicles with arms extended out the driver's side windows, hands clutching papers. She saw the torch flash and shine. Then, they were next, close enough for Isabelle to see the face of the officer as the taxi crept forward.

The driver heard Isabelle's gasp, and knew the officer must have as well.

The torch lingered on the driver's face, blinding him, and then moved to illuminate the back seat where Isabelle sat rigidly, staring straight ahead. She fought the urge to turn her face away from the glare and dared not look into the eyes she felt devouring her.

"*Passer.*"

At the officer's command, the driver allowed the taxi to creep forward.

Perspiration trickled from underneath her arms as Isabelle fought to remain still. Her mind raced with fear, shouting silent commands to go faster.

Courir! Courir! she screamed on the inside.

Were they moving at all?

It was then the driver turned his head and asked, "You knew him?"

"Yes," Isabelle replied. "His name is Richard. He was a policeman I once met in Paris. He used to walk me home from the opera."

Once through the checkpoint, two automobiles made their way to a café in Lyon, where they parked with motors running while one passenger from the lead car got out, going inside.

When he emerged from the car, Isabelle recognized the profile of Guedon.

While they waited, Isabelle struggled to imagine such a scene playing out in Paris.

This freedom of movement was foreign to her, and regret began to creep into her mind as she saw how easy it could have been to leave with Martine. Within only a moment or two, it seemed, Guedon reappeared, and the cars sped off together.

Unlike Paris, Lyon did not prohibit the use of automobiles by its citizens. The traffic was light due to the hour, and they made good time, arriving at the safe house south of the city. Their host was a farmer, and there was plenty to eat. Isabelle was the only woman in the group, but no one seemed to notice. They had mattresses to sleep on for a few hours before departure. During the muted conversations in the group, Guedon came to Isabelle where she was laying. He spoke quietly, letting her know their destination was Marseilles. Questions burned within her, but she kept her peace, realizing the answers, if any, would come in time.

"Adolphe" was the name used in the introductions when they arrived Marseilles. Evacuated from Dunkirk almost two years before, on his return to France, he had been captured by the Coast Guard and imprisoned at Saint-Hippolyte.

More than one story surfaced of his escape from the prison.

Some said the British had arranged his escape. Others were certain he escaped using bribes and diversions. However done, he had contrived to stay in Marseilles.

During the last six to seven months, his escape line had allowed many Allied servicemen to escape into Spain and then over to Portugal or Gibraltar. From there, many escapees made their way to the States. British servicemen could eventually make their way back home, where they would be first welcomed as heroes and, in a short time, put back into the war effort.

After the meeting broke up, small groups of evaders clustered together, discussing what they had been told. Guedon took Isabelle aside, and together they moved outside where their conversation could not be overheard.

"It may not be possible, what you desire, *cherie*," Guedon began apologetically. "To Spain, over the mountains, yes. That can be done. To Portugal, certainly. But when and how from there, it cannot be known."

Isabelle knew from Adolphe's instructions that her dream of getting to London might remain just that. She was a mere citizen, not a soldier who was valuable to his country in the many ways she could not be.

"It is understood," she replied.

Her introduction to Guerisse had been surprising in one respect. He was not overwhelmingly dynamic or assertive. Rather, he seemed to be quietly confident, humorous, and generous. There was no denying his matinee idol looks, Isabelle thought. Balanced by widely spaced intelligent eyes, an aquiline, aristocratic nose split his face in the middle, below which a firm, full mouth seemed set in permanent amusement.

More remarkable in her view was the presence of the doctor, George Rodocanachi. At the age of sixty-four, he had come to Marseilles with his wife, Fanny, to aid the escapees from Dunkirk who did not make the evacuation. With his lined, mustachioed face, bushy eyebrows and short hair graying at the temples, he looked every bit his age, but did not act it.

"You will be in charge here, 'Rodo.' Nouveau and Prassinos will do the overland work. I will be back in no time," Guerisse ordered.

Rodocanachi knew Guerisse, code-named Pat O'Leary, and known to Isabelle as Adolphe, had to go to Gibraltar.

There was the matter of how to dispose of the traitor, Cole, and more importantly, getting the SOE's support of the mass evacuation plans.

Over the last two years, an escape line had evolved, allowing evaders to escape from port areas, such as Dunkirk, Calais, and St. Valery en Caux. Converging on Marseille, they initially found refuge at the Seaman's

Mission at Rue de Forbin. Run by a Scottish minister who had escaped from Paris about the same time as Martine, the Reverend Donald Caskie agreed initially to harbor only civilian refugees.

"Rodo," using his own home, soon established another safe house, and it was in June of 1941 that O'Leary joined him after escaping from prison. Their mission was the evacuation of soldiers—soldiers of all the Allied forces who would find refuge and a way to return to the war.

The principal overland routes used by the evaders traversed the eastern Pyrenees and, once across, led down to Barcelona. From there, several routes were used to get to Gibraltar and then England. In addition, feluccas, crewed mostly by Polish seamen, were used to ferry evaders along the French coast to Gibraltar. Two British ships operated at different times as mother ships for the operations.

Since Pat O'Leary was the dominant leader, the routes came to be known as the Pat Line.

"How laughable!" O'Leary observed, but with no mirth in his voice.

He had just learned of MI6's decision prohibiting the elimination of a known traitor.

While fleeing from accusations that he had stolen from Pat Line funds, Paul Cole, a courier and guide for escapees, had been arrested and interrogated by the Gestapo. His betrayals had cut deeply into the network in Northern France and endangered the entire southern operations.

The object of O'Leary's derision was James Langley, who had flown over from London for their meeting.

"It's all very well for one to sit in London and act humanely, but this man's betrayal has cost us the lives of brave, devoted agents. People on the ground are being hunted down and shot, as we speak," O'Leary reminded Langley.

Langley nodded his understanding. He was not in agreement with his boss's decision. He now looked with interest at a letter O'Leary handed him.

"This letter is from a prisoner who was in jail with Cole during his interrogation. All you need to know about his betrayal may be found there," O'Leary assured, then watched Langley's face while he read the letter.

Seeing no change of expression in Langley's face, O'Leary's despair rose as he contemplated the ongoing cost of this unchecked betrayal. Langley's very next words put his mind at ease.

"All right. Kill him." Langley continued, "Now, tell me about your evacuation plan."

O'Leary believed that the success of the Greek-crewed feluccas, which could evacuate five to ten men at a time, demonstrated that hundreds of men might be evacuated without increased risk. As for the French navy, it frequently looked the other way, as long as no sabotage was attempted. The boats of fishermen were available, captain and crews would cooperate for the right price, and all O'Leary needed was the funding to make it happen.

"And I believe you have one other need," Langley smiled.

A new man joined their group.

"May I introduce M. Drouet, your new radio operator," Langley said.

Drouet, trained in London for the mission, now shook hands all around. O'Leary, releasing his grip, was surprised at the nervousness the man showed. Soon, their group adjourned, and, over dinner, O'Leary resolved to address his concerns.

"Join me for a whisky," he said to Drouet, "and we'll discuss your new job."

Drouet continued to exhibit a furtiveness that was disturbing, even alarming to O'Leary, when he considered the levels of stress that came with the job Drouet was undertaking. His lips quivered when he talked, his hands shook when he gestured, and he had difficulty sitting still. Even under the influence, he seemed a thoroughly frightened man.

"Tell me more about your reasons for wanting to join our network," O'Leary said.

Pausing to consider the question, Drouet looked at the man for a moment. *What the hell*, he thought. You have to trust somebody.

"My wife is in the south, near Nimes, I last heard," he finally mentioned.

O'Leary pondered this news for a moment. "And, of course, you want to do everything you can to rescue her as well."

– § –

HMS *Tarana* moored silently just off Canet Plage. Two passengers were ready for a swift disembarkation.

During his time in Gibraltar, O'Leary had experienced some success, but his mind was freighted with the burden of the incompetence he felt was represented by the figure standing beside him.

Once Drouet had given his primary reason for returning to France, O'Leary had concluded the man would be nothing short of worthless in the clandestine, tension-filled, and dangerous environment they all lived in.

In his conversations with Langley, he had achieved only one of his goals: approval for the elimination of Cole. His plan for mass evacuations went nowhere, and, in addition, he was saddled with a radio operator who even Langley agreed might prove to be problematic.

O'Leary eyed the man standing next to him. He saw his perspiring face glistening in the flickering light of a cigarette lighter held with two trembling hands.

Soon, "Seawolf" (one of the fellucas) pulled alongside, and a rope ladder lowered for their departure.

– § –

Kept busy by Guedon, Isabelle spent her time greeting and mingling with the hundreds of evaders descending upon Marseilles. Allied servicemen from all of Great Britain, French soldiers who refused to surrender or had escaped from workers' prisons, Norwegians, Belgians, and any number of civilians sought refuge and escape. Her job was to help interview, take notes, and aid in determining the order of evacuation.

Soldiers first! continued to be their byword.

Arriving at Rodo's safe house, and asked immediately to assemble his communication gear, in under an hour Drouet had radio messages going out to safe houses and other parts of the network that had receivers. Since there was a backlog of information to send, Drouet found himself busy the entire day.

He moved his gear to the basement of the Seaman's Mission during a two-hour period after he was told to shut down to avoid detection by Vichy police. From that location, he worked well into the night of his first day in Marseilles. O'Leary was too busy himself to take note of the first day's good work, and, standing alone, the results might have given him reason for doubting his first impression of their new radioman.

Isabelle found herself in Drouet's presence often, and she came to sympathize with his longing for a reunion with his wife. She did not mention Martine or the ache in her heart that accompanied the memories of their time together in Paris. When Drouet would get emotional about his fears and concerns for his absent wife, Isabelle understood. O'Leary did not.

After the first month following Drouet's arrival in Marseilles, O'Leary began to lose patience with what he came to see as his radioman's hectoring. He wanted time off to go and look for his wife.

Told his presence was required and that his daily tasks would occupy most of his waking hours, Drouet exhibited his displeasure by malingering. He then began insisting that O'Leary allocate his guides and couriers for the purpose of finding and bringing his wife to Marseilles.

Just a few hours of free time, Drouet argued, would be enough to visit the government's offices, where he could learn of his wife's location. At this, O'Leary finally lost his temper and excoriated his radioman over his lack of common sense, after which there developed a level of resentment between them that, despite Isabelle's efforts at reconciliation, could not be overcome.

The message went out from O'Leary to his contact in Gibraltar about the need for a new radioman. As Drouet sent the message, he smiled inwardly. His persistence had paid off. Now, he would be free to do what he came to do. He told O'Leary he would be leaving once his replacement arrived.

The pistol that O'Leary produced was a large one. He placed it on the table where the two men sat, while Isabelle and two security men stood nearby.

"If you try, you will never leave this building alive," O'Leary began. He did not think it would take much to frighten the man.

He was right.

Obviously nervous, with hands shaking so hard he could not get his lighter to work, Drouet accepted O'Leary's offer of a light and inhaled deeply.

"What you will do is remain here until your wife can be found."

As O'Leary continued to talk, Drouet leaned forward expectantly. What he learned both surprised and pleased him more than he thought possible.

Guedon, speaking in hushed tones, had been in conversation with O'Leary.

Outside the room, Isabelle waited.

Instructed to come to a meeting, she sat cooling her heels while the two men talked. It was more curiosity she felt, rather than frustration or resentment.

After all, who was she to complain? Her time in the Vichy-held zone had gone by without incident. She had been able contribute something, she thought. It was not much, in the larger sense of what had gone on around her. But it was *something*.

Suddenly, the door opened, and Guedon came out to invite her to join them.

She went into the room to find O'Leary sitting at a table, where he asked her to sit. For a brief moment, she watched as he looked at a few pages he held in his hand. When he put them down and looked directly into her face, she had a sudden premonition that her life was about to change.

"There is a need that you can fulfill, if you are willing," he began.

Isabelle listened while inside her body feelings similar to that of an electrical shock began to flow. She had once shocked herself during a careless moment in her Paris flat, and she thought the burning, numbing feeling she felt just then to be very similar.

"I will try," she heard herself say. "But I do not know if I can meet your expectations. I have my doubts," she finished.

"You would be unwise to believe differently at present," O'Leary said reassuringly. "Robert tells me you are used to memorizing and delivering the verbal message."

She allowed herself a chuckle and looked fondly at her mentor in all things espionage.

And so, in the end, it was all agreed. She would leave that very evening for Nimes. Once there, she was to contact Madame Drouet and inform her of her husband's presence nearby and his desire for a reunion. Isabelle was to judge not only the woman's response, but even before meeting her, make inquiries regarding her loyalties and her associations.

"So, you have known of her whereabouts all along," Isabelle said.

O'Leary nodded.

"Why did you not tell him?" Isabelle asked.

For a moment, all O'Leary did was stare at her. His handsome face began to change. When he spoke, his voice had an edge to it that went with the grim expression that formed on his mouth. Gone was any trace of humor and in its place was something closely resembling rage. She was even frightened for a brief moment until she realized his anger was not directed solely at her.

"Do you have any idea what is at stake here? Or what has been going on?" he asked with a vehemence that startled her. He was speaking of Drouet's behavior, of which Isabelle knew nothing.

To her great relief, Robert came to her rescue, interjecting his assurances that Isabelle did indeed know, and even if she did not fully understand everything, she was willing and able to do what was needed.

O'Leary seemed to relax a little and the moment passed. It was a moment that Isabelle would never forget, and ever after, made her wary of the unseen tides of emotion that flowed beneath the surface of the dangerous waters of espionage they were navigating.

– § –

During all her time in the unoccupied zone, Isabelle struggled with remaining alert to the dangers around her. Unlike Paris, here, they were hidden out of sight and simmering below the surface of her daily living. In Paris, the presence of the enemy was suffocating; now, it was nearly invisible.

O'Leary's instructions were for her to make her way by rail to the rendezvous point with the agent who had discovered Madame Drouet's whereabouts. Together, they would take up their vigil and, in time, her interrogation.

She found wherever she stopped, her papers allowed her to pass on without undue delay. In a few short hours, she arrived to make contact with her colleague. After a couple days of observing Madame's habits, which included where she lived, where she worked, and with whom she associated, Isabelle was ready for her first contact.

Madame Drouet was surprised to see the woman sitting literally on her doorstep, as she turned the corner to make her way to her home. Coming to the gate, through which the woman had to have come, she paused to consider what she should do.

To say that she was frightened would have been understatement.

For her, life, even without her husband, had gone on almost normally. She had her work, and she had a few friends to rely upon.

This woman, who had risen from her own doorstep to come toward her, was not one of them.

"Madame Drouet?" the woman asked.

"Who are you, may I ask?" Madame replied in a tremulous voice.

The two women were just a few feet apart when Isabelle stopped and spoke quietly. "I have a message about your husband."

Madame thought her knees might give way at that moment, and she clutched at the top rail of the gate. Seeing her faint, Isabelle moved quickly forward.

"Please tell me he is alive," she whispered.

Isabelle nodded and took a deep breath. "May we go inside?"

It took only moments for Isabelle to determine that the attractive young woman she knew as Madame Drouet was definitely in love with and willing to do whatever was necessary to reunite with her husband. Soon, both women were moving quickly to pack a few clothes and personal items for the passage to England that had been booked for the couple. Isabelle made certain her papers were in order, and within an hour of their first meeting, the two women were underway.

They went not by rail, but by automobile, and for only short distances. At successive safe houses along the way they changed cars and drivers, until the following day, when they arrived at Marseilles.

"You did well, *cherie*," Guedon said affectionately, "so why the long face?"

"That was the easy part. It is the rest that troubles me," Isabelle replied.

Looking into her eyes and seeing the doubt plainly on her face, Guedon began to have his own reservations.

Seawolf gingerly came alongside *Tarana*, delivering her three passengers bound for Gibraltar, with connections to London. Along with the three civilians were a number of Allied servicemen, all with destinations of their own.

– § –

Martine sat behind his desk, working with a pencil to edit a letter he had written out earlier in the day. His secretary was at lunch, and the clerk was eating in, covering the reception desk for anyone who might come to the office.

Although he heard the office door open and his clerk exchange greetings, he paid little attention, trying to finish a letter to his client—a friend who had written of his concerns about the status of Martine's business affairs at his Cape offices.

The content of the letter was of a sensitive nature.

It would not do… No, he thought, *it would not do at all for it to come known at this time.* There was a firm knock on his door, and he saw the clerk put his head in.

"A gentleman to see you, sir."

Formal introductions exchanged, the French officer accepted Martine's offer of a chair. He said he was an aide to General de Gaulle and wished to extend to M. Martine his best wishes, adding that the general would be pleased if M. Martine would do him the favor of a visit to the London headquarters of the Free French Army.

"*Qui*," the officer replied to Martine's question.

Yes, right now would be perfectly agreeable.

– § –

HMS *Tarana* had not always been a British ship.

A French trawler, she had been interned at the beginning of the war and recommissioned in 1940. With the departure of HMS *Fidelity* (formally,

Le Rhin) for convoy duties, *Tarana* had stepped in to take over the ferrying of soldiers and supplies to and from Gibraltar.

The trip took just over three days, and, upon arrival, the Drouets and their companion were taken ashore and from there to the headquarters of MI9, after which they were promptly escorted to the offices of Donald Darling.

Darling's code name was "Sunday," a name that did not match his disposition as he addressed the young couple sitting quietly across from him.

"Normally, I would address you individually and separately about the matters at hand. As the rest of the world and we know, these are not normal times. Besides, I find that I have very little interest or time at present to engage in the niceties of conversation."

Having concluded his introductory remarks, he placed a piece of paper in front of them and began again. "What you see here is a statement that you each are required to sign in the presence of witnesses. The most important part of the statement refers to the confidential nature of the business in which we are now engaged."

Looking directly at Drouet, who found it hard to meet the man's eyes, he continued, "You, sir, are fortunate indeed to have served, although very briefly, with our colleague, Mr. O'Leary. I say fortunate, because neither of you would be sitting here, soon to be taken back to England by His Majesty's conveyance, if not for the good graces of Mr. O'Leary."

Picking up the page, he held it in front of their faces for a moment before concluding his remarks. "You are signing a promise to keep confidential all affairs related to what you have heard, seen, done, or been trained to do. You are acknowledging that a violation of your vow of silence may be punishable by death.

"Sign where indicated."

Afterwards, Darling and the person who had accompanied them on the ship from Marseilles witnessed the statement and several copies. Soon, the Drouets took their leave, while Darling and their escort sat down for another, very different conversation.

"And so, Guedon has made it very clear what you must be prepared to do?" Darling asked.

Isabelle nodded.

Darling looked at the woman sitting next to his desk and tried to take the measure of her. After a moment of silence, he continued, "Guedon has told me of your time together in Paris. He said you were willing to kill, then…"

"Yes, but that was different," Isabelle replied, with the strain obvious in her voice.

"Different? In what ways?" Darling asked, looking unflinchingly into her face.

Isabelle could not meet his unrelenting gaze, and, looking away, her eyes focused on two photographs hanging on the wall behind Darling's desk.

"It was easy then to hate the Bosch, and in any event, I did not have to kill." Isabelle's voice failed her, and she looked down helplessly at her folded hands in her lap.

Darling sat for another moment before opening a drawer in his desk, retrieving a file and placing it before Isabelle. At first, she did not understand, and then she found she could not believe what Darling wanted her to see.

"Where did you get these?!" she gasped.

"Gestapo files," Darling replied unemotionally.

"But, how? When?" she cried.

Darling paused to savor the moment as he saw the flickers of emotion in his reluctant assassin's eyes.

Photographs of Martine and her were in the file she saw, along with some taken of her with Guedon sitting at a table apparently in one of the cafes they had frequented. Darling then produced a photograph of her friend, who had come late to *la resistance*, and, in the end, betrayed them.

"You did not know?" Darling asked incredulously.

Shaking her head vigorously, Isabelle kept staring at the photograph of her friend.

"She was with them all along," Darling said with an edge to his voice. "She simply pretended to pull away so she could fool anyone who might think—"

"The bitch!" Isabelle screamed as she looked into Darling's face with that murderous intent he sought.

Seeing what he wanted, he continued his instructions. "It is very simple, really," he said reassuringly. "In all likelihood, you will not have to use this." He handed her the small automatic pistol.

Isabelle saw it fit neatly into a vest designed for the purpose of concealment. Putting on the vest and then pulling her long coat on, she saw there was no identifying bulge that would give alarm to the Drouets or anyone else.

– § –

"At my age? You are serious, sir?" So began Martine's response to the Free French official.

He admitted to being sixty years of age, and the Free French official said that he looked not a day over fifty. He said that he was out of shape and no longer fit. The official said they could get him into shape.

There were special needs at that moment, the official had told him, which only a man of his…um, experience and wisdom could perform.

His thoughts went back to Isabelle's words: "from, not of," and they rang with accusation.

He had not seen de Gaulle after all, and he was relieved that was so.

Martine had said he would think on it and, leaving the office, headed straight for the nearest pub.

What a day, he thought as he threw down his first whisky.

– § –

The sail from Gibraltar took them too close to the western border of France for their comfort. The tenseness she felt was not as great as she had feared it might be. She realized now the need to kill grew more remote with every mile that brought them closer to England.

Ever since the "Channel Dash" in mid-February, the German naval forces had put into port for safety or repairs. There were the U-boats to consider, but the ship transporting them had been fitted with depth charges and deck guns to counter the threat. She found the presence of the pistol in her vest pocket to be more reassuring and less threatening as the danger subsided. She had been told the need to kill Drouet would come only if the *Tarana* was captured.

"He cannot be allowed to fall into enemy hands," Guedon had said.

They said he was too weak and would not be able to resist any form of interrogation. In the end, Isabelle had to agree, as she reflected on the affection and sensitivity the Drouets exhibited when together. That had been what made the assignment so difficult when Isabelle first realized she was being asked to kill what she so desired for herself.

And Martine.

In normal times, at its average speed of ten knots, *Tarana* would make the trip inside a week's time. But the peril the ship faced caused the captain to take every precaution, and it was ten days after leaving Gibraltar that they arrived in London.

Parting company was sorrowful neither for the Drouets nor for their companion. She had been a kind of warder, they thought, and they were anxious to set foot on the tattered soil of freedom to begin their new life. Arriving in the passenger reception area, Isabelle heard her name called and moved quickly to the ubiquitous information desk.

– § –

The meeting, scheduled for ten o'clock that morning, Martine had risen early to prepare for.

What choice did he have, really? Would they really deport him? If so, how?

It was a given that all shipping had been allocated for military use.

Almost immediately, there came into his mind the image of a troop transport ship—complete with brig. The answer to his question arrived, bringing with it a rising level of discomfort.

The consulate's office was full of people who, for the most part, were sitting quietly, waiting their turn to seek redress, or the continuing, relative safety of their present domicile. He was, to his pleasant surprise upon arrival, invited to follow an attractive young secretary to an office door, upon which she knocked. Being invited to enter, she opened wide the door for Martine, closing it quietly behind him.

A tall man sitting behind a desk on the other side of a sizable room rose, inviting him to join another person already seated before him.

"I believe the two of you have met before," the consulate said as Martine and Isabelle came face to face.

The consulate kept his counsel as the couple embraced.

Seeing both were feverish with excitement, he watched and waited until his presence registered. Slowly, he brought them back to the reality they faced, beginning with an explanation of Martine's obligation.

Isabelle could see a rising despair in her lover's face, and she rose to the occasion by interrupting the consulate.

It went as he had hoped. The consulate listened to Isabelle insist on accompanying Martine on his mission.

Dinner at Josephine's had not been a quiet affair.

Within a fortnight of their arrival, Isabelle and Martine, nearly exhausted from their time off together before beginning training, were in the library at 32a Wildwood Road.

"And so a date has been set," Josephine confirmed.

Seeing their nodding heads, she went on. "Assuming for a moment that I shall be invited to the wedding, I feel inclined to ask what might be considered a suitable present for the newlywed couple." Crossing her arms, she briefly placed her forefinger aside her nose before continuing. "I believe silver to be a most traditional gift, but, then, there is the problem of your future address. I believe, at present, yours is unknown."

Isabelle let out a howl of laughter, joined by Martine, who had been giddy at the start of the evening, and a surplus of William's finest had served merely to prolong his state.

When they paused to catch their breath, Josephine continued. "There is, of course, crystal to consider, but it is bulky when wrapped properly for travel." Pausing, she added, "And it is subject to breakage."

"So, now, I think I have it!" she suddenly exclaimed.

Sharing looks of wonder, the pair watched as Josephine disappeared from the room.

"What could she be up to?" asked Isabelle.

"I wonder," Martine began, "at how buoyant she is. William gone less than a year, and yet, she is wonderful. So charming, so…"

Their dialogue ceased as Josephine returned to the library. She arrived carrying a shoebox, which she placed on the table in front of Martine.

"It was William's. I found it in his closet, and there is a note inside addressed to you," she offered.

Martine sat looking at the shoebox for a moment before his sense of humor told him what he must say.

"This is very nice, to be offered something of William's, but if I remember correctly, his shoe size would be impossibly small for me."

He stopped, realizing his joke was falling flat. Taking the box in his hands, he removed the top and gazed inside. There was a small envelope, just as Josephine had said. Under it was a pistol. A pistol he immediately recognized. With no more joking, he opened the envelope and began to read.

My Dear Louis,

You will remember giving me this during my hour of need. And you may then remember the many hours we spent together, and with others we cherish and admire. Josephine no doubt is with you now, and my hope is that you are not alone.

So many years have passed since that wonderful time in Paris when you first introduced Isabelle. You did not have to tell me of the sorrow of your parting, or the terrible loneliness you felt in her absence. I could see in your face the evidence of your love.

As the world moves forward into the unknown that fate holds in store for each of us, I can only think hopefully of your reunion. I have even prayed for such. I have also prayed that when you receive the return of this pistol, there will no longer be a need of it.

In the end, when it comes time for me to go, I want you to have something to remember from all the days we knew and loved one another. For I did love you as I would have loved a brother, had I one. In his infinite wisdom, God gave me you as a friend instead.

Fondly, William
Nov. 1941

"God is my witness! I did not know," Martine wept.

In a short time, his composure restored, Martine sat back and smiled at his lover and their friend. "I meant, of course, that I did not know William was religious."

"He wasn't. At least, not that I knew," Josephine said, nodding her understanding. "Then, one day, he came back from a walk on the Heath with Hinch. I later found him in the library with a Bible in his hands. I think I went over to him and asked something like, 'What's this?' He looked up at me with that little smile that had always meant a tease was coming; so, you may be sure that I was surprised by what he said.

"Something happened out there on the Heath. It was not a vision or anything like one. He said he was sitting on a bench resting and admiring his surroundings when, all of a sudden, he realized that nothing of what he was looking at or any of the things that had happened in his life could have come purely by accident. There were reasons, some of which he could not explain.

"He said he had begun to look for answers."

– § –

The top-secret training facilities at Beaulieu in New Forest was Isabelle and Martine's new home.

Their training was round the clock, and sleep came to seem like a luxury. Along with dozens of other handpicked operatives, they were learning how to survive behind enemy lines in a country they both called "home." Escape and evasion measures seemed mostly common sense at first, and Isabelle had impressed with the knowledge gleaned from her days with *la resistance*.

Taught how to resist interrogation, perform escape planning, read maps, master code systems, and avoid detection, they received no weapons training. In this, they were both surprised and disappointed. Making inquiries, they were told the answer would come later, at the end of their training.

The weeks went by, during which Martine shed much unwanted weight and, it seemed, some few years. He knew he was in the best condition of his life. Isabelle did not struggle with the physical demands as much due to her extensive training for the ballet.

With the end of their training coming fast to its end, they began to think about their assignments and the answer to their question. It came, along with all their gear, which included the tools of their new trade: a two-way radio, compass, torches, maps, clothing, spare shoes, and kits for personal use.

In each kit, they found small, carefully marked packets sporting a skull and crossbones printed over the word *poison*.

They had decided that, for the moment, marriage did not matter. If they survived, there would be time enough later for that, and thinking beyond their immediate future was…uncomfortable.

Waiting for their Lysander, with gear on their backs, they shared a conspiratorial smile. Near the bottom of Martine's bag was the pistol Josephine had returned to him. Isabelle wore the vest that Darling had given her, concealing her automatic.

They would be flying from Newmarket to their destination in the north of occupied France and, hopefully, a welcoming reception by new friends. However their mission went, they would try to do what they had been trained to do. They would join up with resistance forces and raise havoc. No matter what happened, they had vowed their ending would not be a suicidal one.

There was not a full moon, but there was enough light for the pilot of the Lysander to see that he had crossed the water and was now over land. He flew at the prescribed altitude toward his landing zone. The winds had been favorable, and he feared at first that he might arrive too early. He did not have enough fuel to circle for long, and the wind would not be in his favor for the return.

Then, he thought he saw the first of the fires.

As he drew closer, he could count the four torches designating the landing field. Holding the stick off until it was nearly full aft, he settled with a very mild bump onto the grass. The direction of the wind suddenly shifted, and he slowly turned the Lysander a full 270 degrees to prepare for takeoff. Sliding open the side window on his left, he motioned for his passengers to get out. Isabelle looked at the pilot's face, and the nervous, impatient look she saw there was starkly different from the dashing bravado she had imagined.

Struggling to their feet, pounding on their legs to restore circulation and feeling before climbing down the ladder affixed to the side of the aircraft, they forced themselves to move more quickly to please the pilot as he began gesturing wildly for them to get out.

Setting his trim wheel, the pilot revved up the engine to begin his takeoff. He whizzed past them without so much as a wave of goodbye or good luck, quickly going airborne in a three-point attitude.

Then they were alone.

It was not long before they saw the torches begin to go out, one by one. Straining their eyes in the darkness, they were just able to see a lorry coming toward them with men walking alongside. Together, they stepped forward to meet their reception. Code words exchanged, they were instructed to climb aboard.

It might have been twenty minutes, but it seemed longer before they arrived at a building that, by its outward appearance, suggested a garage.

Suddenly, the doors of the lorry flew open as hands reached for their gear.

From inside the garage there came out slowly a long, black vehicle, the alarming rumble of its powerful engine filling the stillness of the night. Car doors opened, and a voice from inside the vehicle ordered them to get in. Entering the back seat, they saw the windows of the automobile rolled down. Isabelle stuck out her hand and Martine took what she gave him. Nodding, he reached for his packet with the skull and crossbones and threw both packets out the window of the vehicle as it began to move slowly forward.

As they positioned their gear and secured their weapons, they heard voices in the dark from the men they were leaving behind, nearly inaudible at first and then rising just loud enough to hear.

"*Vive la France! Vive de Gaulle!*"

Sources and Acknowledgments

MANY PEOPLE AND INSTITUTIONS, ALONG with the published works of other authors, contributed substantially to my understanding of William, his life, and his times. Writer Andrew Cameron, who knows as much about William as anyone, and Des McCagherty of Signatory Vintage, were both instrumental in getting this project underway. My appreciation for their help is boundless.

My thanks go out to the following individuals and the institutions they represent: Guy, at the London Metropolitan Archives; the staff at the National Archives, Kew; Michael Moon and his bookshop, Whitehaven; Kate at the Leeds City Museum.

The following authors and their works provided a great number of insights into the times and events occurring during William's life: *The Myth, The Mafia and The Magic*, Andrew Cameron, Matador, 2015; *Canada's Rumrunners*, Art Montegue, Altitude, 2004; *Frank Costello*, George Wolf, Bantam, 1979; *Last Call*, Daniel Okrent, Scribner, 2010; *Night Flight to Dungavel*, Peter Padfield, University Press, 2013; *London: The Biography*, Peter Ackroyd, Anchor Books, 2003; *The English Experience*, John Bowle, Phoenix Press, 1971; *Aircraft of WWI*, Jack Herris and Bob Pearson, Amber Books, 2010; *The Second World War*, Winston S. Churchill, Six Volumes, Houghton Mifflin, 1951.